FIRESTORM

The Sons of Templar MC #2

ANNE MALCOM

The Sons of Templar MC #2
By Anne Malcom
Copyright 2016 Anne Malcom

Edited by: Mary Yakovets
Cover: TRC Designs
Cover image Copyright 2016

To all my girlfriends, without you I'd be lost. Thanks for being just as crazy as I am and always making me laugh.

PROLOGUE

GWEN

I watched my baby girl sleep peacefully with my hand on her chest, the rise and fall of her breathing giving me a sense of calm. I was pretty sure I had the most beautiful child on the planet. Considering I had the most beautiful husband on the planet, it wasn't a surprise.

Though, if Cade knew I was calling him beautiful he would have something to say about that. The sentence would most likely include profanities. To me, my rough, badass biker was nothing short of beautiful. He had provided me with an amazing life, brought me back from some dark places and made me feel safe and cherished. Not to mention gave me the best orgasms I'd had *in my life*.

Like the one he had given me an hour ago on the kitchen table...

A spluttering sound interrupted my sex flashback.

I narrowed my eyes and focused on Belle — she was still sleeping, but she was making a weird sound. Was that normal?

Shit, I didn't know.

Maybe my baby wasn't sleeping peacefully, maybe that

splutter was a symptom of some obscure life-threatening disorder. I pulled out my phone, almost hyperventilating.

Since I had already called Mum twice today I didn't think I could disturb her again. Plus, it was two a.m. at home. I would call her if Belle didn't stop making that noise. It was freaking me out. I hadn't been around babies until I popped one out right after I shot and killed a man.

I didn't know what were normal sounds and what weren't. I put my phone to my ear, needing to be calmed down, or at least distracted.

"Hey, this is Amy. Text me. If I don't reply it means I don't want to talk to you."

"Fuck," I whispered.

Since I was desperate, I made a risky call.

"Good afternoon, Abrams residence," a brisk voice greeted.

"Um hi, could I please speak to Amy?" I asked quietly, keeping an eagle eye on my daughter.

There was a pause. "Miss Abrams? Whom may I ask is calling?"

"This is Gwen Alexandra...no wait, Fletcher. I mean, my last name used to be Alexandra, then I got married so I changed it to Fletcher. It's a new name I'm not used to it yet," I babbled, my lack of sleep catching up on me.

"One moment."

I relaxed. Well, slightly.

I frowned down at Belle. She wasn't making the noises anymore, she was quiet. Too quiet. Was that a thing? I was pretty sure babies weren't meant to be that still.

"Gwenevere?"

My attention snapped back to the phone. Amy never called me by my full name, only my family and one other person called me that.

"Mrs. Abrams? So sorry to bother you, I was expecting Amy."

I was sure I asked the maid for Amy. Maybe I didn't. My mind was mush. Existing on coffee and orgasms was not a good long-term plan, but was necessary when you had a two-month-old daughter and a sex god for a husband.

"Oh yes, Vera informed me you were looking for Amy. I wanted to let you know she isn't here. I haven't seen her for months," her cultured voice informed me.

That shocked me out of my freak-out. "*Months?*" I repeated. That couldn't be right.

"Why yes, we both know Amy isn't too fond of communicating with her mother unless she is forced. In fact, she actively changes her phone number whenever she becomes aware I have it." Katherine's voice dripped with disdain.

I resisted a giggle at this. It was true, Amy routinely changed her number in order to avoid talking to her mother. Or, she had.

Now she just had two separate phones, one "safe" and one she specifically bought to communicate with her family. And only when she was faced with no other option. Her cold relationship with Katherine had always made me sad, which was why I had been shocked when she had told me she was staying there.

"But that's not possible. Amy told me she was staying with you. She left for Europe right after my wedding. She got back two weeks ago, and said she was staying with you and Harold in the city," I explained, getting a bad feeling in the pit of my stomach.

Katherine laughed without humor. "I'm sorry, my darling, we both know my daughter has an aversion to the truth. I wouldn't worry. She's probably sunning herself on some pop star's yacht and forgot she was meant to be back at home facing responsibility. Although I don't recall her making arrangements to come here," she added thoughtfully. "I must go, I'm late to a charity luncheon. Lovely talking to you, Gwenevere."

She hung up before I could say anything else.

My stomach churned. No matter what Amy's vile mother said about her, Amy wasn't irresponsible and she certainly wasn't a liar.

I automatically thought about the one and only time my best

friend had kept something from me. A lance of pain ripped through my stomach.

She hadn't told me about her and Ian. About being in love with my brother. When I found out she had kept it a secret, I took it a little badly. Okay, a lot badly since I tackled her on our front lawn. But when I got used to the idea I was happy, ecstatic for them both.

Then things got complicated. Brock, the biker badass who rocked a serious man bun, got Amy twisted up enough to question her relationship with Ian. Not that I could get much out of her. But I knew Ian had been determined to get her back. I was pretty sure his decision to finish out his tour was largely to do with her.

My eyes glistened thinking about what would have been had he not been...killed. I still couldn't say it. I could barely think it. My brother was dead. My best friend was heartbroken and she wouldn't talk to me about it, no matter how hard I tried.

Plus, there was something going on with her and Brock. The months we had been back in Amber she refused to talk about it. They didn't talk to each other, apart from some broody alpha male looks Brock had directed at Amy when fate put them in the same room.

I had been sidetracked with my reunion with Cade and my growing belly, so I didn't give her the attention she needed. Then Belle was born in the clubhouse after I killed a man who was going to kill me and drama ensued. Life hadn't exactly slowed down for me.

Cade had pretty much demanded we get married once I woke up in the hospital. He would have happily done it right then and there, but I convinced him I wouldn't get married while wearing polyester. I managed to hold him off a month, a freaking *month* after Belle was born and he expected me to squeeze into a wedding dress. It was a good thing I was in love with the man or I would have been seriously pissed.

Luckily, through a combination of breastfeeding and being

too anxious about the growth of Belle's hair, I hadn't had much of an appetite, which meant I didn't look like a beached whale at my wedding. Not that Cade made me feel like that for a second. The look he gave me when I walked down the aisle made my insecurities melt away. That and the kiss he landed on me as soon as I made it to him. I had been ready to forego the ceremony and demand he whisk me away and ravish me.

Arms went around my middle and I jumped, being too deep in my thoughts to notice another presence.

"Baby?" Cade questioned. His deep voice was quiet, noticing the fact our daughter was sleeping.

I was about to tell him about Amy when Belle made the noise.

"Did you hear that?" I whispered, narrowing my eyes.

"What?" His body turned taut, instantly alert.

"That noise she's making. It doesn't sound normal. I think we should take her to the doctor," I declared, frowning at my baby.

Cade relaxed and gently pulled me away from the crib, turning me to face him. He grasped my neck with his hands, his gray eyes meeting mine.

At any other moment I would be drooling at his hotness. His shoulder-length inky black hair, sharp and stubbled jaw and sexy gaze were a pot of male deliciousness. I appreciated it, but I had bigger fish to fry. Namely making sure my baby wasn't suffering from some kind of deadly snuffling attack.

"Gwen, she's fine. She's perfect—you need to take a breath. And a nap," he said firmly.

"Are you crazy? How can I take a nap? What if something happens to her while I'm asleep? I'm her mother, I need to protect her," I replied, my voice bordering on hysterical.

"That's what I'm here for, babe. It's my job to take care of both of my girls. You are the most precious things on the entire fuckin' planet. I would never let one thing hurt either of you. I'd die first," he promised, hands tight at my neck.

My stomach plummeted. "Don't say that," I pleaded. "Don't say die."

Cade sighed and pulled me into his arms. "I'm sorry, baby— you've been through so much shit. You amaze me how strong you are to pull through it and still be who you are." He grasped my hair, meeting my eyes again. "But that shit makes you aware of all the things that can go wrong. Now that you know it can happen you're convinced it's gonna happen again. It won't." His words were a promise, his eyes were so intense I believed him.

I realized how neurotic I had been.

"I'm sorry, honey. I'm just terrified," I confessed. "After Ian I was so sure I'd never feel truly happy again. And now I am. I'm so happy that I'm terrified that something's going to happen. Because no one can be this happy, not without something ruining it." My voice broke at the end and a single tear trailed down my cheek.

My hard biker's face softened and a callused hand stroked my cheek.

"Baby, the shit you've been through, the shit you've survived? You deserve a lifetime of happy and I'm going to make fucking sure you get it." He finished this with a kiss.

Plastering my mouth against his, I moaned as his tongue explored my mouth, my worries about Belle fading away.

I pulled back abruptly. "Amy," I muttered.

Cade's face was blank. "Not too sure I'm happy you're thinking about Amy when I'm doing that, babe."

I shook my head. "That was great. Amazing. Obviously. But it's Amy...I don't know where she is. She's missing."

Cade's body tightened at this and he instantly turned into the alert, macho alpha male. "Explain," he ordered.

I recounted what Katherine had told me. "That means she's been MIA for *two weeks*, Cade. I've talked to her since then but maybe only twice. And both times she said she was busy and had to go. I'm worried." I chewed my lip.

Cade brought his thumb up to my mouth, lightly brushing it.

"She'll be fine, baby. She's probably just getting some time away from it all. I know something happened with Brock that might've had her wanting to disappear for a bit."

I raised my eyebrow threateningly. My man had better not have been withholding information from me.

"I don't know any specifics—put your claws away," he said, reading my glare. "I just know that he's been a grumpy mother-fucker. Not that that's really news over the past year, but more so than usual. Something went down—maybe Amy just needed to get her head straight."

I chewed on this for a moment. "But why wouldn't she tell me? She's my best friend and she's going through all of this on her own." I gazed up at him, tears welling in my eyes.

She was the one who would tell me I was being a crazy person worrying about things like snuffles and hair growth. She'd pour me a cocktail and distract me with Celine's latest collection or some inane celebrity gossip.

The tears fell. "I don't make sense without her. Where is she?"

CHAPTER ONE

AMY

I slung back my fifth shot, savoring the burn at the back of my throat and the tingling in my fingers as the alcohol seared into my system.

"Another." I pushed my glass at the bartender without looking up.

He didn't say a word, nor did he raise a judgmental eyebrow that I was drinking alone in the early afternoon. I was pretty sure it was barely past lunch. This was most likely due to the kind of establishment I was currently welcoming oblivion in. It was dark, with an old wooden bar and equally old chairs and tables scattered around the place. The paint was crumbling at the walls and the clientele was as rough as the bar itself. Not that I cared. As long as they provided alcohol that let me escape into blissed numbness I did not give a shit.

"Here you go, darlin'." The bartender pushed the drink into my waiting hands and I downed it.

"Want to talk about it?" he asked in a gruff voice.

I glanced up at him. He was older, probably late fifties with dark graying hair and a greying moustache. He was wearing a plaid shirt undone, with the sleeves rolled up and a wife beater underneath. Faded tattoos were scattered up his arms. I met his eyes, they were brown and crinkled at the sides. He was staring at me with a kind expression that looked out of place on his otherwise rough exterior.

"Talk about what?" I replied, managing not to slur my words.

"Whatever's got a beautiful lady like you in a shithole like this, drinking her troubles away." He pulled out another glass and poured the clear liquid into it before refilling mine. "Can't let you do it alone."

I paused, clinking my glass with his and drinking. "Guess I just felt like being anonymous for a while, and this place seems as good as any to be no one," I replied, glancing around at the patrons. There weren't many, the few that were scattered around were keeping to themselves.

The bartender nodded, regarding me. "Fair enough, girlie. Want my advice, best person to be is always who you are. Might not be perfect, might be hard as hell, but you ain't got nothing if you ain't got yourself." With this sage wisdom he left me the bottle and walked down the bar.

I regarded the tequila bottle through blurry eyes. I wasn't quite ready to be myself. If I was, that would mean I had to face all the issues that came with being Amy Abrams. Currently there was a shit ton of those. I didn't feel like facing reality, like feeling the pain that had been my constant companion for almost a year. I didn't feel like masking it through fake smiles and inappropriate jokes. I had played a part for eight months and I was exhausted. I didn't want to *feel* anymore.

I thought back to what brought me here, to a dive bar in the middle of New Mexico, after driving aimlessly around the country for two weeks trying to get my head straight. If I thought back ... I had to go way back, to the reason I wanted to be in a dive bar in the middle of New Mexico. The day that changed my life forever and that could have turned me into an alcoholic.

TWO YEARS AGO

"Gwen!" I shouted as I slammed the door to our apartment shut, dumping all of my bags at my feet. "Hello, Gwen? I am so fucking late—I need to borrow your Jimmy Choos."

I kicked off my shoes and yanked my dress over my head, trying to save time while I rushed towards Gwen's bedroom. I dropped everything at my feet with the vague intention of picking it up at a later date, Gwen was anal when it came to shit like that.

"Seriously, why my mother makes me go to these stupid things I do not know," I yelled to her. "She knows I would rather chew tin foil than go on a date with one of the trust fund assholes she always pushes on me the moment I walk through the door. If I was going to go home with anyone, it would probably be the bartender, considering he's the one I spend the most time with. Speaking of bartenders, do you remember that one—" I stopped my blabbering when I reached the living room and there was strange man standing in it.

A seriously sexy strange man with a buzz cut, strong jaw, and the most amazing eyes I had ever seen. But that was neither here nor there. I definitely hadn't left him here this morning and I didn't order tall, dark, and delicious, which meant he was an intruder.

Man, burglars had gotten sexy. This one even had the audacity to smirk at me, green eyes on my underwear-clad body. In my rush, I had divested myself of my clothes.

Shit.

I didn't scream. I wasn't a screamer, outside the bedroom at least. What I did do was grab a heavy candlestick holder from the table beside me and waved it threateningly.

"Okay, pal, you have twenty seconds to get out of my apartment before I bludgeon you with this solid silver candlestick."

I gripped my weapon, willing to attempt to do as I said. I didn't think I would be very successful, considering the pretty darned impressive muscles bulging out of the intruder's t-shirt, and the fact that disfiguring such a picture of male perfection would be a crime to humanity.

The thief continued to smirk at me as if I was some kind of amusing child. I did not appreciate the fact he didn't consider me a worthy foe, regardless of the fact he had about two feet, fifty pounds on me and he wasn't only wearing heels and La Perla.

I glared at him.

"I'm guessing you must be Amy," he stated causally, shamelessly eyeing my barely clad body.

I stood straight, refusing to cover myself — this was my freaking apartment, after all. I also refused to acknowledge the flutter of desire that came with his gaze. Getting turned on by a man who had just broken into your apartment?

That's fucked up, Amy, no matter how hot he is.

"How do you know my name?" I snapped.

Shit, maybe he was here to kidnap me and hold me for ransom. The hottest guy I'd laid eyes on in my life and he wasn't around to date me, but kidnap me. Great. But then again, that accent sounded familiar.

The hunk crossed his arms and I failed not to appreciate the way his veins bulged when he did that.

I mentally shook myself. Focus. *Strange man in house, not good.*

"Every time I talk to Gwen she mentions you at least four times. Although she failed to quite accurately describe you." His voice was full of manly appreciation and so was his gaze, which had my nipples in danger of popping out from the seriously flimsy material encasing them.

That should not have been my main concern, considering my brain was the one in control of this situation, although my ovaries were fighting for the opportunity to rub up against him. Something flared at the edge of my mind while I battled not to have weird burglar sex fantasies.

"You're Gwen's brother," I said slowly, doing a mental forehead slap.

I had completely forgotten he was arriving today, regardless of the fact Gwen had informed me this morning. But in my defense, I had only had one cup of coffee, which meant my brain only had control over limited motor function. It was only number three at which I processed and retained information.

"Amy, don't forget that Ian's arriving today. I've left a key with the doorman, so don't be freaked if you come home to a strange man in the apartment—he is not there to rape or murder you. And try not to walk around naked, either."

Shit.

"Ian." Gwen's seriously hot brother shocked me back into the present moment.

"What?" I asked, trying to figure out if there was anything in the immediate vicinity to cover up my nakedness. I subtly glanced around for a robe, a throw... hell, I'd settle for a rug. I was out of luck. In any other situation I would have been happy to be in such a state of undress in front of a sex god, but meeting my best friend's brother for the first time was something that required clothing. And in his case, a chastity belt.

"The name's Ian. I would shake your hand, but I'm figuring you might want to put away the deadly weapon and put on some clothes before we exchange pleasantries." He nodded to my body, eyes teasing. My panties dampened at the underlying sexual hunger in his gaze.

Not appropriate, Amy.

"Not that I don't appreciate the view," he continued cheekily. My face flamed and I guessed it might match my hair. I threw the candlestick back on the side table with a clatter without breaking eye contact with Ian.

"Um, yes, I think that would be wise. I'll just, ah...." I pointed with my thumb to the direction of my room while sidestepping, really not wanting to share the fact I was wearing a G-string.

"You do that," Ian responded, eyes sparkling.

I made it to the edge of the room with Ian watching me the whole time, even though the polite thing would have been to avert his gaze or excuse himself to the corner. But no, he just kept the edge of his attractive mouth up, his green eyes had both rendered me mute and sparked a flame of desire that made me want to jump him then and there.

I was not a woman who gets rendered mute. Especially with men. I've always thought of it as my kind of superpower. I could flirt my ass off and pretty much use my feminine wiles to mold men into my little puppets. I didn't mean to be vain or anything, but it's the truth. Some people are math geniuses or brilliant artists — I'm a man whisperer.

But not with this one. Oh no, I wouldn't have been surprised if I spent the entirety of my journey to my bedroom slack-jawed and drooling. This guy had a presence, an air about him that screamed *male*. His hungry male gaze maintained eye contact with me as I edged into the hallway, then rushed into my room.

In the safety of my bedroom, I gathered my scrambled thoughts. The first one being that Gwen's brother was hot. I shouldn't have been surprised, considering Gwen was a total babe and I'd seen photos of him. Hotness ran in the family. But photos seemed a poor representation of the real thing.

His dark hair was shaved close to his skull in a military buzz cut, which didn't make him look like a skinhead or a lice victim. No, it made him look like a bad ass. Channing Tatum in *G.I Joe* times a thousand. He had a square masculine jaw and freaking amazing green eyes like Gwen's. His face was not classically handsome, it was rugged and masculine as fuck.

His body.

I couldn't get stuck on that thought for too long or I would turn into a drooling mess on the floor. He was built, like *built*. Broad shoulders and some crazy defined arms, it looked like he bench pressed cars for shits and giggles. His tee unfortunately didn't give me a view of his abs, but I knew they were there. He'd probably have that amazing 'V' that pointed to the most important part on a male. Unfortunately I hadn't gotten to check out his no doubt amazing jean-clad ass, but I bet I could've eaten a steak off it.

My dreamy gaze wandered to the Tiffany clock on my dresser. Shit. This guy had the ability that made me completely forget about the prior engagement I was seriously late for. That was a feat in itself, the horrific night ahead of me was as easy to forget about as genital warts. I turned my thoughts to my closet and directed my body toward it, picking out an outfit on autopilot.

I slipped on a silk Calvin Klein gown, one that I knew looked amazing on me. I may have been trying to position my second encounter with Ian on more even ground, ground which I planned to be standing in designer footwear. Plus, designer armor was essential when going into battle with my mother. A fire-breathing dragon would be ideal, but I worked with what I had.

I hurried to my bathroom and commenced in doing a day to night transition of my makeup and hair. Luckily I was one of those women who could throw her hair in a messy bun and make it look artfully mussed. My talents, although useful in everyday life, did not really make me capable of contributing anything valuable to society. Something my mother loved reminding me of.

After finishing I moved to my full-length mirror for a quick inspection.

My soft grey metallic dress was cut on the bias and hugged my body in all the right places before falling softly to my feet. Its spaghetti straps snaked way down low on my back. My red hair escaped from the bun artfully, falling in wisps around my face.

I regarded my face in the mirror. As a natural redhead I was plagued with freckles. Some days I cursed them, others I liked them. Today I had let them peek out from under my makeup, just a light dusting on my cheeks. With a subtle smoky eye and a light pink gloss on my lips, I deduced I looked good. Good enough to face Ian again, and hopefully regain my ability to turn a phrase.

———

I entered the living room to a glorious sight. A view of Ian from behind. I was right, you could totally eat a steak off that ass.

"Yeah, Ace, she just arrived home about half an hour ago. I think I gave her a bit of a fright," he chuckled.

I cleared my throat before he could recount the rest of our encounter, which Gwen would no doubt find hilarious.

Ian turned slowly, phone to his ear, smirk on his face. Did this guy have a permanent sexy grin on his face? If so, the chances of me pouncing on him increased exponentially.

When he turned to me the grin disappeared. It was replaced with a dark gaze so full of lust I struggled not to run over and hump his leg. I guess my dress had its intended effect. I mentally high fived myself.

"Sorry, Ace, didn't quite catch that." Ian spoke huskily, eyes still on me.

Now that I had recovered from the power of his male gaze, I smirked and cocked my hip.

"Yep, that's fine—I get you got to work late. I'm sure I can find a way to entertain myself."

Breaking our eye contact, I moved through the living room while he spoke to gather things into my purse, feeling eyes on my naked back.

"I don't think Amy can act as my babysitter tonight, Gwen.

She looks like she's off to some fancy 'do,'" he exclaimed, his accent seriously hot and rugged. I didn't even care that I had no idea what a "do" was.

I shelved a borderline sick babysitter fantasy and had a brilliant idea. I whirled around and ignored the panty-dropping stare I was getting, snatching the phone from Ian.

"Hey, Gwen, don't worry. I've got Ian sorted for tonight—he can come to this charity gala with me," I told her, watching as Ian raised his eyebrows.

"Really? Oh, thanks so much, Ames. I'm sure he'll hate it as much as you do, but at least he won't be sitting in an empty apartment on his first night back from a warzone. Fucking work. I can't believe I have to stay and sort out this order. On the day my big brother arrives," she whined.

"Um, sorry to put a spanner in the works here, but I can't go to any 'galas' on account of the fact I don't have a monkey suit stuffed in my duffel and by the way you're dressed, I don't think my jeans and tee will cut it," Ian interrupted, watching me.

"You're perfect as you are," I replied, phone still at my ear. He seriously was perfect. If I had the ability, I would've sculpted him out of marble. Maybe I would commission a miniature of him for my own personal use.

"You're so using Ian to piss off your mum and all the stuffed shirts at this charity thing, aren't you?" Gwen knew me too well.

"I can neither confirm nor deny that, Gwen. Got to go—we are *so* late already. Don't work too hard." I cut the call off, knowing Gwen wouldn't actually mind I was using her brother as a pawn in my constant battle to beat the Botox in my mother's face to get it to form a frown. She'd just be angry she couldn't be there. I was kind of glad she wouldn't, considering I'd probably be drooling over her brother the entire night.

The drool-worthy brother was watching me with a raised eyebrow. "You're telling me that you're going to a party dressed like that and I'll be okay in this?" He gestured down to his attire with a skeptical gaze.

I didn't look down, for if I did I might just pull up his shirt to inspect his abs. I needed to make sure I didn't do things like that, he was my best friend's brother. Off limits. Which only made him so much hotter. This was going to be a huge test on my willpower, even worse than that time I decided to do a raw food detox.

"You'll be fine, trust me. My mother's the one throwing the execution."

He smirked. "You mean party."

I smirked back. "Oh, no I don't."

————

We pulled up to the party in the town car I'd had waiting outside our apartment. Luckily since I was so late there were only a few photographers loitering around. I usually didn't mind getting snapped, I shared an easy relationship with the paps. I wasn't famous enough to get followed around or anything, but at events like this they loved me. I didn't mind getting on page five either, it helped get me some serious designer duds.

But tonight for some reason I didn't want Ian to see that side of my life. It all seemed so silly now, with him being the sexy man who fought terrorists and saved the world for a living. The life I had been so content with hours ago now seemed superficial and shallow. I was almost embarrassed. I turned to him.

"Wanna have some fun with these stuck-up stock brokers and trophy wives to spice up the evening?" I asked with a smirk.

"Bring it on." Ian winked at me and got out of the car, rounding it to open my door for me.

I clasped his outstretched hand and almost gasped at the spark I felt touching his skin. He pulled me up and the look on his face told me he felt it too. That moment, everything seemed to fade away and it was just the two of us. There was a connection, something I couldn't explain. An attraction tethering us together as if we hadn't just met two hours ago.

"Amy!"

"Miss Abrams, who are you wearing tonight?"

"Over here, Amy! Give us a pose!"

The voices of photographers shook me out of the moment, which was good. I couldn't be having some freaking "insta-lust" type shit with my best friend's brother. I needed to focus on the mission at hand.

I stepped forward to give the photographers a quick snap, but I was stopped with a hand on my back. I tried to ignore the desire that spread through my body from that touch as Ian directed us towards the doors, shielding me from the camera flashes.

"Who's the new man, Amy?"

"Does that mean the rumors about you and the prince aren't true?"

The questions died away as we reached the doors.

"You didn't have to whisk me away like that. I have plenty of experience with this stuff—heck, it's a normal Friday night for me," I told Ian as I presented the man at the door with the invitation. Not that I needed it, he knew who I was. He gave Ian's attire a speculative look before nodding.

"Have a nice evening, Miss Abrams."

Ian raised an eyebrow at the guy and gave him a casual chin lift.

"Yeah, well, if you've been with the right man you wouldn't have had to deal with that stuff. A real man wouldn't let his woman get ogled like that, especially when he knew what the fuck those photos were being used for," he bit out, directing us to the main room as if he'd been here hundreds of times.

I turned my head to look up at him. "Seriously? The only thing those photos will be used for is determining if I'm ending up on the worst dressed list."

I had never ended up on the worst dressed list. I wouldn't be starting today.

Ian glanced down at me, eyes twinkling. "Trust me, I'm a

man. Those photos will be used for a fuck of a lot more than that."

I scrunched up my nose. "Ew. I didn't need that image."

"Yeah, well, neither did I. It's going to be hard enough looking at all the stuffed suits scramble over their Botox-filled dates to talk to you," he replied stiffly, scanning the room and leading us toward the bar.

Ah, a man after my own heart.

I struggled to comprehend the meaning behind his words. They certainly seemed protective and almost angry, but that didn't make sense. I was his kid sister's best friend, we barely knew each other. That did not warrant this reaction.

I chose not to believe he was feeling the same freaky attraction I was. Even if he wasn't Gwen's brother, I didn't do relationships. I knew they only caused a world of hurt. Caring, feelings, that fricking four-letter word. They all amounted to pain and heartbreak. I was in control over my heart and it would belong to no man... apart from Karl Lagerfeld.

I scanned the people at the party and my eyes fell on my mother. The look she was giving me, and more precisely Ian, was evidence that she had spotted me far earlier. She started to make her way over to us, smiling at her society friends tightly.

I glanced up at Ian. "Can you do me a solid and grab me a martini from the bar? Dirty." I paused, gauging the expression on my mother's face. "Make that two," I amended.

Ian raised an eyebrow. "Sure thing, sweetheart."

I sighed in relief as he escaped just before my mother arrived.

I took a deep breath. Katherine Abrams was a beauty, no one could dispute that. Her hair was the same red as mine, but colored to disguise any gray hairs. It was expertly coiffed into a chignon which accentuated her sharp cheekbones. Her makeup was flawless, like always, applied by her makeup artist. Her face was free from any lines thanks to surgery and injections. She was wearing a jade green gown that accentuated her trim figure, due to the fact she counted calories and barely ate more than one meal a day.

"Amy, darling, glad to see you could *finally* make it. I'm sure I told you countless times to be here at seven. Did your watch break? You know, your father and I got that for you to remedy your inability to monitor time passing."

Fate was a cruel mistress to make me face this creature sober.

"Mother, how lovely to see you," I lied, giving her air kisses.

I shook the pricey timepiece my parents had gotten me, which I wore to every event they forced me to go to. "You know, these days watches have become obsolete. I merely think of this as a pretty bracelet," I declared airily and watched my mother's eyes narrow.

"Darling, you must let Anna do your makeup for these events. She would give you the perfect powder to cover up those freckles—they make you look common." My mother eyed my cheeks in disdain.

I didn't have time to reply as she glared at Ian's jean-clad back. Her face was tight and expressionless. But I swear a vein in her eye twitched. This only helped cement my theory that she was a cyborg incapable of human emotion. The normal reaction of a human woman would be drooling, or at least swooning over the male specimen in front of her.

"Really, Amy? Is this your latest attempt to embarrass me?" she asked, her judgmental gaze now focused on me. "You bring some hoodlum to my event dressed like a drug dealer?"

"Oh, but he is a drug dealer, Mother. You know how hard it is to get good blow at these things. I thought I'd just cut out the middleman."

My mother raised an eyebrow. Well, as much as was possible with the amount of Botox in her face. "When are you going to grow up, Amy?" she sighed.

I pretended to think about that. "If by grow up you mean buy a closet full of Burberry, play tennis, head ridiculous charities and have a stuffy banker husband, I'm going to say... never," I told her. "And plus, I thought the idea of aging in any way shape or form is utterly distasteful to you, considering the amount of surgeries you've had to stop the evidence of time's passing."

God, I wished I had a drink. Or at least a hammer to whack myself in the head with.

Katherine scowled at me, preparing a no doubt scathing retort when Ian approached us. He handed me my two drinks.

"Here you go, Ames," he said softly.

"I love you," I muttered under my breath, cradling my precious drinks.

My mother's eyes went to my multiple cocktails and she opened her mouth. Ian, the sweetheart, beat her to it.

"You must be Mrs. Abrams. I'm Ian Alexandra, it's a pleasure to meet you. I apologize for my lack of formal attire, but I just got back from deployment and Amy wasn't expecting to have to babysit me tonight." Ian cut in smoothly, taking my mother's hand in his.

His rough accent and veiny arms transfixed me, and I struggled not to stare. Or drool. I focused on sipping my drink.

"Oh, that's quite all right. It isn't your fault at all—Amy has the entire Upper East Side on speed dial. She could have wrangled you up a suit. I'm sure the thought never occurred to her. She always has so many pressing matters on her mind, like the next club opening she has to attend." My mother delivered that barb with a smile and continued. "Deployment? You're in the Army? With that accent you must be Gwenevere's brother. Your parents must be so proud to have two such *successful* children. I only wish Gwenevere could influence Amy a little more."

I took a deep breath and willed myself not to react to my mother's apparent disappoint in me and my accomplishments. It didn't matter I had just graduated from Columbia or that I helped facilitate one of the biggest business deals my father's company had ever had. I was a constant disappointment. If I had found a cure for cancer she would have replied with, "Only cancer? You couldn't cure HIV too?"

Ian's face turned hard and he moved to stand beside me. "Our parents are proud of us no matter what, Mrs. Abrams. That's what makes them such good parents—they would never judge or criticize Gwen's and my decisions. If you'd excuse us, it was a pleasure to meet you."

Without letting my mother get a word in, Ian swept me away toward the bar. I whipped my head around to watch my mother's frozen face staring after us. I gazed up at Ian in awe.

"That was freaking awesome. I may just promise to carry your firstborn for that," I joked.

Ian gave me a long and serious look that wiped the smirk right off my face. The intensity behind those green eyes was scary as hell. It also made wetness pool between my legs.

"I'll remember that, sweetheart. Your mum, she always like that?" His face was focused on mine with... concern?

"That's damned near warm and cuddly from her. I'm surprised she didn't eat me at birth," I replied, going for breezy. Gwen was the only one who knew the effect my mother's disdain had on me.

Ian raised an attractive eyebrow. "I don't like that for you, sweetheart. Someone as beautiful and funny as you could not have come out of that." He scowled over at my mother. "You must have had a rough fucking childhood," he muttered as he took my empty glass out of my hand.

I locked eyes with Ian. "Yeah, my life was so hard with a private chef and birthdays where I got gifts like a BMW baby racer," I joked.

Ian frowned at me. "That crap doesn't mean shit when you've got parents who treat you like that."

I stilled. How could he see through the blasé attitude toward my mother's indifference—or let's face it, straight up hostility?

"Yeah, well, I made it out alive and I didn't turn into a designer-clad vampire like the rest of them, so it's a win."

I scanned the room, observing the usual suspects, some of

whom were glancing in this direction. Well, almost all of the female population was salivating at Ian.

Back off, bitches, he's mine.

Wow. Where did that come from? I was not a jealous person and Ian was most certainly not mine. Maybe this martini was spiked and causing me to have weird thoughts. I frowned down at my glass. Surely Ian wouldn't roofie me, he should have known he could click his glorious fingers and I'd be his.

Those glorious fingers lightly grasped my chin, and with his other hand he put my drink down.

"Look at me, beautiful. Trust me, from someone who knows how lucky he is to have two loving parents, I'm sorry you didn't have that. And I'm fucking amazed you are who you are, having been brought up like that."

"You don't even know me. I could be a raging bitch, just one surgery away from becoming like them," I whispered to him, transfixed with his stare.

"I know enough. And I know who my sister is and what she's told me. I know you're special. Knew it the moment I laid eyes on you."

Okay, this was serious shit. Like DEFCON level five type shit.

Battle stations! Do not let the sexy soldier with the endearing accent in! At all costs, people!

"The first time you laid eyes on me I was in my underwear brandishing a candlestick. I'm sure you knew I was *some* kind of special," I replied with a raised eyebrow.

Ian smiled, but his eyes darkened.

The moment was charged with a sexual tension that I didn't know was real outside of romance novels. I was so fucked.

"Amy, you love to make our mother's blood pressure rise, don't you? Just once could you come to one of these events and not cause some kind of stir?"

My brother's superior tone interrupted the moment. For once I was glad for the patronizing little shit's scolding.

"Tripp, what would be the fun in that? She's already got her Stepford son. I'm just keeping her on her toes, making sure all that plastic surgery and hairspray doesn't fry her brain," I replied, giving my brother a sweet smile.

He frowned at me disapprovingly. Where I was the imprint of my mother, Tripp was the imprint of my father. You would never even guess we were related. Where I had pale skin and red hair, he had olive-toned skin and dark locks. His eyes were dark and his jaw chiseled.

He was expertly groomed like always, down to suspiciously manicured eyebrows. His short hair was styled perfectly, and I knew it would have taken him longer to do than mine. His suit was of course designer and tailored expertly.

My gaze moved to the woman hanging off his shoulder and I struggled not to roll my eyes in distaste. Okay, maybe I didn't struggle.

"Penelope, so lovely to see you," I lied through gritted teeth.

"Amy, darling, it's so good to see you too. You look great. I would be too nervous to wear something as revealing as that to an important event such as this, but you really make a statement." Her voice was sickly sweet, but the thinly veiled insult was clear.

I despised this woman. I had known her since we were kids, on account of our parents being friends, which meant I unfortunately was forced to be in her presence a lot. Her only aims in life were to snag herself a well-to-do husband that Daddy approved of and to make other girls feel terrible about themselves.

She was a snake. A pretty one at that, with blonde hair, blue eyes, and an hourglass figure, but a Gucci-clad reptile she still was. I was less than impressed she was latched onto my brother. Although hardly surprised. She had been after him since we were kids.

"Who's your date, Amy?" she purred, eyes roving over Ian.

"Sorry, how rude of me. Ian, this is my brother Tripp and this is Penelope," I stopped myself from elaborating further as I was worried I might label Penelope as man-eating bitch and Ian as a sex god.

"How do you know my sister, Ian? Did she pick you up from a bar on the way here? It wouldn't be the first time," Tripp asked, disdain dripping from his tone.

"Of course I didn't, he's my bodyguard," I interrupted sarcastically. "He's here to make sure one of the silicone socialites doesn't shiv me in the bathroom." I gave Penelope a pointed look.

Ian coughed beside me, I was pretty sure he was doing it to cover up his chuckle. I was happy he was on board with my flavor of humor.

Tripp scowled at me. "Can you take anything seriously?"

I glared back at him. "Can you at least pretend you have manners and treat my guest with respect? I'm doing the same with yours, despite her being Satan's mistress," I bit out, ignoring Penelope's fake gasp.

"It's okay, Amy, I'm sure your brother is just being protective. I understand. I'm Gwen's brother, Ian." He held out his hand which Tripp shook.

Penelope was glaring at me. I smirked at her, daring her to come at me. I'd been itching to bitch slap the evil little twat for years. Unfortunately, she was far too image conscious to pounce on me in front of so many "well-to-do" types. She was more likely to slip arsenic in my martini when I wasn't looking. I glanced at my brother, whose small manicured hand was still encased in Ian's large one.

Tripp's eyes bulged slightly at Ian's no doubt firm grip and I smirked into my glass.

"If you would excuse us, there is someone I would much rather talk to over there." I gestured vaguely to the other side of the room, grabbing Ian's hand.

"Having fun yet?" I asked dryly.

Ian grinned. "I know some battle-hardened soldiers who

would prefer to be in a gunfight than this situation." His voice was teasing.

"You ain't seen nothing yet, soldier boy."

———

Two hours, four martinis, and some nonexistent canapés later, I was feeling pleasantly buzzed. Also supremely horny. Like I almost wanted to jump on Ian and beg him to take me in front of the entire party horny.

Ian and I had been having a blast all night, trying to get the masks of the image conscious attendees to slip at our risqué conversation topics. I was finding it hard to focus on the current conversation I was having with some investment banker. No, wait. Even if I wasn't struggling with impure thoughts over a sexy but off limits man, I would be bored to death at this conversation.

"The way the economy is at the moment, most people are struggling to turn a profit. Not me. It all comes down to instinct."

I restrained a snort. More like he had Daddy's checkbook.

"Speaking of instinct, I have a certainty I must take you out for dinner tomorrow night. I own the nicest little Italian restaurant, plus we could take my jet to wine country." His hand trailed down my arm and I inspected his manicured nails with indifference. He was like a clone of every guy in here. Money, good looks, arrogance, and a certainty that the female race should drop at their feet.

Gag.

"I'm going to have to go with my instinct and give you a resounding no on that one," I informed him.

The banker was unruffled, arrogance making him unable to fathom the fact someone was saying no to him. "No one can say no to Italian," he urged.

"Trust me, it's not the Italian I'm saying no to."

"Oh, come on," he pressed and I was starting to get seriously irritated.

"I believe the lady said no, mate," a rough voice declared from behind me.

Callused hands on my arms gently pulled me out of the banker's reach.

He glanced at Ian and dismissed him just as quickly, opening his mouth to no doubt spit something patronizing before trying to lure me away with a description of his stock portfolio.

Thankfully, I was directed away by the same callused hands that brushed my bare back. I tried to ignore the increase in my heartbeat, the flames that burned underneath his hands, the pool of desire settling between my legs, but I couldn't.

"As much fun as I've had tonight watching you shine like a fucking supernova amongst all these idiots, I think it's time I took you home." Ian's mouth brushed my ear as he directed us towards the exit.

My breath hitched at the suggestion. Did he mean what I think he meant? Was "take me home" code for sex, or did he just mean escort me back to the apartment I shared with his sister? Ugh, my man whisperer powers had left the building and I seemed to have reverted to an awkward teenager incapable of speech.

"Slugger! Don't tell me you're running off so soon! The bar is still fully stocked and nothing's on fire—that's not like you." A booming voice carried over the soft-spoken socialites, who looked over their shoulders in distaste.

I grinned wide. "Uncle Garrett! I thought you were in India." I reluctantly pulled myself away from Ian to be hauled into my uncle's embrace.

"Oh, fuck no. I got out of that shithole as soon as I could. Not my idea of a good time—dirty filthy place," he declared into my hair.

"Good to see you are as politically incorrect as always, Uncle G," I responded dryly.

I loved my Uncle Garrett with all my heart, he was the only reason I didn't consider myself adopted. And the only reason I couldn't say with certainty my mother was an emotionally stunted cyborg.

Garrett pulled away to hold me at arms'-length and inspect me. "You are looking stunning, as always. The plastic surgery monsters don't hold a fucking candle to you, Slugger. Speaking of my sister, where is she?" Garrett asked, scanning the room with a gleam in his eye.

To say they didn't get on would be like saying the *Titanic* only grazed the iceberg. But, like me, Garrett reveled in pissing my mother off, especially by acting decidedly uncouth at these events. We were usually partners in crime, getting drunk off the open bar. And there may have been an incident with a small fire, only teeny tiny. That woman's eyebrows grew back, I was sure.

"Oh, I wouldn't know. I paid my obligatory dues and caught my share of veiled insults for the night, so I guess she's done with me," I responded, feeling Ian's heat at my back.

Garrett's eyes moved from scanning the room to inspect Ian. He grinned. "Well, the fact you aren't wearing a goddamned monkey suit makes me like you already, whoever you are. Amy didn't drag you off the street, did you?" he asked cheekily, holding out his hand. "Garrett Lucas, the closest thing Amy has to a blood relative, on account of the rest of them being blood-sucking vampires."

Ian shook his hand, firmly like all men seemed to do. I got distracted looking at the muscles in his arms pulse as he clenched. My mind wandered to other types of clenching, like the kind his ass would do as he pounded into me.

"Ian Alexandra, pleased to meet you, sir. Amy did not drag me off the street, although you aren't the first person to ask me that tonight." Ian regarded me with a raised brow.

I tried my best to look innocent. I was afraid that didn't work, considering I had just been daydreaming about getting fucked by the man standing in front of me. While in front of my uncle. I needed to see a psychiatrist.

"It's only happened once before," I argued, trying to get my head in the game and away from thoughts of Ian's penis.

Garrett raised his eyebrow.

"Okay, maybe twice," I conceded, feeling red creep up my cheeks.

I never blushed. I was beginning to worry Ian was the catalyst for some kind of medical condition. Was pheromone poisoning a thing?

"This one's a handful, my man, but she's worth it." Garrett winked at me and I cringed.

For some reason my favorite uncle thinking I was involved with this sexy piece of male deliciousness was a blow. Maybe it was because he actually cared about my personal life, unlike the rest of my family, and would ask about Ian the next time we talked. I would then have to correct him in telling him who Ian really was and how he was *so* off limits. Like carbs or refined sugar.

I opened my mouth to correct him, but someone beat me to it.

"I know she is," Ian declared, gazing down at me intensely and not at all platonically.

So maybe tonight could be my cheat night. I did it for diets, why couldn't I do it for socially off limits men?

"As much as I would like to stick around and shoot the shit with you two, I've got to go and embarrass my sister. Have a good night." Garrett winked at me again, pecked me on the cheek, then strutted off in the direction of my mother.

I almost wanted to stay and watch the drama unfold.

"Time to go home." A rough voice tickled the nape of my neck, sending shivers right down to my happy place.

I glanced up to meet Ian's eyes yet again, about to say something when the hunger in his gaze stopped me short. I only managed to nod stupidly and let him lead me out the door.

The promise in his eyes, in his tone, the hand on my back, it all spoke a language I was fluent in. Sex. I wanted Ian more than I had ever wanted another man. I had never felt this attracted to anyone before. And that was saying something since I'd dated a couple of seriously yummy Calvin Klein models.

Ian was just so *male*. Not just in the way he looked, but how he acted, so different than all the men I had in my sexual past. Maybe it was because he was from New Zealand — an exotic, different kind of male than I was used to. Masculinity seemed to waft off him. If that's how they breed them in New Zealand, I was seriously considering moving there.

I had to fight it, no matter how freakishly strong our connection was. It would be a seriously uncool thing for me to do to my best friend. Ian and I would have amazing mind blowing sex, then something would happen, we'd end it and it would be supremely awkward for the rest of time. I wouldn't do it.

"You hungry?" I asked Ian as he opened the door for me.

"Fucking ravenous," he answered in a gravelly voice, eyes flaring.

I gulped and tried not to picture the fact his eyes were not talking about food. Nope. I failed. The image of him in between my legs, using that beautiful mouth to make me come made my knees buckle.

I shook my head.

"Me too. For food, I mean. Yes, food," I stuttered, trying to find my cool.

Ian watched me with a smirk.

"There's an awesome pizza place in Brooklyn that boasts the best pie in the city. The least I can do is buy you dinner after subjecting you to that horror. I bet you wish you were back in the warzone now," I joked.

Ian stopped us at the curb, hand on the door to our car. "You have no idea how happy I am to be right here. All that," he gestured to the hotel, "was worth every fucking second 'cause it meant I was with the most beautiful woman in the room. Every guy in there wished he was in my shoes."

I stared up at him, unprepared for that response and unprepared for the emotions it garnered within me.

Luckily Ian didn't wait for a verbal reply, which I was thankful for. He opened the door. "And there's no way you're paying a dime for the pizza."

I couldn't argue because the door shut behind me. I sighed and leaned back into the seat. I wondered how I wasn't going to pounce on this guy.

————

"So, tell me what it's like being a big, badass, alpha soldier," I asked, munching on my second piece of pizza, enjoying the carby goodness.

I was hoping that since I was binging on something off limits in the food department I would have some willpower left to resist Ian.

Ian watched me a beat then answered. "I don't know about the 'big, badass alpha' bit, but I enjoy the Army. I work with some decent guys who are like brothers." He shrugged. "It's what I've wanted to do since I was a kid and I couldn't imagine doing anything else."

His answer was so not satisfactory.

"Come on, you've got to give me more than that. Do you know how to disarm a nuke? Do you chop the blue wire or the red wire? Can you kill a man in twenty different ways by touching a specific pressure point on their body? Give me the deets."

Ian stared at me a moment, then burst out laughing. Boy, was that a wonderful sight. I watched the cords of his neck move and started to squirm in my seat.

"Jesus Christ, you're a laugh, woman—you're not at all what

you seem. You growing up to be who you are is like a flower growing through a crack in the sidewalk."

I tried my hardest to ignore the power behind Ian's gaze, the connection that seemed to be buzzing between us.

"I bet I seem a lot more interesting than I actually am due to the fact you probably haven't seen a woman in a while," I said awkwardly, trying to deflect the compliment.

Usually I lapped up praise from the opposite sex, but it was always about my appearance: my tits, legs, and hair. Ian saw past all of that, it made me uncomfortable and feel warm inside. It was dangerous.

He frowned. "Trust me, you're nothing like any woman I've ever met. You've been an amazing friend to my sister. I'll be forever grateful for that alone."

I relaxed at him steering the conversation back to a safer subject, one that might douse the flames of my out of control libido.

"Gwen's the one that saved me from suffocating in the stifling Upper East Side cult. She's real, honest and loyal—I'm lucky to have her."

From there the conversation seemed to flow and although there was a sexual undertone, the topics were general.

We talked for hours, talking about nothing and everything. Ian told me about having four-wheeler races with Gwen on their farm back in New Zealand. I told him about the time I signed my mother up to attend a drag queen benefit without her knowledge. I talked with him like I had never talked with anyone before. It felt easy, normal, right. Dangerous.

The easy banter and extreme attraction I felt for this man did not bode well for my future. I had only been in his presence for a couple of hours — how could I stand the two weeks he was here without pouncing on him? I would just have to ovary it up and find a way to resist it. I was a grown woman, after all. I wasn't a slave to my baser instincts.

———

"Fucking hell, you're beautiful," Ian growled while his hand traced my breast.

"No talking," I commanded, pulling him back to my mouth.

Okay, so it had taken my resolve about five sexually charged minutes to waver on the car ride home. Ian seemed to be struggling too and as if we had reached some kind of mutual agreement, we had pounced on each other.

Luckily the car had a privacy screen so the driver wouldn't be getting a free amateur porn show. Not that I cared at this moment. Hell, he could pull up to Times Square and sell tickets, I didn't give a shit.

He yanked me up to straddle his lap, bunching the fabric of my dress so my almost bare core rubbed against his hard length. I moaned into his mouth. Calloused hands snagged against the silk of my dress, playing with my nipples as they hardened under his touch. I ground my body against his, desperate to feel closer. To meld myself against his rock hard body. I almost came from the friction of his jeans against the lace of my panties.

"You're gonna have to stop doing that, beautiful, or I'm going to lose control and fuck you right here," Ian bit out.

I opened my eyes and gazed at him through my lashes, "I *want* you to fuck me right here."

Ian seemed to struggle for a moment and he let his forehead fall against mine.

"You're too good to fuck in the back of a car. I want you in a bed where I can take my time, taste every inch of your body, then fuck you slow and watch your face when you come," he hissed, palming my breast.

I grasped his hand and directed it into my soaking panties. His jaw clenched as his fingers brushed my clit. I barely restrained a scream.

"You're testing my willpower, Amy," he grunted, rubbing me in delightful circles.

My eyes glazed over as he brought me close to the edge, his other hand grasped my neck, pulling me to face him.

"I want to watch you come," he declared, eyes bright.

I was about to treat him to the Abrams orgasm show when something broke the moment.

"Sexy Bitch" blared from the flimsy material of my Gucci.

"Fuck," I muttered.

I tried to scramble off him, the reminder of what I was doing like a bucket of ice water. Hands gripped my waist, keeping me in place. I frowned at them before reaching for my purse.

"Hey, Gwennie," I greeted as I answered the phone.

I watched Ian stiffen slightly. Good, we both needed to calm this shit.

"Hey Abrams, where are you guys? I got home and I figured you would have ditched that snoozefest by now. Don't tell me you've dragged Ian out clubbing, he hates that crap. Actually I could use a drink or ten. I can meet you?" Gwen greeted with her usual speech.

"Um, we're actually on our way home." I squirmed, uncomfortable having this conversation in Ian's lap. I felt like I was betraying Gwen.

Scratch that, I was totally betraying Gwen.

"Okay, no worries. I'd rather put on sweats and get drunk off homemade cocktails. I'll start making them now. See you soon, bitch!" She hung up before I could say another word.

I stared at the silent phone, willing someone, anyone to call to rescue me from this situation that turned awkward with the sound of one song. Even my mother or Craig, the stage-five clinger who I was trying to shake. I'd welcome Craig right now. But alas, crazy stalkers never called when you wanted them to.

I was forced to face the music when Ian grasped my chin and gently directed my gaze to him.

"Gwen's at home. Making cocktails as we speak," I whispered.

He smirked. "I wouldn't expect anything less."

I paused. "She can't know about this." I gestured between us. "This can't happen again."

It pained me to even say it, feeling in Ian's arms felt so right. Ew, did I seriously just think that? I hated girls who said cheesy shit like that. I wanted to tit punch girls that said shit like that.

"I agree, Gwen probably shouldn't know I pashed her best friend within hours of arriving," he grinned.

"What does pashed mean?" I asked, wondering if it was New Zealand slang for some sort of sexual wizardry.

"It means I've tasted how sweet your mouth is, felt how amazing your body feels, and it means I want to taste all of you. Feel what it's like to slide inside you."

Holy fuck. What does one say to that? Especially when one is feeling the impressive length of what could mean multiple orgasms if this guy's kiss was anything to go by.

"I'm going to be straight up here. This is complicated. You aren't just a fuck for me, I can tell you that already. You're more. But I can't give you more. I'm here for two weeks and then I'm gone. I won't be back for another year. My job is dangerous. Who knows if I will come back?"

I tensed at the thought of Ian getting hurt. I tensed even more when I realized how deeply this thought affected me.

He brushed my cheek. "All of that means I should be keeping my distance, not complicating things, not putting you through this. That's what I *should* be doing. But if my job's taught me anything, it's to make the most of every day, every second. Even if it's just for one night, I want the memory of your face, your body to think of when I'm in the next hellhole." His fingertips grazed the edge of my panties. "It may be selfish as fuck, but I want to remember how tight your pussy is whenever I look at you, know what it feels to have you pulse around my finger. I want you, all of you," he murmured.

I exhaled. Wow. I wanted all of that. Hell, after that speech I'd offer to carry his firstborn child and to sell my entire Loubie collection if that's what he wanted.

So after that night, that's what we did. We made the most of every moment, and against my wishes I fell head over red-soled heels in love with him.

We attempted the long distance thing. We tried to keep it casual, to keep it a secret from Gwen, with stolen moments and late night rendezvous. But it wasn't casual. It couldn't be. Not with us. I was prepared to wait. To try. But Ian had something else in mind. Namely yanking my heart out of my chest and stomping on it.

CHAPTER TWO

PRESENT DAY

A presence violating my personal bubble shook me out of my trip down memory lane. It was probably a good thing too, that was a dangerous place for me to venture. I was tempted to thank the space invader but stopped short as my eyes met his. His blue eyes were full of menace and danger, not the good kind.

"Pretty lady like you shouldn't be drinking alone. Next one's one me," he drawled.

I waved my tequila bottle at him unsteadily. "No thanks, I'm set."

I turned my back to him, hoping that sent the message, but at my other side was an equally sinister looking man, eyeing me with that same stare. I was used to attention from men, but this stare was not sexual in any way. It was predatory and cold.

I regarded them both as well as I could after half a bottle of tequila. It was safe to say they were blurry. Both were wearing seriously expensive suits, the kind that cost as much as a second-hand car. Ditto for the gold jewelry.

I may have been halfway to blotto, but I'd have to be unconscious not to register fashion and accessories. One was young and not unattractive, with dark hair and dark features, slim and about my age. The other was older and balding, no matter how good the tailoring was, you couldn't hide the paunch hanging over his belt. They had money. They were not at home in a place like this. I didn't get good vibes as to why they were here talking to me.

"How about we take you somewhere a little more respectable, somewhere a woman like you belongs," the older one addressed me.

Warning bells sounded in my inebriated brain. This didn't seem like it was going any place good. I searched for my friend the bartender, hoping he would be my knight in dirty plaid, but he was down the other end of the bar unpacking boxes.

Guess I had to take care of myself.

"Look, I don't know what kind of sick father-son fantasy you two have going on, but I don't want to be any part of it. Go and check the yellow pages for hookers who specialize in ménage a trois." They continued to stare at me. "In other words, fuck off." I attempted to sound strong and unruffled at the proximity of the men and their not so subtle intentions. The slurring of my words might have screwed with that attempt.

"Well, this one's got spice." The younger one raised his eyebrow, almost amused at me. The way a cat was amused with a mouse before it gobbled it up.

"'Fraid we're gonna have to insist you come with us, sweetheart," he continued conversationally.

"'Fraid you're gonna have to go screw yourself. I am not going anywhere with you two weirdos. Leave me alone before I scream at the top of my lungs." I hoped the patrons of this bar were more chivalrous than they looked.

Paunch Man stepped closer and something hard pressed into my back. I didn't think it was on account of him being happy to see me.

"You better rethink that, Red. I'd hate to blow a hole in such a perfect little body, or splatter the brains of that nice bartender all over the walls." He nodded his head at my tequila-giving friend who was heading our way with a frown.

I gulped. This was a serious situation, one that required some serious brainpower if I was to get out of it. Unfortunately, my brainpower had left the building three shots ago.

"Everything okay there, darlin'? These guys bothering you?" he asked with a skeptical eye at my Armani clad kidnappers.

I swallowed and struggled not to throw myself across the bar and cling to the safety this man represented. The hard barrel at my ribs stopped me.

"Yeah, I'm fine. These are...." I trailed off, trying to think of some secret code I could use that would alert him to my situation. Then he could call the cops and they would hurtle into the building and save me.

It happened in movies.

"We're her cousins, come to take her home. It's not safe for a woman to be drinking alone out here. Who knows what kind of sickos could take advantage," the fat one cut in.

The barman eyed them skeptically, no doubt eyeing the lack of resemblance. He didn't have time to inspect it thoroughly as I was roughly pulled to my feet.

"Come on, cuz, let's get you home." Blue Eyes grasped my upper arm tightly.

I swayed as the bar spun, but I didn't have a chance to get my balance as I was dragged across the room. I managed to put one foot in front of the other without face planting — no mean feat in six-inch heels and a belly full of liquor. My eyes burned as I was pulled out the door and into the sunlight. I put my hand up to shield my face from the rays and the grip on my arm tightened.

"Keep walkin,' Red. Don't want a bullet hole to ruin your outfit, do we?" Blue Eyes yanked me along the street in the direction of a blacked-out SUV.

The sunlight may have temporarily blinded me, but it also sobered me slightly. I glanced around at the small but busy street. I couldn't remember the name of this town, but I knew where my hotel was, not too far away from this bar actually. I also knew that a police station was two doors down from my hotel.

I didn't doubt these guys had a gun, but I also wondered if they'd actually use it on me. They were obviously kidnapping me for a reason — either that or they were going to kill me somewhere and dump my body, in which case I had nothing to lose. Or they needed me for some unknown reason, and then they would need me breathing. In any case I wasn't going to let them have me without a fight. I was Amy Abrams, for fuck's sake.

The SUV was getting closer so I had to act quickly. I pretended to stumble, pulling Blue Eyes back around.

"What the—" he started, but I interrupted him by jamming my heel into his shoe.

That move would not work on some of the bikers I had been hanging around lately, on account of their steel-capped boots. It worked a treat on soft Italian leather loafers. My heel went straight through and into his foot. He screamed in pain and let go of my arm. I pulled my foot back and turned on Fat Guy, who was standing frozen. I kneed him in the nuts, satisfied at the grunt of pain he emitted.

People on the street were looking now, but I didn't want to put any of them in the potential crossfire. I ran in the direction of the police station, adrenaline replacing some of the alcohol in my system. Not all of it. I still swayed a bit, but I managed to stay upright. I heard people yelling in concern but blocked it out, pushing my legs to go faster as I crossed the street.

I started to feel elated and pleased with myself for my escape without the need for a rescue. *I am a strong, independent woman who don't need no man to rescue her from a kidnapping.* On that thought, someone tackled me to the ground. I felt a dull pain from the impact but thankfully alcohol provided a pain cushion.

"Not smart, Red," a voice hissed in my ear.

That's when everything went black.

———

I woke up slowly with a thumping headache and aches all over my body. I kept my eyes closed for a few moments, trying to will myself back to sleep so I could sleep off this giant hangover. Unfortunately I was to suffer conscious. Great. I cracked my eyes open, intending to reach over to my nightstand for some water, but stopped short.

The plush ceiling was not what I had at my mediocre hotel. I glanced around at the luxurious bedding, realizing I was not in anyplace familiar. I also realized that my hands were above my head and were handcuffed to an ornate bedframe. Why this wasn't the first thing I noticed, I had no idea. Hangovers did weird things to me. Speaking of weird things, what kind of guy did I go home with last night?

I racked my brain and tried to retrieve some memories, ignoring the sick feeling I had at sleeping with a strange guy. There hadn't been anyone since ... *him*. That feeling was quickly replaced with dread as the previous events washed over me. My worries consisted of something a whole lot bigger than a *Coyote Ugly* situation and more in the realm of a fucking life or death situation. Fear crept up my throat and I struggled with the cuffs, trying to manoeuver them off the frame.

"She's awake," a voice declared and I jumped.

A man strolled from the edge of the room to stand over me, a phone to his ear and a frown on his face. His blue eyes looked familiar.

"Got it." He ended the call and regarded me coolly.

I gulped, fear crawling up my throat. "What do you want with me?" I demanded, meeting his gaze. I was proud that my voice didn't shake.

He stepped closer to the bed and leaned toward me. I failed to hide my flinch, expecting a blow of some kind. The pain I expected never came, instead my hands were released from the handcuffs. I rubbed them, eyeing the angry red welts that remained.

"Up," Blue Eyes commanded.

I glared at him, scrambling up and over to the opposite side of the enormous bed, thankful for the barrier between us. It was an illusion of safety, but I clung to it.

"What do you want from me?" I repeated, eyes darting around the tastefully decorated room for a weapon.

He ignored me yet again and nodded to a door in the corner of the room. "That's a bathroom—got towels and a change of clothes. Clean yourself up, put on the clothes. You got twenty minutes." He stared at me for a moment then turned to leave.

"Wait a second, asshole, why should I do a single thing you say? You fucking *kidnapped* me," I snapped.

Blue Eyes stopped and turned slowly, his expression not cold or detached as it had been moments ago. It was dangerous, sinister.

"You're going to do as I say because if I come back here in twenty minutes and you aren't showered and dressed, I get to shower and dress you myself. I can assure you I will enjoy every second of it. I can't promise you the same. Your choice, *cara*."

My stomach dropped at his words, they were a promise and a sick grin decorated his face. He turned again and walked out of the room. I heard a click as he locked the door behind him.

"Fuck!" I yelled to the room. This was some serious shit. I pinched myself. "Ouch," I hissed.

Okay, so I wasn't dreaming or in a drug-induced hallucination. At least I didn't think I was. I tried shrooms once and the trip I experienced was nothing like this. I had been convinced my hair was made of plastic and spent three hours crying because I wouldn't be able to use a straightening iron without melting my hair. I swore off any kind of drugs after that.

I had to face the fact that this was all most likely real. I had been kidnapped by some well-dressed Italians. Glancing around at the décor, which screamed money, I deduced I was in some sort of mansion. It was reminiscent of my childhood home, a prison of a different kind. I darted toward the window and tried to push it up. It wouldn't budge. Shit. I should've listened to Gwen and done those gym classes.

I looked through the glass and gathered I was at least two stories up. Men roamed the well-kept lawn with guns, there was not another house in sight. The sparse desert landscape seemed to stretch on forever. I decided I wouldn't go unnoticed if I smashed the window and tried to climb down a drainpipe. Escape via window was out. I was locked in.

I leaned against the wall and racked my brain trying to think of a miraculous escape plan. But my lack of experience in kidnapping situations coupled with a whopping hangover hindered me. I assessed my options. Waste my twenty minutes turning this room upside down for weapons or secret passage-ways and subject myself to possible rape? Or I could shower, dress, and prepare myself for what was coming. If they were going to kill me I doubted they would care about what I was wearing or my state of cleanliness. I deduced my life was not in immediate danger and my best bet was to comply.

For now.

The bathroom was just as impressive as the room I had woken up in. Opulent with black granite flooring, a huge spa bath, and shower stall. A big window treated me with a view of a broad desert landscape and barren mountain ranges. I was in the middle of nowhere. I swallowed the panic at that thought and focused on the task at hand. One thing at a time. Turning into a blubbering mess would not do me any good.

After trying the window and searching the bathroom for any possible weapons, I got in the shower. The blissful hot water and amazing pressure did little to calm me, but I busied myself with getting clean using the seriously expensive bath products.

Being mindful of my twenty-minute time limit, I stepped out of the shower and found the clothes I was to put on, a clingy Versace wrap dress and Stella McCartney underwear. I hoped the lingerie was not chosen with a purpose in mind. My stomach dropped. Holy shit, was I going to be sold into a sex slavery ring? My dad was not Liam Neeson, he was a Wall Street businessman, the chances of him rescuing me were slim to none.

I failed to forget about my biker family. They would not hesitate to come and rescue me. I couldn't control my yearning for one man in particular to be my knight riding a Harley. Too bad he didn't know where I was. They all thought I was in New York. Even if he did know where I was, I doubted he would come to my aid after the past year. He hated me. No, it was worse than hate. He was indifferent.

I couldn't think about him now. I had to focus on the more pressing scenario, the one that may involve me being sold into a sex slavery ring. No one was coming to save me, of that much I was sure. My family in Amber thought I was in New York and my family in New York couldn't care less about where I was. I was on my own.

I put on the dress and accompanying heels before pulling my damp hair into a French braid. My reflection stared at me blankly as I regarded myself in the mirror. Free of makeup I looked vulnerable, my freckles making me look childlike. I didn't need that. I needed my war paint to look strong. Stronger than I felt. A sharp knock on the door made me jump.

"Time's up, Red."

The bathroom door opened and Blue Eyes appeared, inspecting me in a way that made me want to hop right back in the shower.

"It's a shame you had to be a good little girl and do what you were told. I was looking forward to teaching you a lesson, *cara*," he sneered, grabbing my arm roughly and directing me out the door.

I noticed he was limping slightly and smirked. "It looks like you're the one that got taught a lesson. Seems like your kidnapping skills aren't up to par since you let a half-drunk woman put a hole in your expensive shoes. How's your foot?" I asked sweetly.

He stopped me abruptly and his grip on my arm tightened painfully.

"You're not going to be so mouthy once I'm allowed to play with you. I promise you that, bitch. I'll enjoy making you scream." His attractive face morphed into a sneer and I refused to let the fear I felt show.

I stared at him silently and ignored the throbbing in my arm. He gazed at me a moment longer then yanked me along.

After a silent journey through the expansive and impressive house, I was roughly pushed into a dining room. It was huge and sliding doors opened onto an outdoor terrace and a pool. It looked like paradise, apart from the men strolling around with guns. Oh, and the fact I was being held against my will.

My gaze moved to a man sitting at the far end of a long table. His graying head was bent reading a paper, a plate of untouched food sitting in front of him. The entire table was full of delicious looking breakfast platters. My stomach rumbled on cue, I couldn't remember the last time I ate. My hangover, coupled with my abduction, made me hangry.

"Sit," Blue Eyes commanded, shoving me toward the chair at the opposite end of the table.

The man still hadn't lifted his head. Deciding to do as I was told, I sat gingerly, ignoring the plate of food in front of me.

"Miss Abrams, good morning. I see the clothes are a perfect fit. You look stunning. Please eat. I had some *pain au chocolate* flown in from Paris—I understand they are your favorite. And of course coffee." The man waved his hand and a woman bustled into the room.

She was Mexican, older and looked like someone's grand-mother. She smiled at me as she poured fragrant coffee into my cup. I struggled not to salivate, I needed ten gallons of coffee right about now. I resisted the urge to cling to this woman's skirt, knowing there was not much she could do to help me. I wondered if she knew she was serving a kidnapping victim. I sat stiffly as she walked out, fighting the urge not to clutch the coffee.

"Who are you? What do want with me?" I demanded, glaring at the man at the other end of the table.

"Eat, Miss Abrams. I imagine you are starved, considering it's been almost twenty-eight hours since your last meal. I'm sure you need your coffee. We will talk after." The man didn't look up as he sipped his own cup.

My hand twitched, my need for caffeine messing with my brain. I felt like an addict going through withdrawal, my fix within arms' reach. I resisted. I had bigger fish to fry.

"I will not sit and eat while I'm getting held against my will. This isn't a fucking brunch date. You *kidnapped* me. What the fuck do you want?" I hissed, clutching the arms of my chair. Fury had momentarily replaced my fear.

The man glanced at me over his paper, his gaze almost disinterested. He sighed and put it to the side, clasping his hands together. "My reports are not wrong—you are spirited." He seemed almost amused.

"Well, *excuse me* for not praising you on what a lovely kidnapping you've thrown—it's the best I've been to. I'll be sure to let my friends know the caliber of pastries present. What do you want with me?" I continued to manage to keep the tremor out of my voice. I was proud.

The fact this wasn't your traditional kidnapping didn't take away the reality of what was going on here. If anything it made it scarier, I didn't know what was going on. The man in front of me seemed familiar. Not in the fact I knew him personally, but I knew his type. I grew up surrounded by men like him. He could have been one of my father's golf buddies or business associates.

His graying hair was cut close to his head and styled expertly. His suit was Tom Ford if I wasn't mistaken, a gold Rolex adorned his wrist and he was wearing a pocket square. He just didn't fit the role of kidnapper. Not that I really knew what your run of the mill criminal looked like, but I expected tattoos or at least a greasy haired man wearing thick gold chains. Not someone this sophisticated and not someone who looked a lot more like George Clooney than Dr. Evil.

"I apologize for the unpleasantness, Miss Abrams, but unfortunately this was necessary," George Clooney replied, as if he was talking about a mistake in a dinner reservation.

"Unpleasantness?" I repeated. "You call your two goons dragging me out of a bar at gunpoint, then tasing me and waking up handcuffed to a bed *unpleasant*? I think the word you are looking for is illegal—seriously fucking illegal. You need to let me leave right now," I commanded, wishing it would be that easy.

"I'm afraid I can't do that, Miss Abrams. I admit this was a last resort, which was unfortunately necessary. I assure you no harm will come to you if you comply, and you will be able to return back to the bar from in which we found you once I get what I want."

I eyed the man across the table with a raised brow. "Sure. I bet you say that to all the girls. What is it that you want?"

George maintained eye contact, he seemed vaguely disinterested as if this was a meeting he wanted to get through. My conclusion that I was being sold into sex slavery was becoming less likely. Or maybe that was just wishful thinking. One thing was for sure ... I wasn't going to do as this wacko said and hope for the best. I'd be getting out of here if I had to tunnel my way out with a spoon.

"Your father is a business associate of mine. We had a mutually beneficial arrangement—that was, until recently. I won't bore you with the details, but I will say all other civil attempts to persuade your father against certain courses of action have been unsuccessful. So here we are." He held out his hands. "I imagine your wellbeing is of great importance to your father, and the continued health of his only daughter might prove as a motivation to change his mind." George took a sip of his coffee, pausing to let this all sink in.

My father. He was the reason I was being kidnapped? The man who summered in the Hamptons and screwed his nose up at newspaper vendors was business associates with a criminal? Granted, he may not know about said criminal activities, but my father was far from stupid and I doubted this guy went from law abiding to Class A felony in one fell swoop.

I let out a small giggle at the absurdity of this entire situation. Given the company I had been keeping over the last year or so, I had thought if I was going to be kidnapped by anyone it would be by someone wearing a cut and jeans, not a ten thousand dollar suit.

"Something amusing, Miss Abrams?" George asked me, eyes more alert.

I waved my hand. "Not amusing. In fact, this is not funny *at all.* Just ironic. In all the scenarios I would imagine a kidnapping going down, this is the least likely."

I sobered at the memory of my best friend almost dying after being kidnapped, then coming home battered after it happened again nine months ago. We had some bad freaking luck when it came to this shit.

George narrowed his eyes. "Yes, well, I imagine with the company you keep you have been exposed to some more *unsavory* criminal activities. As long as you are well behaved and your father is obliging, there is no reason for this to get uncivilized," he said with an air of superiority.

I sucked in a breath. "Are you serious? The man who just had me kidnapped is doling out judgment on the 'company I keep'? You've got to be fucking kidding me. Let me tell you something, you *Soprano* wannabe, those men are each worth a hundred of you and your tacky watch, which I can assure you screams new money," I hissed at him, momentarily forgetting the power balance in this conversation.

George's eyes flared slightly, but his face betrayed no emotion. "I imagine this has been an unsettling few hours for you, Miss Abrams, so I'll let that little outburst slide." He leaned forward slightly. "But if you ever speak to me like that again, you'll be very, *very* sorry." His tone was soft and I shivered at the promise underneath it.

"Now," he carried on, "please eat something. I would hate for my guest to go hungry." He moved his attention to his own plate, reopening his newspaper. Apparently I was dismissed.

Deciding my hangover coupled with severe caffeine deficiency made me slightly loopy, I pushed my plate away defiantly. It was a struggle with my mouth watering at the sight of the pastry of the gods, but I managed. The coffee cup was another story, I had to actually clutch my hands to my lap to stop from reaching for it. But I was determined.

I was not going to accept this situation and eat a (albeit magnificent) croissant and sip (medically necessary) coffee with my captor like this was a weekend retreat. I could handle skipping a couple of meals and foregoing coffee for that. I did the master cleanse, for crissake. I did however slip a butter knife into my lap while pushing the plate away. I wasn't too sure what I would do with it, it wouldn't be effective in deflecting bullets, but I needed to start somewhere.

"Not hungry?" He didn't look up from his paper.

"I'm afraid captivity messes with my appetite," I replied sweetly.

There was a long pause until he spoke again. "Well, I can only hope your appetite returns sooner rather than later. I'd hate to see you starve." His thinly veiled threat had its effect and he moved on. "If you do not want your food then I will consent to you leaving the table."

"How gracious of you," I muttered sarcastically.

He ignored this. "Rafe will show you to your wing. There is a library, a TV room, and a home gym. You have the freedom to move about them as you please."

I restrained a snort. If they wanted to hurt me they could have just forced me to use the home gym. I'd be much more compliant under the threat of imminent exercise.

"I will inform you that all exits will be locked, and I'm sure you've seen my employees." He gestured outside. "Just in case you have any ideas about wandering off."

I held a hand to my chest in mock shock. "Me? Never! Why should I want to leave such a pretty cage?" I didn't even think about my sarcastic remark, it just came out.

George ignored me again as if I was a troublesome teenager. "I also expect you to join me for breakfast every morning and dinner every evening. Whether you consume them is up to you, but I must insist on your presence, as well as you wearing the garments I supply you with." His eyes moved over my dress, interest obvious in his gaze. I felt as if spiders were crawling over me.

George was a silver fox, no doubt about that, but he was also a crazy psychopath who may or may not try and kill me. My taste in men had gotten me into some shitty situations lately, but I wasn't insane.

I decided to ignore him, getting up to remove myself from his presence and to plot an escape using only a butter knife. I turned to leave.

"Oh, Miss Abrams? I would appreciate it if you left the knife here. I wouldn't want my mother's silverware getting lost," he remarked casually.

Fuck.

I turned slowly and placed the knife on the table quietly. I spun to leave the room to plot my escape sans butter knife. My stomach swirled at how precarious my situation was. My spirits did lift slightly when Rafe limped toward me, scowling. If I could do damage to a career criminal's goon with only a Louboutin I had to have faith.

———

I paced the long stretch of room in "my wing's" library for the hundredth time. It had been hours since my little breakfast meeting with George and I was going stir crazy. I was also pissed. Anger was a much better coping mechanism than fear. Fear was not productive. If I gave into the fear curled at the bottom of my stomach I might be crouched on the floor rocking back and forth right now. Walking back and forward for two hours was arguably just as bad, apart from maybe wearing down an expensive looking Persian rug. I sank down on a leather armchair in exasperation.

I had explored the rooms of my prison earlier this morning, looking for possible escape points and for any potential weapons. I had come up dry on both points. Even if I had found a way to slip out into an unguarded area of the property, I would be facing a long trek in an unforgiving desert landscape. And who could forget Rafe following me around all day, his blue eyes burning into me with anger and a sick desire.

The rooms I was free to explore were exquisitely furnished and spotless. The man had a good decorator. Considering where I came from I knew how to spot serious wealth. To tell the difference between a cheap imitation rug for instance, or one that cost more than a down payment on a house. This man was hideously rich. Which made me wonder what the heck he did to accumulate all of this wealth to contribute to the need for an around the clock security detail that rivaled the president's. All of my guesses were not good.

What the fuck had my father been thinking getting involved with this guy? I wondered what my father was doing now. Was he cooperating with the demands? Or had he called the police? I doubted my mother would want the "scandal" of her daughter being kidnapped. I imagined her greatest worry right now would be how bad the lighting would be in a police press conference.

I couldn't imagine my father becoming outraged or out of his mind with worry for me. He never really expressed much emotion toward me. We got along okay, even had some enjoyable conversations. My father had a dry wit and I enjoyed his company when he was around, which wasn't often. He was never affectionate with me, but didn't hesitate in getting me whatever I wanted and he did drop everything to help me when I needed it. He loved me in his own detached sort of way. He would do what it took to get me home, I hoped.

My thoughts moved to someone who would have an entirely different reaction to news of my kidnapping. Or he would have. Before. Maybe six months ago before I had come home and refused to talk to him. Avoided him at all costs. And when he had finally had enough of my evasion and silence I had to flat out lie to him.

I'd never forget the look in his eyes after I uttered words that broke my own heart. So maybe after that he might not have the reaction I would have thought. He might not have any reaction at all. I was solely to blame for that. I sabotaged any future I had with him. It would have been a fucked up future anyway, with the shadow of a dead man between us. No, it would have been doomed. I did us both a favor.

But now, while I was imprisoned, facing the grim reality of my own mortality, I couldn't help but think back to when I first saw him.

Brock.

CHAPTER THREE

ONE YEAR AGO

It wasn't love at first sight. Fireworks didn't explode between us, nor did my angelic good looks and womanly wiles ruin him for anyone else. Pure sexual attraction was what it was at the start. Nothing deeper. No romance novel, "you are mine for the rest of eternity" crap. All that magic was saved for my best friend. Not that I begrudged her, not for a second. She deserved every inch of that fairy dust that was sprinkled between her and Cade. I made sure none of that shit settled on my designer clad shoulders.

I had been all sparkly eyed and struck dumb by love. By her very brother, in fact. I had been there, got the t-shirt and the kick to my lady bits. Okay, maybe more like a gunshot wound to the heart. The pain was as fresh as it was the day Ian yanked my heart out of my chest and stomped on it before handing it back to me.

"Ames, we had fun—it was amazing, in fact. You're an incredible person, beautiful inside and out. You're special. I love you. But this can't work. You can't pine for me while I'm thousands of miles away. I might

not come back. I can't be thinking about you. I need to stop this before it's too late and shit gets complicated. You'll thank me later."

I gripped the cocktail shaker in my hand tightly at that memory, anger a more comfortable companion than heartbreak. Pining. Me? That was exactly what I had been doing for a fucking year. There had been men. I hadn't been a nun. I wasn't one of those girls that said goodbye to orgasms because she was hoping her "true love" would get his shit together. I was, however, a hugely toned down version of my former sexual self. There had been men. But not many. And every time I took someone to bed I felt like crying. Heartbreak had turned me into a sniveling mess.

So I had decided as well as leaving New York, I was leaving the sad and pathetic Amy Abrams behind. I wasn't becoming a new person. I was going to be the old Amy. Pre-Ian. That Amy knew what the deal was. Friends, high heels, designer threads, great cocktails, and sex. Just sex. No messy strings, no emotional attachments.

I had originally thought this decision was ironic, considering I was moving to a tiny town where the fuckable men pool would be small. Miniscule.

But I had been pleasantly surprised after my first few days here. It was as if this town attracted beautiful men. If I was a conspiracy theorist I would have been suspicious at just how a town this small managed to get such a great selection of men.

I was not.

What I happened to be was horny. I didn't care if they were a government experiment gone wrong (or incredibly right), or aliens from another planet. The last time I had sex was months ago. That had to change.

I doubted that I would be finding any eligible bed buddies at our store opening, but I was delightfully surprised. My eyes flickered to the sexy policemen that had waltzed through the door not ten minutes ago. They were hot. But they were clean cut, handsome, good guys. Well, I didn't know if they were technically *good guys*, but they represented them. They were a little too close to a certain soldier who I was trying to get over.

No, I didn't need a good guy. I didn't need someone who would treat me right and tell me I was beautiful. I needed an asshole. Someone who would fuck me and then not call me until he wanted me in his bed again. Someone who I wouldn't fall in love with.

I was passing a beer to one of the cops, fluttering my eyelids just a little (just because I wasn't going to sleep with them didn't mean I wasn't going to flirt) when my eyes flickered to the door. Or more precisely, the leather clad hunks who had just walked through it. I recognized Cade straight away and followed his murderous stare. It was aimed at Gwen, or more precisely Luke's hand, which was at Gwen's hip.

In any other circumstances I would be tickled pink at Gwen flirting with a member of the opposite sex. But right now I was thinking it might be conclusive to a brawl erupting in our store. Not that I wouldn't pay to see those two men wrestle — that shit would be awesome. I just didn't want it happening so close to all of those innocent accessories.

I caught Gwen's eye and tried to give her a look. We could usually communicate pretty well with a look, we had an uncanny connection. But unfortunately *"the hot biker who seems a tiny bit obsessed with you is currently storming over to potentially smack down with the local cop who also seems obsessed with you"* was not something that could be communicated with a mere look. We had to work on some kind of sign language.

I shrugged and settled in for the show. Unfortunately my front row seat was interrupted.

"Three beers. Thanks, sweetheart," a rough voice requested.

I didn't move my gaze from Gwen and Luke, who had just been joined by a furious looking Cade. Uh oh.

"I'll be with you in a sec," I told the voice, wishing I could read lips.

"You got something better to do than give out drinks? I'm

thinking maybe you shouldn't be standing behind a bar," the voice replied dryly.

At this point, Cade grabbed Gwen's hand and pretty much dragged her out of the store. I grinned at her as she went past, amused at the turn of events.

My grin disappeared and irritation flared at the deep voice's last statement. I reached into the fridge and grabbed three beers, turning to thrust them at my unhappy customer. They were free, for fuck's sake, who was he to act all snippy?

"Here. I assume you haven't died of thirst in the minute you've been waiting," I started, turning to meet this guy's eyes.

I stopped short. This guy was hot. Granted, there were a lot of hot men peppered around this room, but this guy was *hot*. He looked like a cross between a surfer and an outlaw. His sandy blonde hair was pulled back into a messy bun — holy crap what an awesome man bun it was. He had tanned skin, which was contrasted by some serious blue eyes. I felt them pierce my soul.

Okay, my ovaries.

His nose was slightly crooked like it had been broken a couple of times too many. It seemed to make him hotter, to contrast the clean cut surfer look. Well, that and his tattoos. I could see one snaking up his neck and his hands had letters on his knuckles. Unfortunately I couldn't get a good look. I did know his hands were big and you know what they said about big hands. I took a quick glance at his body, which was hidden under a leather vest and shirt, but there was no hiding the bulk. I swallowed, feeling my mouth water.

Don't drool in front of the biker.

"I would recommend you not quit your day job, sweetheart —I don't think bartending is your calling. Your barside manner needs some work." He smirked, revealing dimples.

Dimples!

He also reached over and snagged the bottle opener, his hand lightly brushing past my stomach. His touch felt like an open flame that spread south of the spot he had just made contact with. I was certainly attracted to him. His body at least, not his mouth. Actually his mouth was equally as attractive as the rest of him, just not what came out of it.

"Yeah, well, no one else seems to have a problem with my bartending skills," I retorted, ignoring him pointedly opening the bottles.

He raised an eyebrow and looked me up and down. I felt like his was doing something incredibly naughty and he wasn't even touching me.

"I can see why, Sparky. I'm thinking most men would drink cold piss if you served it up wearing that. Tits like yours, who cares if you're a bitch?" He winked and walked off.

I let out a breath and welcomed the flame of irritation this man had kindled. He had just called me a bitch seconds after meeting him! I wanted to pour a beer down his front and simultaneously lift up his tee and lick his abs.

"Holy crap, did you see that? I totally thought Cade was going to pummel Luke for a second. But now I see he is channeling a different emotion." Lucy peered at the door Gwen and Cade had just exited, leaning on the bar.

I snapped my gaze away from the jean clad ass of the surfer and turned my attention to Lucy, who was joined by Ashley and Rosie.

"Well, it looks like my brother has decided that Gwen is his and she shall talk to no other man," Rosie joked, sipping her cocktail. "Seriously, I wouldn't have been surprised if he started beating his chest grunting 'Gwen mine,' before he dragged her off."

I smirked at them "I don't think the two of them will be doing much talking either. I'd bet her new dress is getting snagged on a brick wall right now." I paused for a moment, feeling sad about the brutal treatment of such an innocent dress.

Rosie giggled. "It's about time Cade set his sights on a woman who has class... and someone who doesn't think belts can double as skirts."

I glanced at the three girls with a smile. Our arrival in Amber had been so much better than I expected. Not only was our house amazing, the men unnaturally hot and the town actually nice, but we had also seemed to fall right into rhythm with a kick ass girl posse. These chicks not only had good taste in clothes and cocktails, but they were genuine and friendly.

I felt more comfortable with them than most of the girls I grew up with. They were real. Their fathers didn't own banks and I didn't think they summered in St. Tropez, which was exactly what I liked about them. They didn't live their lives in order to impress or incite jealousy in others. They just *lived*. I dug it.

"I'm just happy Gwen has chosen a guy with so many delectable friends," I replied, gazing back over at the bikers who didn't look at all uncomfortable at being in a woman's clothing store.

Rosie followed my eyes. "Yeah, the guys are freaking hot," she sighed. "It's a shame my chances of getting into any of their pants are hampered by the fact my brother would most likely cut the dick off any of his brothers who touched me."

I gazed at her with sympathy. "That seriously sucks, babe. Having men like that in such close proximity and not even being able to sample their wares?" I shook my head. "It's a crime to humanity. I'll be sure to give you explicit details of what happens when I get into bed with one of them...or all of them." I winked.

———

I spent the rest of the night serving drinks, chatting with the locals, and drinking cocktails. I also managed to give Gwennie a good-natured ribbing about her hot guy faceoff and subsequent make out session with a sexy biker. Not that I saw her make out with said biker, but by the looks of her when she came back in, she definitely played tonsil hockey with Cade. Not to mention the panty-dropping kiss he slapped on her once they got back. I think she had been officially claimed. I was happy for her. She deserved it.

Despite her reservations, I thought she was going to go for it. I supported her wholeheartedly. That was of course, after I had gotten my Uncle Garrett to get the lowdown on this Cade Fletcher and the "Sons of Templar."

He had friends in high and low places and didn't ask any questions. What he had come up with was slightly troubling. they were on ATF and Fed radars for suspected gun running, but hadn't been charged with anything in years.

Cade had priors, but again he hadn't been charged for over two years. More importantly, his rap sheet had not contained anything to do with hurting women. In fact, one assault charge had been for *protecting* a woman. Granted, he had broken the jaw of the guy he assaulted. And the arm.

Not that lack of evidence proved he didn't hurt women, it could simply mean he didn't get caught. But I had met him. And Gwen had given me in depth descriptions of their encounters. Although he was no doubt involved in some nefarious things with his club, I got a good feeling about him. And about the way he looked at Gwen. It was intense, that was for sure, and it was something that would set my panties on fire if it was directed at me, but it was good.

Not like the way Jimmy looked at her. Like she was a possession. An object. I had never liked him. From the moment I met him something didn't seem right about him. His smiles never met his eyes, he was too charming. But I didn't say anything to Gwen. I didn't even follow my gut and look into him. I knew Gwen was besotted with him and didn't want to invade her privacy. It would also put a huge strain on our friendship. So I said nothing. Well, maybe not nothing, but I didn't scream at her to run from the sociopath as quick as her Manolos would take her.

That's what I should have done. It was something that would forever be on my conscience. So I wasn't taking any chances. I would watch Cade carefully, although I didn't think he would be a danger to Gwen. Her heart and her capacity for how many orgasms she could handle may be in danger, though. I would do everything in my power to make sure my best friend didn't get hurt again.

Just because I had a watchful eye on Cade, did not mean I wasn't glancing at my own biker. I had caught his eyes a couple of times during the night and he had grinned at me. I hadn't grinned back, but I think my vagina had. By the end of the night I was convinced that our silent conversation had resulted in a mutual agreement. One that meant I was going home with him tonight. And Gwen had informed me that she wasn't coming home. We were both getting laid tonight. High five for Team Abrams and Alexandra.

The party had wound down, only our newly-formed girl posse and the small group of leather clad gods remained. After I had cleaned up my workstation (cleaning up accounted to me draining the last of my drink and sweeping everything to one side), I had expected to see the sexy surfer again for more beer.

Since he was a man at a clothing store, he would be needing booze, but all of the men had sat on their single beers for the entire night. That had puzzled me. I owned the joint and I was halfway to blotto. I speculated they didn't want the cops in attendance, who had been watching them, to have any reason to pull them over.

I had met all of the other men on the night of Rosie's party. Heck, I had grinded up on Dwayne (christened this because of his uncanny resemblance to my crush The Rock) half of the night. Unfortunately, despite his similar looks to my celebrity crush, there was not much of a spark. Sure, he was hot and I wouldn't kick him out of bed, but I didn't want to climb him like a tree either. The same could not be said for Brock. He was someone I hadn't seen at the barbeque, so Rosie had introduced us when our two little groups had merged.

"Amy, this is Brock. He was MIA on the day of the barbeque

and he has only just made it back into my good graces," she teased, smirking at him.

"Oh, we've met and had a discussion on Amy's lack of future in the bartending field," Brock remarked, face blank but tone teasing.

"I don't know, brother, if our bar had a woman that looked like that behind it I think I might just take up residence there." Lucky winked at me.

"Like you don't already," Dwayne shot at him.

I smiled at the kid warmly and raised a triumphant eyebrow at Brock. Of all the people I had met in the club, Lucky was my favorite. He was a freaking funny guy, which was interesting since on first glance he looked like he drop-kicked puppies for fun. He was Hispanic with a bald head, harsh features and tattoos covering everything but his face and neck. Once he smiled, which was often, all of his menace melted away.

We had formed a bit of a huddle and I was currently squeezed with Rosie on one side and Brock on the other. I didn't miss the way his arm brushed mine, nor did he miss the way I leaned into him. We didn't speak, well, apart from him whispering in my ear, "Need a ride home tonight, Sparky? Think you've been sampling your wares a bit too much."

I failed to hide my shiver at his breath at my ear and glanced up at him, nodding. We both knew he was giving me much more than a ride.

Or maybe more than one kind.

His hair had been released from its bun and was falling in waves around his face. Seriously hot. I wanted to rake my fingers through it. I had to form my hands into fists so I didn't do just that.

"Okay, I think I need to go home now. The room is spinning and not in a good way. For future reference Amy has a heavy hand with the liquor when making cocktails," Rosie declared, wobbling slightly.

"I'll take you home, Rose. I'm dropping the heavy-handed bartender off, you're on the way," Brock said.

"Oh, right on. Thanks, Brocky. Do you need my car? I don't fancy trying to fit two of us on the back of your bike," Rosie replied, smiling vacantly.

"Got a cage, babe. Knew you girls were bound to suck back too many cocktails. We had contingency plans," Brock declared. "And I thought we talked about you calling me that," he added, frowning.

"Calling you what?" Rosie asked innocently.

"You know what."

"No, I don't," she argued.

Lucky and Dwayne shook their heads, grinning.

"For fuck's sake, just get your ass out the door and into the truck," Brock ordered, running his hands through his hair.

I followed their journey, entranced.

Rosie stayed put, frowning at Brock. I knew from experience that no matter how drunk a woman was, she did not respond well to getting ordered around. Well, outside the bedroom at least.

I turned to let Gwen into the circle, my movement pushing me closer to Brock. I felt his hand brush my ass and my eyes flared in surprise.

"Are you okay to get home?" she asked me with concern, unaware I had just been fondled by a cocky biker.

I swallowed, ignoring the flames of desire that had followed said fondling.

"Yeah, girl, Brock here is taking me and Rosie home," I informed her, eyes on Brock. His gaze was hot on mine.

"Thanks, Brock," she said, her voice a little breathy. I didn't blame her, this guy had a presence. An air of sex, if you will.

"No problem, Gwen. Kick ass brownies, by the way." He grinned at her.

That's it, I deduced. I was making brownies if it got me a smile like that. It didn't matter that I couldn't boil an egg. I'd figure out a way.

At that moment, tattooed arms circled around Gwen and Cade pulled her against him, whispering in her ear. I gaped at them for a second. The fact that Gwen was wearing a thousand dollar dress, made up to the nines and Cade wearing jeans and a leather cut was inconsequential. They looked right. Like they fit. A little ball of happiness settled in my gut. Gwen deserved this.

At that point we said our goodbyes, me leaving my best friend and her biker to start what looked like a romance for the history books. Brock opened the door for Rosie and she glanced up at him.

"Thanks, Brocky," she said, shooting out the door.

"Jesus Christ," Brock muttered. He turned to me, putting his hand at my waist. "Let's get you home, Sparky." His eyes locked onto mine and my stomach flipped at the erotic suggestion behind them. I couldn't get out the door fast enough.

Rosie chattered throughout the journey, it was pleasant and Brock obviously thought of her as a younger sister. He even got out and walked her to her door and helped her inside when we made it to her place.

Biker gentleman. Who would have thought? But I didn't need a gentleman. I'd had one of those. That didn't work out. I would be really pissed off if Brock was a nice guy hidden underneath tattoos and leather.

We had been driving in silence. It wasn't uncomfortable, but it was loaded — you could cut the sexual tension with a knife. I squirmed slightly in my seat, feeling turned on already and he hadn't even *touched* me. I felt his eyes turn to me, then lower to my exposed legs.

"Fuck," he muttered.

I would have smirked at the statement had he not sounded ... disappointed? Something in his tone puzzled me. We pulled up my driveway and he turned off the engine. Good sign.

"Do you wanna come in for a drink?" I asked, not intending

on offering him any actual refreshment once we got into the house. But we needed the pretense. I couldn't very well ask 'Do you want to come in for some no doubt mind blowing sex? Never mind the fact we just met.' Well, I *could*, but I was going to act like a lady until we got inside at least. Then I'd release my inner nympho.

Brock ran his hand through his hair and locked his eyes on mine. The desire was unmistakable.

"Yeah, I fuckin' do," he started, and I sensed a *"but."* "But I just gotta get a couple of things straight first. Then I'd like nothing more than to taste every inch of you, see if you're as wild in bed as I think you are, Sparky." His voice turned rough at the end.

"Wha ... what do you need to get straight?" I stuttered, fighting the wetness in my underwear and the little voice that was telling me to pounce on him.

Brock's face turned suddenly blank. It transformed so quickly I had to blink a couple of times. "You've been looking into the club," he said flatly.

My stomach dropped. And not in the good way. "I don't know what you're talking about," I replied.

Brock scowled. "Don't play dumb. You think we don't know when someone's looking into us, pulling files, asking around about us?" His voice was quiet, but it had an edge. A dangerous edge.

I suspected I might be in a slightly hazardous situation. No matter how nice their sisters or how easygoing the members, these guys were still dangerous. I had the files to prove it.

"You and Gwen turn up, both fuckin' knockouts. Your friend gets the instant attention of my VP and get yourselves an invite to a club gathering. You get half the men gagging for you, not to mention Gwen getting my brother tied up in fucking knots. What's your play here?" His voice was flat and threatening.

"There is no play," I said quietly.

There was no way I was revealing anything about my reasons for looking into the club. Especially not to do with Jimmy. Gwen had left him behind. No one here knew about it. Gwen didn't have to live with the "victim" label. No one was going to know until she decided she wanted to share. If she ever decided to tell them.

"Bullshit!" Brock's voice rose with impatience and I jumped. "Two high class pieces like you don't just come along and decide to slum it with bikers for no reason. We're not your *people*. So I repeat my question. What is your play? Keep in mind I'm going to find out either way. It's just quicker and better for you to tell me straight up now. You ain't fucking up my club, Sparky, no matter how sweet your ass is. And my VP may be blinded by gash right now, but he's got me to find out what's going on."

I stared at him as his words sunk in. Did he seriously just refer to Gwen as a "gash"? No fucking way. Anger blossomed in my stomach, replacing the desire and fear that had been there moments ago.

"Okay, Rocket Power, let's just get one thing straight here. You refer to Gwen in a derogatory way one more time, you'll need a surgeon to remove my Jimmy Choo from your balls. Secondly, there is no 'play.'" I finger quoted his ridiculous phrase. Who spoke like that?

"The only thing there is is my concern for my best friend," I continued. "She's getting involved with someone who doesn't look all that safe on the surface. I'm all for not judging a book by its leather bound cover, but I'm also not an idiot. We're new here—we don't know anything about you or your 'club.'" I finger quoted again. "You could help old ladies cross the road in your spare time or you could manage a cock fighting syndicate. I don't know. Therefore I did a little background check on you. Not to hurt your club but to protect my girl. Your reaction right now makes me sure I made the right choice, asshole." I delivered my speech in a scathing tone and accompanying glare. When I was finished I grasped the door handle, intending to storm out.

Does one storm out of a vehicle? Maybe I could climb out aggressively.

A hand on my arm stopped me. I glared at it. "Let me go," I hissed.

His grip was firm but not painful and if I was honest, the same electric current flowed through me than when he had brushed my stomach.

"Wait a second, Sparky. You don't get to spew all that shit, then storm off. You were protecting your girl, I'm protecting my club. You don't know us, we don't know you. You arming yourself with information—there's nothing wrong with that. I'm just trying to do the same, though I'm asking it to your face instead of going behind your back and digging up dirt."

I moved my glare from my arm to his eyes. They were hard, determined, but still held a note of desire. I ignored that. "Oh, so the big bad bikers are scared of two *women*? You don't want that to get out. It might damage your street cred," I shot sarcastically.

"Sons aren't scared of nothing, Sparky. What I do know is what the right woman can do. She can get under your skin, either in a good way or a bad way. Either one, it affects the club. Trying to figure out which category Gwen falls into." His calm and even tone juxtaposed my biting one.

"Gwen would never do anything to hurt anyone. She doesn't know anything about me learning about the club. I'd like it to stay that way," I requested sharply.

Brock watched me a second. "Your secret's safe with me. That don't mean I won't be watching you—not that that's a chore." His eyes travelled down to my legs. "But I find out you're lying, that you are doing anything that jeopardizes the club, it won't be good, Sparky," he warned.

"Watch away, Otto. I don't have anything to hide. Unlike you. I won't be digging into you or the club anymore, but I suggest if you do have something to hide make sure it's buried nice and deep. And that it doesn't touch my friend." I gave him a warning of my own. It took a lot more than veiled threats delivered from a sex god to scare me.

He nodded stiffly. "I guess that offer for a drink is rescinded?" His tone had turned playful but his eyes were dark with desire. I was dangerously aware of his hand still grasping mine.

"Yeah, the offer was rescinded the moment you referred to my best friend as a 'gash,'" I hissed. "If you do so again, make no mistake—I'll rip your balls off."

On that note, I yanked myself out of his grasp and stormed into my house, slamming the front door behind me. I sank against it, breathing hard. Not from fear, but arousal. I had really gone and done it. Wished for a hot asshole to come into my life and make me forget about a certain someone.

Be careful what you wish for, Amy.

————

After that encounter, I had not been able to get Brock off my mind. Every time I thought about him I got pissed off. What kind of arrogant asshole alludes to the fact that he thinks Gwen and I are some kind of spies here to infiltrate a biker gang by sleeping with the members?

Although that would make for a kick ass TV show. Two undercover agents attempting to bring down an outlaw motorcycle gang using only their wits and their feminine wiles, with the added bonus that the men they seduce are sexual demons. My mind wandered to plotlines for the TV show, or more specifically the sex scenes between the Brock and Amy characters.

"Amy!"

I jumped, looking guiltily at Gwen who had just called out to me. "I wasn't thinking about an erotic TV show," I declared quickly.

She frowned at me. "Okaaay." She looked at me like I was insane. "I was going to ask you if you wanted more wine, but obviously you've already finished your own bottle." She shook her glass at me then wandered out to the porch with a book in her hand.

I wanted to talk to her about the whole Brock thing, she was my best friend and I told her everything.

Almost everything.

She had been seriously grilling me. She knew something went on with Brock and I hated keeping things from her, but I had to. If I mentioned why I was so pissed off at Brock I would have to mention that I had someone look into the club. She wouldn't be mad I did it, I knew that much. She'd probably be unhappy I kept it from her. That wasn't the main reason for my reluctance, though.

If I told her I looked into the club because I was worried about her, she would think it meant I didn't think she was strong enough to make her own decisions about Cade. She would take it as me handling her like a victim, treating her like she needed someone second guessing her choices. It would break her heart, not to mention it was wrong.

Gwen was strong. She was the strongest person I had ever met. She was beaten within an inch of her life, almost gang raped by her boyfriend and his buddies, and she somehow still managed to come out the other side. Sure, her smile had a shadow every now and then and it has taken a lot for her to be around groups of men, but she was still *her*. She was kind of my hero.

Plus, if I told her about Brock she'd deduce he was an asshole and then question my reason for wanting to be with an asshole in the first place. Then I'd have to tell her about falling in love with her brother, not telling her about it, then getting my heart broken by him. *That* she would get mad about.

Keeping secrets from Gwen was like keeping secrets from the other half of myself. But it was over with Ian. No need to bring it up. That got me thinking. All of my weird thoughts about Brock had taken up my headspace, I hadn't once thought about Ian. Four days. That was a record.

Since it looked like I was leaving heartbreak city in my rearview, it was time to ovary up and get out there. Since shit had recently gone down with Gwen and Cade, I decided that motorcycle men were not the way to go for us. This brought me to the conclusion we needed to gussy up and check out the nightlife this town had to offer. But first I had to get Gwen out of that awful football shirt.

————

Sipping delightful cocktails, talking to some attractive men in well-tailored suits ... I mentally slapped myself on the back. I had divested Gwen of her shirt, replaced it with Gucci and taken us to Laura Maye's chic bar.

I was impressed with the tasteful furnishings and sleek décor, not to mention the view. Within minutes of getting there we had scored free drinks from our current companions.

Now, a couple of hours later, I was completely happy. And also reasonably drunk. I didn't think the two were connected. I was sitting very close to an advertising executive whose name I had forgotten. Not that his name was important. He had been telling some boring story that I was half listening to, I was trying to figure out what kind of body hid under that shirt. He looked lean, like one of those guys that did marathons regularly and had wheatgrass growing in their apartments.

"Do you run?" I interrupted, needing to sate my curiosity.

He stopped talking and looked confused. "Excuse me?"

"Are you a runner?" I repeated. "Like marathons and stuff. You look like a runner."

He stared at me for a second and then smiled confidently. "Why yes, I am. I just completed a 20k last weekend," he declared with a slightly puffed up chest.

"I knew it," I whispered, almost to myself. I was about to ask how his wheatgrass was growing when an angry male voice penetrated the conversation. I was glad. Who ran 20k voluntarily? This guy was nuts.

"You won't be buying her any more drinks."

I blinked up to see Cade glowering down at the guy Gwen had been talking to. I started to smirk until I spotted Brock directing the same look at Marathon Guy.

I got what Cade was doing here. I was even happy about it, I had hoped he wouldn't be stupid enough to let Gwen get away. Plus, she had been pining around the house for him for *days*. She needed Cade. They had a freaky deaky connection. Anyone could see that.

But I didn't get why Brock was here. I had met him once, shared some sexual chemistry with him, then argued with him. He certainly didn't need to back up Cade, he could wipe the floor with these guys. Not that he needed to, since he was currently directing Gwen toward the restrooms. Kinky bastard.

"Sparky." Brock spoke to me and I glanced up at him.

I still didn't know why he called me that. I hadn't gotten around to asking. Last time we spoke I was concentrating on not scratching his eyes out or jumping on his lap. I couldn't remember which.

"Brock," I returned politely, sipping my drink.

"A word," he commanded evenly.

I looked back up at him, hopefully with a disinterested expression. If he tried to drag me off I was totally dragging Marathon Guy along for the ride.

"Sorry, I'm sharing drinks with my new friends and it would be awfully rude of me to just leave," I countered, glancing around at the table.

The men looked slightly uncomfortable. Who wouldn't be with Cade and Brock directing badass death stares in their direction?

"Fine," he declared tightly, "I'll join you."

To my horror, he sat down in the seat Gwen had just vacated, next to Trent or Troy or whatever his name was.

He flagged down our waitress. "I'll have a Bud, darlin.' Thanks."

Brock leaned back in the booth, casually slinging his arm along the seat. He grinned at me. I scolded myself for being momentarily stunned by how hot he was. Hotter than I remembered, if possible. His hair was in a bun again and with his cut, tattoos, and bulging muscles he put these suits to shame.

"What are you doing?" I hissed at him quietly, even though the men at the table were practically silent, watching us awkwardly.

Brock's grin widened. "I'm sharing a drink with my new friends here." He gestured to the table. "By the look of those suits I'm guessing you boys aren't from around here."

Marathon Man cleared his throat. "No, we're just passing through on business," he said, eyes warily inspecting Brock and his cut.

"On business? So what is it you do? Lawyers?" he guessed, eyeing their suits. He didn't give them a chance to answer. "If you are lawyers I might be interested in hiring you. Providing you're defense attorneys. You see—" He retrieved a long knife from his jeans and the suit clad runner's eyes widened. Thankfully he didn't start disemboweling anyone, he just started using it to clean his nails. Which was gross, but I knew for a fact his hands were clean as I had inspected them upon his arrival.

"I've found myself in some hot water in regards to the law. I'm sure I'll be found innocent. Especially once they see the reason I broke that smarmy bastard's jaw. And ribs," he added with a smile and his possessive gaze moved to me. "After all, you gentlemen have had the pleasure of my lady's company—you can see just how special she is. And why a man such as myself would be inclined to teach any man a lesson if he thought he could try and touch what's mine." He raised an eyebrow at the runner who seemed to have scooted as far as humanly possible away from me.

"Brock," I hissed again, glaring at him.

He ignored me. "So any of you men willing to give me some representation?" he asked mildly.

"Actually," the runner from beside me stuttered, glancing at his Rolex, "we've just realized we've got to get on the road."

Brock nodded. "I think that might be a good idea." He stood up to let the guy beside him out of the booth. "You have a nice night now." He tipped an imaginary hat as the men scrambled out and walked away without a backward glance.

I didn't protest throughout this because I was still processing the fact it actually happened — plus I was secretly glad I had an excuse to escape the clutches and wheatgrass laden breath of whatshisname. I wasn't going to tell Brock that, though.

"What the fuck was that?" I snarled, leaning across the table.

Brock took a pull of his beer, leaning back against the booth, his huge knife safely stowed back in his belt. He shrugged. "Seems your choice of company scares easily."

"Does you waving that big knife around compensate for other areas you're lacking in size?" I asked him spitefully, surprised I wasn't breathing fire.

Brock's face turned abruptly serious and sexy. "You'll be learning I'm more than well-endowed in that area, Sparky."

I toyed with the olives in my martini. "Why? You in any porn I watch? Because the only place I'll be seeing any more of you is a TV screen," I informed him, ignoring the wetness pooling between my legs at his statement.

Brock eyed me for a second. "You want it. I know you do. I know by the way you're biting you lip, by the way you're flushing delightfully red. And I know your panties are dripping right now," he murmured softly, his gravelly voice full of sex.

"Are you seriously saying that to me after you waltz in here and scare away my dates for the night?" I shot back, my voice breathy.

Brock gave me a look. "Babe, I did you a favor. Those guys were pussies who scampered off the moment it looked like their suits would get wrinkled. They were nowhere near good enough for you. You want a man who would fight tooth and fuckin' nail at just the prospect of getting into those panties of yours. One who would tear any motherfucker down who got in the way of the chance of tasting your cunt when you come."

I swallowed.

Ignore the way his words make you squirm in your seat, Amy.

"What gives you the right to think you can decide who is worthy enough to get in my pants?" I sneered, superbly impressed I hadn't launched myself across the table at him.

Brock leaned forward, his eyes turning dark and serious. "Because I fully intend on getting into your panties. I would be more than willing to tear down a thousand of those suit-wearing pansies, because sweetheart, if your pussy tastes as good as I think it does, its fuckin' worth it," he murmured.

Okay, so I didn't know what I'd done to make this guy think I had a golden vagina, but the promise of sex in his tone made me reluctant to correct him. I only hoped my lady parts didn't get performance anxiety. That was if I did actually decide to go home with him.

"You really think talking to me like that and acting like a possessive ape is going to get me to go home with you?"

It totally would.

Brock's eyes twinkled for a second then darkened. "I think we both know it's a matter of time before I get that sweet ass in my bed. I just don't wanna wait. I wanna get you on the back of my bike and fuck you till you don't remember your own name."

I tried to think of a witty response or even to find some willpower to get up and walk away from the infuriating sex god, but neither happened. I worried about my ability to strut off effectively due to the potency of the cocktails I had consumed. Those very same cocktails caused me to get up. Screw it.

"Okay then, let's go," I said to him as he got up too, anticipating an escape attempt.

His eyebrows rose at my statement, as if he expected some kind of catch.

"Your place or mine?" I continued impatiently. Now that I had committed myself to the idea of sleeping with Brock I was tingling with sexual anticipation.

His gaze turned hooded. "Mine's closer."

"Right," I said, losing my breath at the carnal look he was devouring me with. I pointed at him. "Let's get one thing straight. I am not 'yours.' I do not belong to anyone. This isn't the prelude to some intense biker relationship you all seem to be so fond of. It's just sex."

Brock stepped forward into my space and it felt like the air crackled. "Works for me. As long as I get inside you in the next thirty minutes."

We stared at each other for a couple of moments. His hand rested lightly on my upper back and he guided me out. My only focus was on the hand that was currently setting my body on fire as he directed me toward the exit. I did notice Laura Maye's knowing grin and not so subtle thumbs up. I grinned stupidly back at her.

The brisk breeze of the night caused me to sober up slightly, but it didn't affect what Brock's sex hormones were doing to me.

"Fuck it, I can't wait—especially when you're wearing a dress like that," he mumbled.

His hands tightened at my waist and he yanked my body flush against him. I let out a little sound of surprise before he covered my mouth with his. His kiss was brutal, unrelenting and a hundred and twelve on the hotness scale. His hands moved down to cup my ass and I ground into him, quite prepared to have sex on the street the way things were going.

My plans for indecent exposure were foiled when he released me.

"Jesus," he muttered.

In the streetlights his eyes glowed and a fierce look crossed his face. "We need to get you on the back of my bike."

He grabbed my hand, pulling me towards his Harley. Of

course I had known a biker would be driving a motorcycle, but I hadn't factored that into tonight's transportation.

Brock handed me a helmet. I glanced down at it, not taking it. "I can't get on that," I declared.

Brock's eyes narrowed in disapproval. "The little princess too good to ride on the back of my bike?" His voice was low.

I shook my head. "Not at all. Given proper warning and enough time to put together a suitable outfit I'd be jumping on. But this," I gestured down, "is Alexander McQueen."

Brock eyed me. "I don't give a fuck what that is. Get on the fuckin' bike so I can take you home and eat your pussy until you pass out," he commanded roughly.

I shivered at his words. Alexander who? I snatched the helmet.

The ringing of a phone interrupted my efforts not to jump him on the sidewalk. Brock glanced down at the display. "Fuck," he muttered. He glanced up at me. "A second, Sparky."

"This better be fuckin' important," he hissed into the phone. I watched him silently listen to whoever was on the other side with a hard jaw. "I'll be there in twenty," he bit out furiously.

I pouted at him like a sullen child after hearing his last comment. He ran his hand through his hair. "We're gonna have to raincheck, babe, something's come up."

My vagina and I both frowned at him. Actually, I think it was safe to say I glowered.

He stepped forward, lightly grasping my hips. "Fuck, normally I wouldn't let anything interrupt me getting in there." His palm crept to my ass. "But this shit is pressing and it's something that can't wait." He sounded genuine and supremely pissed. But I was drunk and horny and his sincerity meant sweet fuck all at this moment.

"Get on, I'll take you home," he said, stepping back.

"No way," I responded quickly and with venom in my tone. I stepped back, out of his grasp. I needed to be out of range of his male pheromones in order to practice the feat of extracting myself from his presence without humping his leg.

"Pardon?" He frowned at me.

"I said no. I bet that's not a word you're used to hearing due to your impressive muscles and inhuman kissing skills," I said. "Now, I was willing to risk couture for the promise of what those muscles could do, considering you went to all of that effort to scare away my dates. But leading me on, ordering me around, then bailing on me? Not okay. So I'm going to call a cab and go home to my vibrator, who never disappoints. You go and take care of whatever you need, and enjoy your blue balls."

On that note I turned on my heel and walked away, ignoring Brock's shouts and curses.

CHAPTER FOUR

After nursing my disappointment and rejection, I was back to being supremely pissed at Brock. No matter what his reasons were, he still got me all hot and bothered only to ditch me for his little club. It might've been childish or immature, but I didn't care. I maintained my healthy dislike because the alternative was to drive over to his house like some sort of doormat and beg him to fuck me.

That was not me. I didn't beg.

So I dodged unknown numbers on my phone, avoided any place where leather clad men might frequent and kept myself busy. Gwen was currently all loved up with her own biker so I couldn't even suggest nightly cocktail sessions with her. Luckily Rosie and Lucy were happy to comply.

After days of probing, the girls convinced me to head to the weekly club party, promising me there would be loads of hot men from out of town visiting. I complied with only the slightly evil plan of flaunting my Upper East Side version of biker chick in front of him.

Okay, maybe I was thinking of doing a little bit more than flaunting. I could only stay angry and sexually frustrated for so long, and I wasn't about to jump into bed with any other bikers.

Not that I didn't want to, I just didn't want to be the girl that caused shit between friends. And by Brock's possessive behavior the other night and descriptions of Cade's actions from Gwen, I guessed these were a special breed of men.

The type of alphas that decided a woman belonged to them and them only until they decided otherwise. I didn't agree with this. Not one bit. But I wasn't going to be the Yoko Ono to this band of outlaws. I had no choice but to sleep with Brock. I was doing it for the good of the community. It was the charitable thing to do.

So when I arrived at the club with Rosie, Ashley, and Lucy I wasn't intending on being anything other than friendly to whatever hot men I encountered. That was until I saw a sandy-haired girl sitting on Brock's knee. I didn't consider myself a jealous person. But right then, I was considering ripping the girl off Brock with my freshly manicured hands.

"Ames?" Rosie questioned, following my death stare.

"Oh shit," she muttered. She thrust a beer in my hand. "That'll help. And let's go over and have a chat with the guys from the New Mexico charter."

I glanced around at the party. I had been to a lot of parties over the years, ranging from stuffy society parties where they served five hundred dollar champagne to raves in Europe where I had to dodge used needles on my way to the bathroom. I had never been to a biker party. I guessed I suspected burning tires, men throwing knives at a prospect chained to a dartboard and maybe some public sex.

What was in front of me was a slightly rowdier version of Rosie's barbeque. Granted, there were a lot more leather clad men and the women were decidedly skankier. My eyes darted back to one skank in particular. It was unfair of me to think of her that way. She could have been a perfectly nice girl, but right now all I could see was her hand on Brock's chest.

Rosie successfully defused the situation and led me over to some very attractive men. I drained my beer quickly and it was immediately replaced by the dark haired man I was chatting to. He wasn't bad looking. Not at all. He was Hispanic, he wasn't tall, but he had the obligatory muscles and a seriously awesome goatee which made up for what he lacked in stature. I respected any man who still looked hot with a goatee.

"You belong to anyone here, Red?" he asked bluntly, a glint in his eyes.

I smiled and opened my mouth to reply when a deep, pissed off voice beat me to it.

"Yes, she fuckin' does," Brock snapped, hand at my elbow.

Goatee Guy held up his hands. "Sorry, brother, wasn't aware this one was yours."

"I am not his," I argued and Goatee Guy just smiled.

"When you're able to convince him of that you come and see me," he said, ignoring Brock's growl.

I didn't get the chance to argue further when the hand at my elbow tightened and Brock started dragging me toward the parking lot. I struggled, but it turned out his muscles weren't just for show.

"What are you doing? Let me go!" I hissed, debating on smacking him with my beer bottle. I decided against it, not because I didn't want to maim Brock, but because I sensed alcohol might be needed in this interaction.

"I'm taking you home to do what I should've done the first night I met you," he declared, not turning back.

"Introduced me to Goatee Guy so I could have gotten laid like I planned?" I retorted.

He stopped in the middle of the lot and turned. He face was tight with fury at my statement. "No, I should have dragged you to my bed and fucked you so hard you felt me in your throat," he said, eyes moving over my body.

I couldn't even restrain the shiver I had at his gaze. "Sorry, you lost the opportunity to do that when you passed me up for some 'club business.'" I accentuated my distaste with said business with sarcastic finger quotes. I glared at him. "I'm sure the blonde who was draped over your lap would be a willing partici-pant," I continued, leaning in, "though she will be *nothing* compared to me. I'm guessing fucking her would be like throwing a sausage down a hallway." I was surprising myself with such spiteful words, my jealousy turning me into a screaming bitch.

"You jealous. Sparky?" he asked with a glint in his eyes.

"Jealous? Yes, actually I am—she had on some kick ass heels that I was coveting. If you'll excuse me, I have to go and find out where she got them from."

I attempted to turn and walk back to the party, but he grabbed my hand.

"Not that I don't love it when you've got your claws out, but I think this extended form of foreplay has to stop. This is going to happen. We're going to happen."

I glanced at the bike that had just roared up, one Gwen was on the back of. I really didn't want to have some scene in front of her. She'd be nervous enough about a party full of men without me adding to it by bottling her boyfriend's best friend.

I snatched my hand away. "Sorry, you had your chance and you passed me up. I don't wait around for anyone."

I turned and strutted toward the party, swinging my hips a little because I knew my ass looked amazing in these shorts. I smiled when I heard the frustrated curse from behind me.

———

The night passed with a fair amount of drama, including me almost getting into a second catfight and I hadn't even been there an hour. The second one was due to some other bee-atch draping herself all over Cade. The hurt in Gwen's eyes had me ready to pass Rosie my earrings and go full skank bash on her ass. That again was foiled, this time by Gwen.

I didn't like the fact that her man had left her at a party full of bikers and then let a woman who should have been jailed for her fashion choices sidle up to him. Well, admittedly he pushed her away, but he had disappeared when he should have realized how intimidated Gwen felt by a party full of men who reminded her of the ones who attacked her. I was *so* giving him a piece of my mind later.

Apart from my worry for my best friend, I had an amazing night, cementing the fact that Ashley, Lucy, and Rosie were all seriously cool chicks. The more drinks I had, the more I felt like it was a good idea to waltz up to Brock and demand he take me to bed. Who cared about the reasons why not? Him being seriously sexy and not taking his eyes off me was reason enough.

I was talking to Dwayne, trying to distract myself from the urge to go and lick a certain biker's biceps when I felt heat at my back. A large hand gripped my hip tightly. I didn't even have to turn to know who it was, the flames that ignited from the simple touch told me.

"We're going. Now," his rough voice ordered in my ear.

The erotic promise in his tone plus the fact I was suffering from the female equivalent of blue balls had me nodding.

"Bye, Dwayne." I waved at him and he smirked at the nickname Gwen and I had christened him with.

"Bye, babe." His eyes cut to Brock. "Lucky bastard," he muttered.

Brock turned me around and I almost gasped at how freaking hot he looked, all broody and turned on.

"Got your shit, babe?" he asked impatiently.

I waved my Chanel at him.

"Right," he murmured pulling me by the hand to his bike. I followed dutifully, my panties already wet with anticipation. We arrived at his bike and he turned to give me a head to toe inspection. The heat from his gaze almost had me spontaneously combust on the spot.

"You need a jacket," he said with a frown.

"I do not need a jacket," I argued.

"Babe, it's a twenty-minute ride to my place and it's cold on the bike once the sun goes down. You need a fuckin' jacket."

I crossed my arms. "Well, let's got to my place. It's like two minutes away," I suggested.

Brock gave me a look. "I intend on fucking you for the entire weekend. I don't want to have to worry about the neighbors hearing you scream after I make you come harder than you ever have in your entire life."

"Okay, your place it is," I said immediately, voice husky.

Brock shrugged off his jacket and handed it to me. I immediately put in on, inhaling his manly scent. He'd make a killing if he figured out how to bottle that shit.

"Now you'll be cold," I pointed out.

"Sparky, with your hot little body pressed against me it'll be like riding through a fuckin' firestorm," he declared, handing me a helmet.

Well, alrighty then.

The ride out to Brock's was *awesome*. I didn't want to advertise it, but I had never ridden on a motorcycle before. You would think during my campaign to piss my parents off in my teenage years, a boy with a motorcycle would have factored in somewhere. It was the ultimate "fuck you" to Upper East Side parents. But I never got the chance.

I still had plenty of "fuck you" moments for my parents to remember fondly. Like the time I replaced all of the catering staff at one of my mother's charity events with strippers. That was a fun night.

I didn't want to advertise my bike virginity to Brock so I had just done what I always did in life: faked it till I made it. I had jumped on the bike like I'd done it a hundred times before and swallowed any anxiety. The thrill of hurtling down the road under the stars while pressed up to arguably the hottest guy I'd seen up close was beyond words.

And a very special kind of foreplay. One that had me almost breathless from the vibration of the bike between my thighs. I had slipped my hands under Brock's tee and run my nails up his rock hard abs. I had no choice in the matter.

By the time we turned up at Brock's place, it was safe to say I was sufficiently turned on. I guessed Brock felt the same because once he had turned the bike off, instead of hopping off, he reached around and lifted me to sit on his lap.

While sitting on the bike.

It didn't topple over or anything. I was impressed. He unclipped my helmet and discarded it.

He seized my head and his mouth crashed onto mine, plundering it, mercilessly fucking my mouth with his tongue. I ground against his hard on with a moan, the friction nearly causing me to burst into flames right there. His hand went to my ass to press me harder against him while his other tweaked my nipple through my shirt.

Not many times in my life did I ever regret an outfit choice, but right now I cursed myself for wearing leather shorts. All I wanted right now was a dress so Brock could slip my panties aside and fuck me on his bike. Brock must have come to the same conclusion about the lack of easy access because he stood us up and dismounted.

"Next time I'm fucking you on the bike," he declared roughly.

I didn't argue.

He didn't move his mouth from mine as he carried us inside, me grinding on him impatiently. It seemed like it took him hours to get to his bedroom.

He threw me on his bed roughly and leaned over to yank off my shorts.

I hurried with the clasp of my top, opening it to reveal my braless chest.

Brock let out a hiss. His eyes devoured me. "Jesus Christ, baby, you're even better than I imagined. Your tits are fuckin' perfect." His eyes moved to my heels. "They're staying on. I've visualized fucking you with those things on all night."

He covered my naked body with his, still fully clothed. I struggled to pull off his cut as he kissed me again, moving down my neck.

"You need to get naked, like now," I ordered.

He glanced up from between my breasts, hands cupping them roughly. I moaned.

"No, Sparky, first I'm going to taste both your nipples, then taste your cunt until you come. I want your orgasm on my tongue while I fuck you," he growled.

My aforementioned lady bits did a whirl. "As you were."

His eyes turned dark as his mouth closed around my nipple. He wasn't gentle. Nor was he tender. But the pain was even better. I almost came from just his mouth on my nipple. My eyes rolled into the back of my head as he thrust a finger inside me.

He growled. "Fuckin' soppin'—that's my girl."

Again his fingers weren't gentle as they plunged into me, they were brutal and fucking amazing. When his mouth settled between my legs I struggled not so scream. With all of the pent up frustration and the fact he was seriously good with his tongue, it felt like I came in less than a minute.

I went temporarily blind, or at least blacked out because the next thing I knew Brock was naked and lifting me to turn my back to him. He latched my hands onto his wrought iron head-board. "Don't move these hands, Sparky," he ordered hoarsely.

I vaguely nodded and he kissed me fiercely, pushing himself into me, his body plastered to my back. He was big and it had been awhile, so it was intense at first, especially at this angle. I had expected him to thrust into me hard and fast, but he pushed in slowly until he filled me to the hilt. He moved his body off mine and grasped my hips roughly.

"You ready for this, Sparky?" he asked.

"Fuck yes," I replied.

He was hard, brutal, unyielding. It was magnificent. I held onto the headboard for dear life as he pounded into me. I could feel another orgasm building and he gripped my neck lightly, making me arch my back and give him more leverage to go deeper. The different angle set me over the edge and everything exploded.

My orgasm didn't cause him to pause, nor did he slow down. He kept pounding into my sensitive skin, the feeling bordering between pleasure and pain. His fingertips bit into my hips so hard I was sure they'd leave a mark. I wanted a mark. I wanted evidence of where his hands had been. Suddenly, they tightened and his body went taut as he had his own climax.

We both stayed like that, breathing heavily, coming down. He pulled my body up so I let go of the headboard, my back was to his front and I was on my knees.

"That defied my fuckin' expectations, baby, and knowing you, looking at you, I expected a fuck of a lot," he murmured in my ear.

"You weren't so bad yourself," I replied huskily, still floating back down to earth.

His hands tightened around me and I felt him harden inside me.

"Oh, we're far from fuckin' done, babe."

———

"I think I have literally had my brains fucked out," I declared, lying back after about the millionth orgasm I'd had this weekend.

Brock chuckled. "I hope I've at least fucked some of the sass outta you, babe. Increases my chances for a repeat performance," he replied, tucking me into his shoulder.

"How can you have a repeat performance in the next decade? I think we've emptied you," I said.

I let myself relax, his strong tattooed arms surrounding me. We had pretty much had a sex marathon, not leaving his bed except to get sustenance. It was late on Sunday morning, or maybe afternoon. I wasn't aware of time passing. I was in a sex vortex. Nothing happened outside of it.

We hadn't spoken much during the sexfest apart from the obligatory "harder" and "faster." You know the drill. It was good. I didn't want to keep comparing things to Ian, but he was a shadow in the corner of my mind that didn't seem to go away.

In fact, the other two dalliances I had since him, I'd thought about Ian *during* sex, even tried to pretend it was him. But not with Brock. It was him the whole time. He ravaged me, mind and body, which was why I was glad he didn't try for the heart to hearts in our little breaks. With those came feelings. I needed those like I needed to be shot in the face.

"Can I ask you something, babe?" he asked softly, his arms still tight around me.

I was running my hands across his chest, tracing the line where he had a magnificent tattoo of an old clock morphing into a skull. It was intricate and amazing, along with most of his other tattoos.

"Mmhmmm," I muttered distractedly.

"Who's Otto and what the fuck is Rocket Power?" he asked.

I paused and rested my head in my hand to meet his eyes.

"You're kidding me. You don't know what Rocket Power is?" I asked, baffled.

Brock grinned and shook his head, seeming more relaxed than I'd ever seen him.

"That's right, you're an old man. Color TV probably wasn't around when you were a kid," I teased.

Brock continued to grin and shook his head at me.

"It's just some stupid cartoon show I watched when I was a kid, a freaking awesome one at that. Otto was some surfer dude who was arrogant and thought he was in charge of everyone." I smirked "Sound familiar?"

Brock shook his head. "Only you could pull off referencing a fucking cartoon show in the middle of an argument." His tone was light.

I giggled slightly, turning my gaze back down to his chest. "It seemed appropriate."

He stroked my back. "You don't seem to me like you would have been the type of kid to sit around watching TV shows about surfing, babe. More like taking horseback lessons and walking around with a book on your head."

I snorted. "Yeah, trust me—it wasn't for lack of my parents trying, but I excelled at disappointing them," I informed him, not looking up.

We were silent for a bit. I was glad he didn't probe about my parents. I hated talking about them. Hated thinking about them. Plus, I didn't want to sob on his tattooed chest while I told him how my mother would lock me in my room for days after I embarrassed her at some function or another.

Hence my familiarity with a plethora of television shows. Once I grew old enough, though, she couldn't pull that shit with me and settled for indifference and the occasional scathing insult.

Brock ran his hand along my shoulder. "Want to put some clothes on, baby, and go and grab some grub? Maybe ride up the coast somewhere?" he asked softly, breaking the silence.

I stiffened and stopped my perusal of his colorful tattoos. "Actually I really should go," I declared, getting up. I was thankful his arms hadn't stopped me. He sat up in bed while I scoured the room for my clothes.

"Are you fucking kidding me?" he shot softly with a hint of menace. The playful tone was long gone.

"No, I'm not kidding. I've got things to do," I replied, clasping my top on.

I couldn't find my panties so I slipped my shorts on commando. I didn't miss Brock's pointed gaze at this.

"I don't think we should do things like that," I continued, not making eye contact as I scoured the room for my purse.

Brock stood, pulling his own jeans on commando. My mouth watered slightly at the sight of him wearing jeans and no shirt.

"Like what?" Brock asked briskly, interrupting my gaze by pulling on a shirt.

"Like going out for Sunday breakfast together, going for romantic rides along the coast," I said flatly. "This," I gestured between us, "is just sex. Nothing more. We shouldn't confuse it."

The memories of my less than stellar childhood were the perfect reminder of why I should get the fuck out of here now before I became vulnerable.

Brock's gaze turned thunderous. "So you don't want your precious reputation to be tarnished by being seen in public with a biker?"

I furrowed my brows. "No, it's not like that," I tried to argue. I might want to distance myself from him emotionally, but I didn't want him to think so little of me. I didn't want him to believe I thought so little of *him*.

"Shut it. I know what it's like. You think you're better than everyone here. You come waltzing into my town with your fancy shit, your long legs, your big tits and smart mouth and drag me around by my dick. I can't get you off my mind. All I think about is how I'll pull that red hair while I'm taking you from behind and how I'll fuck that smart mouth. We fuck like rabbits for two fuckin' days and you're suddenly Queen Bitch again?" He shook his head. "Fuck that. Your pussy's good, but not good enough for you to get away with acting like an entitled bitch."

My temper ignited. I stepped forward. "That is not even remotely what this is about. I couldn't give a flying fuck that you're a biker. I don't think I'm better than anyone!" My voice rose to a screech at the end.

"You're not—the way you're acting right now, you're no better than the club whores," he shot cruelly. He pulled his boots on. "I'm assuming you wouldn't want to be seen in the daylight on the back of my bike?"

I couldn't care less. In fact, I would've loved to roar around the freakin' state pressed up against him and have the event televised. "I'd rather get my hair cut with a butter knife," I shot back icily.

"Suit your fuckin' self," he muttered.

He walked out the door, slamming it as he left. I flinched as it rattled the hinges. I stood there, one shoe in my hand, not moving until I heard his bike roar off.

———

"Thanks so much for this, girlfriend," I said to Rosie for the millionth time in five minutes.

"No problem." She glanced at me across the car. "I'm guessing you don't want to talk about the reason you were stranded at Brock's for two days after he dragged you away at the club?" she asked perceptively.

"I'd rather not," I answered quietly but with a small smirk.

I had decided to call Rosie for the extraction mission from Brock's for two reasons. One, because I didn't know whether Gwen was off with her own hunky biker, despite the obvious fight they had at the party. Two, I wasn't quite ready to spill the beans about Brock. Somehow I knew if I spilled about Brock, I'd keep babbling and let loose about Ian. That couldn't happen.

"Just tell me one thing," Rosie ordered as we pulled up at my place. "How was it?" she asked with a grin.

I turned to her. "I was amazing."

She laughed and waited expectantly. I gave her a fake wide-eyed look. "Oh, you meant him?" I paused. "My vagina will never be the same again."

———

"I hope Gwen and Lucy haven't crashed on the way home from getting booze," I slurred slightly, wondering why they were taking so long. "I would be really upset to miss out on more margaritas," I added and Lily cackled with laughter.

After coming home and finding Gwen halfway to smashed at three in the afternoon, I deduced things were not well with her and Cade. Since the Sons of Templar were pricks, we decided to get drunk. Then we decided to throw a party with all of our new girlfriends. No dangerously hot men in leather cuts allowed.

That's how I came to be sitting on a sun lounger in my bikini, well after the sun had gone down, shooting the shit with Lily. For someone who seemed shy and prim, the girl could sure drink a margarita. And swear like a sailor.

On that note Lucy appeared from around the corner.

"Hurray! I was getting worried about the fate of our tequila," I shouted at her, getting up from my lounger. I was focused on staying upright so I only realized her hands were empty once she got closer. "Where's the precious, precious alcohol?" I asked her slowly.

She smirked and opened her mouth, but I didn't hear what she said, considering I was focused on the hot biker I was currently furious at strutting into my backyard. He was followed by more equally hot bikers.

Upon inspection, I saw that Brock was carrying the liquid that was necessary for my mental health. He approached, his gaze setting me on fire head to toe. The picture of him plunging into me from behind hurtled into my addled mind. I felt desire pool in my stomach.

Stop it, hormones!

I was struggling on how to handle the situation, since I didn't actually want to talk to him, but I needed the booze in his hands. I needed it even more so now if I was to resist the fact he looked hot as shit with his hair loose and down, wearing all black and his cut. Even his glare was sexy. I turned around as he approached.

"Lily," I whisper yelled.

Her eyes had been wide at all of the men approaching and she fixed her gaze on me. It looked like she was struggling. I didn't blame her. It was like *Magic Mike* met "Sons of Anarchy" up in here.

"What?" she whisper yelled back.

I glanced over my shoulder to see Brock had been waylaid by a wasted Rosie. I did an internal fist pump. Rosie was the best. His dark glare met mine. I quickly turned my head back.

"Come here," I ordered quietly.

"What?" Lily was at my side.

I turned to her, realizing Brock had disengaged from Rosie and was pointing his motorcycle boots in our direction. He was joined by some younger kid I didn't know whose eyes were locked on Lily.

"I need you to get the booze off Brock," I ordered quickly.

Her eyes bulged. "I've never even spoken to him—he kind of scares me. Why can't you do it?" she asked, looking terrified.

"It's a long story. It involves a sex marathon and his stupid man bun," I explained. "Will you do this for me? Please?"

I gave her a little push toward him, she stumbled forward, shooting me a panicked look before striding in Brock's direction. I should have felt bad about sending a shy, drunk, twenty-year-old girl over to a biker to get booze off him, but I just didn't have it in me at the moment.

I sank back into my lounger, watching her chatter nervously to him. The younger guy, the one with dark hair, was eating her up with his eyes. He looked about my age and surprisingly didn't have any visible tattoos. Not surprisingly, he was muscled and hot.

After shamelessly pushing her into the company of gruff bikers, my conscience made its appearance. I felt slightly protective over the shy, beautiful girl who worked in the store. Well, I'd fucked that up. It was like sending a mouse into a viper's nest. I so shouldn't have children if this was any indication of maternal instinct.

I turned my attention back to her exchange with Brock. It

seemed to be all going well until she gestured to the bottles he was holding and then to me. All eyes turned in my direction.

"Shit, don't point at me," I groaned under my breath, looking for something to hide behind.

Brock shook his head, said something to Lily then started his way over. She looked like she was going to make her own escape when the remaining biker lightly grasped her elbow. I was worried for a second, but Lily's blush and tiny smile quelled my fears. I had my own shit to worry about as I noticed Brock had almost reached me.

"Fuck," I muttered.

I tried to quickly scramble up from my seat so I could run away. I didn't know where to. Serbia possibly, but it seemed a lot harder than it had been two seconds ago. I somehow got my foot tangled in the feet of the chair and stumbled. I was about to eat shit on the concrete when a strong arm caught me.

"Easy, Sparky," Brock said, pulling me upright.

I yanked my arm away from his touch, refusing to believe it turned me on. I had only had sex with the man this morning. My body should've been sick of him by now.

Brock took in my bikini with a scowl. "It's nine o'clock at fuckin' night. Want to put some fuckin' clothes on?" he growled.

I raised my eyebrow and cocked my hip. The pissed off woman stance didn't work as well after countless cocktails and I wobbled slightly. "This is *my* freaking house. And it is *my* freaking party. There is no way in hell you can come in uninvited and have comments on my attire, no matter how sexy your man bun is."

Shit. I hadn't meant to say that last bit. The asshole had the audacity to smirk.

I snatched the bottles out of his hand. "These are *mine*. You can go now," I declared, turning my back on him and storming into the house.

Thanks to tequila I wasn't articulate enough to have a verbal sparring match with him so I deduced escape was my only option.

I got into the kitchen and started slamming bottles down, my blurry eyes looking for the right ones to go in the blender. At this point I didn't care, I poured various liquids in, thinking of names for my concoction.

"Amy Juice." I tried it out loud. No, that wasn't right. "Abramtini!" I declared, feeling like a genius.

Hands at my hips interrupted my train of thought. I jumped as they whirled me around, bringing me face to face with Brock's hungry gaze. His mouth was on mine before I knew what was happening.

"Fuck, it should be illegal for you to wear that little red bikini," he growled, his hand palming my breast roughly.

"I'm still mad at you," I panted in between kisses.

"So am I," he said, pushing me towards the bathroom. "Doesn't mean I can't fuck you, though."

———

"I think sex is the best cure for a hangover," I announced after Brock had returned to the room after getting rid of the condom.

He joined me in bed and pulled me to him. "Babe. Sex with you could cure fuckin' cancer."

I laughed. "Oh yes, scientists should study my magical vagina," I joked.

We were silent for a while and I didn't like how comfortable and right it felt lying in bed with Brock, cuddling and joking.

"About last night—" Brock began.

"About you fucking me in the bathroom while a party full of people made cocktails in the kitchen only a few feet away?" I finished for him, teasing.

"No. But that was fuckin' hot," he said, squeezing my ass. "No, this was more about you prancing around the whole night in what was equivalent to your fuckin' underwear. In front of my brothers." His voice had lost the teasing tone.

I stiffened. "I didn't prance," I argued. "And it's called a bikini. I don't know if you've heard of them—invented by a fellow named Louis Reard, been around for almost seventy years?" I asked sarcastically, trying to pull out of his arms.

Brock tightened his hold. "Calm down, Sparky. I'm not saying don't wear a bikini. I'm just saying for future reference, put some more clothes on once the sun goes down. I've never wanted to pummel my brothers before. I don't want to have to because of the way they're looking at my old lady."

The pit of my stomach dropped at that statement. I didn't entirely know what that label meant, but I knew it was one I would never wear.

Like Roberto Cavalli.

"Let's get one thing straight here. I am not going to alter my fashion habits in order to make you happy... ever. I'm happy with how I look. I'm proud of it, in fact. I don't count calories and deprive myself of chocolate so I can don an ankle-length one piece. One thing I'm also proud of is belonging to no one." I pulled myself out of his arms and he let me. "I'm not going to be anyone's 'Old Lady.' Frankly I'd rather shave my eyebrows than become some biker's possession," I spat.

Brock's gaze turned deadly. "You did not fuckin' just say that," he said quietly.

I stood from the bed, crossing my arms. "I did just say that. Just because you're good in bed does not mean I want to jump into any kind of relationship, and it sure as shit doesn't mean I want you to lay some kind of fucked up claim to me!" I shouted at him.

He leapt out of bed, shoving his jeans on. "You have no idea how many bitches are fuckin' gagging to be my Old Lady—how fuckin' important that title is," he yelled back at me.

"Well, go and find one of those no doubt classy ladies to

bestow your oh so important title on," I screeched, shoving my nightgown over my head.

He stepped towards me, eyes blazing. "You're afraid," he hissed. "You're fuckin' terrified cause you know what you feel with me is actually real. It means you really have to feel something, put yourself out there. You're being a bitch so I'll act like a jerk, and you can feel better about yourself for me getting sick of it and bouncing."

The anger I felt at that statement had me wanting to scream. Also, the fact he was right on the money had me terrified.

"Fuck you!" I yelled, opening my door. "Get out of my house this instant before I call the police and inform them some biker *asshole* is trying to rob me."

Maybe I was being a touch dramatic, but the fact his words hit close to home was a stark reminder of the last time I opened myself up. I wasn't getting hurt again. I had the feeling this one had the potential to hurt me a whole lot more than Ian.

"Calm the fuck down, babe," Brock responded to my hysterics with an even voice, his eyes on me. He seemed almost amused. "You don't threaten to call the pigs on me ever. Do that again and I'll put you over my knee."

The erotic glint in his eyes had me wanting that. Bad. I shook my head. This guy was arrogant and infuriating.

"Ugh, I can't believe I even considered letting a Neanderthal, cocky, criminal asshole into my bed. I won't be making that mistake again. Now get. The. Fuck. Out."

I was breathing heavily, expecting him to rush at me and spank me. I'd be lying if I said I didn't want it. But I was serious. I did need him to get out. This was an emotional overload I didn't need.

Brock's face hardened at my words. "I can't believe I bothered sticking my dick in some uppity, snooty bitch. Don't worry, sweetheart, I won't be coming near you again." His voice was as cold as his expression as he stormed out of my room.

I started to go after him, to say what I didn't know, but I stopped outside my door as his words sank in.

That had escalated way too quickly. I still had hot fury running through me at his macho possessive actions and his assurance that I was "his" after having sex a couple of times. I wasn't ready for someone to claim me, to own me. I didn't know when I'd ever be ready for that. I might know what dress I'd wear if the time ever came, but I didn't know much else.

"Sweetheart, you okay?" a soft voice asked. I whipped my head around to see Gwen standing in her robe, looking at me with concern.

"Yes, I'm fine. Brock's just an asshole," I said quickly, trying to act breezy. I was pretty sure I fell flat.

Gwen furrowed her brows. "You've been avoiding this subject around me for too long, Amy." Her tone meant business as she directed me into our sitting room.

Due to my delicate emotional state, it only took gentle prodding for me to spill the entire Ian situation to her. Well, not the entire situation. I may have told a white lie and said his name was Tom and that he was one of Tripp's friends, but the premise was the same.

I told her I met him, had the whole "love at first sight" thing and he broke my heart after ditching me for the war. I wasn't ready to tell Gwen about her brother and me. I just didn't know how to tell her since it had been so long. So I was a coward and lied again. It felt even worse when she blamed herself for not being there for me during the whole ordeal. My guilt weighed even heavier as she gave me advice and was just an all-around awesome best friend.

I did feel a little bit lighter having shared some of my secrets with Gwen, albeit not the full story. That didn't last for long when she casually mentioned Ian's arrival this week. Fate was cruel. Maybe it was karma for the time I drank all of my father's thirty-seven-year-old whisky and replaced it with colored water.

Or when I was fifteen and scratched my mom's Mercedes and

then let the valet take the heat. Whatever it was had me feeling sick all week. I couldn't sleep knowing I had to face him. Especially now when I was so confused with what was happening with Brock.

I was so fucked.

CHAPTER FIVE

PRESENT DAY

"Senora?" A timid voice penetrated my thoughts.

I blinked and sat up in my chair, bracing myself for something, anything. I had been so deep in my memories I hadn't even noticed that someone had entered the room. Not the best when being held captive.

Note to self: be more aware of surroundings.

My alarm was quelled slightly when I met the kind eyes of the Mexican woman who had served me at breakfast. She was now smiling nervously at me.

"Lunch. You must eat, Senora."

She put a tray down on the table beside me, my mouth watering at the smell of the food. Without conscious effort my hand snatched the cup of coffee off the tray. Well, I guessed my hunger strike wasn't going to last. I'd probably go through withdrawals if deprived of coffee much longer.

I glanced up at the woman, who was standing in front of me as if to make sure I was going to consume the food she had presented me. "What's your name?" I asked her, picking up my fork.

"Lucy," she responded nervously, watching my hand as I speared a piece of chicken off the plate.

"I'm Amy," I told her, putting the food in my mouth. I felt rude, but I was starving and it was either that or start gnawing on my own arm.

"Yes, Miss Abrams, I know." Her face had relaxed a bit after seeing me take my first bite.

"Did you make this?" I asked, pointing with my fork. She nodded nervously.

"It's delicious, thank you." I told her genuinely. The poor woman's shoulders sagged at this, as if her fate depended on her chicken salad.

"Are you....?" I started to ask her if she was a captive as well, but I didn't quite know how to word it without spooking her. "Do you work here?"

She nodded again. "Yes, Miss Abrams, I have been working here for five years."

"Call me Amy, please," I requested.

Five years? She didn't seem comfortable with having a kidnapping victim in her presence. I didn't know what to make of that. Mr. Clooney obviously wasn't a first time offender, but Lucy was decidedly skittish.

"And you work here by choice?" I asked Lucy carefully, taking another bite.

She nodded vigorously. "Yes, of course. This job is very important to my family and I."

I chewed for a moment. "I'm not here by choice. I'd very much like to be back with my family, or at least let them know I'm okay. Do you think you could help me?"

Lucy's eyes widened and she shook her head frantically. "No, no. You don't want to ask me that. You can get in trouble. I'll forget you asked. You just do what Mr. Devon says and you will be okay." She scurried out of the room before I had the chance to reply.

"Drat," I muttered, throwing my fork down. I had succeeded

in scaring the already terrified maid off. I only hoped she would be back to serve me again so I could work on gaining her trust.

So I could get the fuck away from my kidnapper, and more importantly, my memories.

———

"Time's up, Red," a familiar voice called before the door was opened.

I had just zipped up my midnight blue evening gown when I came face to face with Rafe. I resisted the shiver I felt from his gaze. It was not a good shiver. It was the kind that made me feel like I had spiders crawling up my skin.

"Well, Rafe, if you had come a couple of minutes earlier you would have caught me naked," I remarked sweetly. "You see, the underwear provided with this outfit just wouldn't work. I don't do VPL." I gave him a suggestive eyebrow raise and twirled to make my point.

The skintight sheath hugged my every curve. Although I hadn't abandoned breaking through to the housekeeper, I was going to explore every option I had to get out of this place. Unfortunately, that included seducing Hannibal Lector over here.

"You might regret being such a cock tease once I'm allowed to play with you," he hissed, pulling my body flush to his. I fought the bile in my throat, feeling his hard on pressing against my stomach.

"I'll enjoy every second," his mouth brushed my ear, "but I can't say the same for you. I can't even promise you'll be able to walk after."

I met his eyes, hoping he couldn't see the fear in mine. "Maybe I like it rough," I whispered hoarsely.

He paused a second then blinked, stepping back from me but keeping hold of my arm. "You're late for dinner."

His demeanour may have changed, but I could tell when I'd

gotten to a guy. Maybe my man whisperer skills might save my life after all.

I was taken to the same dining room as this morning, but this time the table was set with candles and wineglasses and Clooney wasn't hiding behind his paper. He was standing right by the chair I had sat in hours ago, eyes on me.

While he was inspecting me I returned the favor. He had changed his suit and was now wearing a black Burberry with a black shirt, no tie. Up close he was handsome, even in his mid-fifties. His skin was tan and he had bright blue eyes. He was clean shaven and could definitely be a certain movie star's brother.

"Miss Abrams, you look stunning. I must say you get more beautiful every time I see you," he declared.

I stopped in front of him. "Well, this is me in captivity—you should see me in the wild, Mr. Devon," I replied icily, enjoying his slight surprise as I addressed him by name.

He recovered quickly. "I'm afraid since emotions were running high this morning I wasn't able to properly introduce myself. I'm Clark Devon." He grasped my hand and kissed it lightly.

I didn't snatch it away but glared at him.

"I'll remember that for the police report. It's Clark with a *C*, right?"

Clark smiled. "I see we haven't lost any of our fire. I'm happy you feel safe enough to be so brash, Miss Abrams. Others in your situation might refrain from such statements, fearing for their own wellbeing." He pulled my chair out politely while he threatened me just as courteously.

"What can I say? I'm special." I sat down without glancing back at him.

"Can I offer you some wine?" he asked, holding up a bottle. "It's an excellent vintage."

"I'll pass. I'd like to keep my wits about me. You know, in

case you've slipped some roofies in there. Kidnapping may not be enough—maybe you want to violate me too," I replied acidly.

Clark shook his head as if he was dealing with a petulant child. "No matter how much you like to convince yourself otherwise, Miss Abrams, I mean you no harm. I've tried to make you as comfortable as possible. I do wish you would at least eat something," he said mildly.

I crossed my arms. "And I've told you, no matter what you wrap it up in, no matter how many tiny meals of fancy food you serve me, this is still a kidnapping. I'll eat when I can do it of my own free will and when you're in prison."

Clark sighed. "As you wish. I do hope you will come to reconsider in time."

The stress on the "in time" part had me feeling decidedly uncomfortable. I didn't like the insinuation that I'd be here for an extended period. I needed to get an escape plan in place, stat. I couldn't rely on the fact the cavalry was going to come in and save me. I had to rely on myself.

———

The days passed agonizingly slowly, with the routine the same. Rafe came to get me every morning to drag me to breakfast. I refused any food, like I always did when Clark offered it. It may have been stupid to basically starve myself, but it was the only thing in this entire situation I had control over. Plus, I didn't want to play into this whole civilized kidnapping fantasy that seemed to be Clark's goal — I wanted to piss the guy off. Unfortunately my refusal to eat didn't seem to bother him, and he still made me endure mealtimes with him.

Luckily Lucy knew I wouldn't eat in front of Clark, so she seemed to try and give me as much food as possible throughout the day while he was gone. I knew he was gone because the window of my library faced the circular driveway and I watched him leave every morning for the past six days at precisely eight-thirty a.m.

I wasn't into starvation so I tried to eat most of what she gave me. But one main meal and a couple of snacks throughout the day wasn't enough, I was losing weight. Fast. Not a diet I would recommend to anyone.

I tried my best to get through to Lucy, to convince her to let me get some kind of message out to the world — a smoke signal, Morse code, anything, but she scampered whenever I raised the subject. I deduced that putting the kind woman in danger for my own sake was extraordinarily selfish. I knew even if I did manage to escape with Lucy's help, Clark would most likely punish her and her family. I couldn't have that on my conscience.

Since I was left to my own devices during the day and exercise was out of the question, I spent most of the time in the library. I didn't read much, more like plotted the ways I could murder Rafe and escape this place.

I watched the guards outside as much as I could trying to memorize the schedule. I did this at night also, since I didn't sleep much either. I made subtle advances on Rafe, as much as my skin crawled doing it. He was a vital part of my plan. I knew trying to seduce him outright would be obvious, so I opted for small displays. Like purposely not being ready when he came to get me, or brushing up against him as he directed me to my meals.

It was working.

As I sat watching Clark one night eat his dinner and drink his wine, I hoped it was for the last time.

"I have some unfortunate news for you, Miss Abrams," Clark said, wiping his face with a napkin.

"You didn't win the best kidnapping of the year award?" I asked seriously. "Don't worry, I'm sure you'll be nominated next year."

He ignored this like he did most of my remarks of this nature. "Your father, although he is cooperating, is thinking of turning to the authorities." He sipped his wine. "Now I explicitly advised against this action, informing him that the consequences of this would be *unpleasant* for you. It seems he needs reminding."

He nodded to someone behind me. Rafe came into view with a look that made me taste bile. His grin was different than what I had ever seen before. It was triumphant, expectant ... evil.

I swallowed.

"Now I cannot say I agree with Rafe's tastes, nor do I approve of them, but I can't fault their results."

I listened to Clark but kept my eyes on Rafe, who pulled my chair out roughly. I failed to hide my flinch.

"Open your legs, Miss Abrams," Clark instructed me mildly.

My stomach dropped. "No way in hell," I snapped.

"I must urge you to reconsider," he requested, nodding at Rafe again.

I felt cold metal at my temple.

"I think my value as a hostage goes down significantly if I have a bullet hole in my head," I declared with a bravery I was faking.

"You have courage, I'll give you that. But no self-preservation. Bring her in."

Dread bloomed in my stomach as Lucy was pushed into the room, a man holding a gun to her head.

"Now, as you have pointed out, your life is very important in this situation. But there are many others in this house who are disposable." Clark gestured to Lucy who was crying, her face a mask of terror. "I would persuade you to change your answer to my request," he stated mildly.

I glared at the evil man sitting calmly in front of me, vowing silently I would kill him if I ever got the chance.

I opened my legs.

———

GARRETT

Garrett Morgan sat in a conference room of a hotel, one that looked similar to the many he had sat in before. He had lost count at the amount of mind numbing meetings he had to sit through in rooms like this. Boredom was a feeling he associated with them.

Fear was not.

But right now, he felt terror sitting at the bottom of his gut. It had nothing to do with the three men sitting in front of him. He was sure they incited their fair share, but he was not afraid of them. Fear had been his constant companion for the last week, since he had watched the video of his niece being handcuffed to a bed while unconscious, then witnessed her throw sass at one of the most dangerous men in America.

It was that fear that had him sitting in front of these men. Murderers, he speculated. Gun runners, he was certain. Despite this, he also sensed they were decent men. This was largely because Amy thought so and he valued her opinion. There was also the fact that one of them was married to Gwen, and he loved and respected her as well.

"Can you tell me why we're here, Mr. Morgan? You went to significant effort to seek us out," Cade, Gwen's husband, stated casually.

The men on either side of him were silent but deadly, he knew. Garrett had not been in touch with Gwen upon his arrival in Amber, nor did he let these men know who he was when he set up this meeting. He had only just offered them his name.

"I'm here because I need your retrieval services," Garrett replied calmly.

Cade's face was blank and he was silent, so Garrett carried on. "My niece has been taken. I need you to get her back."

Garrett watched as surprise flickered in Cade's eyes as he sat back in his chair. "Shouldn't you be going to the law with this?" he asked mildly.

"I have been well informed that you and your brothers have exactly the skills needed for a hostage extraction. I believe some of you are ex-SEALs?" His gaze flickered to the blond one who didn't display any emotion. "I also believe you retrieved your wife from a dangerous situation," Garrett added.

Cade sat forward, blank expression gone. "How the fuck do you know about my wife?" His fury was barely restrained.

Garrett was happy at this man's obvious protection for Gwen. He hoped that would translate to Amy.

"She's my niece's best friend," he said quietly.

Cade stilled and understanding flickered on his face.

"What the fuck are you talking about?" The blond man beside him growled, his emotionless façade gone, fury replacing it.

"Amy was kidnapped from a bar in New Mexico six days ago by a man named Clark Devon," Garrett explained as he watched the men's faces pale.

He reckoned that these men rarely felt fear, but the look of alarm on the blond's face mimicked the terror that was eating him up inside. He cared about Amy a great deal.

Garrett knew about this man. He made sure he had as much information as he could on these men. His name was Brock Vaughn, and he'd patched into the Sons of Templar after two tours as a Marine. He grew up here, was best friends with Cade Fletcher and was in love with his niece.

The last part he didn't find out from his files.

"*Six days?*" Brock yelled, banging his fist on the table. "Six fucking days and we're only hearing about this now? How the fuck is that possible?"

"My brother-in-law has been insistent on keeping this quiet —he believes it is the best way to help Amy. I respected his wishes." Garrett paused. "Until now."

Heavy silence hung in the room. The blond ooked like he was ready to kill someone with his bare hands, his eyes intent on Garrett.

"What's changed?" Cade asked evenly, flicking his gaze to his friend.

Garrett noticed at first glance, Cade may have seemed calm and unruffled by his revelation. But on closer inspection he could see his knuckles were white from the intensity at which they were being clenched, and the stiff posture showed he was containing his rage.

The man who had been quiet during this exchange spoke up. "How do you know she's alive?" he asked.

Before Garrett could answer Brock shot a death glare at his brother. He looked like he might break his jaw.

"She's alive," he bit out.

"Brother, you know this guy. Fuck, he's notorious. We've all heard the stories—without proof of life he could have—"

"She's a-*fucking*-live!" Brock exploded.

"She's alive," Garrett interrupted quietly, not wanting a brawl to erupt. He needed these men focused.

The three men looked at him and he could feel the tension in the room dissipate slightly. He opened his laptop and turned the screen toward them. "Six days ago my brother-in-law was sent this email, informing him that his daughter had been taken and if he wanted her back alive, he would have to do as he was instructed."

"What were the demands?" Brock interrupted.

"That Harold continue to support a business deal that will give Devon significantly more money and power than he has now," Garrett answered. "Harold suddenly got a conscience, decided he didn't want to be doing business with a criminal no matter how clean he was on paper. This is Clark's way of telling him that isn't going to happen."

Garrett opened the first photo they received. Amy lying unconscious, handcuffed to a bed. Once the men had seen it he felt the air turn dangerous.

"Fuck," Cade muttered.

Brock stayed silent, but he was shaking with rage.

"Shortly afterward we received the first video. He has streaming cameras in his dining room. Of course he is smart enough not to show his face."

Garrett played the video, Amy's voice through the speaker still a blow to his stomach.

"Well, excuse me for not praising you on what a lovely kidnapping you've thrown. It's the best I've been to. I'll be sure to let my friends know the caliber of the pastries present."

"Jesus Christ, Amy," Brock muttered.

Garrett had almost laughed when he had heard her say that for the first time, but the knowledge of just how dangerous Devon was sobered him. "We get one of these every day to prove Amy is still alive. She is unharmed in each of the other ones, although her language stays colorful," Garrett explained once the video ended.

"Does she even fuckin' know how dangerous this guy is? She's playing a game with her life every time she opens her smart mouth," Brock bit out, shaking his head.

Garrett laughed. "I don't expect she does know what Clark is capable of. I'm thankful for that—her stubbornness and sarcasm are better than terror."

"You said something changed to make you come to us," Cade addressed him, his tone was flat.

"Yes," Garrett sighed. "The last video we got." He paused, not wanting to choke up in front of these men. He cleared his throat. "The last video has led me to believe Clark doesn't intend on letting Amy go anytime soon. Nor does he intend to keep her in one piece."

He played the clip that had broken his heart.

He watched the men instead of the video. He didn't need to look at the computer screen, he saw it every time he closed his eyes. They all stilled at Clark's voice.

"Open your legs."

"No way in hell." He heard Amy's strong tone.

He was so proud of how brave his girl was.

Brock's hiss and Cade's curse informed him they were watching a gun being held to Amy's head. They kept their eyes glued to the screen until it abruptly turned off the moment Amy did as she was asked. The clip then jumped to Amy being carried out of the room with blood staining her thighs. He had lost his lunch upon seeing that, and had barely been able to eat since.

A loaded silence followed the end of the clip.

Abruptly Brock pushed out of his chair, his face blank. He picked up the chair, walked to the wall and smashed it against the concrete. It shattered into pieces.

He paused before walking back over. "He's fucking dead," Brock declared flatly.

For the first time in six days, Garrett smiled.

———

AMY

I awoke to fire. My legs, they were burning up. The pain was so intense I was afraid to move. What I was feeling was on par with how bad it was when I sustained these injuries, when Rafe's knife had torn through my skin. At first I was relieved when I had discovered he wasn't planning on raping me. But after he had sliced the skin on my inner thigh, down through the muscle, I found myself wondering whether I would have preferred it.

He had slid the knife up my thigh and I had been terrified, horrified at the prospect of what he might do with it.

"Do you know that one tiny incision, deep enough in this exact spot—" he dug the tip into my leg, just enough to break the skin. "It can cause you to bleed out in a matter of minutes. Unfortunately, the reason I know this is from experience." He smiled at me in a way that made me want to vomit. "Don't worry though, sweetheart, I've had enough practice. You'll live through this. Not like the others."

Then he began cutting. Running the blade lightly along at

first so I felt a sting, and a thin trail of blood marked his progress. Then the next time he went deeper and I struggled not to cry out, not to move. He was slow, drawing out the agony of having the steel rip open my skin.

Rafe glanced up. "I wouldn't squirm if I were you, Red. One wrong move and I might nick the artery. We wouldn't want that."

His hand ran lightly, almost gently up my thigh in a caress, lapping up the blood. I was sickened to see the hard line in his slacks. The fucker was getting off on this.

"Someone really did a number on you, huh, Rafe?" I bit out through clenched teeth. "Your mom never hug you enough? Or your dad just a little too much?"

The hand on my thigh tightened on my wound and I whimpered despite myself. "You won't be quite as mouthy once I'm finished with you," he sneered, turning his attention downward.

It turned out Rafe was right. I had no more sarcastic remarks, no words at all actually. All of my focus was on not screaming, not pleading, not begging for him to stop. I guessed it didn't actually last for long, but it felt like hours with no respite, only increasing amounts of agony.

When he was done, I was close to passing out. Clark, who had been watching intently from his spot at the table, was in front of me all of a sudden. "You're strong," he remarked, stroking my cheek.

I still had enough energy to flinch away from his touch.

"I apologize for that, Miss Abrams. As I said, it was necessary. You continue to surprise me, though—I have had grown men reduced to tears from similar experiences."

"Well, maybe you need to get yourself a new torturer," I answered faintly. "This one's getting a bit soft." I gestured with my head to Rafe who was cleaning my blood off his knife, still sporting a hard on.

Clark chuckled. "I might just have to keep you, Miss Abrams. You interest me."

On that disturbing note, he left. Upon his departure two men approached me, with blank faces and carrying what looked like first aid kits. At that point I passed out.

Which brought me back to now. I gingerly lifted the blankets to reveal my legs. My inner thighs were bandaged, and I pulled back the coverings with a flinch. Three cuts were stitched closed and they looked angry and red. They were also long, about six inches. I checked my other leg which sported identical incisions. Only six? When it was happening I was certain he made half a dozen incisions on each leg, not in total.

"I wouldn't move too much if I were you. Those incisions are dangerously close to your artery—one wrong move and you could tear it." Rafe stepped out of the shadows and I jumped. The pain that blossomed in my legs caused me to regret that sudden movement.

"Oh look. Jack the Ripper's back for round two," I muttered sarcastically. It sounded sad even to my own ears, fear saturated my tone.

Rafe gazed at me with an emotion I couldn't place. It couldn't be regret. Sociopaths weren't capable of that.

"It had to be done, Amy. I won't say I didn't enjoy marking your milky white skin, but I did wish I could have been doing it to someone else."

He reached the side of my bed and pushed the hair off my face tenderly.

"You're strong and I know you want me. We could be perfect together. Once Clark is done with you I could convince him to let me have you. You'll learn to enjoy the process." He nodded to my thighs. "You'll even beg for it."

My stomach rolled at the prospect. This guy was fifty shades of insane. But insane could be good in this situation.

"Of course I want you. I'm just not used to such a powerful man controlling me," I responded, eyes locking with his crazy baby blues. My gaze flickered to the clock on the table beside me. "How long has it been?" I asked, changing the subject.

Rafe stared at me a moment longer before he answered. "Almost twenty-four hours. They gave you something to help you sleep. I've been here ... watching you."

Okay, can you spell *creepy?*

"I like that you were here," I purred, inwardly gagging. "I want you, but I need some more time so I can properly show you how much."

Rafe's eyes flared. "I can't touch you again, not until Clark decides."

"He doesn't have to know. It'll be our secret," I said quietly.

Rafe looked uncertain so I grasped his hand.

"Come tomorrow morning early... sunrise. No one will be around. Just one time, then I'll wait." I pulled his finger into my mouth and bit down softly.

Rafe groaned.

"Tomorrow," I whispered.

He nodded stiffly and turned to leave.

I sagged down in my bed, anticipation overwhelming the pain in my thighs. Tomorrow. Tomorrow I might actually stand a chance. Okay, it was slimmer than a model at fashion week, but it was a chance. I had watched the guards religiously the past week, looking for some kind of weakness.

I knew that Rafe or some other burly mute was outside the door of whatever room I was in. From my wing there was a short walk down a hallway, then down a huge staircase which led to the foyer. Past the foyer was a sitting room and through that was the dining room which I now knew doubled as a torture room. Kind of unsanitary if you asked me.

When I was escorted to my meals with Clark, I had watched for any other guards. Apart from whoever was with me there didn't seem to be any. I knew there was one directly outside the front door, I knew this from watching from my library. What I also knew was that at precisely twenty minutes after sunrise, a van came to the front door to deliver what I guessed was groceries. Or it could be drugs. Or freaking Beanie Bag toys for all I knew.

It wasn't important. What was important was this truck came every day at the same time. That truck was my ticket out. All I had to do was somehow overpower Rafe, get his gun, silence the guard at the door and commandeer the truck. I'd put on false eyelashes after five cosmos, I was sure I could manage a simple escape.

I couldn't sleep. Partly because I had been unconscious for twenty-four hours, partly because I was anxious as hell about my plan and partly because my legs hurt like a motherfucker. How I was going to manage this when I was barely able to walk was a mystery to me. But I had committed. Rafe would be here any second and I'd rather take my chances with escape than actually sleep with the sicko.

Yuck.

I had gone over my plan continuously throughout the night and I knew what little chance I had. I was relying on a lot of shoddy information and uncertainties, and the fact I was injured would hamper me. Chances were I would probably get caught, I might not even make it past Rafe. But I had to try.

In waiting for dawn to arrive and for whatever preceded, my mind wandered to Ian, the way it did when I lay in the dark and the memories crept in like demons in the night.

CHAPTER SIX

It was the day. The day Ian was going to arrive in Amber. I was a mess.

"Are you high?" Rosie asked me curiously as a customer left the store.

"What? No," I replied in shock.

I wished I was high. Maybe a joint would take the edge off. I wondered where I could get some weed in this place. I was sure Lucky would give me some. He had to be my best bet. No one was that happy all the time without some help from a pal called Bud.

"You just gave that lady a hundred bucks change instead of ten. And you looked for a sweater for ten straight minutes until you realized it was in your hand," Rosie said lightly, part teasing, but concern flickered in her gaze.

She knew something was up. "What's going on?" she asked. "Has it got anything to do with the fact Gwen's brother is arriving today?"

My eyes bulged. Maybe she was a mind reader. "How did you know?" I asked quietly.

She raised an eyebrow then gave me a sympathetic gaze. "It's not hard. Every time Gwen mentions how excited she is to see him, you go a delightful shade of green and make some excuse to escape."

My stomach dropped. "Do you think Gwen noticed?"

Rosie shook her head. "No, she's too excited to see him, plus she's like encased in a cocoon of infatuation with my brother."

I let out a sigh of relief.

"Want to talk about it?" she asked.

I shook my head, but before I knew it the whole damned story came tumbling out, along with my very confusing feelings for Brock.

"Wow," she said when I had finished. Her mouth was open slightly.

"I know," I said sadly. "You don't think I could convince them to have a reverse polygamy type situation and they could be brother husbands?" I joked weakly.

She smiled dreamily. "Imagine having two bad ass men doting over you."

I thought for a second. "I think I have my hands full with Brock at the moment. Literally. He is very well endowed." On that thought my head snapped up. "I'm sorry, I know he's your friend, I haven't meant to be such a witch to him."

Rosie waved her hand. "Don't you dare apologize. Brock's a big boy, and by the sounds of it he's been an asshole. This isn't all on you. Unfortunately, I have a feeling they might meet. And I don't think the first thing on their mind will be becoming brother husbands."

I put my face in my hands. "Why can't I be a lesbian? I feel like my problems would be so much easier if I liked girls."

"I agree—if it wasn't for the fact I liked sex with men I would have turned a long time a ago," Rosie said, folding some sweaters. She glanced up at me, her face turning from joking to serious. "What are you going to do?"

I looked at her, feeling overwhelmed. "I honestly don't know.

I was getting over Ian. I was at peace with the fact we weren't going to be together. And Brock...." I trailed off. I couldn't articulate my feelings for him right now. They didn't exactly rival the feelings I had for Ian. They were different. Raw and all consuming.

"I need to go for a walk," I declared. We had been quiet all morning. "I'll take my cell. You get busy, call me," I said.

"I'll be fine. Go and clear your head. But you can't take off to Canada, no matter how enticing the prospect," she joked.

I had been tossing up the merits of leaving the country and seeking asylum. She was totally a mind reader.

A few minutes later, I walked along the beach, carrying my heels in my hand and letting the water kiss my toes. I was sure I'd regret it later when I got sand in my seven hundred dollar shoes, but right now it was therapeutic. I was letting the water wash all my man troubles away when it washed something else right up in front of me. Running out of the surf, holding a board and looking all wet and delicious was Brock.

I stopped walking.

"Shit," I muttered.

We hadn't spoken since our yelling match four days ago and I was surprised to realize how much I had missed him. I itched to go running into the surf and pounce on him, no matter the fact I was wearing a white lace Chloe dress that would not survive salt water.

It must've been serious if I was willing to risk couture. The fact that his abs looked great dripping with water and his long wet hair framing his attractive face had me willing to throw my entire wardrobe into the ocean if need be. I had already decided to turn and remove myself from the situation when Brock's head turned my way and his eyes locked on mine.

At that moment, while he changed direction and strode towards me, I was locked in place. It was as if his gaze had turned the sand underneath my toes into quicksand.

"Sparky," he greeted me softly.

"You surf," I replied, drinking in his sculpted body.

"As much as I can," he replied.

"I've always wanted to surf," I continued.

"I can teach you." He seemed to not be perturbed by the weirdness of my greeting.

"You'd want to drown me after five minutes."

Brock's face went dark. "Maybe. But I'd want to fuck you after five seconds. Especially if you wore that red bikini that makes your tits look good enough to eat."

Silence descended at the mention of the red bikini and the argument it represented. "I'm sorry I was such a bitch. It was all a bit ... intense," I blurted, feeling generally sorry.

"Shit, babe, I'm sorry I came on too strong with the whole old lady thing. It's too fast for you, I get it." He ran his hand through his damp hair and I followed it intently with my eyes. "It's too fuckin' fast for me as well. But I can't stop fuckin' thinkin' about you, babe. Your body, your hair. That bikini, the way you taste." His eyes were dark on mine. "Fuck it," he muttered.

He speared his board into the sand and grabbed the back of my neck, pulling my body against his damp and hard one.

I melted into the kiss, submitted to the firestorm that followed his touch. As his hand squeezed my ass roughly I was able to gain some coherent thought.

I pulled back. "We need to stop," I said breathlessly.

"Yeah, if by stop you mean go to your place so I can fuck you against the wall while you're wearing that virginal fuckin' dress ,I agree," he growled and I almost complied. Hell, I almost suggested the sand at our feet.

"We can't," I said firmly. More to myself than him.

He frowned. "Why the fuck not?"

"We can't do this for ... a while," I declared, not wanting to end it entirely. It was selfish and possibly cruel, but the thought of never feeling Brock's explosive touch again had me feeling vaguely nauseous.

Brock's frown turned into a glare. "What are you talking about, Amy?"

"We just can't, okay?" I said quietly.

Brock's hands tightened at my hips. "That's not a reason, and not something I'm going to accept, baby."

I huffed at him. "Well, it's my prerogative to end something without giving a reason if that's what I want," I shot at him.

A hand moved from my hip to graze the side of my breast. "Yup, it may be your prerogative, but it sure as shit isn't what you want. Tell me what's going on," he demanded.

I let out a breath. I really didn't want it to come to this. "Someone's coming to town today. Someone I need to ... sort some things out with before I can even consider taking this—us —further," I said quietly.

Brock's face turned cold. "A man."

I nodded, unable to say anything else. I felt like a massive bitch.

"So you've just been using me as your personal fuck toy until your real man comes to town? That it, Amy?" he clipped. "The man who wears an expensive suit, earns enough money to keep you in your fancy shit and someone you can take him to Mummy and Daddy?" he yelled.

"No! Of course not. How could you even think that? We're not together. Not anymore," I defended. "And wearing a fancy suit and getting my parents' approval would be two things that would make me run a mile," I told him honestly.

Brock glared at me in disbelief before his face turned blank. "Yeah, well you do whatever you gotta do. I don't need your shit fucking up my life." He grabbed his board and walked off.

"Well, that went well," I said to myself.

———

It was safe to say the drive home that night had me feeling like utter shit. Not only had I felt like a terrible person after the train wreck run-in with Brock, I also had just gotten off the phone with Lucy and she had told me somehow Jimmy had called Gwen. My worry for my friend permeated everything else. I was terrified that sick fuck got into her head and bulldozed all of the progress she had made over the past year. That was not going to happen. I would make sure of it.

I dialed a number I usually avoided like the plague.

"Amy, how are you, my dear?" My father answered the phone pleasantly.

"I'm not the best, Father, since I just found out that piece of shit Jimmy somehow called Gwen's cell phone and threatened her," I responded with a shaking voice. "I need you to find out how that happened and get whoever was responsible fired," I ordered. "I also want you to make sure that that piece of shit is in solitary for the rest of his miserable life."

My father was silent for a moment. "Consider it done. How is Gwenevere?" His concern almost sounded real for a moment.

I paused. "I don't know, I haven't spoken to her yet. I'm pulling up at home now so I've got to go." I turned off the car, bracing myself. "And Dad ... thanks," I said after a moment.

"You're welcome, Amy." My father sounded taken aback at my thanking him, but I didn't have time for my estranged family drama. I had my real family to worry about.

Promptly, as I was walking up our driveway in fact, my worry turned to anger.

I stormed in the door, slamming it behind me, eyes narrowing on Gwen as I hurtled into the dining room. "You!" I accused, pointing my finger. "I cannot believe The Prick Who Shall Not Be Named called and I had to find out from freaking *Lucy!* I mean, I love the girl, but I don't want to find this shit out secondhand. You should have called me the moment you got off the phone with that maggot so I could call him back and reach down the phone and castrate the fucker," I said fiercely, meaning every word. I would gladly de-ball that man, given the opportunity.

Gwen looked at me blankly, and I was happy to see she looked ... okay. She didn't look like she was on the verge of breaking down. She wasn't that shell she was a year ago. She looked strong. I let out a teeny breath.

"Hello, Amy, how's it going? Want to say hello to Ian who just got home from an unknown warzone?" was Gwen's sarcastic response.

Okay, so she was fine.

I swallowed, unsure if I could glance his way without laying all of my feelings on my sleeve for Gwen to see. The room felt like it was crackling with electricity, I could feel his presence, the heat of his gaze on me. I willed myself to glance in his direction with an impassive stare on my face. I focused on why I was mad.

"Sorry, Ian, didn't mean to be rude. I was just a little preoccupied with the whole 'Gwen getting a phone call from a murderous psychopath' situation." I decided sarcasm was the best form of defense.

But as my eyes locked with Ian's everything fell away. I drank him in greedily as he pushed up from his chair, striding toward me, not breaking eye contact. He was bigger, his muscles more defined. His eyes glowed with intensity.

Then I was in his arms. I battled with the feelings that came rushing with his touch and then relaxed. He was whole. Safe. No bullet holes in sight.

When he released me, I wasn't ready to let go of his touch. I also wasn't ready for the tender, intimate gaze that penetrated my soul when he looked at me. It was one we had shared in the stolen moments of our fleeting courtship. I inwardly winced at the pain it caused.

"Looking great, Ames," he said softly after his eyes had roved my body.

The look wasn't wild or animalistic like the ones that Brock directed at me, neither did it make me feel like flames licked my body. It was soft, reverent, though there was a tinge of sexual hunger in it.

I was glad I looked good today. Well, I tried to look good every day, but I was happy with my outfit of choice. My white lace dress had long sleeves, but its hemline finished well above my knees. My hair was braided so it fell long over my shoulder, and my Manolos almost had me meeting Ian's chin. I was clad in enough designer armor I might just survive this encounter.

I turned my thoughts outward, or more particularly to rove over Ian's body. A dull hunger thrummed through me as my gaze ran down his muscled expanse. I stopped at a scar on his eyebrow with a frown. A sick feeling quickly replaced the desire, a brutal reminder of his chosen profession. The thing that could get him dead in an instant. The thing that had already killed us.

"Just another one to add to the collection," I remarked dryly.

Something passed in his expression before he schooled it and I realized we were showing way too much of our confusing non-relationship in front of clueless Gwen. I tried to turn my face into an emotionless gaze and removed myself from Ian's vicinity.

Interestingly enough, the worrying situation with Gwen had done nothing to derail my runaway freight train of emotions about Ian. When I tried to bring Jimmy up again, Gwen refused to discuss it. She instead changed the subject to something arguably more dangerous.

"How about we talk about where you've been all day, Abrams?" she shouted from the kitchen where she'd gone to dump the dinner dishes and my stomach dropped.

Don't mention Brock! I mentally shouted at her. I was having enough trouble trying to sort out my feelings without making Ian aware of the man who had worked his way under my skin.

"Having makeup sex with Brock maybe?" Gwen teased, walking to the table with dessert in her hands. Our telepathic connection left a lot to be desired.

Ian's face turned to granite. "Who's Brock?" he growled.

The anger in his tone caught me off guard. Then pissed me right off. *He* was the one that called it off between us. *He* was the one who pushed me away. He had no freaking right to play the jealous, angry, macho man.

Gwen, bless her, continued to feed the fire without knowing. "Oh, just some guy that won't take Amy's shit but is completely under her skin," she said with a smirk.

Great.

Ian's glare was in danger of turning me to stone. I did my best to ignore it as the conversation with Brock came into my mind. He wasn't likely to be a problem anymore anyway. I ignored the stab to the heart that was.

"He's no one. No one special and I certainly won't be talking to him again. Subject closed." I was trying to convince myself more than anyone else.

I eyed the decadent looking cake Gwen had placed in front of me. I cut the hugest piece I could then dumped it on my plate. Maybe if I become two hundred pounds heavier I wouldn't have to worry about man problems. Only the crane that they would need to get me out of the house would be an issue.

Gwen's disbelieving gaze at my food choice had me feeling defensive. "It's my cheat day," I shot at her.

Luckily the roar of a Harley took the heat from me and the fact I was consuming two days' worth of calories. Gwen's face got all dreamy and happy and I couldn't help but feel pleased at this. My love life might be a steaming pile of shit, but my best friend was happy. That was good enough for me. The stormy look on Ian's face had me feeling instantly defensive of Gwen's well-deserved happiness.

I pointed at him with my fork. "Look here, Mr. Soldier, don't you dare try any of your macho man bullshit and be a dick to Cade. He can handle it, I have no doubt about that, but we don't need the drama. He cares about your sister and makes her happy. That's all you need to know," I told him snippily.

I may have also been using this opportunity to not only let out the anger I had toward Ian for shooting me accusatory looks at the mention of Brock but for breaking my goddamned heart in the first place.

I glared at him. The soft feeling I had towards seeing him again without any shrapnel wounds had dissipated and reality was setting in. He glared back at me then nodded.

He chose that moment to retreat with his plate of food. I struggled not to perv at his ass as he was walking away. I failed.

I realized that Gwen's eagle eye was on me as I dragged my own gaze away from her brother's glorious behind. "What the hell was that?" she shot.

Oh shit.

"What?" I tried for innocent.

She wasn't having it. "You know what. You and Ian—what the hell is going on? You guys were acting weird."

"No, we weren't." I went for denial.

"Yes, you were," she pressed.

"Were not."

At this juncture, she let out a frustrated groan and then in a flash my plate was whisked away. My eyes narrowed. You did not take away chocolate from a woman who was suffering serious love life troubles. Granted, Gwen was oblivious to these troubles, but my emotions didn't know that.

"Hey, what the fuck?" I nearly snarled. I needed that chocolate. It was that or heroin. And I didn't like the way addicts wore their hair.

"You don't get any more until you tell me what's going on," she declared, holding the plate out of my reach.

Gwen did not know how close I was to tackling her. Cade entered the room and I directed my scowl in his direction. "Your girlfriend is evil," I informed him.

I used his arrival as an opportunity to push past Gwen and snatch my plate of sanity before escaping up the stairs. "That will go straight to your ass," I heard called after me.

"Fuck you!" I shouted back.

I slammed the door to my room and tucked myself in bed,

shoving cake into my mouth and trying to sort all of my emotions out. Seeing Ian again made me painfully aware I wasn't over him. I still loved him. He was strong. Caring. And extraordinarily sexy. He also broke my heart.

My mind wandered to Brock. Also strong. Also sexy. But he was different. He made me furious. Irritated the shit out of me. We hardly went five minutes without arguing. What we had was raw and real, he didn't romanticize me and put me on a pedestal like Ian did. He ravaged me body and soul, but he didn't take shit. Didn't treat me like I was some delicate "China doll" who needed to be handled with care.

These thoughts rolled around in my head until well after my plate was licked clean. Well, after the lights turned off and a Harley roared away.

I was painfully aware that Ian was in the same house as me. I had wished for him to be this close, pleaded for it. Now I didn't know how to handle it. I even had the evil thought of wishing he was still over fighting some unknown war so I didn't have to face the grim reality that was staring at me through the darkness.

I was in love with two men.

"Fuck this," I muttered, throwing my covers back and slipping out my door.

I wasn't intending on going anywhere near Ian's room, not with Gwen in the house. My mission was to locate either vodka or chocolate and either drink or eat my problems away. Said mission was foiled when I reached the kitchen and came upon a shirtless Ian sitting at the breakfast bar.

His eyes flared as he took in my nightgown. I self-consciously yanked it down. I don't know why, the man had seen me naked for crissake. Plus, I should have felt a little satisfaction at the hungry gaze that flickered over my lace-clad body. Instead I felt panic.

"What are you doing?" I whispered at him accusingly.

"Waiting for you. It's about time," he replied casually, but his voice was gruff.

I crossed my arms. "I didn't come here to see you," I said.

"Yeah, I can guess what you came down for." He shifted slightly to reveal the bottle of beer he was drinking and a glass of vodka. "I know you, Abrams."

I narrowed my eyes. "You *used* to know me. Then you left and chose an unwinnable war over me. I've changed," I snapped at him, snatching the glass from his outstretched hand.

His eyes didn't leave mine. "Not from where I'm sitting. You're still beautiful. You're still fiercely protective of my sister and you're still sarcastic as hell. You're still my Amy," he said hoarsely.

"I'm not yours," I snapped, "You made sure to let me know that a year ago."

Ian sighed, standing. "I wanted to protect you, Amy. I wasn't ready to leave the Army. My duty. I didn't want you resigned to the life of a soldier's wife. Waiting for sporadic phone calls, only half living your life because of the way I chose to live mine." He stood, moving toward me. "I wanted you to be happy, to have a chance to move on—not be stuck in one place waiting for me."

I stepped towards him, pointing my finger at myself. "No, you didn't do it for me. You did it for you. So you didn't have to feel guilty for going over and satisfying whatever it is that makes you leave and risk your life." I glared at him. "You didn't even give me a chance. Didn't give us a chance. You didn't believe I was strong enough to handle it. I was. I would have been. Or I would have tried my fucking best. It might have worked. It might not have. But you took that choice away from me," I finished on a whisper yell. "And then after Gwen was hurt you came back and those nights—" My voice broke slightly remembering the silent, desperate way we made love, trying to comfort each other. "Those nights that we shared, I thought it meant something to you. Made you realize it was something worth waiting for. But no. It was off to war you went again, without a fucking backwards glance!"

"I know!" he shouted.

His raised voice echoed through the quiet house. I winced, hoping Gwen didn't wake.

He stepped into my space and I held my breath. "I fucked up. When I was over there I knew it. The second I left the airport I knew it. I thought I was doing it for your own good." He caressed my cheek.

I flinched away from his touch. "Oh yes. Chivalrous freaking martyr Ian. He knows what's best for me because sweet delicate Amy couldn't possibly have a brain between her ears. Don't patronize me. I'm not some little flower that needs protecting."

"I know that." Ian kept his voice even, controlled.

It pissed me off. It was always like this. We never had arguments. He didn't react. Didn't fly off the handle. I would yell and scream and he would just stand there stoically with his iron clad control. That was it. The control. With Brock there was no control. It was pure, unbridled passion. He didn't worry about hurting my feelings. He threw the anger right back, not caring whether I could handle it or not.

"What are you expecting from me, Ian?" I asked.

My anger hadn't lessened, but I needed to know. I was tired. Tired of the pain I had been carrying in my heart. Exhausted from the weight of keeping this from my best friend. I wanted this finished.

"Everything," he said quietly. "I want everything we had. I want you. I want to make love to you like the world is going to end. I want to feel you break apart in my arms. I want to have you. I want to go to sleep in whatever shithole I'm in knowing I've got you waiting for me at home." He stepped forward again, his eyes intense, but I retreated.

They were the words I had been dying to hear. When my love for this man had torn away all my dignity and I had begged him to give us a chance, all I wanted to hear was this. But now ... I didn't know what I wanted. A part of me wanted to jump into his arms and be engulfed in the comfort and strength of his love.

"What am I supposed to say to that?" I hissed. "You are a

year too late, Ian. Did you think you could shatter my heart, then expect me to be cradling the pieces waiting for you to put them back together once you finally decided you wanted a woman waiting for you on the other side of this war? Fuck you." I shot a venomous gaze at him, downing my drink and storming off.

————

The next morning I awoke early. I felt like shit. I had shut my eyes for about two minutes, but my mind hadn't been able to turn off. All of Ian's words last night whizzed around my brain like an annoying mosquito in the night. He wanted me. He wanted us. It's a shame he had to stomp all over me in order to come to that conclusion.

I had been up since six a.m. consuming copious amounts of coffee and distracting myself with online shopping. Nothing cured heartache like a new handbag. Or five.

Gwen had ventured off to get more precious java since I had emptied the house of our supply.

"Morning, beautiful," a rough accent greeted me.

I whipped my head up from my iPad. Ian stood in the doorway, shirtless and looking rumpled and seriously sexy.

His body was cut. He looked like he had rubbed oil on his six pack to make it glisten. It felt weird seeing a body free from tattoos, I had become accustomed to it. It didn't make me any less turned on as I drank him in, remembering that body pressed against mine.

Ian's body had momentarily distracted my caffeinated mind and I remembered I was annoyed with him. I jumped off the barstool, glaring at him.

"There's food in the refrigerator—help yourself. Gwen's gone to get coffee. She should be back soon." I informed him, walking toward the living room. I couldn't be in the same room as him when he was half naked, I was afraid of what I might do. Or what my hormones might do.

"Wait, Amy."

I ignored this and kept walking. A strong hand grasped my arm, stopping me.

"What—" I started to say, but the arm whirled me around and yanked my body to a hard one.

Ian's mouth was on mine and I struggled at first, but I quickly melted into the embrace. My willpower shattered at his familiar touch, at the intensity simmering between us.

The kiss was wild and tender at the same time. His hand delved into my hair, the other gripping my ass. I let his tongue explore mine, savoring the slow burn that ignited with his touch. I shouldn't be doing this. I was sure there was a multitude of reasons why I shouldn't. I will stop it. In a second.

"Oh my god, my eyes!" A dramatic screech made me yank myself away.

Gwen's horrified and disbelieving face darted between the both of us before she slammed the front door shut again. I didn't miss the look of disappointment she shot at me before the door slammed.

"Fuck," Ian muttered.

I ignored him and ran outside to try and repair the damage that kiss had done. This was not how I wanted Gwen to find this out. Ideally, I would have rasped it out to her on my deathbed so I wouldn't have to face her wrath. That plan was foiled.

Gwen was pacing the lawn when I emerged.

"Gwen, stop—listen to me. I'm sorry I didn't tell you. It's just —" I ran toward my friend, hoping the perfect explanation would pop out of my mouth, but Gwen cut me off, her face wild.

"It's just what, Abrams? You've been screwing my brother and lying to me about it?" Her yell was accentuated by a hard shove to my chest. I stumbled back, shocked at the fact she was getting physical. She didn't stop her rant. "We never lie to each other. Ever. Jesus, how could you not tell me?"

Ian emerged from the house and tried to forage into the fray.

"Stay out of this, Ian, this is a chick thing. You don't have a vagina so you don't understand," Gwen snapped at him.

Gwen had been glaring at her brother so the full weight of my pissed off stare didn't penetrate with her. She was mad. I understood that. I expected that. But that didn't mean she needed to go all "Jersey Shore" on me. I decided if she was going to get physical then so was I.

I pushed her back, hard.

"Don't push me!"

I didn't know what I expected her to do, but tackling me to the ground shouldn't have been a surprise. I tried to struggle, but for a tiny person she was scrappy as fuck.

"It's my brother, Amy. Do you not think I would've been happy for you two, you stupid idiot?" she screeched breathlessly as I struggled in vain to get the upper hand. I pinched her.

Her eyes flared. "Ouch! You bitch!" She looked like she was about to go for my hair when suddenly she was pulled off me. Cade had her in his arms, restraining her. I hadn't noticed him pull up, deep in catfight mode. Ian helped me up before I flinched away from his touch.

"Why didn't you tell me?" a small, hurt voice asked. I turned my thoughts away from Ian to my more important hurt best friend. I sighed.

"Shit, I don't know, Gwen. First it was because I didn't want to even admit how I felt, let alone admit it to you. Then things got complicated, you got hurt and there was never a right time," I replied.

It was a huge oversimplification of it all, but I really didn't want to pour my heart out to our current audience. They had already witnessed me lose a catfight. That was enough for today.

My gaze wandered past Cade and my breath caught in my throat as it landed on Brock. He had his shades on so I couldn't see his eyes, but by the set of his jaw I could tell he was pissed. He was leaning against his bike, seemingly casual, but I could tell by the way he held his body he had figured Ian was the guy I was talking about yesterday. What a clusterfuck.

Ian must have caught the stare off and made a connection of his own because he moved from behind me to stand in front of me, shielding me from the field of vision, and for all intents and purposes laying his masculine claim.

I narrowed my eyes. Gwen got in before I could unleash my feelings for that gesture.

"This is not the time to discuss any of this, okay? Go back inside and put some clothes on, Amy, the neighbor's boys will be snapping photos of you with their phones."

I looked down, remembering my lack of attire. Luckily I hadn't slipped a nip.

"Ace, we'll talk inside, okay? Just calm yourself first—we don't want any more brawls in the living room." Ian stepped in, his voice level and calm, like always.

He directed me into the house with his hand on the small of my back. I reluctantly let him, hating the intimacy of the gesture at this point in time. Hating that I couldn't go to my friend and pour everything out to her. And also hating the look Brock had directed at me.

"Why didn't you just pee in a circle around me, Ian? Then everyone in the neighborhood would know to stay away," I bit at him sarcastically as the door closed behind us.

Ian turned to me with a hard expression. "That was him, wasn't it? Brock." He spat out his name like it tasted bad. He didn't give me time to answer. "Do you love him?"

"That's none of your business. He is none of your business," I said, crossing my arms.

"It is my fucking business. You're my fuckin' business because I love you!" he yelled.

I stood silently, taken aback at the sudden slip in his usual iron clad temper. He ran his hand through his short hair, it was a gesture I saw a lot when he was frustrated or stressed. He stepped towards me to lightly put his hands on my hips. His green eyes met mine. "I love you, Amy. You're all I think about when I'm over there. I tried to let you go. To forget you. So you could move on. I can't. I want you. You want me too," he said gently.

"I used to," I admitted quietly. "You can't expect me to jump into your arms after saying something like that. You left. You left me."

The person saying that wasn't the independent, strong Amy Abrams. This was the vulnerable little girl who had been neglected and left behind too many times.

Ian's face hardened. "It's because of him, the *biker*."

I shook my head. "It's because you broke my heart and now you're acting like I should be ready to jump back into things with you. I can't." I pulled out of his grasp.

"Amy," he said.

"I need to think. I need time," I declared.

His face softened. "Take all the time you need. I'll wait for you. Forever if I have to." It hardened into a grim look of determination. "And I'll fight for you. I'm not going to do the polite thing and stand down. I'll fight tooth and fuckin' nail to make you mine. For good."

CHAPTER SEVEN

I did need time. I needed space. I needed to breathe, away from all of the stifling emotions that cropped up from being in the same room as Ian ... and from being in the same zip code as Brock. I could feel the heat of his fury.

So I took a drive. I drove down the coast and tried to clear my head. It didn't work. My thoughts bounced around the interior of my car.

The way it felt with Ian when we were together was easy, right. Then there was the way I felt when he left me. How excruciating the pain of a broken heart was. How debilitating the sting of his rejection was. Then it was back to Brock. He was the fire to Ian's ice. Ian was cool, calm, never lost his temper. Brock ran wild and hot and his emotions simmered on the surface.

When I got back home hours later, I still didn't know what to feel, but I did know I wasn't going to run back into Ian's arms. Too much had happened. Ian was drinking beer in the kitchen when I arrived home, he stood, eyes on me.

"You're back."

"You're perceptive. Bet that's why they've got you in the Army, huh, soldier?" I remarked dryly.

He grinned. It was his cheeky grin with the side of his mouth and it made his hard army façade crumble and remind me of the playful guy underneath. He tapped his head "I've got it going on up here." After an expectant look he asked, "So, you've thought?"

Irritation bloomed. "Really? You think after I go for a drive I'll have it all wrapped in a tidy bow and ready to give you what you want, after you've decided you want it?" I snapped.

Ian's brows furrowed. "Well, I know it's what you want too. The way you kissed me this morning, babe, you still want me. I sure as shit still want you." His eyes darkened and I ignored the flutter between my legs.

"You're a hot guy. Of course I want you. That doesn't mean I'm going to forgive you and decide to wait on the sidelines patiently for you to finish playing war."

"I'm not playing war, Amy. It's my job, it's my duty! It's been my life for ten years—it's not something I can just walk away from," he argued. He stepped forward and his gaze turned feral. "This is about the lowlife biker. He's in your head," he growled.

"Don't talk about him like that! You have no right to act jealous. You gave away that right when you dumped me," I hissed at him, hurt seeping into my tone.

Ian looked frustrated. "I told you, I thought I was doing the right thing, what was best for you."

"Oh yeah, keep telling yourself that," I muttered.

The roar of a Harley interrupted the conversation and I realized Gwen would have questions. And maybe a semiautomatic weapon.

"Gwen," was all I said.

"I'll deal with my sister," he declared.

"You'll have more luck dealing with whatever war you're fighting," I replied. "She'll either be pissed as hell or come in planning our wedding. I don't really know how to explain to her that's not going to happen."

Ian got a weird look on his face. "Sit. I told you I'll handle her."

I frowned at his order but did as he said. We sat in uncomfortable silence to wait for Gwen to come in.

Ian was right, he did handle it. He handled it by distracting his sister with the news he was quitting the Army. His little declaration had Gwen squealing and laughing after he told her.

I was a little more conflicted. I still loved Ian. I loved Gwen. Of course I was happy he was leaving a job that endangered his life every day, but I was also angry. More like furious. He decided *now* he would leave the Army? Not when I wanted him to, not when I pleaded with him to. Not when his sister had been recovering from a traumatic attack. But now.

Now when I had started to move on. Started to recover from the wounds I had sustained with him. Now I had Brock. Or maybe I didn't have Brock. Fuck, I didn't even know if Brock wanted me. But I knew the situation was complicated enough without adding Ian to the mix. I wanted him back safe. I also didn't. I wanted the geographical buffer that I had once cursed. I was a terrible person. I felt all the more terrible when Ian looked at me across the table with a heartbreakingly tender expression on his gruff face.

"Ames?" he said softly.

He expected me to jump for joy. To kiss him. I would have. Two years ago. Heck, even three months ago. Before Brock.

"Fuck you, Ian," I spat, pushing out of my chair and storming into the house. I made it to my room when Ian grasped my arm.

"What was that, Amy?" he growled, whipping me around. "I expected a different reaction, babe."

I glared at him. "What were you expecting? Me to scramble over the table and jump into your lap with joy?"

His face was impassive, but a small spark of amusement danced in his eyes. "I wouldn't have complained," he replied.

I ripped my hand out of his grasp. "Why now?" I asked, the fight gone from my voice.

Ian stood close to me, penetrating my space and letting his large hands span my hips. "Because I realized what I want out of my life. I don't want to die over in some sandbox. I also don't want to continue living in one, devoting my life to it then coming back to nothing." His eyes searched mine. "I want a life where I can see my sister more than once a year. I want to stop my mother from going grey with worry." His grip tightened on my hips. "And I want a certain beautiful redhead to be mine. To sleep next to her every night. To wake up to her every morning. To laugh at all the funny shit she says. To slide inside her and forget everything else but the two of us exists. To marry her, to grow old with her."

Holy shit. I stared at Ian, unable to believe he just said that.

"We were together for two weeks, you've been gone for a year and all of a sudden you're expecting marriage and a white picket fence?" I said, shocked.

Ian stroked my face. "The amount of time we were together doesn't mean shit. I've known you for years."

I stepped out of his grasp. "You've known certain parts of me for years, Ian," I shouted. "You've only been around long enough to see what you want to see, not everything I am. You've formed some ideal opinion of me based on things you've seen in a short amount of time." I paced the room. "You don't know the bad things about me." I stopped, deciding to enlighten him.

"I don't hold elevators for people—in fact I purposely close the doors when people run for them. It's evil and mean, but I hate sharing an enclosed space with strangers. I pretend not to notice people waiting at crossings when I'm in a hurry. Heck, I don't even slow down. I'm lucky I haven't hit anyone yet. I hate old people. They annoy me, and it irritates the fuck out of me when they act like I should find them adorable. Same thing with kids. They're dirty and loud and always seem to have sticky hands."

I stopped and stood in front of him.

"There's plenty more where that came from. You can't say all that stuff about marriage and forever when you haven't even spent an entire weekend alone with me," I declared.

Ian looked amused. "I know enough. All that other shit I find out along the way will just be a bonus."

I let out a little scream. "You're acting like we're a foregone conclusion, like my protests are amusing to you and you're just waiting for the little female to calm down and then she'll be wowed by your sexy accent and impressive ass. You said the reason why you dumped me is because you didn't want me stuck in one place waiting for you when that's exactly what you've expected me to do!"

Ian started to look frustrated. "That's not what I expect. I expect to spend a long time making it up to you. I expect that things aren't going to go smoothly." His eyes darkened. "But you are mine and you know it."

I threw my arms up in the air. "Stop it! I'm not 'yours'—I'm not anyone's. I'm my own person. Belonging to a male does not define me and it sure as shit isn't going to happen." My anger threatened to turn me green as this whole freaking situation was hurtling out of my control.

Ian stepped forward. I held my hand up. "You need to leave," I ordered, sidestepping him and opening my door.

He glared at me. "I'm not going anywhere until we sort this out," he declared.

"There's nothing to sort out!" I snapped at him. "You think we have some kind of future because now you've decided you want it. I disagree. Subject closed."

Ian crossed his arms over his chest. "The subject is not fuckin' closed, Amy! I'm going to apologize a thousand times for the way I treated you, but I'm never going to apologize for loving you. I'm going to do it until the day I die, and I'll do everything I can to make you give me another chance." He stared at me a moment longer before he strolled out the door.

I slammed it, resting my back against it. I sank to the floor, holding my head in my hands. This was a disaster.

———

The next few days were spent dodging Ian. This was hard, considering he had commenced his "make Amy forgive me and remember how much she loves me" mission. He cornered me every chance he got and did all this chivalrous stuff like opening doors for me while blatantly checking me out and doing his best to touch me in some way.

I did my best to scowl at him, but I was only human. A woman could only be trapped in a house with a seriously hot soldier who she used to be in love with without something happening. That something was either pouncing on him or spontaneously combusting.

I did my level best to be at the store as often as possible and out of the house. I didn't see or hear from Brock, which I was conflicted about. He was serious about being "done" and I was upset. Then I felt guilty about missing him when I had a kind and extremely sexy man declaring his undying love for me. I didn't know what to think about the whole situation, so I did the adult thing and tried to ignore it.

I couldn't ignore it, however, on Ian's last night when Gwen dragged me out to dinner with her, Ian, and Cade. It was torture, he sat across from me the whole night staring like I was his dinner. It didn't help that his legs kept touching mine. He would purposefully brush them together, rubbing my ankles with his. He wasn't even fazed when I attempted to kick him, only succeeding in spilling my cocktail.

The attraction between us was something not to be denied, neither was the reality of the fact he was leaving the next day. As much as I wanted to ignore the entire situation, I couldn't when he was running back off to war and I would regret not laying it all out when I could. I couldn't spend six more months obsessing over him while he was God knows where. I had to do it now. I was about to creep into his room after the house went quiet later that night, but my door slowly opened, showing he had beat me to it.

I had planned on saying a lot of things. On explaining why it wasn't going to work after everything that had happened. On telling him I couldn't open myself back up to him again. On letting him know that I had feelings for another man. I had a speech and everything. But it all tumbled out of my mind the moment he closed the door, the moment our eyes locked.

He was leaving the next day. I didn't know whether I would see him again. He strode toward me purposefully and clutched my body to his, crashing his mouth on mine.

Ian kissed me tenderly, taking his time like he was savoring me. The feeling of his lips against mine, his hands on my waist had me pressing myself against his hard body. I poured every single bit of emotion I had into the kiss: all the love I had bottled up, all the anger I had already unleashed, everything. Ian directed me towards the bed, lowering me down and covering my body with his.

He peeled off my clothes slowly, worshipping every inch of my body. When I was naked he sat up, his eyes full of hunger and desire.

"You don't know how much I've pictured this." He ran his hand across my nipple slightly and I shivered. His mouth moved to cover it. "How much I craved the taste of your nipple," he whispered. His mouth moved lower. "I thought about how sweet you tasted, how perfect it was when you came on my tongue," he murmured, putting his mouth on me. I held back a scream as he brought me to climax, his tongue working magic between my legs, slowly and tenderly.

He stayed there for a moment, gazing at me. His rough face was soft and full of emotion. He seemed to shake himself out of the moment and pushed himself up to undress, not taking his eyes off me the entire time. When he was on top of me, divested of his clothes he stroked my face.

"I've dreamed of making love to you. When I was sleeping,

hugging my rifle, fearing I'd wake up with a bullet in me, it was you I pictured to get me through," he growled, pushing inside me.

I moaned as he moved slowly, making love to me. His huge hands cradled my face and his mouth moved against mine as he slowly built me up to explode in his arms. Every inch of his hard body was touching me, his eyes locked on mine. It was beautiful, tender, and the perfect way to say goodbye. To put an end to everything between us. To get closure.

———

I awoke the next morning to Ian's arms around me and I felt conflicted. Extraordinarily guilty. Like I was betraying Brock. Then I felt like I was betraying Ian by thinking about Brock. I didn't doubt that he was probably waking up next to some club slut right now, but what I was doing was worse. There was an emotional connection with Ian. I loved him. He loved me. He wanted a future with me. Commitment. The thing was I didn't want that anymore.

I didn't want it with Brock, either. Not right now. We were too volatile. I loved Ian. Last night was proof of that. But it wasn't the right type of love. Forgive the cliché, but I wasn't "in love" with him. There was something missing with us. Something I wouldn't have missed had I not met Brock. It was the fire, the passion, the wild urgency that made me feel like bursting into flames.

I felt dirty. Like a bad person. Like a dirty whore playing two men. I needed a scarlet letter to sew onto my clothes.

I tried to creep out of bed so I wouldn't have thoughts about one man while wrapped up in another man's arms. No such luck.

"Morning, sweetheart." A gravelly voice scratched my ear as arms tightened around me. I couldn't help but melt back into his warm embrace, my self-deprecating feelings fading away.

"You should get out of here before Gwen wakes up," I muttered, getting distracted by his mouth at my neck.

"Babe, this is the last time I'm going to feel you in my arms for a long while. Shut up and let me make the most of it."

I admit I was a coward and let myself relax into his arms. I let his muscled arms hold me. I let us descend into a comfortable silence. For too long. I should have spent the time setting him straight about us. About what last night was. It wasn't the prelude to Ian and Amy 2.0, complete with commitment and strings. It was closing the page on us once and for all. It was saying goodbye.

"Ian," I started softly.

He rolled so his body was on top of mine. "Shh. Don't say anything, babe. Don't make any decisions about us now. I want to leave with this perfect, untarnished memory of you. It'll get me through," he said, drinking me in. "When I come back I'll have time to win you over, to show you what it'll be like. Right now I don't. So just think. While I'm gone think about us. And know I'll never do anything to hurt you again. I'd die first." His eyes were intense.

His words shattered the resolve I had been so firm on moments ago. The promise of life with Ian was enticing. I knew he meant every word. He wouldn't hurt me again, not purpose-fully, anyway. Life with him would be stable, safe. He'd treat me right and give me mind blowing orgasms. It wasn't a shabby life. It just wasn't one I was sure I wanted anymore.

He kissed me softly. "I've got to go get packed," he said quietly.

My stomach dropped. No matter what conclusions I drew about us being together, bottom line was I cared about him. The thought of him going back over to the place from where so many people never came back had me feeling nauseous.

He seemed to read my mind. "Don't worry, babe. I'm comin' back. I promise." He looked at me a beat more before pushing up from bed.

"You gonna come to the airport?" he asked, pulling on his tee.

I stood, wrapping my robe around me. "Fuck no," I declared. The thought of saying goodbye to him, being around a blubbering Gwen ... no, I couldn't do that.

He nodded as if he knew this. He gave me one last look then slipped out the door. I emerged later, when he was all packed and Gwen was readying herself to take him to the airport. Her eyes had moved between the two of us as if expecting some kind of performance, but Ian had banished her to the car. She protested weakly then gave me a look before walking out the door.

Ian stared at me a moment, then crossed the room. "This is it, then," he murmured, gripping my hips.

I nodded, not trusting my words.

"I love you, babe," he said. He didn't wait for a response and he kissed me with a furious intensity as I clung to him to stay upright. He pressed his head against mine, then he was gone.

CHAPTER EIGHT

Ian's departure had left a bitter taste in my mouth. I lost any strength I'd had when he declared I was the person that was going to get him through the last of his tour. How could I say anything to that? I was a coward. His visit stirred up feelings I had been previously ready to let go. The last night between us had totally fucked me up. I felt sick over the fact it happened. I felt sick at the reverent, tender way Ian had made love to me. He didn't know my mind had also been on another man after the sweet performance.

I felt sick over the fact I hadn't seen nor spoken to Brock since Ian left. It had been weeks. Gwen had tried to extract information out of me regarding the entire train wreck I had created, but I had refused to speak of it, mainly because I was ashamed at how it all had played out. Also because I was terrified she would be disgusted with me about the way I had treated her brother.

So I tried to forget it all once again. I tried to pretend I didn't crave Brock's touch while dreaming of Ian's smile. That I didn't wish for the flames I felt from Brock's lips on mine while I wondered about what life with Ian would be like. I tried to forget it all. Unfortunately fate had decided to thrust Brock and

I back together when Gwen got a death threat from a dangerous gang.

The fact she was delivered a box of tarantulas creeped me out and terrified me. I hated the thought of my best friend being in danger once again, so I supported the club going into "lockdown." I supported it until an unsmiling prospect had turned up at my door.

"Gwen's already been escorted to the biker fortress, kid. I think you're a bit behind the eight ball," I informed him.

Regardless of the fact he couldn't have been much other than twenty, he didn't look like a kid. He looked mean and dangerous.

"You've got to come with me to the clubhouse," he said by way of reply.

"You're kidding, right?" I scoffed at him.

His face was blank. "Do I look like I'm kidding?"

"Well, you look like a kid who's used to extracting lunch money with little or no argument. I'm telling you now I'm not going anywhere."

He scowled slightly. "I've been instructed that if you refuse I'm to tie you to my bike," he informed me without humor.

My anger peaked. "That's the only way you're going to get me to go with you," I declared, calling his bluff.

The prospect had raised an eyebrow and unearthed rope out of his cut. "You sure about that?"

Shit. The little fucker was serious. "Cade is so getting his ear chewed when I see him next," I snarled under my breath.

The prospect stared at me. "It wasn't Cade that ordered you in," he said.

I paused.

Brock.

———

I had been pacing the floor in his filthy room for what felt like hours. Tequila had done little to quell my rage — actually, it fed it. How dare Brock force me to not only be locked in this godforsaken place, but sleep in his room? The asshole. We hadn't even spoken since the whole Ian debacle, but still he thought it was appropriate to play possessive male? He would be getting a rude awakening. I had initially planned on trashing his room, but it was so messy I doubted he'd notice.

In the deep recesses of my furious mind, a little part of me acknowledged that maybe it was nice that he cared about me, worried about me enough to face what he knew would be my wrath to keep me safe. But unfortunately that little piece of me didn't have control at the moment. Tequila did.

Midstride, the door opened and my eyes snapped to the figure walking through it. "You!" I shouted, stomping forward to poke my finger at his chest. I didn't register the tired and weary look on his attractive face.

"How dare you get some freakin' kid to basically force me onto a bike with barely enough time to pack a makeup bag, let alone a sufficient variety of outfit choices?" I paused for a moment, I wasn't sure that was what I was mad about. Turned out tequila had more control than I originally thought. I continued, "Actually, how dare you have someone drag me off at all? And then demand I sleep in this ... *dorm room!*" I glanced around at the messy room in distaste. "I'm not yours! I do not belong to you. Hell, we don't even sleep together anymore. You can't lay some fucked up claim on me!" I had moved right to his face and was breathing heavily.

Brock's expression was blank. "Sorry this isn't five-star accommodations that you're used to, Sparky. We'll get the maid to leave a mint on your pillow in the morning if that helps." His eyes searched mine. "But you are mine. No matter what shit you pull, no matter who the fuck turns up and tries to tell you any different. You may not be my old lady, but you're mine. I know how sweet your pussy tastes, I know how your mouth feels around my cock, and I know that if anything fuckin' happened to you I'd lose my shit."

He paused and it was enough time for me to register the wetness between my legs and the fact we were so close our mouths almost touched. I could smell the tobacco on his breath.

"I've had a long night. I can't be fucked dealing with your mouth tonight, unless it's on my cock. How about I fuck you and we pick up this argument in the morning?" he asked with a growl.

The erotic promise in his eyes, the hand that suddenly clutched my hip sending fire through my body dissipated the rage that I was feeling. Or more accurately channeled that rage into desire.

Brock must have read the silent change in my body because his hand thrust into my hair and he yanked my mouth onto his. The kiss wasn't gentle. It wasn't loving. It was raw and it took everything from me.

He lifted me up and roughly threw me on his unmade bed. The carnal, animalistic look in his eyes excited me. It had been weeks since we had last been together and all I could think about was getting him inside me. Evidently he had the same idea, because as he leaned over me his hands went to the middle of my shirtdress and ripped it off me.

I barely registered the buttons flying off and scattering everywhere. All I could think of was Brock's mouth, which had settled on my breast and was sucking my nipple over the lace of my bra. He yanked the cup down to lightly brush his teeth over my peak, the mix of pain and pleasure nearly sending me over the edge. Rough hands plunged into my panties and I cried out as he rubbed me.

"Fuckin' drenched," he growled.

I whimpered as his hand rubbed in circles and his mouth worked my breast. Without warning, an orgasm shattered me and Brock's mouth was on mine, silencing my scream.

I vaguely registered him pulling his jeans off, but I was in a sort of dream. My focus sharpened as he plunged into me, filling my sensitive flesh. I moaned as he settled on top of me, moving hard and fast. He gripped my neck.

Something changed in his eyes and he stopped, turning me around so he could plunge into me from behind. The new position meant he could thrust into me deeper and it was so intense it bordered on pain. I felt him lean over me, pushing into me hard and slow.

"This is us, baby," he growled in my ear. I moaned as he flexed his hips and thrust into me. "We're real—we're not hearts or fucking flowers. It's you and me and it's raw and magnificent."

I whimpered as he pounded relentlessly. But I met him thrust for thrust, desperate for it.

He leaned back up, fingertips biting into my ass. "You are fucking perfect for me, baby. All gloss on the outside, but a dirty bitch who likes my cock hard from behind on the inside," he growled, moving faster.

I felt myself build at his rough words and exquisite friction. "You're mine," he grunted. "Your cunt's mine," he added, clutching my hair and pulling it slightly.

I shattered at his words combined with the small eruption of pain that came from his hand in my hair. I felt him jerk inside me as my muscles milked his release.

I collapsed on the bed as he gently pulled out of me, feeling delicate but sated. Brock pulled me up gently, gathering me in his arms. We lay like that for a second, breathing heavily. Brock kissed me on the head.

"Go clean up, baby, then we'll sleep," he commanded softly.

I was too mellow from my orgasms to argue. I just nodded meekly, wandered to the bathroom, did as he said and curled up with him in bed. With his strong arms around me I relaxed.

"You're still in trouble tomorrow," I murmured sleepily.

Brock's arms tightened. "Baby, I'm in trouble for the rest of my life."

The words didn't sink in as I fell asleep.

———

I woke up with only a slight hangover but feeling happy and warm. Warm because of the familiar muscled tattooed arms around me. Happy because of the familiar muscled tattooed arms around me. I felt tender between my legs, a reminder of the mind blowing sex from the night before.

I snuggled into the iron clad chest that I was currently using as a pillow, my leg thrown over his thighs. Then the events pre-sex rushed into my mind. I stiffened.

"Fuck," a gravelly voice muttered.

The arms around me tightened and I was pulled up Brock's body. Before I could utter a word, he pressed his mouth against mine. Groggy from sleep, and still not able to get sufficiently pissed, I relaxed into the kiss, letting it set me on fire.

The moment his mouth released mine my temper came back. "What was that?" I snipped.

"I wanted to kiss you before we started arguing," Brock declared, arms still around me.

I struggled out of his embrace and clambered off the bed. I was aware of my nakedness as I searched the messy room for my seriously under packed bag. I spotted it in the corner, picking it up.

Thank God Brock's room had an attached bathroom. I would have climbed out the window rather than face the prospect of communal showers. I would need a penicillin shot after using his facilities as it was.

"No screaming or swearing this morning, Sparky?" Brock teased. "Maybe I fucked the angry out of you. I didn't think that would be possible."

I glared over my shoulder at him. "I'm not speaking to you."

I tried my hardest to peel my eyes away quickly from the vision of him in bed but I couldn't. I would have to be a robot, or my mother to not appreciate what my eyes were feasting on.

He was lying in bed, the sheet at his waist covering his

impressive manhood. Luckily his six pack was on display, complete with that delicious V. His muscled arms were clasped behind his head, his hair messy and unbound. His blue eyes were devouring me, a hungry look not matching his teasing tone. I gulped as I saw his hard on tenting the sheet at his waist.

I snapped my eyes away before I forgot every reason why I was angry and rushed into the bathroom. I hopped in the thankfully clean shower and let the hot water melt away some tension. It didn't work with the sexual tension. I was considering taking care of that myself when the shower curtain opened and Brock's huge body took up the rest of the stall.

"What are you doing?" I demanded.

Brock frowned at me. "We're not arguing yet."

His mouth descended on mine and he proceeded to take care of the tension.

Twice.

After reluctantly getting out of the shower and doing the best I could with the limited provisions I had, I was ready to face the day. No way I was hanging around here, potentially getting Stockholm Syndrome. I was tagging along with Gwen to the store.

Brock's eyes roamed appreciably over my outfit as I walked out of the bathroom. I was wearing a skintight khaki sleeveless turtleneck jersey dress with tan heels and my hair tumbled in messy waves.

"As much as I love how fuckin' sexy you look in that outfit, babe, I'm afraid I'm not gonna let you out of this room looking like that. I can't have you hanging around the clubhouse all day teasing the men and giving them a serious case of blue balls," he said with a smirk.

I fastened a gold watch on. "I'm not sticking around here — I might catch an STD. I'm going into the store with Gwen," I informed him.

Maybe the bitchy comment wasn't necessary, but I was still pissed at the whole getting dragged here thing.

Brock's eyes narrowed and he stood. "You're not going to the store. You're not leaving this compound," he bit out.

I regarded him for a second, cocking my head. "I'm sorry, did you mistake me for someone that you can order around? Because last time I checked this isn't Saudi Arabia, which means a man does not dictate what a woman can and cannot do," I said calmly. "On that note, a man certainly does not command another man to practically drag a woman from her home to deposit her in a biker clubhouse then detain her in his room."

Brock raised an eyebrow, his jaw hard. "Well, that woman didn't mind it when I was fuckin' her."

I didn't know what to say to that so I picked up my phone to text Gwen.

Brock strode forward to snatch it out of my hands. Luckily I had already sent it.

"Hey!" I exclaimed, reaching for the phone. "Give that back."

Brock crossed his arms. "I said you're not going anywhere. It's not safe."

"And I said you're not the boss of me. We're not together, I'm not your old lady." I used condescending air quotes. "We have sex. That's it. You don't get to play the protective male card when it suits you, then act like an asshole when it all gets a bit rough. We aren't together so stop acting like it."

Brock's face turned hard. "Is that what you want? Just sex? So you can have someone to fuck you every now and then while you wait for Ian to come home?" he asked bitterly.

I was taken aback.

Is that what he thought? I was using him as a human fuck toy to keep me occupied? If only he knew the truth. The fact was I was keeping my distance because I was afraid of what would happen if I didn't. Afraid of the feelings that threatened to consume me, unlike anything I felt for Ian.

He took my silence as agreement and he shoved the phone back into my hands. "Do what you fuckin' want. You and your crazy shit aren't my problem," he growled.

He threw open the door, which a shocked looking Gwen was standing in front of, her hand in the air poised to knock.

"Bitch," he muttered under his breath.

I didn't let the pain of the verbal blow show. "Asshole," I retorted to his back.

Gwen's face was curious and I didn't even want to try and explain what happened. All I wanted was to leave before I chased Brock and spilled my heart to him. That would be worse than anything else because then he could trample all over it.

———

Hours later I wished I had listened to Brock, wished I hadn't dismissed the danger Gwen was in. Because maybe if I had, I wouldn't have wandered into the back room of our store looking for Gwen, only to find the back door open and no best friend.

When I realized Gwen had been kidnapped, I lost my mind. I mainly swore at any biker that happened to be around the club-house – where I had been imprisoned – and tried not to cry. I had wanted to steal someone's gun and break out of this hideous place and look for her myself.

Images of her in that hospital bed after Jimmy attacked her preyed on my mind. At first she had been barely recognizable, her face black and blue, half of her head covered by a bandage. She had a tube in her mouth because she couldn't breathe on her own. I had stood around helpless while I waited for the most important person in my life to either wake up or fade away. It had been beyond a nightmare.

The fact that I faced the prospect again had me terrified, especially since I had the knowledge of what the gang who kidnapped her had done to their last victim—Laurie, Bull's old lady. Raped her. Stabbed her repeatedly, tattooed her face. Then dropped her off in front of the clubhouse just so the man who loved her could watch her die in the hospital the next day. I tasted bile at the thought of this happening to Gwen.

I recalled the look on Cade's face when he had arrived at the store after I had alerted the club of the fact she was missing. It was wild, feral, and resigned. Beyond his strong façade was a glimmer of resignation at the prospect Gwen might face the same fate as Laurie.

He had punched the prospect who was meant to be protecting her. Pummeled is a better description. He would have killed him had Brock and Lucky not pulled him off him.

"Cool it, brother. Killing this piece of shit isn't going to get us to Gw 1. We'll do that when we get her back," Brock had told him ev nly.

Cade seemed to shake himself and nodded. He then spat at the prospect's prone body and stormed out the door. Lucky had followed him. Brock and I had stared at each other for an inordinate amount of time.

"Don't let her out of your sight," he instructed the men left watching our stare off. With that he had left.

That was hours ago, and had it not been for Rosie and Lucy, I would have gone insane with worry. Or at least murdered a prospect. They had been amazing, plying me with enough alcohol to calm me but not enough to get me drunk. I could tell by the shadows in their eyes that they were battling with demons of their own. Laurie had been their friend.

We all abruptly stood when we heard motorcycles approach. I ran to the door and a prospect stood in front of me, blocking the exit. "I can't let you go out there," he said firmly.

I glared at him. "Either you let me out there or I make sure you are never able to have children," I informed him coldly. He stared at me, not looking like he was going to back down.

"For fuck's sake, Tiny, let her fucking past. I doubt anything will happen to her in the parking lot of the clubhouse. I'd be more worried about your immediate safety," Rosie said from behind me.

Tiny gave me another look before stepping aside.

I ran out to where Brock had gotten off his bike, a weary look on his face.

He caught my expression when I made it to him and steadied me with hands on my shoulders.

"We got her, Sparky—she's fine."

I stared at him a moment then threw my arms around him. My entire body sagged at the relief from his statement. I heard Rosie and Lucy's sighs from behind me.

He pulled back slightly. "I'll take you to her." He handed me his helmet and I took it silently.

When we arrived at our place, Brock had barely stopped the bike before I flew off it. I had to see for myself ... make sure she was okay and in one piece. Physically and mentally.

"Jesus Christ, babe," I heard Brock's mutter from behind me. I ignored it and burst through the door, finding Gwen and Cade in the living room. Everything inside me relaxed when I saw her safe and breathing.

"Gwennie! Oh my God. Oh my God," I chanted as I rushed towards her, hugging her just to make sure she had all of her body parts accounted for.

Once I was satisfied I pulled back to inspect her. My eyes rested on purple bruising covering half of her face.

"Those fuckers," I hissed as fury burned through me.

"Amy, it's okay," her soft voice tried to reassure me.

That only made it worse. How could my tiny, five foot nothing friend get subjected to violence yet again? Hadn't she been through enough? Didn't she deserve a life where she wasn't in danger of getting kidnapped or brutalized?

"Those fuckers!" I yelled, wishing I had the person responsible in this room so I could tear their fingernails off. "How can this be happening to you again, Gwen? You've been through enough! Jesus, you've been through hell. You almost died at the hands of crazy fucked up men. Now after finally healing some other bastards get their hands on you. Um, no. This is not acceptable."

My eyes darted around the room to rest on Cade. He was watching the exchange with a grim face and his arms crossed. He was looking all badass and dangerous. What was the use of a dangerous badass if he didn't prevent kidnappings? For fuck's sake, he was the *reason* she was kidnapped in the first place.

"What have *you* done about this?" I shot at him. "Are you going to make sure this isn't going to happen again? 'Cause if you don't, I'm calling my father and he's going to send his jet to come and take us to an island far away where there are no men within miles." I changed my mind. "Actually, fuck that. I'm calling him now."

I was deadly serious as I whipped out my phone, scrolling through my contacts.

"Babe, cool it. It's sorted. Put the fucking phone down and chill the fuck out," a familiar deep voice commanded at my shoulder.

I whirled around and directed my glare at yet another biker involved in this freaking mess. How dare he dismiss this like it was nothing now that Gwen was back? Did he not realize what she had been through trying to recover from her last attack? How horrific it was for her to be able to even walk down a fucking street after it?

"Cool it?" I repeated quietly, my voice shaking. "Cool it?" I shouted at him. "Are you fucking *kidding* me? Did you see Gwen lying in a hospital bed, hooked up to monitors on life support? No. Did you listen to a doctor say she might never wake up? No. Did you sit by her bed for almost two weeks, waiting, thinking over and over how you could've stopped this, seen the signs, maybe saved her from the horror she endured? No, you didn't! I did!" I finished my rant with tears streaming down my face, all of those ugly memories surfacing.

Brock didn't say anything, didn't yell back or argue. He just stepped forward and pulled me into his arms. I relaxed into them, thankful for the strength and support they represented. I barely noticed him lift me and carry me out of the room, his mouth in my hair.

He made it to my bedroom and lay on my bed, positioning me so I was curled up tightly in his arms. I clung to him. We were silent for a long while.

"Are they dead?" I asked quietly.

Brock moved his head down to make eye contact with me.

"Every last one," he declared fiercely.

"Good," I murmured.

With that his arms tightened around me and I drifted off to sleep.

————

ONE MONTH LATER

A month passed after Gwen's kidnapping. Things were quiet, there were no car bombs, drive-by's or fashion emergencies, so things were good. Well, for Gwen and her overprotective, seriously hot, seriously into her biker things were good.

Me? Not so much.

I had woken up alone after falling asleep with Brock on the night of her kidnapping. I had barely seen him since, and when we did bump into each other, things were tense. He had come to the wrong conclusions about Ian, and I was at a loss as to how to set him straight. I craved his touch. I missed him like crazy, but I was also happy for the time to get my head together.

A surprise visit from Ry and Alex had done wonders to distract me from my disastrous love life. Gay best friends seemed to have superhuman emotional healing powers. And a heavy hand when making cocktails. It had taken a turn after an argument with Brock at a strip club where I had just gotten into a catfight with Cade's ex.

I had almost melted at the look he had given me after the smack down I wasn't aware he witnessed. I then stiffened when he thought he could order me around after ignoring me for the past month. In front of my friends no less. Not okay. So I threw sass. Asserted my independence. It felt good until he had sworn and stormed off with a waitress, his intentions clear. This had been a swift kick in the ovaries.

No matter how much I tried to convince myself I didn't care, I did. I felt like vomiting at the thought of him with someone else. I then loathed myself for thinking that — I had done the exact same thing with Ian, worse in fact.

The month sucked majorly. My friend was happier than I'd ever seen her, our business was booming, we had a beautiful home and awesome new friends. I should have been ecstatic. Instead, I was miserable. I could hardly sleep, hardly eat with all the shit churning through my mind. I couldn't keep this up. I had to do something, make a decision about all this.

I did. I came to the conclusion that no matter how much it made sense for Ian and I to be together I couldn't do it. I wanted Brock. I needed him.

I wanted to make a go of being an "old lady", no matter how much I despised the label and the connotations of ownership that went with it. Gwen seemed to be wearing it as easy as she wore Prada, so I could give it a go.

I only faced the prospect of swallowing my pride, or more accurately my fear, and telling Brock this. I was terrified he would reject me. Crush me, humiliate me. Memories of my desperate vulnerable childhood hampered me.

I had attempted to seek him out at the clubhouse days ago, but when I had gotten there I had seen him with a blonde. Needless to say I had blanched when our eyes met, happy that I had the pretense of picking up Rosie. I was pissed at the fact he was pawing some other woman, but I couldn't really be, since I had slept with Ian.

We weren't together. I had made that abundantly clear. He was free to do as he wished. I had wished he'd be like one of those men in romance novels who waited patiently and chastely for the heroine to get over her shit. But this was real life. He was a biker. It was a miracle he had even wanted to commit. So I couldn't bring myself to blame him, no matter how much I wanted to scratch the blonde's eyes out.

Luckily I got the distraction of finding out Gwen was knocked up. I was seriously ecstatic at the prospect of a little kid to spoil and dress up. I was less than ecstatic that I couldn't enjoy cocktails with my best friend for nine months, but I would manage.

The day after the announcement of Gwen's little bundle of joy I decided to take a drive to LA to get a jump on baby shopping. I hated that I had to do gender neutral, and on the drive I had decided to buy an equal amount of boys' and girls' shit. I'd donate the loser gender to charity once they found out. Plus, shopping was a welcome distraction to what I was planning to do that night. Confront Brock. The prospect of it vaguely brought me out in hives, but I had to do it.

What I had to do first was call Ian and tell him he wasn't coming home to me. That was something else that curdled my meager breakfast. I cared about him. Loved him. The idea of hurting him sucked. The fact that I was telling him this shit over the phone had me wanting to punch myself in the face just a little. It was a seriously crappy thing to do. But stringing him along was worse. I was in the process of finding a way to get in touch with him and was waiting on my info.

I was about halfway to LA when my phone buzzed. I thought it would be my Uncle Garrett with the deets, but instead it was Gwen's mother.

"Hey, Lacey, I'm currently on my way to LA to start the shopping," I greeted, assuming she was calling after hearing Gwen's news.

I knew she'd want to coordinate and was excited to talk to her about it. I thought of her as my mother too, and loved the woman with all my heart.

"Amy, it's Dave here." Gwen's father interrupted me, his voice sounding funny.

"Oh hey, what's up, Mr. A?" I greeted him fondly. Although he was a man of few words, he was the father I wish I'd had, instead of the cold and absent one nature had lumped me with.

There was a pause and something about it made my stomach drop. "Sweetheart, I'm assuming you're not with Gwen so you don't know," he said softly, his usually gruff voice sounding wrong somehow, broken.

"Don't know what?" I asked, dread building in the pit of my stomach.

"We just got news...Ian was killed last night...a roadside bomb," he told me, his voice breaking. The weight of the anguish and pain in his voice was hard to listen to.

I didn't hear anything else, thanks to a dull roar in my ears. I might have said something else to Dave, I didn't know. Everything was a blur. I must have said my goodbyes because my phone wasn't in my hand anymore. My hands started shaking on the wheel and my vision got blurry. I pulled over, on autopilot, then stumbled out of the car to be sick on the side of the road.

I didn't know what to do. I stayed on my knees for a second, not caring about the rough stones that were cutting my knees, not feeling anything but the heavy weight on my chest. The weight that threatened to suffocate me. I tried not to hyperventilate. If I continued sucking in air at the rate I was, I would pass out.

"Get it together, Amy," I muttered to myself.

Slowly, I managed to get to my feet. I stumbled back into my car and my blood ran cold. Gwen. Shit. She would be a mess. The baby. Fuck.

I broke every traffic law in the book speeding back to Amber, frantically dialing Gwen's number as I wove through traffic. On getting her voicemail for the fourth time I was about to call Cade when Rosie called. me.

"Rosie, are you with Gwen?" I asked her as soon as I picked up.

"I take it you know."

"What?" I snapped, my stomach threatening to roll again at her tone.

"Gwen's in the hospital, Amy," she whispered. "She didn't take the news real well—we don't know anything just yet— "

"I'll be there in ten," I declared, putting my foot on the gas.

Five minutes later, after parking half on the curb of the hospital, I burst through the doors. I had broken down for about a minute on the drive, letting the tears fall while I sped through the streets. I had made myself stop once I realized I would have to be strong for my best friend. For her kid.

I stormed through the waiting room to be greeted by half of the club. My eyes rested on Brock, who stood upon seeing me, but Rosie got to me first, throwing her arms around me.

"I'm so sorry, Ames," she whispered into my hair. I stood in her arms stiffly and waited until she let me go.

"Where is she?" I demanded.

Tears welled up in Rosie's eyes. "They weren't letting anyone see her, but Cade just went through those doors." She pointed to where two pissed off looking orderlies had emerged.

"Right," I said, pointing my heels in that direction. I ignored everyone around me until Brock stepped in my path.

I glared up at him. "Get out of my way," I said quietly.

"Sparky," he murmured softly, his eyes on mine.

I couldn't do it. I couldn't let the soft, sympathetic look in his eyes penetrate. If it did, I would fall into his arms sobbing. I had to find my friend.

"Get out of my way!" I screamed at him, my voice breaking at the end.

I didn't care that my voice caused the hushed chatter to cease and put all eyes on me. I only cared that Brock frowned at me a beat then stepped aside. I burst into the room where my best friend was and held onto her for dear life.

———

The next day, after being assured Gwen was fit to fly, I sped around franticly organizing our trip to New Zealand. I called my father, and upon hearing the news, he made sure we had everything we needed, including his jet and a doctor to fly with us. No matter what his emotional shortcomings were, he was there with his money and connections when I needed him. They were a poor substitute for a father's love but useful nonetheless.

Because I had been so busy sorting everything out, I had the luxury of a busy mind, which meant no free moment to let reality come in and tear me to pieces. I could feel it, though. The cold, sharp grief puncturing the frail sense of sanity I was clinging to.

I was determined to shelve my own grief and focus on getting my friend home safe and away from the traitorous dirty cheat of a biker that was hovering around her.

After finding out Gwen had found him in bed with a club whore, I had seriously debated the merits of stabbing him with a scalpel, but I deduced Gwen didn't need the drama and I didn't want bloodstains on my outfit. I was toying with the idea of accidentally plowing into his motorcycle while he was on it.

All of these plans had to wait since I pulled up to the hospital, bags packed, flights booked, ready for Gwen and I to fly out of this freaking town.

I stopped the car and took a deep breath. Brock was following Cade, who was pushing Gwen in a wheelchair. I did not need that.

I glared at Cade hotly as I rounded the car, wishing looks could kill. I softened my gaze to smile weakly at Gwen. "I've got everything we need for our trip, Gwennie. Daddy's jet is waiting for us at a small airstrip outside of town and it'll take us to LAX where we've got the next plane to Auckland. Daddy also insisted we take his doctor with us on the flight. Just in case."

I glanced down at her stomach and tried not to let my worry

for the little being in there show. I tried to help her out of the chair, doing my best to ignore the heavy stare of two angry bikers. I couldn't ignore the hand that fastened on my wrist, unfortunately.

"What the fuck do you think you're doing, Amy? You can't just take the mother of my child halfway across the world. Wherever she goes I go," Cade clipped.

Oh no, he didn't.

He could not play the concerned father and boyfriend bit after fucking some slut. I was wishing I had sharp objects in the immediate vicinity, couture be damned. I settled for a piercing glare.

"You can take your hand off me right now." My voice was pure ice.

Luckily for him, he complied. He was muscly and tall and all that, but with the cocktail of fury and grief running through my system, I figured I could take him.

I helped Gwen up and then my gaze shot back to him.

"I can and I will take Gwen back to her family and her home, to the people that love her. In case you've forgotten, she's going to attend the fucking funeral of her only brother," I hissed at him, ignoring the sharp stab I felt as I uttered the words. "It just happens to be convenient that her home is as far away from you as humanly possible, and a silver lining in this fucking nightmare is the fact that you are a criminal with a record which means you aren't going *anywhere*," I finished on a slight snarl.

I flicked my attention away from him. Now that I said my piece, he did not exist.

"Jesus, Gwen, wait," I heard him plead.

I was totally ready to drop the motherfucker if he tried to stop me, but Gwen put her hand on my arm.

"It's okay, Amy."

I managed not to flinch at the flat, dead tone of her voice and complied in letting her turn back to Cade. When this happened, Brock advanced on me, yanking me away and pulling me flush to his body.

"Sparky, wait a fucking second before you fly halfway across the world," he hissed in my ear.

I gazed at him flatly, trying to disguise my yearning for him. I was disgusted with myself. All I wanted to do was jump into his arms, to grieve the loss of another man.

His hand went to my hips, and his face softened to a look so tender I had never seen it on his rough face. "Baby, let me sort some shit out. I'll come with you. Be there for you," he said softly.

I yanked out of his arms, his suggestion like a bucket of ice water. "Yeah, how do you think that will go down? Me bringing the guy I've been sleeping with to Gwen's brother's funeral. That's poor fucking taste," I hissed at him and his eyes hardened.

"I'm more than that and you know it," he replied roughly.

"This isn't the time to discuss semantics of our past relationship. I've got a flight to catch," I snapped.

I turned my back on him, but not before I saw his face turn to stone. I swallowed my feelings and got Gwen into the car, using all of my willpower not to look back. Not to fucking turn around and beg Brock to come with me.

I did it. Barely.

———

It was two weeks after that scene at the hospital. Two weeks of being at Gwen and Ian's home in the beautiful countryside of New Zealand. We had to wait to get Ian's body shipped back before we could have the funeral. These two weeks, I had been in a weird state of limbo. Without a funeral, without a goodbye, I could almost pretend none of this was real. That Ian was alive and well in some unknown location. I prayed for it. Prayed for Dave to get a call informing them the Army had made some kind of mistake and Ian had just been misplaced on the battlefield.

No call came. Only a coffin. Containing the man I once loved. The man I still loved. The man who had declared his intention to love me until the day I died. The man whose heart I had been planning on breaking.

"Need some company, sweetheart?" a voice asked me quietly.

I glanced up to see Dave staring at me with a soft expression on his face. "I'd love some," I told him sincerely, needing a respite from the thoughts in my brain.

He sat and I marveled at the strength of this man. He had stayed strong among the countless amount of female tears around him. He had remained standing while his only son was lowered into the ground. He comforted his wife and daughter as they broke down when the dirt started covering the coffin. He even opened his arms to me when I finally let the tears fall. This man was my hero.

Right now though, sitting next to me in the dark corner of some pub where the wake was being held, his mask slipped. The pain and despair in his eyes was harrowing to watch and his whole frame seemed to sag under the weight of his loss.

He unearthed a flask from his coat pocket and offered it to me. I took it with a grin, taking a long swig and handed it back to him.

He grinned through his grief. "A woman who can take a decent drink. I see why he liked you," he said lightly.

I froze at Dave's words.

His large hand settled over mine. "He talked about you. Called me up two years ago and told me he met the girl he wanted to marry." His eyes twinkled as he seemed to recall the conversation. "Wasn't till a few months ago he told me it was you."

"He told you about us?" I asked weakly.

Dave nodded, smiling slightly. "Yeah, sweetie. He told me a couple of years ago about this amazing girl, but how he wasn't ready to leave the Army, didn't want that life for her. I told him if she was the one she would happily wait for him." He shook his head. "Damned boy didn't listen. He thought he was doing the right thing. I had to support his decision."

He took another swig of the flask and offered it to me again. I was thankful, I needed the alcohol to anesthetize the agony that this conversation was causing.

"We never spoke of her again, this mystery girl. Then six months ago out of the blue he talks to me about it. Tells me it was you." His eyes focused on me.

I swallowed broken glass.

"When I found out I told him to get his ass out of the Army and to the USA so he could marry you before some other bastard snapped you up. Couldn't believe he was going to let someone as special as you slip through his fingers."

His grip tightened on my hand.

"You were perfect for him. You're strong, loyal, frigging beautiful, best Yank I've ever met," he joked. "Couldn't have asked for a better friend for my girl and I couldn't have asked for a better daughter-in-law," he told me softly.

I choked up at this, at this man's heartbreakingly kind and beautiful words. I felt guilty and disgusted with myself, unable to verbalize the fact that I'd had no intention of becoming his daughter-in law. That I instead had planned to break his son's heart.

"Just want you to know, sweetheart, even before Ian told me I already considered you a daughter and I always will."

I couldn't speak, I only nodded with tears in my eyes. Dave sat there with his hand on mine, letting silence descend and we remained there, drinking from his flask and trying to shoulder the weight of our grief.

———

For the two months Gwen and I had stayed in New Zealand, Dave had been true to his word. He treated me like a second daughter, and although the walls of their home were soaked in grief, I never felt more at home. More part of a family. I wasn't in some fancy loft on the Upper East Side. I was in an impressive farmhouse at the edge of the world in an unfamiliar country. Home wasn't a place. It was a feeling. And I had that, something to salve the burn of loss.

There was something missing. Something that I needed to make me feel at home, complete.

Or someone.

After that, I had vowed I would never let Gwen or a member of her family know that things were not as they seemed with Ian and me. I would rather them think he died with the vision of a future. He died happy, if anyone could die happy.

I was never going to tell Gwen he wasn't my true love. And that meant nothing could ever happen with Brock. I couldn't stand Gwen secretly resenting me for disrespecting her brother's memory. She would never say a thing, but she would always remember.

So I didn't speak to Brock, even when he called repeatedly. I ignored him when I got back home, acted emotionless towards him. I ignored the physical pain it put me in to see the cold looks he directed back. I struggled with staying upright when I saw him with the club women, which was thankfully only a couple of times. I put on my mask. I should've won a fucking Oscar for my performance.

———

Everything changed on the night of Gwen's wedding seven months after we arrived back from New Zealand. Gwen and Cade had patched things up after the disastrous confrontation at the hospital.

Cade had flown to New Zealand to bring her home to Amber

and to set her straight on what really happened with Ginger. Or what didn't happen. She set the whole thing up. The little twat. I had to seriously resist the urge to run her over with my car.

I may have been a little biased, but it was the most beautiful wedding I had ever seen. Gwen had always been insistent she would get married at the Plaza in New York, wearing custom Vera Wang.

It wasn't the Plaza, it was Cade's backyard. Granted, his backyard was the ocean. She did wear Vera Wang, though. I threw myself into planning it and it had been perfect.

Wooden chairs sat in the sand and at the end of each row was an antique steel lantern with a candle inside. Huge bouquets of flowers dotted the aisle in soft ivory and whites. At the end of the aisle was a rustic arch made of driftwood that had white roses threaded through it and white fabric that billowed in the wind.

Cade had stood at the end of it wearing all black, including his cut. A small white flower poked out beside the *President* patch. He was cradling a tiny baby Belle in his arms. He was flanked by Brock, Bull, and a grinning Lucky.

I had walked up the aisle and my eyes had been locked on Brock. I didn't know if it was the salt air or wedding fever, but every reason I had to stay away from him disappeared and I wanted to jump on him then and there.

Unfortunately, that would have been slightly inappropriate so I restrained myself. He didn't help matters with his hungry gaze falling over my strapless lavender figure-hugging gown.

I had dragged my gaze away from him when Gwen started walking down the aisle. I wasn't looking at her, like everyone else was. I already knew she looked beautiful. Her gown was form fitting to her waist, delicate lace covered the ivory dress. It draped down her body, flowing like a waterfall to her feet. The back dipped low, exposing her back and a train trailed behind her.

I was looking at Cade, who froze the moment he laid eyes on

her. The look he gave her was impossible to describe. It was like she was the only thing holding him to this earth, that she was his oxygen, his lifeblood. She grinned at him as she wandered down the aisle, unbridled happiness on her face. He remained staring at her as if his life depended on her reaching him, he looked like he wanted to run to her, but he was frozen in place.

When she made it to him, he gently handed Belle to a surprised Dave and yanked Gwen into his arms, kissing her soundly. Dave had laughed, shaking his head, sitting carefully beside a crying Lacey with Belle in his arms. The crowd whooped and even Bull cracked a smile. Brock and I had been silently staring at each other.

This continued throughout the entire ceremony and into the photos that Gwen insisted we do. No one dared argue with her. She may have been five foot nothing wearing an intricate white dress, but she was a force to be reckoned with.

After she was satisfied with the amount of photos, we moved to an area where long tables had been set up in the sand under billowing tents. Fairy lights lit up the canopies and countless lanterns were dotted in the sand. When it was time for my speech, I took a deep breath, ignoring Brock's gaze on me.

"I heard once that true love is recognizing the soul's counterpart in another," I started, omitting I heard that in the movie *Wedding Crashers*. "Anyone who knows me realizes I'm not huge about soulmates or true love or anything along those lines." I smiled at Gwen. "I didn't believe in 'other halves' until I met Gwen. She is my other half. She knows me better than I know myself—she probably has more memory of some of the things tequila has made me forget."

There were a few chuckles at this.

"Saying Gwen is my best friend doesn't seem adequate. She's my sister, my wingman—she's the best person I've ever met. The strongest person I've ever known." My voice broke slightly. "She's my hero." I swallowed. "So naturally, all I want in this world is for my best friend to be happy, loved. When I saw her and Cade together, I knew it. Maybe even before she did—definitely before she admitted it. Gwen's soul had found its counterpart." I moved my gaze to Cade. "I want to thank you for making my friend happy. For cherishing her. For giving her a life she deserved and a love she is worthy of," I finished to applause and kisses from a tearful Gwen.

I only half responded, the weight of Brock's gaze burning into me. When we had farewelled the couple and their baby, Brock had seized me, dragging me into the darkness.

No words were spoken as he plastered his mouth to mine, kissing me with a ferocity I barely survived. I was ready to lie on the sand and beg him to fuck me, despite what a logistical nightmare sex on the beach was when he released my mouth.

"My place now," he growled.

I nodded and was about to suggest transportation options when he threw me over his shoulder. I squealed and he smacked my ass, hard.

"What are you...?" I started to ask, but I got another firm smack in response.

"No talking. We always fuck shit up when there's talking. I need to get inside you and neither of us are going to say a word to fuck it up," he growled, striding through the sand.

I pursed my lips, listening to him for once. My thighs had instantly quivered at his tone. I hadn't realized how close his and Cade's houses were until we walked up the passageway from the beach to his house.

He opened the French doors to his bedroom, which opened out with a view of the ocean and threw me on the bed. "How fond are you of this dress?" he asked gruffly, standing over me.

"Um—" was all I managed before his hands went to my bodice, ripping the thin fabric off me.

"Omigod!" I whisper yelled, "That was Elie Saab!" I exclaimed, my sadness for such brutal treatment of couture momentarily jerking me out of my sex haze.

Thoughts of the sadly departed dress went away when

Brock's mouth went to my breast. He wasn't gentle or sweet —
he was rough and urgent, desperate. I moaned at his touch, his
body on mine and his fingers which touched my sweet spot.

I writhed underneath him as he brought me to climax with
his hands between my legs and mouth at my breast. He wasn't
tender, he was brutal. It was perfect.

"Brock," I muttered, needing him inside me.

"No fuckin' talking," he ordered, knifing up to take off his
clothes.

I complied ,and for the rest of the night we made silent, frantic, intense mind-blowing love.

I fell asleep in the early hours, drunk on his touch, happy to
be with him. I let my guard down. I let my façade fall and let
myself be bewitched by the wedding juju.

"I love you," I whispered to his sleeping body as I drifted off
to sleep.

I was too far gone to recognize his body stiffening and his
arms tightening around me as I dozed into dreams.

———

*I was driving my car. I didn't know exactly where to, but I knew the
direction and I knew I had to get there fast. I knew if I didn't something
terrible would happen. My foot flattened on the accelerator as the landscape whizzed by. I was going to make it. Suddenly ringing sounded on
my phone and a voice sounded through the car. "He's dead, Amy. He's
dead," Dave's voice informed me flatly.*

"No, no, no" I chanted my world falling apart around me.

I awoke with a jerk. I registered the strong, tattooed arms
that encircled mine, the comforting smell of tobacco and the
ocean. I felt relief, relief that it was just a dream and that Brock
wasn't dead, it was Ian.

Then the prickle of guilt settled over my skin. How could I
think that? What was *wrong* with me?

I had to get out of here. Through some great act of fate, I

was able to slip out of Brock's bed and pick up his shirt. The tattered remains of my dress left that as my only option.

"Where you going, Sparky?"

I jumped and turned to see Brock, sitting up, his impressive boy on display and looking all sexy and rough from sleep.

"I've got to go," I answered quietly.

His face hardened. "You're fuckin' kidding me?" he growled.

I shook my head. "I've got to."

"Fucking save it," he snapped, getting out of bed and storming toward me. "You aren't running off after last night, after we finally put all the shit aside and I got you back again. You're mine. I'm not letting you shut me out anymore," he declared, snatching the hand that I had been using to button his shirt.

I knew him well enough to know he was serious. To know I couldn't run anymore. So I had to do it. I had to lie. I couldn't let him convince me to do what I wanted to and stay here with him. Because with all of the fucked up shit going on in my head I would fuck us up eventually. I didn't want him to have to deal with the guilt I was feeling. He didn't deserve that.

"I'm not yours," I declared coldly. "We both know that."

He jerked at my words but didn't step away. "That's a fucking lie, Amy," he snapped. "You're mine. Every inch of you. You're not perfect. You can be annoying as fuck, irritating beyond belief and as stubborn as a mule. But you're perfect for me. You're meant for me, Amy. Don't spout shit to me to the contrary."

"It's not shit!" I shouted, yanking myself away from him. "I'm not yours. It was never you," I finished cruelly and I watched him jerk as if I struck him.

I swallowed my tears as his expression turned blank.

"Whatever," he bit out finally. "You wanna fuck up your life by pining over a dead man, be my fuckin' guest."

I paused a second and then walked out the door, my heart shattering.

CHAPTER NINE

PRESENT DAY

The door opened quietly and Rafe slipped in. The look of antici-pation and arousal on his face was enough to make my skin crawl. I ignored it, I had to if I was getting out of this place. I stood up, restraining a wince at the pain.

"I haven't been able to sleep all night thinking about you." I smiled at him seductively as he crossed the room.

"Fuck. I've wanted to do this since the moment I laid eyes on you, Red. You're a feisty little bitch. You need me to tame you, don't you?" he growled, grabbing my head roughly.

I nodded and he dragged me in for a kiss. It was sloppy and disgusting and I really wanted to bite his tongue off, but I had a mission. He was wearing his gun on a belt holster, but I needed to render him immobile for this to work.

"Lie down on the bed. Let me take care of you," I purred, gazing at him through hooded lashes.

He grasped my chin roughly. "You don't order me around. Got it? For that I'll punish you ... later. First, you're going to take care of me."

He dragged me toward the bed, yanking me on top of him. I

struggled to ignore the pain in my thighs as I straddled him. I kissed his throat, undoing his shirt at the same time. I raked my hands across his chest and heard him groan, my hand moved lower toward his belt. I took a deep breath. It was now or never. I quickly moved my hand to his gun holster, yanking it out.

"What the...?" Rafe started to yell, taking him a second to fathom what was going on.

It was the second I needed. With all of my strength I smacked him in the temple with the butt of the gun. I prayed it would work like it did in the movies, rendering him unconscious. Luck was on my side, he was out cold.

I had to move quickly. I didn't know how long people stayed knocked out for since I didn't have much experience in that department. My hands reached under the pillows for the ripped up sheets I had stashed there. As quickly as I could, I fastened Rafe's hands to the headboard. I hoped they held for long enough.

Just to be safe I wadded up some sheet and stuffed it in his mouth. I deduced he could just spit it out. My eyes moved to his belt and I had an idea. I quickly whipped it off, fastening it around his head so it kept the fabric in place. Even if he did wake up, he couldn't yell for help. I mentally patted myself on the back. Just call me MacGyver.

I jumped off the bed. I felt something warm trickling down my leg and glanced down to see blood seeping out of my bandage. The pain in my thighs was excruciating, I gritted my teeth and willed myself not to black out. This was it, my only chance. I would crawl out of here if I had to.

Holding the gun to my side I crept out the door, poking my head out. I half expected to see armed men storming toward me, but all I saw was an empty hallway. I took a deep breath and tiptoed out. My bare feet were another hitch in the plan, but Clark had only provided me with heels.

Although I didn't doubt my abilities to carry out any task while wearing heels, I didn't think they would couple too well with stealth and marble floors. I hurried down the hallway as fast as I could with my injured legs, ignoring the blood trickling down in a steady stream. I paused just before rounding the corner to the staircase.

"Shit," I whispered, hearing soft footfalls. I clamped my hand over my mouth realizing being silent was an integral part of a stealth escape.

Trying to ignore the dread pooling in the bottom of my stomach, I raised my gun with a steady hand. Was I ready to shoot someone? Hell no. But I wasn't ready to give up on freedom either.

A figure rounded the corner and I took a deep breath, hand on the trigger.

"Amy?" Brock whispered in disbelief as he rounded the corner, lowering the gun he had pointed at me.

Holy shit.

Relief flooded through me, but I was in shock so I didn't think about lowering my gun. I was blinking furiously, praying this wasn't a hallucination.

"What are you doing here?" I asked him, looking him up and down. He looked as good as ever. This may have not been the time for me to check him out.

"I'm here for a tea party ... what the fuck do you think? I'm here to rescue you. What are you doing? Lower the gun, Sparky, I'm not fond of getting shot," he said dryly, but I could see the tension in his features.

"I'm rescuing myself—I couldn't wait around for you. I'm not fond of how they treat their guests here," I replied, lowering the gun to my side.

Brock's gaze moved down my body and he stilled when he focused on my legs.

"Jesus Christ. You're bleeding."

I glanced down, seeing a red line staining my bare thighs. Much more than had been there moments ago.

"I'm aware," I replied, feeling lightheaded. "My stitches ripped when I was tying Rafe to the bed."

Brock's face turned to stone. His eyes were haunted. "Stitches?" he finally bit out. "Where the fuck is this Rafe?" he added, looking ready to kill someone.

"Can we maybe have this conversation when we are away from a big mansion full of gun toting psychopaths?" I asked mildly.

Brock looked like he was about to answer when we both heard movement from the direction he came from. He moved quickly, pushing me behind him and raising his gun. I noticed it had a long attachment on it and realized it was a silencer. Nifty.

To my amazement, Lucky appeared in front of us, his own gun raised. Both men quickly lowered their weapons.

"Jesus Christ, Lucky, I almost shot you."

Lucky grinned. "Ditto, brother, we need a fucking bird call or something."

He lost his grin when he locked eyes with mine. "Can't tell you how glad I am to see your beautiful face, darlin.' Things have been mighty boring without you around."

"Yeah, well, I'm glad I could put some excitement back into your life, Luck, but for now can we blow this joint?" I asked, swaying slightly. I was feeling a little lightheaded. I chalked it up to the fact I hadn't eaten in twenty-four hours.

"I think we've outstayed our welcome anyway," Lucky stated as I heard the faint sound of gunshots. "Boys are downstairs with the wheels. Let's go."

Brock turned to me, his eyes hard and determined. A concerned glance flicked to my legs. "You going to be able to walk?"

I puffed up my chest, trying to garner some strength. I had to ignore the pain, let Brock focus on not getting shot. "I'll be fine, lead the way."

"Stay behind me, Abrams. If anyone starts shooting get

down," he ordered. His eyes moved to the gun in my hand. "And don't point that at me again."

Despite the circumstances irritation bloomed in me. "I can't make any promises," I snapped.

"I hate it when Mom and Dad fight," Lucky whined. "Can we save the domestic squabble for when the probability of us getting shot is considerably lower?" he called over his shoulder.

Brock stared at me for a second, then he grasped my head, pulling my mouth to his. It was a quick kiss, closed mouthed and urgent. His forehead dropped to mine for a moment and he turned. "Stay behind me," he repeated over his shoulder as he started walking.

I felt dizzy and disoriented, and not just from the kiss. Although it was safe to say my feelings for him had not dulled a bit, I had a sinking feeling my light head was due to the throbbing in my legs. I stayed silent, we would get out of here first, then I'd address the blood loss situation.

As we were descending the stairs, both men glanced around, guns raised. The sounds of gunfire had subsided and now there was only a disturbing silence. Weirdly, I didn't feel afraid. That might've been because Brock had grasped my hand and used it to pull me close to his back, and he hadn't let go. We made it to the bottom of the stairs without incident and I let out a breath I hadn't realized I was holding.

Lucky turned. "We should have the wheels right outside. Everyone think happy thoughts and let's hope we aren't greeted with bullets when we open the door." He waited for Brock's stiff nod before he thrust open the door.

I squeezed my eyes shut, expecting him to flinch or get peppered with bullets. "'Bout fucking time. What were you doing? Admiring the decor?" A grim voice met us.

I squeezed open my eyes, happy to hear the familiar voice.

"Where's Amy? She okay?" Cade demanded with concern.

I waved weakly at him and his shoulders sagged in relief. "I wouldn't recommend this place for a weekend getaway," I said dryly, fighting the nausea that had just appeared.

Cade's gaze settled on my legs and alarm registered in his eyes. "Holy shit, Brock, you let her walk with her fucking legs like that?" He moved forward glaring at Brock, who had his back to me.

Brock turned and his gaze followed Cade's. I noticed something I had never seen before in his expression. Fear. That was the last thing I saw before blackness claimed me.

———

"Are you sure you know what the hell you're doing, Hansen?" An angry voice seeped into my ears as I struggled to regain consciousness.

I felt foggy. And cold. Really freaking cold.

I felt sharp pain at my leg, but I couldn't move to flinch, my body immobile. I tried not to panic, the familiarity of the angry voice helped.

"Do you want me to bring up a list of references for you to check while she bleeds out or do you want me to save your old lady's life?" a calm voice responded.

"I'm not his old lady," I croaked, finding the ability to speak.

A couple of manly chuckles erupted around me. I slowly opened my eyes to see myself surrounded by my biker family. Cade, Bull, Lucky, and Asher were all looking at me with strained grins. Worry lurked behind their attractive eyes. I moved my gaze to the unfamiliar man bent over my legs, his hands embarrassingly close to my lady bits.

"Gee, you haven't even bought me dinner first," I muttered weakly to a bald head.

An attractive stubbled face glanced up at me, his face tight with concentration, but amusement danced in his eyes.

"How about I take a raincheck on the dinner and stick to saving your life first?" he replied dryly.

"It's a date," I replied, ignoring the frustrated sound that erupted from behind the bald guy. My eyes met Brock's glittering blue ones. His face was tight with concern and he frowned at my legs.

I moved my attention to the fact I was lying in a makeshift bed in the back of a van with a strange man working between my legs. Unfortunately I couldn't say this was the weirdest place I'd woken up. It was safe to say drinking copious amounts of Ouzo in Greece was not my finest hour. Especially when I woke up in Albania.

"What happened?" I asked weakly.

Cade moved closer to my head, stroking my hair tenderly. For such a rough and scary biker man he could be tender when he wanted. Not to mention the fact he was mind numbingly sexy. Gwen was a lucky woman.

"You were kidnapped. We came to get you," he said softly, something moving in his eyes.

"I gathered that part, thanks, Captain Obvious," I retorted and Cade smirked, despite himself. "Why am I currently getting what is getting dangerously close to an exam only my gynecologist should perform?" I asked jokingly, but all of the men in the cab stilled and the air turned dangerous.

There was a beat of silence and Hansen broke it. "Your stitches have torn. Normally that wouldn't be that much of a big deal, but you had contusions dangerously close to your femoral artery. Whatever happened to make you rip the stitches also made you rip the skin. Since the cuts were so deep and hadn't properly healed, it punctured your artery and you began to bleed out. Couple of minutes longer you would have been dead." Hansen looked up and removed rubber gloves I hadn't noticed him wearing.

"Holy shit!" I proclaimed, sitting up quickly. I wanted to get a look at the cuts that nearly got me dead. "That bastard. Not only was that experience high on my list on the most terrible experiences of my life, it totally replaces the time my mother subjected me to that guy who was obsessed with feet. But he has totally messed with my ability to wear hot pants. Not that I would ever wear hot pants, but he took away the option," I ranted. "Now I almost *died* because he's one weird motherfucker with some seriously *whacked* sexual preferences. I should have done more than tie him to the freaking bed." I finished my rant breathing heavily and feeling a little lightheaded.

It seemed all the oxygen in the van had been sucked up when I had mentioned Rafe's sexual preferences. I forgot how protective these macho men could be.

Hansen's hand settled on my shoulder, gently putting pressure on it.

"Whoa there, you've suffered a significant amount of blood loss. I need you to stay lying down for a while." He frowned. "Ideally you need a hospital and possibly a blood transfusion, but for now I'd settle for you being horizontal."

I tried to push against his palm, but I felt weak and my body felt like jelly. My mind started to fog, but my tongue still seemed to be working fine.

"I don't need a hospital. I need to cut Rafe's...." I started, but I didn't get to finish as the fogginess overtook me.

―――――

My eyes snapped open and I felt like I'd been hit by a truck. My legs throbbed and my mouth felt like it was full of cotton wool. I thought I suffered badly with hangovers, but vodka infused sickness had nothing on serious blood loss. It took me a second to realize I wasn't in a moving vehicle and I wasn't lying on an uncomfortable surface.

I looked up at the white ceiling and then moved my eyes around the room I was in. I didn't get far when I saw Brock sitting on a chair close to my bedside, eyes closed. My eyes roved over him and I felt a pang in my heart. He had a rough growth of stubble on his chin which I wasn't used to, he was always clean shaven. His hair was longer, tied into a loose ponytail. My gaze moved to his cut, then down his muscular arms. I stopped short when I saw the tube attached to his forearm. A tube that had red liquid coming from it.

I tried to sit up in a panic.

What had happened to him? Holy shit, did he get shot? Worry washed over me.

I followed the tube up to an IV stand that looked like it held a bag of blood. Ew. Only then did I realize the bag was running into another tube, one that was attached to my arm.

Brock shifted in his chair, eyes snapping open. "Sparky?"

He leapt from the chair, mindful of the tube and he grasped my hand. "How you feeling, babe? You scared the fuckin' shit outta me, passin' out not once but twice." He looked relieved but still concerned.

I blinked at his manner, completely different than the last time I saw him. Granted, the last time I saw him I hadn't been kidnapped and knocking on death's door. I had been a screaming bitch.

"Um...." I started, unsure of what to say.

"Amy Abrams speechless?" he questioned, his eyes teasing. "I never thought I'd see my girl lost for words."

His girl? When did this happen? I hadn't seen him for almost a month. The last words I said to him had me convinced he would never want to speak to me again, let alone throw around phrases such as "my girl."

"I think substantial blood loss is a viable excuse for the lack of my usual quick wit," I countered, almost instinctively. My gaze flickered to the bag on the stand. "You trying to turn me into a vampire or something?" I joked lamely. "Trust me, things will not go well for you if you stand in the way of me getting my tan on."

Brock's face turned serious. His hand came up to push the hair out of my face with a tenderness that stabbed my heart. "Amy, you lost a shit ton of blood. I've never seen someone so pale in my life. You looked—" he stopped, almost choking on his words. "You looked ... dead. You almost were." He shook his head as if his was trying to shake away the image. I'd never seen him this rattled.

"I was ready to go all Eric Northman on your ass and feed you my fucking blood if that's what it took," he smiled grimly and I returned it, remembering my pestering him to watch my favorite vampire TV show with me.

Before.

"Luckily we were close to this place, a place where we had the right supplies." His gaze flickered up to the bag again. "If we hadn't I would've sliced open my arm right there, did whatever it took to get you looking rosy like I love." His gaze softened. "Lucky I'm O negative. Universal donor."

I sank back in my bed, feeling the wind knocked out of me. This was a lot to process after just waking up. The man who I was sure hated me, the man I was in love with, not only rescued me from what was sure to be a fate worse than death was now literally giving me his blood to survive.

"Abrams?" Brock looked concerned. "You feeling okay?"

"Peachy," I replied, feeling like my brain had just consumed a quarter pounder heavy on the fries. I was emotionally bloated.

Brock's gaze turned hard, almost pained. He paused for a second, letting us bathe in the silence before he spoke again.

"We ... well, Hansen has been so caught up in getting blood back in you he hasn't had time to check you over." He paused again, clenching his fist. His eyes met mine and I almost flinched at the pain in them. "Where else are you hurt?" he asked quietly, sounding devastated.

I blinked, feeling confused for a second until the weight of his words sunk in. "You think I was raped," I stated, and he flinched.

He nodded stiffly. "Baby—" His hand found mine. "Clark had cameras set up in the dining room." His voice was soft but somehow laced with fury at the same time. It didn't help that the way he was holding himself that it seemed if I tapped him he'd shatter.

"I know," I responded.

He looked up, surprised. "You know?"

I nodded. "He told me on the first day. I told him my father wouldn't do anything without proof of life and since he hadn't posed me with a picture of the day's newspaper I asked him how he was planning to do it. He pointed out the cameras," I explained.

Brock shook his head, smiling despite himself. "Sometimes I forget just how sharp you really are, Sparky."

His expression turned somber again. I was getting whiplash from the changing of his emotions.

"We saw the footage," he began and I nodded. "We saw the footage from two nights ago" he expanded, voice tight.

Dread washed over me. Duh. Of course. The entire "slice Amy up" stunt was done for the benefit of the cameras and for Rafe's sick pleasure although I suspected that was just a bonus.

"You mean you saw Rafe go all Freddy Krueger on my pins?" I asked quietly.

I wasn't ashamed, it's not like it was my fault the crazy motherfucker decided to slice me up. No matter how Brock felt about me he was a protective guy. Seeing his ex-whatever I was get tortured must have been hard.

Brock's jaw was hard. "No, the footage cut off after Clark ordered you to open your legs." His voice way low, almost a snarl. "Then it cut to you being carried off with blood dripping down your thighs."

The look in his eyes scared me for a moment. He looked like a wild animal ready to go on a killing spree. His eyes focused on me and they softened quickly. They were full of pity and regret. I opened my mouth to reassure him that I hadn't been raped, but the door opened before I could.

"Good to see you're awake and looking a bit more rosy," Hansen greeted as he approached my bedside.

I glanced at Brock's stiff frame for a moment longer then turned my attention to Hansen. I didn't recognize him, which wasn't saying much considering I avoided the club like it was Barney's on Black Friday. He was attractive, not that I was surprised, most of the guys in the club were.

It was like there was an unspoken rule you must be cut and panty-dropping attractive in order to join. Oh, and be a serious badass. This guy was all three. Tall and muscly? Check. Amazing bone structure complemented by a bald head? Check. Not many men could pull that off. A sense about the way he held himself that made you not want to meet him in dark alley? Check.

"Well, I think that's thanks to my blood donor over here." I gestured to Brock with my head, noticing he was dangerously still.

Hansen followed my gaze, frowning. "Yeah, well, I think it's time to stop the transfusion, considering it's highly unorthodox anyway." He started to fiddle with the bag. "But considering you were dangerously low on blood and we didn't have any blood bags lying around it was our only option. Brock would have attempted the procedure himself if I didn't do it." He smiled at me. Boy, what a smile.

Brock's muscly arm grabbed onto Hansen's equally impressive one. "She needs more," he clipped, eyes on me.

Hansen glanced down at the hold Brock had on his arm. "Brother, she's good. If we take much more from you you're the one that's gonna need a transfusion."

Brock glared at him. "I don't give a fuck what I need. I care about what she needs."

I felt a pang at that statement.

"You need to trust me when I tell you she's good. She's out of the woods—her body will take care of itself now."

Brock paused, then let go of Hansen's arm. "You'll be fuckin' sorry if you're wrong."

Hansen chuckled. "I'm never wrong."

I shook myself out of the daze I had been in over Brock's

behavior. "As much as I would love to watch you guys increase your testosterone levels, I kind of want some answers," I interrupted, feeling the eyes of two attractive men on me. If only this was a different situation that would be a good thing. I suspected I was far from looking my best, though. Blood loss would do that to a girl. "Where are we?" I asked.

It looked like we were in a hospital room, or more like someone's bedroom that had been turned into a makeshift hospital room. The bed was comfortable and had a warm quilt on in. Brock sat in a homey-looking armchair, and the walls were decorated with pictures and paintings. There were also cabinets filled with medical supplies.

"In the compound of the New Mexico chapter," Brock answered, rubbing his arm where Hansen had just taken out the tube.

I winced slightly when he did the same to me. Brock's eyes narrowed at this.

"You guys have a New Mexico chapter?" I asked, surprised.

I didn't know why I was surprised, I knew precious little about the club. Well, apart from what Garrett had found out all those months ago. My only connection was the fact my best friend happened to be married to the now president of the Sons of Templar MC.

Oh yeah, and I was in love with the Sergeant at Arms.

"Yeah, Sparky, thought you would have known that. Thought you'd have the location of all the US chapters in your little file," he replied lightly, reminding me of the first night we met.

I grinned . "It wasn't the New Mexico chapter I was worried about."

Hansen cleared his throat. "Now that we've got the most important thing out of the way, that is making sure you didn't die from blood loss—" Brock growled, but Hansen ignored this. I liked the guy already. "I want to give you a proper exam and check you are physically okay everywhere else."

Brock went statue still at this. "You'll be doing nothing of the fucking sort. If anyone's givin' her an exam it'll be a goddamned doctor. A *female* doctor," he growled, standing.

The men stood toe to toe glaring at each other. "You know I'm a doctor, Brock, evidenced by the fact I just saved your old lady's life," Hansen said calmly, but he held himself stiffly.

I really hoped they didn't have a punch up. I didn't completely have my wits about me, and I felt like I wouldn't fully be able to appreciate it. Plus, they didn't have their shirts off.

"You boys gonna kiss or what?" a teasing voice asked from the door.

"Lucky!" I sat up, grinning at the attractive man leaning against the doorway.

Lucky was the funniest biker I knew. He was goofy and love-able as well as deadly and alpha, a combination only he could pull off.

He sauntered into the room followed by Cade and Bull, who didn't share his carefree smile. Both of them glanced at Brock and Hansen then focused on me, concern evident. I directed my grin at them, hoping to appease them.

Lucky skirted past the two men who had broken their stare off to come and kiss my head gently. "Now, I know I said things were more exciting with you around, but let's tone it down a bit, huh, kid? I think you gave me a couple o' greys with the fainting stunt you pulled." He ran his hand over his smooth head. Even though he was smiling it didn't quite reach his eyes.

I punched him, shocked at how weak my limbs felt. "Who are you calling kid, Junior? I'm pretty sure I've got three years on you."

"Oh sorry, would you rather I called you *ma'am*?" he teased, eyes twinkling.

"You wouldn't if you wanted to procreate," I retorted snarkily.

He chuckled. "Good to see getting kidnapped hasn't taken your spice."

His statement was meant to be joking, but the air felt heavy.

Cade approached my bed and he pushed my hair back. "Hey, darlin.'"

"Hey, Cade," I spoke quietly, my teasing tone gone.

"How you holdin' up?" he asked, glancing down at me as if he expected me to reveal a bullet wound.

"I'm okay. It takes more than a punctured artery to get me down," I replied lightly. Cade's face stayed grim.

"Does Gwen know?" I asked quietly, worried about my best friend's state of mind. She had a new baby to worry about, not to mention the events that happened directly before Belle's birth. She didn't need this shit on her mind as well.

"No. I knew I wouldn't be able to stop her from coming up here with us, and I didn't want her going out of her mind with worry until we got you back. I'm gonna call her in a couple o' minutes."

I couldn't help but smile knowing my best friend's reaction. "You're in for one hell of a tongue lashing."

Cade's face was blank. "Don't I know it."

I moved my thoughts away from that situation, knowing I would be getting my fair share of cursing from Gwen. I knew I had a lot to answer for.

"What happened to Clark? I'm guessing he didn't take too kindly to you guys dropping in." My question hung in the air for a moment.

"Fucker's still breathing—he preoccupied us with his laughable security," Cade finally answered, running his hand through his hair in frustration. "He wasn't our first priority going in, but after seeing what the psychopath did, I am regretting not sticking around to get properly acquainted with the old man." His voice dripped with fury.

"Thank you," I said quietly, not just to Cade but to all the men in the room. "I should have said this straight away. But thank you for coming, for saving me. I'm sorry you had to risk your lives coming in to clean up my father's mess."

Cade's face softened. "You don't have to thank us, darlin,' and you sure as shit aren't apologizing to us. You're family. We take care of our family." His tone was firm and it brought tears to my eyes.

"What happens now, though?" I asked, thinking pragmatically. "I'm guessing this isn't the end of it. Clark doesn't strike me as the kind of man who will just shrug this off. It puts the club in danger." My stomach dropped, thinking of any of my adopted family in Amber getting affected by this. "My fucking father. I swear to God I am going to drag him by the collar of his Armani suit to come and sort this out," I declared passionately.

I heard Lucky and Hansen's chuckle at this. I even thought I saw the corner of Bull's mouth twitch. Cade and Brock were the only ones that remained stoic.

"Clark's fuckin' dead," Bull declared passionately.

Cade nodded stiffly. "We're taking care of him, Amy."

My anger bloomed. "It's not your job to take care of him. Don't get me wrong, I'm tickled pink you guys executed the rescue mission when you did, but this isn't your responsibility. Plus this guy seems to be seriously high on the organized crime food chain. You will be putting yourselves in danger for something that has nothing to do with you."

Brock stepped forward beside Cade. "They took you, Amy. They hurt you. You belong to the Sons. You belong to me. That sure as shit has something to do with us. No one messes with us. And they sure as shit don't hurt what's ours."

I refrained an eye roll due to the severity of the situation. "Okay, we're going to circle back to the whole 'Amy as a possession' statement, but for now let's focus on the big stuff. This is dangerous. You guys could get hurt."

"There's no more discussion. What they did to you, Ames...." Cade paused. "They're dead."

I gauged the atmosphere in the room plus the grim looks that had settled back on the men's faces, grins gone. My gaze settled on Bull's haunted expression for a beat.

"Okay, first I need to set something straight," I addressed the room. "I wasn't raped."

I let that statement hang in the air and could hardly breathe due to the fact oxygen had been replaced with testosterone. These guys were beyond protective. Not that I could blame them. Gwen had been kidnapped last year by a rival gang, then held at gunpoint while she was in labor. Plus she had to shoot the guy.

Before we got on the scene, Bull's old lady had been raped and murdered by the same gang that kidnapped Gwen. Violence on women was a sore spot for these men and something that was not tolerated.

"I know you saw the footage, and I can imagine what it was staged to look like." I paused, meeting Brock's hard stare. "But I wasn't raped. Rafe considers knife play to be foreplay and apparently so does Clark. I'm telling the truth when I'm saying that the only thing that touched me was a blade." I thought back to my gross kiss with Rafe. That didn't count, I decided. "Although I don't like to guess what else would have happened if you guys hadn't arrived."

The same loaded silence followed my declaration before Cade filled it.

"You don't know how fuckin' relieved I am to hear that, Amy," he said. By the look on his face I could guess. "But that still doesn't stop the fact they held you for six days," he continued through gritted teeth. "The fact they cut you up like that...." His voice was a hiss. "Bull's right. They're dead." At that moment, this wasn't my best friend's husband speaking. This wasn't the man who doted over his two-month-old baby girl. No, this was the president of a motorcycle club. A deadly one, at that.

CHAPTER TEN

After Cade's declaration, Hansen had insisted the men leave so he could check me out, despite my protests. When he had suggested Brock wait outside Brock gave him a look that could set concrete and no other word was spoken. He gave me a once over, and after declaring I was slightly dehydrated he was happy to leave me be. I was to be put on iron pills and to expect extreme tiredness for the next few weeks.

Great.

He also told me I needed to be horizontal for at least twenty-four hours to help my legs heal, due to the fact my body was too weak to be moving around. I had mentally groaned at this, I had been held captive for a week. I wanted to go and make the most of my newfound freedom, frolic in some meadows, go and buy a Chanel handbag, but it looked like I was stuck for another day at least. Not that the company sucked. Brock had set up camp in the armchair beside my bed. I felt safe with him there, no matter how dangerous it was for my heart.

I had wanted to speak to him after the doc's checkup, my brush with death making some things come into perspective, but exhaustion had overwhelmed me and I drifted off before I could.

I jerked awake, panicking at the darkness and my unfamiliar

surroundings. I had dreamed that Rafe found me and was cutting me all over again. I was scared that I dreamed the entire episode with the club and I was still a prisoner. I sat up, a cold sweat settling over me.

"Sparky?" Brock's voice was alert as he switched on a lamp.

I squinted at the harsh light, then let out a breath at the concerned and attractive face that I saw.

His hand cupped my cheek. "Are you okay? Is it your legs? I'll call Hansen." He made like he was going to move, but I gripped his hand.

"Are you real?" I asked, my voice small.

His face softened and his grip on my neck tightened. "Yeah, baby, I'm real."

"You came to get me," I said.

His eyes searched mine in the dim light. "I'll always come and get you, Sparky. No matter where you are, you can count on that."

"I missed you," I whispered, filling the silence that had descended, my eyes never leaving his.

Brock pressed his forehead to mine. "You have no fuckin' idea how much I missed you, Sparky."

I pressed my lips to his, all of the reasons I had against this disappearing in the moonlight. His response was instantaneous. His grip tightened on my hair as he plundered my mouth, I moaned into him, pouring months of desire into the kiss.

His hand moved to my breast and I arched my back, fire burning through me at his touch. My hand gripped his shirt, attempting to yank him down onto the bed on top of me. Abruptly his mouth left mine and I frowned in the dark, restraining myself from letting out a mewl of protest.

"Fuck," he hissed, voice hoarse.

"Yes, that's exactly what we should do," I murmured, trying to pull his mouth back to mine.

Brock sighed and gripped both of my hands. "You're hurt,"

he said simply. His mouth was still close to mine and his beard tickled my chin.

"I'm fine," I argued, deciding to ignore the dull ache in my thighs and focus on the not so dull ache between them.

Brock detangled himself from me gently and stood quickly, the sound of the chair scraping echoing in the silent room. I watched his silhouette as he paced by my bed. He came back to stop at my bedside and gently stroked my hair.

"You're not fine. Jesus, you're far from fine. The fact that I have to sit here and make sure you're going to be okay is the only thing stopping me from going out to that sick fuck's house and skinning him alive," he said, voice rough from fury.

I screwed my nose up at the visual.

"You don't know how long I've fucking visualized sliding into you again, Sparky." The hoarseness in his voice changed from fury to desire. "But when I fuck you, I want you to be whole and healed. 'Cause trust me, baby, I'm not gonna want to be gentle."

My stomach dipped and I struggled not to squirm at the erotic promise in his words. The uncomfortable bandages on my thighs stopped me from this action anyway. Any residual frustration I felt at him denying me what I wanted faded away due to the tender concern. I felt vulnerable in the darkness, if I couldn't have the connection I craved, then I just needed him. I needed him to make me feel safe, protected. If only for tonight. Tomorrow I could repair my strong independent woman armor, which had been tattered in captivity.

"Will you at least lie with me while I go back to sleep?" I asked softly.

Brock paused, and then I felt him lift me, moving me with such care you would have thought I was made of china. The bed depressed as he settled in beside me, gathering me in his muscled arms. I manoeuvered myself carefully and snuggled into him, reveling in his warmth and musky man smell. We settled in silence.

"This has been all I've thought about for almost a year," I

whispered on the edge of sleep. I felt his body tighten as I drifted off.

————

A full bladder awoke me the next morning, and I didn't have time to make the most of lying with an unconscious Brock. My favorite part of waking up with him was perving at him while he slept. He was mind numbingly attractive and looked peaceful while he slept.

Plus, he hadn't pissed me off yet that day so I always thought of him fondly in those moments. A very close second was the fact he always ravaged me within moments of awaking. The only thing better than a coffee first thing in the morning was an orgasm.

I gently disentangled myself from him, fully expecting him to wake up. He was a ninja sleeper, and in the past, any attempt I made to leave the bed while he was asleep was hampered by his strong arm. This time was no different.

"Where do you think you're going?" he asked, his voice gravelly.

"Oh, you know, I'm off to run ten miles. I'm feeling energetic," I replied.

The arm around my middle tightened, which was not good news for my bladder. "I've never met someone whose first words in the morning were dripping with sarcasm, Sparky."

"Yeah, well, I'm special," I snapped. "Let me up."

I looked over my shoulder impatiently, surprised at the emotion on Brock's face. I couldn't place it, and thanks to my bladder, I didn't have time to ponder it.

"Let me up, I need to pee," I demanded.

Brock did not let me go. What he did do was sit up, and in an impressive yet infuriating gesture got off the bed with me in his arms.

"What are you doing?" I protested. "I assume that's the bathroom." I pointed to a door in the corner. "I think I could have made it on my own two feet."

Brock walked us to the door. "I disagree. Hansen specifically said to stay off those impressive legs until he said any different."

I scoffed as we entered a surprisingly nice bathroom, complete with a decent-sized shower stall and bath in the corner. "I don't think the five paces it takes to get to the bathroom are going to result in any life-threatening issues," I said dryly as he put me down.

"I'm not taking any chances," Brock declared, standing in front of me, hands lightly on my hips. His blue eyes were intent on mine and I blinked, trying to ignore the intensity in them.

I waited a beat for him to leave, but he kept staring. "Um okay, we've succeeded in carting me in here. You can leave now."

His hands released my hips and he crossed his arms, stepping back slightly. "I'm not going anywhere," he declared ridiculously.

I widened my eyes and fought against my pressing need. "Yeah, you are. I'm not peeing in front of you."

"I've fucked you. Multiple times. Multiple ways. I've seen every inch of you. Tasted every inch of you. I don't care."

I ignored the desire that pooled at his words, which was easy as my frustration was mounting. "You're ridiculous. What do you think I'm going to do? Fall in?"

Brock raised an eyebrow. "I know you're going to walk out of here if I leave the room, which is exactly what I'm trying to avoid."

Okay, this was taking protectiveness to a whole 'nother level. "Okay, so you obviously lost a lot more blood yesterday than anyone realized and you've gone temporarily insane," I declared, jiggling my foot just a little. Brock didn't move a muscle and I knew he was serious. "What if I promise I will," I mentally cringed, "do my business and then won't move until you come in to carry me back to my bed?" I couldn't believe I just uttered such a statement.

Brock eyed me and my jiggling knee for a second before

nodding. I expected him to walk out, but he was on me in two steps, plastering his mouth to mine. I immediately forgot about my need and pressed into him. He pulled away far too quickly.

"Mornin,' baby." He smirked and left the room.

I stood, mouth agape for a second before I realized the reason I was standing in the bathroom. I did my business and walked to the door, opening it to a pissed-off looking Brock. I would never admit that the short journey had me feeling slightly breathless, my limbs feeling like lead and my legs throbbing.

"How did I know you'd never do what you're told?" he growled, gently lifting me into his arms.

"Maybe because you actually know me?" I replied sweetly.

He set me onto my bed and frowned down at me, face serious, tortured even. "Jesus, there's nothing left of you," he muttered.

I glanced down at myself. I wasn't wearing a hospital gown, thank God, but a plain nightgown that stopped mid-thigh. I had to agree with him. My meager and self-imposed near hunger strike at the mansion of horrors had taken its toll.

"The 'getting kidnapped and held against your will diet' is not one I'd recommend, but it's effective," I joked, trying to dispel the intensity that had settled in the air.

Brock's frown hardened. "This isn't a fuckin' joke, Ames. Not only did that sick fuck cut you up, he starved you. Jesus," he shuddered. "He's dead."

"Well, you're right about the 'cut me up' bit. But not so much about the second bit," I said carefully.

Brock narrowed his eyes. "What do you mean?"

"Well, it was more of a protest, really. You know, he tried to make it seem like I was there on some kind of vacation. Making me dress up for every meal, serving all this fancy shit, being polite. It pissed me off." I paused. "So I refused to eat any time he summoned me to his ridiculous meals. I refused to participate in his sick game."

"You mean you starved yourself?" Brock asked quietly.

"No, not exactly. Lucy, his maid, served me lunch and snacks. And I ate that. I just couldn't do it in front of him—it would be like agreeing that what he was doing was okay, you know? It was bad enough he dressed me like a high class hooker."

Brock was silent. The silence lasted awhile. I was unsure of what to say to fill it. I racked my brain for an alternate subject. A safe subject. Unfortunately, all subjects between Brock and I were volatile at the moment. In fact, this was the most amount of time we had spent together in months.

Brock decided to break the silence at that point, he did this by calmly walking over to a cabinet full of important looking medical instruments and shoving it to the ground, its contents smashing and scattering everywhere.

"Fuck!" he roared.

"Well, that was dramatic," I declared mildly.

Brock turned to me, his face murderous. "Dramatic? Let's talk about dramatic. Dramatic is you going on a fucking hunger strike 'cause you're too fucking stubborn and hard-headed for your own good." He stepped forward. "Do you have any fucking idea who Clark Devon is?" he asked on a yell.

"I'm guessing he isn't a philanthropist who rescues puppies in his spare time."

Brock's gaze narrowed. "This isn't a fucking joke, Abrams. Devon's one of the most dangerous men in America—mother-fucker kills people for *sport*. What in the hell were you thinking, refusing to eat because you wanted to make some statement?" he yelled at me.

I sat up, crossing my arms, feeling pissed at our uneven positions. "I was thinking that was the only goddamned thing I had control over in that crazy situation. I was thinking how fucking ridiculous it was that I got kidnapped over some shit my father does when the man hardly gives me a second thought. I was thinking I had to do something instead of being scared out of my wits the entire time!" I yelled back at him, breathing heavily.

This was a familiar situation, us screaming at each other.

Brock wasn't afraid to tell me when I was being a bitch and I wasn't shy about informing him when he was being a macho asshole, which was most of the time. What usually followed our screaming matches was some seriously hot makeup sex. I didn't see that happening this time.

Brock's face softened and he swore quietly running his hand through his hair, which had fallen out of its bun. "Jesus, babe, it eats me up inside knowing you were not only kept in that psychopath's house for a week, but you felt you had to starve yourself." He locked eyes with me. "When your uncle told me you had been taken and who by...." He shook his head. "I don't think I've ever been that afraid in my life. And when he showed me the videos, the one from the first morning you were there," he chuckled. "I was equally proud as shit and furious with you for the crap that was coming out of your mouth. Didn't snivel or plead like most bitches would have. Your fire, your spark, it didn't dim. You are so fuckin' brave, Amy." He stepped back toward my bed and grasped my hand. "That last video. When you thought you were about to be violated you didn't beg. You were strong, you fuckin' put your wellbeing below some stranger's. You're one in a million, Sparky."

I blinked. This conversation had done a complete one-eighty. I had emotional whiplash. I didn't know what to say. Brock and I didn't do deep and meaningfuls.

We continued to stare at each other in silence, something passing between us that made me uncomfortable. Not in the squirmy sex way either. This was more like a pivotal shift. Something had changed. The barriers I had built between us the past year were crumbling, and something about Brock's expression made me think he wouldn't let me shut him out any more. What scared me was that I didn't want to.

I opened my mouth to let it all tumble out. My true feelings, why I had been avoiding him, everything. To lay all of my cards on the table. I had almost died, for crissake. I didn't want to have any regrets. "Brock, I...."

"I'm taking from the yelling that we are awake and feeling better?" Hansen asked with a cheeky grin as he entered the room, effectively silencing my imminent declaration.

I moved my attention away from Brock, who looked mildly irritated at the interruption. Okay, considering the tic in his eyebrow he was a lot irritated.

"I'm feeling better than ever," I declared, lying through my teeth.

I felt like I had been hit by a truck, exhausted and drained emotionally and physically. My legs throbbed like a bitch and I had a headache to rival the ones I got courtesy of Pinot Noir. I wasn't going to tell them that, though. I wanted to get out of here.

"Bullshit," Brock bit out, glaring at me. "You're still as white as a fuckin' ghost and you weigh a hundred pounds soaking wet." He turned to Hansen. "She needs to go to a hospital." He looked around the room. "A proper hospital. She needs tests and blood-work and all that shit to make sure she's going to be okay."

My eyes bulged. Brock was taking the overprotective thing way too seriously. "I do not need to go to the hospital for tests, I'm fine!" I protested, feeling pissed at the fact I was lying in a hospital bed sans designer footwear. I needed height to compensate for my lack of tattoos and macho personality.

Brock gave me a sideways glance with a hard jaw. "She also needs a MRI if she thinks she's fine."

Hansen gave him a steady look before strolling over to me. In the light of day, without a room full of concerned hot bikers, I got to fully appreciate his hotness. I felt guilty checking out my pseudo doctor while my, whatever Brock was in the room. I was pretty sure I had enough on my plate.

Hansen eyed me, not in the way that I liked either. It was cold and clinical.

"She does look a little pale, but that's to be expected." He came to my bedside to pick up my wrist. There was silence for a second. "Pulse is remarkably good for someone recovering from serious blood loss." He gave me a soft look, something a little more human. "Do you mind if I look at your stitches?" he asked quietly, gesturing to the blanket covering me.

"Be my guest. It's nothing you haven't seen before," I said casually, though I wasn't feeling as blasé as I sounded.

The grim reality of what had happened to me was starting to set in, and I wasn't at all happy about the label of victim that seemed to be the only one that fit me at the moment. It was how everyone was treating me.

Brock stood slightly to the side of my bed, with his arms crossed and standing like your standard staunch alpha male. His breath hissed when Hansen pulled back my bandages to reveal my little collection of cuts.

"How much pain are you in?" Hansen asked, not looking up from his inspection of my legs.

I bit my lip, aware of the tension rolling off Brock. I wish Hansen had told him to leave before we started this. But I could have predicted that would have ended in him still standing here with Hansen potentially sporting a black eye.

"Um, not much. Maybe like just having a constant bikini wax every time I move," I joked.

I wasn't technically lying, but considering two bikers probably wouldn't have the experience of the excruciating pain of having hair ripped from the roots, they wouldn't gather the extent of the discomfort. The silence in the room told me otherwise.

Hansen pressed around the area gently and I couldn't help my wince.

"I wouldn't be doing that again if I were you, brother." Brock's angry voice was suddenly closer and I glanced up to see him standing right at Hansen's shoulder, glowering.

To his credit, Hansen didn't return the aggression. "Easy. I just needed to see if the pain was localized and if all of the nerves are working as they should. These are deep lacerations." Hansen glanced at me. "Although I don't think you need to go to the hospital for any health related problems, I do think you're going to want to see a plastic surgeon." He gestured carefully and covered up my cuts. "These will scar unfortunately." Needless to say his clinical tone was long gone and an undercurrent of fury rippled through his last statement.

He gave me another once over. "I also want you to go for a checkup in about a week, get your iron levels checked and make sure your body is healing how it's supposed to."

"Well, what are we waiting for?" Brock interrupted, "Let's get to a hospital so a surgeon can look at this shit now."

Hansen pulled off the gloves he was wearing. "She can't actually have the scars looked at until the cuts have healed. Then we'll know the extent of the scarring and what, if anything can be done to reduce them."

Brock stilled. "You mean she could go through all this pain, almost die and still have to live with the reminder of what happened to her?" he asked quietly.

Hansen put a hand of Brock's shoulder. I was impressed with his bravery, Brock looked like he was going to go all Hulk on him. "I'm sorry I can't tell you more, brother. This isn't exactly my specialty. But we're just going to have to wait and see." His voice was grim and he seemed frustrated.

Brock stared at him for a moment then nodded stiffly.

"Okay, now that I'm satisfied you're going to make a full recovery I can report back to some seriously nervous men," Hansen joked, eyes back on me. "You gave everyone quite the scare, beautiful. You're a fighter." He winked at me.

I rewarded him with a smile.

He turned to Brock, who looked unhappy at our little exchange. "We got church in five, brother."

Brock didn't respond, instead he looked at me and if I had been standing up I'm sure I would have toppled over at the amount of concern and emotion in his gaze.

Hansen caught this. "She'll be good, brother, I've got Macy

comin' in any minute with breakfast and a laptop filled with movies and books and shit."

Brock approached my bedside. "You'll eat everything on that fuckin plate, and I don't want you out of this bed." he ordered.

All the warm and fuzzy feelings I had over his loving gaze disappeared in a puff of smoke. "I'll eat what I want to eat and you won't command me to do so ever again, Otto," I snapped. "And I'll get out of this bed if I want to get out of this bed. That is my prerogative, since last time I checked I was in charge of my motor skills."

Brock's eyes narrowed. "You need to turn off the bitch switch for five fuckin' seconds and realize that I'm right. And if you don't do what I say, I'll come in here and *make* you eat every last bite."

"What are you going to do? Knock me unconscious and shove a feeding tube down my throat?" I asked sarcastically.

Brock's gaze changed. "Oh, baby, I won't have to knock you unconscious and trust me, you'll be begging me to shove something down your throat."

My stomach dipped. "You're disgusting," I whispered.

"You know I'm right," he said softly back and then kissed me quickly on the lips before straightening.

Hansen, who didn't look at all perturbed by our exchange, clapped Brock on the back and lifted his chin to me. "I'll be back to check on you later on today. And as much as I respect your prerogative and your right as a woman to not listen to no man, I must request you stay off your feet as much as possible." He winked at me, then he and Brock walked out the door, Brock smirking over his shoulder as he left.

I didn't have much time alone with my thoughts after the door shut. More accurately, I had about three point five seconds to analyze what went on moments before and what the heck was going on between Brock and I before Macy arrived. The door burst open and a small woman thundered through it, arms full with a breakfast tray and a laptop.

"Good morning! I hope you're hungry. Even if you aren't, there is no way you could resist this French toast. Jonah only makes it on like 'special occasions' and I'm talking when the 'Yankees win the World Series' type occasions, and looks like you deserve this orgasm on a plate, my dear. Heck, I'm thinking on getting kidnapped myself so he can make these when the boys come and rescue me." She stopped speaking abruptly, eyes snapping up.

"Oh shit. I'm sorry, that made me sound like a crazy insensitive bitch. I swear I'm not. Well, insensitive anyway. A lot of the guys around here might argue with the "crazy" bit. I am. In a good way, though, you know?" She arranged a plate in front of me and my mouth watered at the smell. She also looked genuinely sorry, which I couldn't help but laugh about. Her brown eyes were wide and apologetic.

"It's fine. If you had told me two years ago that I could lose this much weight in one week just by getting snatched from a bar in New Mexico, I would have seriously considered it," I joked, picking up my fork.

Macy regarded me as if she had x-ray vision. "Girl, I hear that, but you look like you lost fifteen pounds too much. We need to get some meat on those bones, and trust me, French toast is a great way to start."

She settled on the chair beside me, with a plate of her own in her lap.

"Oh shit, I'm Macy, by the way," she said after her first mouthful.

I groaned slightly at my own first bite, this was the best breakfast I had ever tasted. But the sweet taste of freedom mixed with maple syrup may have contributed.

"I'm Amy," I said, recovering from my foodgasm.

"I know. Everybody knows. You're pretty much the main subject around here."

I raised my eyebrows. "Really?"

Macy nodded her brown curls. "Really. The Cali boys rode up

here like bats outta hell a couple o' days ago and everyone got called in. I've never seen the guys that grim and seriously fucked off before. But it was scary. Like in a good way. They were shaking their alpha-ness around and it made for one heck of an aphrodisiac." She winced. "Shit. Sorry, I didn't mean that like it sounded."

I waved my hand. "I get it. If the guys in this charter look anything like the ones back home, I totally get it."

Macy chewed for a while. "Yeah, we've got a couple o' studs, but nothing like the caliber of guys from the main charter. It's like someone spiked the freaking water down there in California. I'm seriously skeptical as to how that many attractive men can be concentrated into one charter. It's cruel, really. They should be sprinkled around so more women can appreciate their beauty, or at least they could take their show on the road." Her eyes went dreamy.

I couldn't help but laugh again at this girl. She was a freaking hoot. And just what I needed to take my mind off things. Ideally, I needed my best friend. I more than needed her, I felt incomplete without her. But Macy would do until I was well enough to travel.

"Whose old lady are you?" I asked in between bites.

I was seriously surprised to see I had inhaled almost the entire plate in under five minutes.

Macy's smile dimmed slightly. "No one's yet, but I'm just waiting for them to realize what a perfect old lady they have under their noses. They just aren't ready."

"They? Or is there someone in particular?" I asked, picking up the meaning behind her words. The fact that this meant she was effectively a club girl didn't faze me, she was sweet and fed me freaking amazing French toast. How could I judge her?

Macy paused a second, looking almost sad. I'd known her for all of fifteen minutes but I could tell that expression was unwelcome on her pretty face.

"Hansen. He's just so freaking stoic and he never does

anything with women. I started to think he was gay, until...."
Macy petered off.

I sat up, reveling in the girl talk. "Until...?" I pressed.

Macy put her plate to the side and I got the gravity of the situation. There was still half a plate of food on there, you didn't put that down lightly.

"Well, one night I stayed late to clean up the kitchen and there was no one around, so I had my headphones on and was dancing and singing and stuff. Next thing I know, he's right there, staring at me. I took out my headphones to say something, something stupid most likely, but he marches up to me and kisses me." She gave me a meaningful look. "I mean *kissed* me. There was no doubt about his sexuality after that. I thought I got pregnant off that kiss."

"So what happened after?" I asked, getting into this story and wanting these two people to get together. They would if I had anything to do with it.

Macy looked seriously sad and it was all I could do not to gather her up into my arms. That was saying something. I'm not a hugger. "Nothing. He just stopped, then basically ran out of the room. He's been avoiding me ever since. And when I tried to talk to him he was just downright mean. Talk about mixed signals."

I felt for the poor girl. I found it hard to imagine the man who had just carefully tended to my wounds and successfully dealt with an alpha male with unnatural testosterone levels being mean to a five foot nothing beauty like Macy.

She definitely didn't look like a club girl. She was short and petite with pixie cut chocolate black hair and tanned skin. She was wearing a lace mini dress with a printed kimono overtop and knee length tan boots. She was a knockout and I didn't get why Hansen would screw her around. But these men were weird. And a lot more complex than they seemed on first glance.

Before I could console her, Macy plastered a smile right back on her face.

"You don't need me unloading on you—we need to get some positive vibes in here." She held up a laptop. "Now of course I am open to any and all online shopping possibilities that this baby presents, but I also have a plethora of movies for us to choose from. We've got some of the classic chick flicks—*Dirty Dancing, Pretty Woman, Bridesmaids*. And if you are feeling like watching a chick kick some serious ass, we could totally watch *Underworld*. Kate Beckinsale is my ultimate girl crush. I want to be her and sleep with her simultaneously." She paused. "Well, if I was a lesbian, of course. But I feel like if you met someone that attractive in person who could pull off skintight leather, you'd be whatever she wants you to be, ya know?" Macy babbled.

I blinked at the rapid conversation and found it comforting and strangely similar to Gwen's ramblings. "Mine's Scarlett Johansson, but I totally get yours. Gotta love girls that kick ass. I think I'm taking kickboxing classes when my legs heal," I pondered and ignored the almost physical recoil my body had at the prospect of exercise. The idea of being able to properly defend myself was hugely enticing.

"Okay, *Underworld* it is," Macy declared, moving her chair and setting up the laptop.

———

"How do you think she moves like that in that outfit?" Macy asked, tilting her head as if an alternate viewing angle would provide the answer.

"Hmm, I don't know. I give her serious props for it though. I feel like I would walk like the Tin Man in something that tight."

A clearing of a throat interrupted our pondering. Brock stood at the door, flanked by Lucky and Bull. "Hey, guys," I greeted, smiling.

Bull gave me a chin lift., "Hey, darlin,' you're looking better."

My mouth dropped open. He not only spoke, but his face looked slightly warm, and I was pretty sure his mouth was curled into a small smile. Before I could return this positively articulate and warm greeting from my usually broody friend, Lucky interrupted.

"Holy shit, is this *Underworld*? Why didn't you guys tell me you were watching it? This chick is fuckin' hot. Plus she kicks some serious ass." Lucky pushed through the doorway to perch himself on the arm of Macy's chair, peering intently at the screen.

"We've already had this conversation," I told him.

"And discussed our change in sexual orientation if we ever met her in person," Macy added casually.

Lucky went quiet and moved his gaze from the screen to dart between both of us, mouth agape. "Holy shit. Well, isn't that the best visual I've had since ever."

"You wanna keep your tongue, I suggest you stop right there, brother, and can whatever thoughts you got of my woman," Brock growled, coming to sit on the bed next to me.

Lucky grinned at him. "Sorry, brother, I can't control what goes on in here no more than you can," he said, tapping his head.

Brock shook his head and smirked good-naturedly. Even his crazy over the top possessiveness was no match for Lucky's easy-going nature. I was pretty sure it was impossible to be mad at him. I decided not to think about Brock calling me his woman so casually. I could face reality later. Right now I was going to make the most of the warm feeling that came from the statement.

"We've got one more to go. You guys wanna watch?" Macy asked.

I almost snorted. These guys were more likely to dress in pink tutus than watch a vampire movie with us. I was sure they had heads to crack or guns to shoot.

Imagine my surprise when Brock gently shifted me over to lie beside me and gather me in his arms and Lucky settled himself beside Macy. Even Bull dragged a chair from the other side of the room to come in viewing distance.

Break out the tutus.

After the movie, the men left us to it. I hated to admit the loss I felt when Brock peeled himself off my bed. We were settling into some kind of couple dynamic way too easily, like the last year and a half hadn't happened. It scared me. And excited me.

Then I got worried about being excited, knowing that something good between Brock and I would never last. Then I felt panic. This was all in the space of time it took for Brock to extract me out of his arms and stand beside my bed.

He must have gauged something in my expression. "I'll be back later on tonight, Sparky. You good?"

The men had declared they had "shit to do." This coincided with a text Bull got which meaningful looks were exchanged once he read it.

I nodded, swallowing the lump in my throat. "Yeah, peachy."

He frowned at me a moment before bending down to kiss me firmly on the mouth. He pulled back an inch so our mouths were almost still touching. "Stay in bed, baby, please?"

The snarky argument I would have normally had for such a command was quashed by the soft tone and tender look in Brock's eyes. I merely nodded.

He stayed gazing at me for a second more before he left the room.

CHAPTER ELEVEN

I jerked awake when I felt a soft touch on my thigh, panic rising from the dream I had been trapped in.

"It's okay, babe, it's just me," Brock's worried voice said from across the cab.

I glanced down at the tattooed hand on my thigh and relief swept through my sleep addled mind.

"Bad dream?" he asked, voice quiet.

I turned to him, emotionally wincing at the look on his face. His jaw was hard and his eyes were glittering with anger. He alternated between fury and tenderness the past couple of days and it was hard to keep up with. Not to mention a stark reminder of the reason for those conflicting emotions.

"Anyone would have a nightmare at the prospect of facing Katherine Abrams imminently," I joked.

My relief at the familiar scenery whizzing past us was quelled by the fact that the closer we got to home, Gwen, Belle, and all my family in Amber was the closer we got to my mother. I had spoken to Gwen on the phone right before we left.

"Amy, I didn't want to tell you this, but every soldier needs to be prepared when going into battle," Gwen had whispered.

"Oh no, what?" I had groaned, thinking I knew what she was

talking about. I just hoped she was referring to someone more tolerable, like Genghis Khan or Hitler.

"Your mother and father arrived late last night. Someone must have told them you were coming home," she said carefully.

I groaned, burying my head in my hands. "Maybe I should go back to Clark's. I like my chances there better."

I was met with silence on the end of the phone.

"Gwen?"

"We don't joke about Amy getting kidnapped until I get to see you in person and hug you and catalogue your limbs to make sure every one is still there. Then we have a stiff drink, you tell me everything that happened and I'll decide whether humor is appropriate." she said quietly, voice breaking.

Needless to say, my chat with my best friend had turned serious then and I had to talk her out of driving six hours to see for herself.

We had stayed in New Mexico for two days, long enough for Hansen to feel happy about me facing the journey home without carking it. I had kept myself entertained with the help of Macy. She wasn't joking, that chick was insane but in a totally good way. Her happiness and easygoing personality was contagious. It helped keep the dark thoughts at bay that included a knife and a seriously fucked up Italian. We had hugged each other goodbye only after I made her promise she would come and visit sometime soon.

Brock had continued to treat me like I was his and he had been uncharacteristically tender. It unnerved me. It also warmed me from the inside out. This wasn't the intense firestorm that it usually was when we were together. This was something different. He would gaze at me with an intensity I couldn't place. Like he couldn't take his eyes off me in case I disappeared.

He held me tight when he squeezed onto the small hospital bed after I awoke from nightmares. He touched me with a familiarity and ease of someone that had being doing it for their entire life, while wearing an expression that looked like he intended to do it for his entire life. It scared the shit out of me. I didn't know how to erect my emotional barriers again. He hadn't kissed me like the first night. He had stroked my face, held my hand, and gathered me in his arms, but his mouth hadn't touched mine since then.

So that brought me to now, pulling into my street, facing an interaction with my mother. I had been terrified to think she might actually be staying in my house, but thankfully they were flying out later today.

Brock grabbed my hand and squeezed. "She can't be that bad, Sparky. She made you."

"Do you have your gun?" I asked seriously, ignoring the tender statement.

His face was blank, but his mouth twitched. "I'm not shooting your mother, babe."

I shook my head. "I'm reasonably sure bullets wouldn't work on her. I'm talking about for me. I may ask you to put me out of my misery if I have to be subjected to her for longer than forty-five minutes."

Brock's blank expression returned, sans mouth twitch. "We don't joke about anyone using a gun on you. Got it?" His voice was hard.

"Sheesh, what is it with you and Gwen?" I said, exasperated at the sobering effect my attempts at humor had been having the past few days. I needed to cling to it, the reality of what had happened to me was too scary to face at this moment in time.

Brock pulled into the driveway, shutting the engine off. He grasped my chin lightly and turned my face to meet his. "For two days we were faced with the very real possibility that something had happened to you. Either you were...." Brock paused a second. "Either you were dead, or something had happened that changed you, made us lose the Amy we knew forever." He stopped and watched me a second as if he was imprinting me on his memory. "When I first saw you in that hallway and you threw your smart ass comments, I've never been more glad to hear that in my life. I could breathe again knowing I hadn't lost my girl."

His other hand moved to bite into my hip.

"When you passed out, when I saw all that blood...." He flinched at the memory. "I was resigned to the fact I'd have to live without breathing. Without oxygen. I was willing to give you every last drop of my blood if it meant the world wouldn't lose you. Then you woke up. Threw the bitch." Brock grinned. "That's when my breath came back. So you see, when I've stared at what the world would look like without you in it, I don't like anything that would remind me of that situation. Nothing, babe."

I gaped at him. "Well, not much can distract me from an impending confrontation with my mother, but that'll do it," I said blandly.

Luckily Brock didn't expect any heartwarming, heartbreaking declarations from me because he smirked and grabbed my head, laying a huge smacker on my lips. I got lost in the kiss and before I knew it we were full on making out, pent up desire flowing through us both. I was about to scramble onto his lap when my door burst open.

"Detach! Detach!" a familiar, slightly hysterical voice demanded.

I reluctantly complied and turned to my best friend. I didn't get the chance to say a word before I was unceremoniously dragged from the car.

"Let me look at you." Her eyes darted up and down my body, searching for something.

She seemed satisfied because she met my eyes and paused for a moment. Gwen then promptly burst into tears, gathering me into her arms.

"Oh my God, I'm so happy you're okay," she sobbed into my shoulder.

I sank into her arms, letting myself finally feel all of the emotion that I had been holding back. Before I knew it, I was bawling along with her. I don't know how long we stayed like that, drawing comfort and strength from one another, but it felt good, despite what the waterworks were communicating. Gwen was the person who knew me better than anyone else in the world. She was my "sista from anotha mista."

She pulled back, hiccupping, before a serious look descended on her face. "Your mother's inside," she said solemnly, eyes darting to the living room window.

"We're going to have to get a priest in to come and exorcise the place once she's gone," I replied.

She nodded. "I spiked her San Pellegrino with some holy water. Imagine my surprise when she didn't burst into flames."

I patted her shoulder reassuringly. "Thanks for trying."

The roar of motorcycles drowned out any further conversation as Cade, Bull and Lucky arrived. They had been trailing us the whole way.

Gwen glared in the direction of Cade, who was dismounting his bike, eyes locked on her. "Don't you come near me," she ordered, pointing her finger at him. "I am not speaking to you. Mad is not a sufficient enough word to describe my feelings toward you right now. Don't worry, I'll think of one and get back to you. Or I'll consult a thesaurus. But for now, stay at least ten yards away from me at all times."

Cade's face was soft as he approached us.

Gwen held both her hands up. "Uh uh! Do not come any closer. I mean it. Your daughter is inside. Go and see her. She hasn't mastered motor skills or the ability to swear at you, so I think your chances are better with her."

"Babe. I haven't seen you in days. I said I'm sorry. I didn't want to worry you until I could do something about it. Let me fuckin' kiss you then you can go on being mad." Cade was standing right in front of us now.

Gwen was still clutching my shoulders and I thought she might use me as a human shield against her husband. "You didn't want to worry me?" she said quietly. "You didn't want to *worry me?*" This time it was louder. "You are not a human censorship machine for poor delicate Gwen. I think I have a right to know when my best friend has been kidnapped!" she yelled. "You do not just get to ride off with a vague excuse and leave me thinking about breast pumps and Belle's baby teeth and lack of them." She cut her eyes to me. "I started freaking out over Belle's mouth full of gums and how weird it was she hadn't started growing teeth yet and it was a big thing." She darted her eyes back to Cade. "Anyway. You don't leave me worrying about things like that when my best friend is being held captive. In no world is that okay."

Cade crossed his arms. "And what would telling you have done, Gwen? Stressed you out even more than you already are worrying about Belle's fucking gums? You would have been beside yourself. And I wouldn't have been able to be there to fuckin' calm you down. So yes, I didn't tell you. I'd do it again. I'd rather have you pissed at me than worried and alone without me."

On that note he grabbed the back of her head and laid a hot one on her, not unlike the lip lock I had just detangled myself from. After what was a smidgeon too long for a kiss outside the bedroom, Cade let her go touching his forehead to hers. He gave her a look. A look that I felt like an intruder even being witness to. One that communicated a shared secret between the two of them that the world didn't know about, nor would ever know about. With that look, he let her go.

"I'm going to see our daughter," he said softly.

"'kay," Gwen replied dreamily, watching him walk toward the house with a vacant look on her face. She seemed to shake herself out of it and turned back to me, clutching my hand in hers. "Let's go inside and get you some tea."

I let her drag me inside, following Bull, Lucky, and Brock. Brock had been watching the little scene unfold, leaning on the truck looking all sexy. "I'll only have tea if by tea you mean vodka," I replied as we walked through the door.

"Slugger!"

Uncle Garrett detached from what looked like an argument with my father, who was standing in the middle of my living room to pull me into a hug. I sagged against him, the familiar smell of cigarette smoke comforting. "Thank God you're okay, kid," he spoke softly into my hair, not letting me go.

The emotion and slight choke in his voice threatened to get me starting with the tears all over again, but they dried up with the sound of a familiar but unwelcome voice.

"Garrett, now that you've pounced on my daughter, do you mind releasing her so we can assure ourselves she is not suffocated?" My mother's cultured voice was dripping with disdain.

Garrett held me a moment longer in rebellion before he let me go. "Oh, I'm sorry, Katherine, did my display of emotion that my niece was living and breathing make you uncomfortable?"

My mother chose to ignore him, casting a judgmental eye over me. My outfit was sure to give her an aneurism. I was wearing loose yoga pants so they didn't compress my bandages. My tee, which I thought rocked, had the Sons of Templar insignia on it and was tight, baring some of my midriff. Brock's eyes had turned dark when he saw me in it and I deduced I would wear the shirt more often. For once, a well-put together designer outfit was not high on my list of priorities. But if she had one comment on it, I might have just tried to strangle her with her pearls.

She seemed to sense this and stayed silent on the outfit front, stepping her pumps forward to stand close enough that I could smell the Chanel.

"Amy, my dear. We're glad you're back." She lightly touched my shoulders, giving me air kisses.

"Yes. Well, Mother, one could only stay so long against their will before it got dull." I matched her tone that communicated we were talking about a spa retreat rather than a kidnapping.

Like Garrett's remark, she chose to let that one fly over her perfectly-coiffed head.

My father stepped around her to stand in front of me. The expression on his face was tortured and even miserable for a second until he disguised it. "Amy. I apologize you had to get caught up in this...unpleasantness," he said blandly.

I raised my eyebrows at his choice of words and felt Brock's body behind me still. Garrett's face also got red. I could tell he was about to let loose, but I thought I'd beat him to it. "You and your business partner seem to operate from the same playbook," I told him, meeting his eyes.

He had the good grace to pale slightly. "Amy, I—"

I didn't let him finish. "You see, Clark Devon also referred to me being tasered, handcuffed to a bed, and being held against my will as 'unpleasantness.'" I used air quotes. "As if being held captive was equal to the valet scratching your car or eating bad food at a restaurant. I think I would beg to differ about the degree of 'unpleasantness' I experienced. I find it ironic that I had to suffer through your indifference as a child and now your business got me taken against my will. How it almost killed me. How are you going to explain that, Daddy Dearest?"

"Do not talk to your father in such a manner, Amy Abrams!" my mother chimed in, looking disgusted.

"Oh, I'm sorry, Mother. I think any respect I had for this man died away when his actions got me *kidnapped* and *tortured!*" I snapped at her.

She assessed me. "You can't lay all of the blame on your father. You were the one sitting in some filthy bar in New Mexico drinking yourself into a stupor. What did you expect would happen to you, Amy?"

Silence followed this statement.

I felt Brock's heat at my back as he stepped forward and I could feel the fury rolling off him in waves.

"Are you fucking serious, Katherine?" Garrett boomed from beside my mother, his normally carefree face distorted in fury.

My mother looked at him aghast. "I understand due to the company we are surrounded by you are tempted to think cursing in such a manner is an appropriate way to talk to me. I assure you it is not."

"Trust me, *Sis,* you're lucky I'm holding myself back," he sneered. "You're honestly trying to lay the blame for all of this shit on your *daughter*? Did they remove your black, shriveled excuse for a heart in your last surgery?"

"Now you wait just a minute—" My father attempted to defend my mother's honor.

"Oh, I would shut your mouth right now if I were you, Harold. The only reason why I haven't broken your nose is due to the fact this girl has come back breathing." Garrett pointed to me with his eyes still locked on my father. "But believe me, I'm holding on by a thread here."

He turned his attention back to my mother.

"I've kept my mouth shut for most of Amy's life. I've watched you ignore her, insult her, and deny her any kind of decent human affection for twenty-five years. And by some miracle, she turned out to be the person she is today, in spite of having a reptile for a mother. What I will not do is stand here and watch you not only try and lay the blame on your daughter for what she went through, but ignore the reason which is standing right beside you," he yelled, gesturing to my father. "I've held on to my connection to you out of necessity in order to give Amy some semblance of family, and through a misguided idea that since we're related by blood I'm obligated to share your air." He looked her up and down. "Now, I have no such urge to ever talk to you ever again, you emotionless bitch," he hissed, his arm still around me.

My mother gaped at Garrett before schooling her expression. "Are you quite done now?" She didn't wait for him to reply. "The reason Amy was taken because she was doing what she always does, acting irresponsibly."

"You're done," a cold voice announced from behind me. My mother looked shocked, as if only just noticing Brock was there.

"Excuse me?"

The way she addressed him actually had me leaning forward slightly, to do what I didn't know, maybe smash a vase over her head, but Garrett's arms tightened around me.

"I mean you and your husband are done spouting this hateful and poisonous shit. I don't know what kind of people you are to stand in front of your daughter days after she almost bled to death and give her as much love as I have for a suicide bomber and frankly, I don't care. What I do care about is Amy. I'm not having her near either of you for a moment longer," Brock growled.

My father stayed silent, but at least he had the good grace to look ashamed. My mother glared at him. "Is this the kind of people you hand around with, Amy?" Her voice was filled with distaste and she didn't let me answer. "Young man, we are Amy's *parents* and you cannot speak to us like that."

"As far as I can see you're not parents. He's a sperm donor and you're the fucking incubator."

Katherine looked at me aghast, "Are you just going to let this tattooed hooligan speak to me like that, Amy?"

"Of course not, Mother," I replied. Katherine's face was smug as she glared at Brock. "He left out the part where I say if I ever have to be subjected to your poisonous presence ever again I'll make sure every last society bitch on the Upper East Side knows all of your dirty secrets, you spiteful she-devil," I said quietly, suddenly exhausted.

Exhausted at the emotional toll my mother took on me. On the little niggling hope I had every time I saw her that some glimpse of maternal love would peek from underneath her surgically enhanced, powdered façade. And the little pinpricks I felt every time I was let down. I wanted it over.

Katherine's eyes narrowed and her face settled into a familiar look. One that meant a scathing insult was heading my way. "Well, Amy, you—"

"Don't speak to her anymore. Actually, shut your mouth entirely. Take your fancy ass out of this house and far away from my town," Brock interrupted my mother, stepping in front of me as if to shield me physically from verbal barbs.

I was happy to see my mother shrink away from his muscled form as he stepped closer to her. My father grasped her arm. "Come on, Katherine, let's not cause a scene. Amy needs her rest."

My mother looked like she was going to argue, but my father's face turned hard. She lifted her chin and a blank mask settled on her face. "Fine." She marched out the door without a backward glance.

My father turned to Garrett, who had been watching the scene with clenched fists, although he had smirked when Brock waded in. He gave him a stiff nod.

And then, to my absolute shock, my father held out his hand to Brock who was still standing in front of me. "Thank you for bringing my daughter home," he said quietly and sincerely.

"Didn't do it for you," Brock replied gruffly, ignoring the outstretched hand. "But if any more of your shit lands on Amy and hurts her in any way, the next time we meet won't be quite so civilized, no matter how much I care about your daughter."

My father's eyes widened, then he nodded. He turned his attention to me.

"I'm truly sorry this happened to you, Amy." I swore his eyes were glistening as he walked out.

"Holy shit, your mom may be a MILF, Amy, but she's a massive bitch," Lucky declared from the corner of the room, breaking the tension in the air.

———

I sank into my bed, sighing at the comforting feel and familiar surroundings. This afternoon had been exhausting, both physically and emotionally. After Brock had kicked my parents out, we had all relaxed exponentially, thanks to the fact we could now breathe without choking on Chanel No. 5 and my mother's disdain. Lucky and Bull had left, Lucky declaring he needed to "get so drunk I can't see and drown in pussy."

I realized there was still a grim reality to face.

"What about Clark?" I asked the group around me later once I had settled onto a couch.

More like once Gwen had forced me onto a couch after she had demanded to see my injuries. After paling slightly, she had declared I wasn't to move or otherwise I would face her wrath.

Brock, Cade, and Garrett all exchanged a look before Cade answered. "He's going to be taken care of."

"Taken care of?" I repeated, raising an eyebrow.

"Yep," Cade stroked Gwen's shoulder absentmindedly. She had allowed him back within touching distance but still scowled at him every now and then.

"Sorry, we're going to have to expand a bit on the vague badass terminology. What does 'taken care of' entail? You're going to give him a stern talking to? Or are you going to off him?"

"No one says 'off,' babe. You watch too many movies," Brock said from beside me.

I turned to him. "Well, obviously not because I didn't think that people said 'he's going to be taken care of' in real life, but the phrase was just uttered from Cade's lips. So there we are," I snapped at him.

"We're sorting it out," he replied stiffly.

"Can you expand on that?" I asked sarcastically.

"No," Brock said.

I sat up. "No? Correct me if I'm wrong, but I'm pretty sure *I* was the one who was kidnapped, so I think I'm entitled to be kept updated on the fate of my kidnapper."

Brock opened his mouth, but Garrett beat him to it.

"Slugger, that's precisely why you aren't going to worry about what limited future that piece of shit has." His voice held a bite I had never heard from my easygoing uncle. "You got a family here that is going to take care of it. We aren't shutting you out because we don't respect your ability to handle what's going on—we're doing it so you don't have to think about him anymore." His voice was soft and I found myself loath to argue with him.

"Okay," I relented. "But you're giving me the lowdown on what kind of business my freaking father was involved in with a crime lord, and how said business translated into me getting carved up by a crazy person," I demanded.

There was a pause and I raised my eyebrow threateningly at my uncle. I was not taking no for an answer.

He sighed. "You know from experience the variety of pies your father has his manicured fingers in."

I nodded. I had helped bake some of those freaking pies, so to speak. My mother may consider me an irresponsible party girl, but I had a certain knack for the business world. Not that I would ever pursue it. It was boring as fuck.

"Well," Garrett continued, "your father has a certain amount of control over certain high-ranking officials thanks to these businesses."

"Let me guess. He owns the notes to more than a few home titles and is a capital investor in many business ventures of certain high-ranking officials." I deduced.

Garrett smirked. "Spot on, Slugger. Your father, despite being a fucking twat, is a shrewd businessman. In addition to making a fuck ton of money, he also gained influence."

"So that's what Clark wanted—Dad to blackmail some city official?" I interrupted. It was the logical conclusion, but I didn't think something that simple would result in me getting involved.

"In part," Garrett replied slowly, his face hard. "Clark was more interested in the Silversdale deal."

I sat up straight, shrugging Brock's arm from around my shoulders. "You mean the deal I closed?" I asked quietly. I ignored the hand at my back and the eyes I could feel on me. I focused on my uncle who nodded, mouth set in a grim line.

"That deal not only had your father's company importing milk products from around the world, it also gave him significant control over the docks. And since he had control over not only what came in but also the people that let it in, he was of particular interest to Clark Devon," he explained.

I was silent for a moment. "I'm guessing Clark wanted to smuggle something into the country and didn't want to declare it to customs," I said dryly. "What exactly was he trying to get in? Elephant tusks? Fake designer bags? Freaking illegal immigrants?" I rattled off sarcastically. In truth, I knew the probable substance that would warrant all of this shit and account for Clark's wealth.

"Drugs," Garrett answered, proving me right, his eyes flaring in distaste. "Clark Devon is a major player in the heroin and cocaine game and had been trying to get access to a deal like the Silversdale one for over a year. When your father's company closed the deal it was a prime opportunity for him."

I got up quickly, ignoring the glare I got from Gwen. "So you're telling me that the deal *I fucking facilitated* was what got my father involved with Devon in the first place?" I said, my voice bordering on shrill as I paced the room.

Garrett's face turned soft. "Slugger—"

I didn't let him finish. "My mother was right, it is my fault I got kidnapped." I laughed without humor. "By trying to prove to both her and my fucking father I was good enough for them I shot myself in the goddamned foot," I paused. "Or more aptly I stabbed myself in the leg." I laughed coldly again.

As I was in the midst of working myself into hysteria, I hadn't noticed Brock get up off the sofa, but strong hands at my shoulders which stopped my pacing got my attention. He pulled me close to face him, his hand going to my neck, eyes intense on mine.

"Don't you dare fucking say that," he ordered roughly. "Don't you ever blame yourself for one minute of this fucking nightmare. None of this shit is your fault," he declared fiercely, his hand tightening at my neck. "The blame for this shit rests solely on your father's shoulders. Sparky, he is the one who got involved

with that piece of shit. He is the reason you almost fuckin' died."
His voice shook with restrained fury, then his eyes softened.
"The only reason you're standing here today is because you're
the strongest, bravest, most stubborn person I know. That's
what you're responsible for—you survived when not many other
people would have. That's the only thing you're responsible for,"
he told me quietly, pride in his voice.

I blinked, my anger fizzling like a deflated balloon. My fragile
emotional state could not handle declarations like this. Luckily
the soppy stuff was short lived.

"Now sit the fuck down. You need to rest your legs and
pacing like a mad woman is a stupid ass thing to do when you
have healing stitches," he growled, directing me back to the sofa.

I glared at him, but did as I was told.

I caught Gwen's eye and her face was hard but determined.
"Brock's right, Ames, none of this was your fault. Don't you dare
blame yourself." She screwed her nose up. "This is all your
father's fault. I wish I had kicked him in the nuts when I had the
chance," she muttered angrily.

I laughed at the frustrated look on Gwen's face, and I wasn't
the only one amused by her angry proclamation. Cade smiled,
shaking his head before he pulled Gwen tightly into his shoulder,
kissing her.

I shook my head slightly, needing more details. I turned back
to Garrett, who was watching Brock and I with a small smirk.
"So what was in it for Harold?" I asked. "I doubt he just said,
'Sure, I'll break the law for you and face federal prison. Just buy
me a beer later and we'll be square.'"

"Money," Garrett replied, his face hard. "Devon paid him a
lot of money. Plus no one says no to Clark Devon. Not without
ending up floating face down in the Hudson."

I chewed on this for a moment.

"No one says no to Clark Devon," Gwen parroted in a
sarcastic voice. "Who is he, freaking Vito Corleone?" Her voice
still held an irritated note.

"He's a lot more dangerous than a movie character, baby," Cade answered softly, his face blank. "He's got serious connections to all of the four families and not someone to be taken lightly."

"Well, maybe you guys shouldn't be looking to 'take care of him,'" I cut in, slightly panicked. "Or else you all might end up sleeping with the fishes."

Despite my use of a corny Mafia quote, I was supremely worried my best friend could become a widow because her husband's club felt obligated to avenge my kidnapping.

To my surprise Cade laughed. "Amy, the fucker may have a shit ton of money and some greasy friends, but we'll burn him and his entire fucking outfit to the ground without breaking a sweat," he declared flatly.

I chewed my lip, my worry not leaving me. Brock's mouth brushed my forehead. "Stop thinking about the asshole, babe. You're here, you're safe. Nothing or no one will ever hurt you again. I got you," he promised softly, his mouth brushing my ear.

The tingles that went down my spine helped to dissolve my worries, as did the strong arms encircling me. Anxiety still swirled in my gut though, and deep down I couldn't shake the fact something terrible was going to happen.

"Enough about that cockroach," Garrett boomed. "Let's talk about my boy here referring to Katherine as an incubator." His twinkling eyes were on Brock. "Fucking hilarious, my man. You've got my blessing with that one after that shit," he declared with a grin.

I ignored the stomach squeeze at that comment and from there, the conversation moved on to lighter topics, the tension in the room dissipating slightly before Garrett declared he had to leave. I was upset that my uncle couldn't stay longer and so was he, it seemed. But he had business in China that couldn't wait and he promised he would be back to see me as soon as he could.

After he left, I lounged around with Gwen and Belle while

the menfolk made themselves scarce. Brock seemed reluctant to let me out of his sight for extended periods of time, which meant he popped his head in every now and then, sometimes coming to press a soft kiss to my forehead. It confused the shit out of me, but I was too emotionally drained to contemplate it.

"Are you sure you don't want me to stay, Amy?" Gwen asked, looking at me with concern.

"I'm sure," I replied firmly. She bit her lip, looking unsure.

"I'm going to be *fine,* Gwennie. You need to go home and get some sleep and we'll talk tomorrow." I put my hand on her shoulders.

"You promise you'll call if you need anything?"

"I promise." I made a cross over my chest.

She threw her arms around me. "I'm so glad you're back. I missed you so much."

I sighed into the embrace. "I missed you too."

She pulled back. "Once this whole kidnapping thing is a little less fresh I'm going to totally kick your ass about the whole taking off thing, and you'll have some serious explaining to do, young lady."

I smirked at her. "Wow, look at you, going all mom on me."

She opened her mouth to retort when Cade joined us at the door, Belle in his arms. "Come on, baby, it's time for me to get my girls home."

Gwen glared at him for a second before turning her attention back to me. "I'll see you tomorrow, okay? Love you."

"Love you, Gwennie," I replied quietly.

I looked up at her husband. "Thanks, Cade, for everything."

Cade leaned in, brushing his lips on my cheek. "Don't need to thank me, darlin,' you're family," he said before directing his girls outside.

I stood in the foyer, wrapping my arms around myself, letting the atmosphere of my home settle around me. This was home for me. Not just this house, but Amber and everyone in it. The cold, sprawling penthouse where I grew up had nothing on this place. I felt safe here, like I belonged. No matter the fact there wasn't a Barney's or Bergdorf's in a hundred-mile radius.

"You should be sitting down," a voice informed me.

I jumped slightly and turned to see Brock leaning against the doorframe. He was really something in his jeans and cut. Tattoos sprawled across his arms, I took in his long hair and handsome face. I shook myself.

"I'm fine," I replied.

"That's why you're standing in the middle of the room staring into space?"

"I just needed a moment," I told him. "You can go now. I doubt I'm in danger of bleeding out anymore and I think my chances of getting kidnapped again are reasonably slim."

Brock frowned at me. "I'm not going anywhere, Amy."

"What do you mean? Your job's done. I'm home. You can go back to your life. We can both go back to the way it was."

"The way it was?" Brock asked in a dangerous tone, pushing off the door. "You mean the fuckin' hell of the past year, trying to get you to talk to me, to fuckin' *look* at me without running off?"

I straightened. "I didn't run off," I argued.

"Cut the shit, Sparky. You've been avoiding me ever since...." He paused.

Ever since Ian died was the unspoken phrase hanging in the air.

"Then after what happened at Cade and Gwen's wedding you spouted all that bullshit and ran off," he continued, smoothing over the 'Ian dying' part.

"It wasn't bullshit!" I protested, for some reason carrying on the lie, protecting my heart.

Brock stepped forward so he was way into my personal space, his presence overwhelming my senses. I hated it when he did that, using his body against me. He knew it distracted me.

"Don't lie to me, Amy. Not again. Not after everything we just went through. Not after I almost lost you." His voice held a warning, but he stroked my face tenderly, staring at me.

"You have to go," I pleaded quietly, feeling emotionally raw.

He shook his head slightly. "I'm not going anywhere, Sparky. I'm not letting you push me away again. We're going to do this, you and me." His voice brokered no argument.

I gazed into his eyes, taking in the determination and emotion in them. They were unguarded.

"I'm afraid," I confessed finally.

His face softened. "What are you afraid of?"

"Losing—" I started, but his fingertips brushed my lips.

"You aren't going to lose me. I'm not going anywhere. I promise."

"I know," I said.

His actions and the look in his eyes right now told me how much he was in this. I had known deep down how much he cared about me, but self-preservation had me in denial.

I took a deep breath, "I'm afraid of losing myself. Of getting so deep in this that I attach everything that I am to you. And if something happens I not only lose you, but I lose myself too."

I told him my greatest fear, what I knew would happen if I gave into what this was between us. Because I knew what we had, it wasn't "hearts and roses warm fuzzy" type of love. It was a soul-wrenching, heart destroying, all-consuming kind of love. It could be the greatest thing to ever happen to me, or it could ruin me beyond repair.

Brock stared quietly for a moment as if he was letting my words sink in. "Baby, you are the most strong-willed, stubborn, brave and irritating woman I've ever met. You're small, but you take up an entire room. You aren't afraid to be who you are and you've got this spark inside you that lights you from the inside out." His hands grasped my neck. "No matter what happens with us, that spark ain't gonna go out. But trust me, I don't intend on letting anything happen between us."

I sucked in a breath, unsure of everything, and certain at the same time. I knew I loved this man who had waited around and still wanted me after everything that happened, but I still hesitated. When I first fell in love with Ian, despite my strong feelings against the sappy emotion, I was ready to jump in, to be with him. Then he broke my heart and I turned into one of those girls who I had strived to be different from. My shield that I had built growing up in a loveless family had cracked. I repaired it with time. But I knew that if something happened with Brock, my shield wouldn't just crack, it would shatter.

"Jesus Christ, you're stubborn," he muttered, sounding frustrated at having to wait through my inner monologue.

He covered my mouth with his, kissing me like he had in the car earlier. But before he had been controlled, the flames that sparked between us contained. Now there was no control and the blaze whipped through me in a frenzy. He plundered my mouth, hands running all over me. He yanked my body against his and I moaned slightly at the feel of his hard on against my stomach. His hands squeezed and kneaded my ass. I ground my body against his, needing friction, needing to be closer. Somewhere in the recesses of my mind I registered him backing us into a wall so he surrounded me, boxed me in. His mouth went to my neck.

"All I've been thinking about for months, fuckin' months, is getting inside your sweet cunt again," he growled in my ear, palming my breast. I barely restrained a moan as he tweaked my nipple. All I wanted was him inside me in that moment. "Fuck, baby, do you know how much I wish I could be in that pussy right now?" he murmured, reading my mind.

"You can," I whispered, running my hand down to his belt.

He groaned and grabbed my wrist. "I'm hanging on by a fuckin' thread here, baby. It's taking all my willpower right now not to rip your clothes off and fuck you against the wall until you feel me in your throat."

Desire pooled in my stomach. "I wouldn't object to that turn of events," I whispered, struggling to undo his belt.

His hand was a vice. I pouted at him.

"I told you before, Sparky. When I fuck you, it's not going to be tender or careful. It's going to be rough and hard and I'm going to possess every inch of you." He swept his free hand up my waist to cup my breast roughly. I whimpered and his hand moved to cup my cheek. "But I'm not doing it while there's any chance I could hurt you." His voice was decisive.

"I'm fine," I declared, yanking at his cut.

Brock shook his head. "No, baby. You've still got fuckin' stitches holding your skin together and you can barely walk. You're pale as a sheet and you're exhausted after walking to the fuckin' kitchen. You're not fine." His eyes blazed in mine. "But you will be. Then I'll fuck you into oblivion," he growled, lifting me in his arms.

"You're using sex against me?" I shot at him with a scowl.

He walked us up the stairs with his eyes on me. "Baby. Fair warning, I'll use anything against you to get you to drop the shit and make you mine. I'm happy to play dirty." His eyebrows rose at the promise behind this.

My stomach did a flip and a thousand dirty images flew through my mind.

We made it to my bedroom, Brock depositing me carefully on the bed. I sank down in the familiar sheets. Brock started to undress, hanging his cut on a chair by my dressing table.

"You're staying?" I asked.

I hoped he was. As much as the independent woman in me hated to admit it, I was terrified of being alone.

He looked at me over his shoulder. "Babe, I'm not spending another night without you for as long as I fuckin' live."

My stomach fluttered at this, but I said nothing. I scared myself with the thought that was all I wanted as well.

Brock joined me in bed, gathering me into his arms. He stroked my shoulder, eyes on me, as if he was cataloguing my every freckle. Weirdly, I wasn't at all uncomfortable under his gaze. Partly because it was so hot it would have made my panties catch fire, if I was wearing any. And also because it was full of emotion, of tenderness. He was unguarded and had dropped all his barriers.

I ran my fingertip across his impressive pec, tracing the lines of one of his colorful tattoos. "Do you think this is going to work?" I asked quietly.

There was silence for long enough that I didn't think he would answer me. I lifted my head to meet his eyes.

"I don't know," he replied honestly and my stomach dropped. His hands tightened around me. "We're going to piss each other off, fight like cats and dogs, and you're going to act like a bitch. I'm also going to love you more than I have anyone on this fuckin' planet, babe. I'd do anything for you, die for you in a heartbeat. I can't predict the future, but I'm going to do everything in my power to make sure my future includes you."

Wow. That was an answer.

We sank back into comfortable silence and my stomach did backflips at his declaration. He reached over to turn the lamp off. "You need to sleep now, Sparky. It's been a hell of a couple of days and it's looking like I'm actually going to get some shuteye with you in my arms."

"Okay, night," I murmured, snuggling into his hard body.

As I was drifting off, I realized I didn't tell him I loved him too, and for some reason, he wasn't acting like he expected me to say it.

CHAPTER TWELVE

"I can't believe you!" Ry's hysterical voice screamed.

I held the phone back from my ear, flinching. Gwen gave me a knowing smirk from the counter.

"Ry—" I tried to cut in.

"Don't Ry me!" he shouted. "What is going on down there? Are you and Gwen just magnets for trouble? Do you have a freaking psycho homing device sewed into your Chanel? Not only that, you don't deem it necessary to trouble your best friend with knowledge you have just returned home from a *kidnapping*!" His voice was getting higher and higher and I worried about the glassware in his immediate vicinity.

"When you drive to LA to go baby shopping you tell me. When you get new highlights in your hair you send me like a dozen pictures. But when you get rescued from being held captive I have to hear it from Dave Simmons, who only knew because his maid is friends with your mother's maid. So if your hired help wasn't such a Chatty Cathy I wouldn't even know!"

"Ry, I would have told you." I bravely foraged into the fray.

He scoffed dramatically at the end of the line. "Really? When? Or do you only inform me about the really bad kidnappings?"

"Ry," I tried again, feeling supremely bad.

"Amy, you could have been hurt, seriously hurt. And I'd be waltzing around Manhattan worrying about the fact my next gig requires me to bleach my eyebrows," he said, his voice returning to a normal decibel.

"You're bleaching your eyebrows?" I asked.

"Amy," he warned.

"Okay, okay, sorry. I was going to tell both you and Alex, I promise. It's just been a lot, being back and dealing with everything," I said honestly.

There was a pause at the end of the phone. "Are you okay?" His voice was concerned, any residual anger gone.

"I'm fine, Ry, I promise," I lied, deciding not to inform my dramatic best friend about the nearly healed cuts on my legs. Not only would he go nutso, so would his super macho, super protective boyfriend. I had enough macho protective nutso-ness at the moment. My eyes landed on a figure leaning on a motor-cycle outside the door, but I focused on the conversation at hand.

"Amy, I don't know what I would have done if anything had happened to you. We've had enough. With what happened to Gwen, what happened to Ian—we've had enough heartbreaking events. We've reached our quota. So if you'll do me a favor and not get kidnapped again and live the happy life you deserve, that would be great," he ordered, sounding slightly more like himself, but I could hear tears in his voice.

"I promise you I'll refrain from getting kidnapped, shot at, or involved in any drug stings," I declared, hoping this was going to be a promise I stuck to.

"Okay. But if you do, God forbid, promise me you'll actually tell me."

I rolled my eyes. "I'll send you live video feeds," I replied dryly.

"I'm holding you to that. I've got to go—they've got the baby oil warmed up now," he said bizarrely.

I wasn't even going to ask. "Okay, love you."

"Love you, babes, kiss Belle for me."

I eyed Gwen, who was flat out laughing at the counter. "It's not funny, Gwen," I complained. "I'm pretty sure he's done permanent damage to my ear." I rubbed it.

"I don't envy you, my friend. I've been on the receiving end of one of Ry's rants, and trust me, I heard ringing for days."

I sank back on the couch I was currently lounging on. The couch was beside the fitting rooms in the store Gwen and I owned in our adopted hometown of Amber. It was doing well, extremely well, despite the fact that we'd had a death threat from a rival gang occur in here, as well as a kidnapping, and Gwen and I had left it for months when Ian died.

So it was a pleasant surprise that after only a year of being open we were not only breaking even, but turning a profit. Not to mention I actually loved working here and hanging out with my best friends all day. My eyes travelled back outside to the "friend" I wasn't so happy to be hanging out with.

"I don't get why Asher has to sit out there like some kind of friggin' sentry," I huffed, crossing my arms. "Not only is it completely unnecessary for him to sit out there looking all broody and badass, but it's affecting our business."

"Yeah, affecting it because after every woman nearly trips over their own feet trying to perv at Asher, they come in here so they can continue perving under the illusion of shopping," Gwen said. "I'm pretty sure we've made a thousand bucks off him so far —he should be getting a cut." Her eyes lit up. "Maybe we could give him a permanent job doing that."

I stared at her. "I think having a baby has messed with your brain. It's bad enough having Brock treating me like I'm going to burst into hysterics or turn into a hemophiliac when we're together, but when we're not together I have a leather clad shadow," I whined.

"You're seriously complaining over a hot guy following you around all day?" Gwen asked disbelievingly.

I thought for a moment. "You're right. I never thought of it like that." I let out a frustrated huff. "I'm so mad at Brock."

Gwen looked up from unwrapping a jewelry delivery. "Don't be mad at him, honey, he's just worried about you. They haven't dealt with this Clark guy yet and it's better safe than sorry."

I waved my hand. "Not about that." I dialed my phone, which was still in my hand after my shouting match with Ry.

"Babe."

"You're such an asshole," I snapped.

"Hello to you too. My day's going fine, how's yours?" he asked dryly.

"I'm so mad at you—you've *ruined* me," I declared, getting up from the couch and pacing.

There was a pause. "Not yet, but once those stitches come out I will."

I ignored my ovaries, which had jumped to attention the moment Brock had spoken in that sexy voice of his. I tried to stay on track, and I wandered to the window to peer at Asher.

"Because of whatever we are now and the fact you are a supremely good kisser and have a nice body and face and stuff, I'm ruined for other men," I complained. "I mean, I've been so pissed off you've instituted the 'make sure Amy and or Gwen doesn't get kidnapped again squad' I haven't even realized that the previously mentioned squad is made up of some seriously hot man flesh."

I peered at Asher, who was sitting on his bike, his muscled but tattoo-less arms on display. His dark shades hid his eyes but totally added to the dangerous and mysterious vibe he was giving off. I narrowed my eyebrows when his shades locked on Lily, who had been out getting us coffee. They followed her as she walked into the store.

Interesting.

"Amy?"

Whoops, forgot I was on the phone.

"What?" I snapped, trying to deduce whether Lily had noticed Asher checking her out.

"I was just asking what *in the fuck* you were talking about. Man flesh?" he bit out, sounding pissed.

"Oh yeah, so I'm too busy thinking about how many more days until my stitches come out and what will follow that procedure that I don't even check out the guys anymore. *Gwen* had to point it out. I'm surprised she doesn't bump into things she's so blinded by her rose-tinted glasses. For her to comment on it, the situation must be serious."

I heard a deep chuckle at the other end of the phone.

"This isn't funny," I snapped.

"I disagree, Sparky. The fact my woman is mad at me because she is too busy thinking about getting into bed with me to check out my brothers is hil-*fucking*-arious," he replied.

"Whatever," I huffed. "I was going to tell you some news, but you're being an ass so I'm not going to now," I informed him, feeling childish.

"Okay, babe," Brock replied, sounding disinterested.

"So you don't even *want* to know?"

"I do want to know. I feel like you'll get over this fuckin ridiculous snit and tell me at some point." He still sounded amused.

"It's not ridiculous. I don't appreciate you calling me that."

"I didn't call *you* ridiculous. I called your reason for being mad at me ridiculous."

I sighed. "We can fight about anything, can't we?"

"One of the many things I love about you, Sparky—you keep me on my toes," Brock teased lightly.

I was silent for a moment, straightening a rack beside me. I still hadn't said the 'I love you' to Brock. He didn't seem to mind, but I could tell it might turn into a problem.

"I'm going to tell you anyway because I've got to get back to work." I looked around the store. It was empty, technically I didn't need to get back to work, but Lily had brought coffee and

I wanted to grill her about Asher. "I'm going to the doctor this afternoon to get my stitches taken out," I said quietly, a sexual undertone to my voice.

It was our unspoken agreement once I got my stitches out we would finally do the nasty. It's not like we hadn't done it. But I felt like a born again virgin it had been so long. I seriously wondered if my hymen had grown back.

No matter how much I had tried to seduce him this week, he had stayed strong. Apart from some seriously hot kisses and the odd boob or ass grope, Brock kept his hands to himself. He didn't even let me take care of him. It pissed me right off.

I was also secretly impressed at his willpower. Not that I'd ever tell him that.

There was a silence. "Were you going to tell me before or after?"

"I'm telling you now," I said, confused.

"No, you're only telling me because you called spouting your crazy shit about Asher, who is not trailing you ever again, by the way. If you hadn't come to your conclusion, would you have told me before or after you went?" His voice definitely seemed angry, I couldn't see why. He was finally going to get laid. I thought he'd be more excited.

"Does it matter?" I felt mildly irritated so I reached for the coffee Lily had gotten me, hoping caffeine would quell the anger.

"Yes, it fuckin' does matter if you were going to go to the doctors and not even tell me, let alone ask me to come with you," he growled into the phone.

"I'm not five years old, Brock, I don't need anyone to hold my hand at the doctor's office. I'm very capable of taking myself. They don't even give me lollipops anymore, which obviously is a mark of my maturity." I sipped my coffee.

"Fuckin' hell," Brock muttered. I could tell he was talking to himself so I decided not to answer. "We'll talk when I get to your place tonight—I've got shit to do."

"I'm not sure I want you coming to my place tonight anymore. You've irritated me," I decided.

"Babe," was his response.

"What is it with you and the word 'babe'? You somehow think you can use it for a greeting and as a substitute for any sentence you feel like. It's one word. It doesn't even have a meaning. It's a term of endearment, so speak like a normal human," I ordered.

He sighed into the phone. "You want me at your place tonight. You want me to push you up against the wall and fuck you against it as soon as I get home. You then want me to walk you upstairs, eat you out then fuck you from behind. I know you want that, and I sure as shit want that. So I'll be at your house tonight." His voice was hoarse and full of authority.

"That's better than babe," I said airily into the phone.

"See you tonight, Sparky."

"Mmmhmmm," I replied, my mind already at the tonight part. My panties dampened in anticipation.

Gwen and Lily were both smiling at me as I got off the phone.

"What?" I asked them defensively.

Gwen looked sad for a moment, then her smile returned. "It's just good to see you happy, to see you and Brock finally happy. You deserve it."

I smiled back at her, but I knew it was a sad smile. "Thanks, Gwennie, although he makes me happy approximately twenty percent of the time and pissed off the other eighty."

Gwen snorted. "Whatever. You love arguing with him. It's like foreplay for you two."

I couldn't disagree with her there.

Things between Brock and I had been good the past week since I'd been home. He had been crazy possessive and protective, would growl at me for being on my feet too much, and was intent on making sure my legs were healing. He got an angry, faraway look in his eyes every now and then when he saw the bandages, but other than that he kept his fury at bay. I didn't get much more out of him as to what was happening with Devon, which pissed me right off.

When I told him this he replied, "Babe, you had to deal with that shit for a week—likely you'll be dealing with it for the rest of your life. Let me deal with as much as I can so it's not on your shoulders."

I argued that it should be on my shoulders since it was my family's problem in the first place, therefore the club should not bear the responsibility nor face the danger that came with "dealing with" Clark Devon.

Brock disagreed.

"You're family. You're mine. Therefore it is my responsibility to sort this shit out and make sure it doesn't touch you again. Plus there needs to be retaliation against someone who harms the Sons."

At this point, the argument threatened to descend into the problem I had with me landing as a possession, but a phone call had interrupted us and he had kissed me firmly before declaring he had club business to attend to.

So apart from that, things were good. He stayed with me every night and checked in multiple times during the day. He was there to hold me when I jerked awake from nightmares of Rafe and his blade. He made me feel safe and loved.

There was an undercurrent to our happiness, though. The least of which was the fact I hadn't uttered those three little words. It's wasn't that I didn't, it was that I wasn't sure I was ready for the giant strings that were attached to it. The potential for heartbreak. The power it gave him. Plus, there was the big elephant in the room otherwise known as Ian. Or more precisely, Ian's death. Brock knew there was a history, I suspected he knew my feelings for Ian, but he hadn't confronted me about it. I knew it was coming.

I had finally broken down and spilled the beans to Gwen about almost everything in regards to Brock. I kept silent about most things regarding Ian because she still flinched anytime she heard his name and I didn't want to upset her. She also was convinced I had missed out on my true love and was ecstatic I had a second chance. I also didn't want to break her heart setting her straight on that one.

Needless to say, she was happy with the fact Brock and I seemed to be together and she informed me that Cade was over the moon. I found it hard to believe that that big gruff man had any strong emotions over my romantic life and told her as much. She had clarified it was because Brock was no longer threatening to disembowel everyone that pissed him off which was, prior to our reconciliation, everyone.

So on the surface at least things were good, apart from the fact I still needed an escort everywhere and the house of cards that Brock and I had built our unsteady relationship on.

————

I was curled up on the couch a few hours later Googling plastic surgery and scar removal. I had gotten my stitches out earlier, although the angry red lines looked seriously scary right now, the doctor assured me they would fade. She did say there was a chance they could be almost fully removed with surgery, so I was looking at my options.

A knock at the door interrupted my web surfing. It was a good thing too, because I was getting worried about the fate of my scarred legs thanks to the Internet.

I expected Brock and my stomach fluttered with anticipation. I frowned to myself. I wasn't a girl that had stomach flutters.

I got turned on.

I didn't get butterflies in my stomach at the prospect of sex. But I couldn't ignore the little fuckers fluttering around in my mid-section.

I opened the door with a grin, planning on pouncing on the hot biker on the other side of it.

"Why are you knocking? You usually just..." I stopped short. The man at the door was not Brock.

He was good looking, that was for sure. He had light brown skin that hinted at exotic origin, just not one I could place. His black hair was close cropped to his head, which accentuated his handsome face. He was freaking tall and had serious muscles.

"Sorry, I thought you were someone else," I explained, meeting the handsome man's eyes.

For once, I wanted to encounter a normal freaking male in this place. One that did not make my womb clench.

The man smiled, it was warm and made his face light up. "That's okay, I'm sorry to turn up unannounced," he said. "I'm Keltan."

"Yes, you are," I muttered, eyes on his tee.

His eyes twinkled. "What?"

"Nothing," I said quickly. "I'm Amy. How can I help you?"

He had jerked in recognition at my name.

Oh shit, please don't be here to kidnap me.

"You're Amy?" he said quietly.

I nodded slowly, recognizing the familiar accent. My stomach plummeted.

"I'm here to see Gwen," he said slowly, "but I was hoping I'd get to meet you too. I'm Ian's best friend—we were more like brothers, really. I was there when..." He paused. "I couldn't make it to the funeral. I've only just gotten leave," he explained, his voice grim.

I blinked, dread settling in my stomach. Not just at the grief in his tone but at his clear deduction of who I was. He thought I was the grieving girlfriend. I could see the pity in his eyes as I shook myself.

"Do you want to come in?" I asked quietly.

Keltan nodded. "Thanks."

I stepped aside and let him in in a daze. "Um, Gwen's not

here. She doesn't actually live here anymore. She lives with her husband and baby now," I told him, directing him into our living room.

Keltan stopped and gazed at me in surprise. "No shit? Gwen's a mum? And married?"

I nodded. "No one's more surprised than I was. I totally thought she'd be doing body shots off strippers until she was sixty. Now it looks like I'll be doing that alone," I joked.

Keltan burst out laughing. "Ian was not wrong, you're something," he told me after recovering.

The mention of his name sobered me. I gestured to the couch. "Please sit down. Can I get you anything? A beer?"

Keltan gave me a grin, "A beer would be great. Thanks, Amy. Shit, I'm sorry. I feel like I know you already—Ian talked about you all the fuckin' time."

I kept my smile, but it was tight. "I'll get you that beer and call Gwen, get her to get her ass over here," I said, ignoring the land mine that was talk of Ian. "Make yourself at home."

Once I made it to the kitchen I sank down, the weight of reality hard on my chest. I took a moment, then grabbed my phone.

"'Sup, whore? I thought you'd be balls deep into a sex marathon by now," Gwen answered.

"Not exactly," I said quietly. "Um, Keltan's here."

There was a pause. "Keltan?" Gwen said in a tiny voice.

I nodded, but then realized she couldn't see my nod on the phone.

"I'll be right there, I'm two minutes away," she declared, hanging up.

I got Keltan's beer and one for myself, returning into the living room.

"Here you go." I gave him the drink, sitting across from him. "Gwen's on her way."

"Thanks," he said, taking a pull of the beer. "That shit's good. Nothing on the stuff we got back home, but a huge improvement on what I got when I was deployed," he told me with a grin.

"When did you get here?" I asked, grasping for topics of conversation that didn't involve his dead friend.

"'Bout an hour ago," he said, sinking back into the couch.

In other circumstances, I would have been appreciating the way his muscles moved at such a gesture and inspecting the tribal tattoo sneaking out from under his tee. Not today.

"Holy shit, you must be exhausted. I should have gotten the whiskey out," I joked. I sure as shit needed something stronger than beer. Like Prozac.

Keltan chuckled. "Nah, beer's good for me. I'm not a hard liquor man myself, just a humble country boy at heart."

I smiled. "So you've known Gwen a long time then?"

Keltan's expression went soft. "Yeah, I've known her all my life — she's like a sister to me. Even used to beat me up when we were kids."

I raised an eyebrow. Teeny tiny Gwen beating up this muscled Adonis?

Keltan saw my disbelief. "She may be small now, but she was a freaking chubby kid, and a vicious one at that," he said seriously.

I burst out laughing at the visual. "I would have loved to have seen that."

Keltan smirked. "Yeah, it's hard to believe looking at her now. Although she could still hold her own against Ian and me, she's something else when she's riled."

I nodded. "Don't I know it."

Silence descended for a moment.

Keltan's face turned serious. "How is she?" he asked.

I paused. "She's good. She's better. She's the strongest person I know," I said quietly.

Keltan nodded, a proud look on his face. "I know, Ian was so proud of her. Wouldn't stop talkin' about how well she was doing after his visit here." He paused. "He mentioned you as well—

fuck, I think you're the reason why we were going to open our security business two hours down the road. Then he could work on convincing you to marry him." His tone was light, but his eyes were haunted.

I swallowed, unsure of how to respond. How did I tell him I had no intention of becoming his best friend's wife?

Thankfully I didn't have to, as the front door opened and closed. Both Keltan and eye looked to it, expecting Gwen. Instead we were treated with a friggin' huge biker. His eyes narrowed at Keltan, who stood.

I stood also. "Hey. Brock this is Keltan. Keltan, this is Brock," I said with a shaky voice.

Keltan stepped forward with a smile. If Ian had told him about a certain biker, he wasn't letting on. "Good to meet you, bro," he said, holding out his hand.

Brock's face was blank, but he shook Keltan's hand. "You too," he grunted.

"Keltan's a friend of Gwen's," I explained once they had released each other's hands.

Brock nodded, moving to stand beside me, his hand lightly coming to my waist.

"You here from New Zealand?" Brock asked with a friendly tone, taking my beer to have a sip.

Keltan watched this, but he didn't betray a thing. "Nah, man, I'm here from deployment. Just finished my last tour," he explained.

Brock stilled, realization flowing through him.

We didn't get to carry on this awkward conversation as the front door flew open again, Gwen bursting into the room. I could have kissed her. She carefully set down her baby carrier and squealed.

"Keltan!" She ran into his arms

I detached from a stiff Brock to get a wide-eyed Belle out of her carrier. She made a snuffling noise as I picked her up, then quieted. I used to be nervous at holding such a breakable human, now I was a pro. As long as she didn't projectile vomit on me.

Keltan grinned and somehow managed not to spill his beer as she descended on him, his arms going around her. "Hey, G," he said into her hair.

They stayed like that for a moment before she released him, smacking him on the arm. "Why didn't you tell me you were coming, you asshole?" she scolded.

Keltan grinned. "Wanted to surprise you. Think you won that one, with your girl telling me you popped out a kid and got hitched," he teased, his eyes going to the baby in my arms.

Gwen's eyes followed, her eyes twinkling.

"Yeah, well, no one was as surprised as I was. I never expected to be a wife and mother at twenty-six, but I wouldn't want it any other way," she said seriously.

"Wanna hold her?" I gestured with my eyes.

Keltan looked slightly panicked as I stepped forward with the baby in my arms. You would have thought I was holding an explosive.

"Shit, I'll just look for now. I don't want to fuckin' drop her or anything."

Gwen laughed, taking her daughter out of my arms. "She's pretty resilient. I heard your mum dropped you as a kid and you're fine—only minor brain damage."

Keltan looked down at the baby in her arms and he softened. His large hand stroked her little cheek tenderly. "Yeah, well, let's not forget the time Ian whacked your head on a car door. It only affected your hand-eye coordination," he shot back, the air in the room changing at the mention of his name.

Gwen's eyes instantly filled with tears and I froze in place, mindful of Brock's arms around my shoulders, which tightened.

"I'm so sorry, Ace, I promised you I would take care of him over there. I fuckin' broke my promise," he muttered, his voice hard.

Gwen shook her head furiously as if she was trying to shake away the tears. "Don't you dare blame yourself, Keltan Brooke. I know you would've taken a bullet for him," she choked out.

"Come on, babe, let's give them a moment," Brock muttered in my ear, his voice flat.

I nodded, feeling like an intruder in this moment.

Keltan's eyes shot to us as we made to leave the room. "Hey, don't go. I've got something for you," he told me, his voice stronger than before. He glanced back at Gwen. "For both of you."

He motioned for us to sit down, helping Gwen and the baby to the couch.

"I've got to make a call," Brock told me quietly before leaving the room with a chin lift to Keltan.

I was left standing awkwardly in the middle of the room, unsure of what to do, so I sat.

Keltan took a deep breath. "Ian and I, we had each other's backs over there in that shithole. Shit, I wouldn't be sitting here today if it wasn't for your brother," Keltan told Gwen, who was as white as a sheet. "As much as we both wanted to get back here in one piece, we knew there was a chance we wouldn't. Knew we'd be leaving people behind if we didn't." He looked to Gwen, then me.

I was finding it hard to breathe.

"Ian was prepared. He was determined as fuck to make it back to his family, but he made arrangements for if he didn't." Keltan reached into his pocket to retrieve two crumpled envelopes. "Made me promise that if anything happened to him that I'd deliver these. And that I'd take care of his girls. I intend to keep both of those promises."

Gwen had tears running down her cheeks and was clutching her daughter.

I was staring blankly at the envelope in Keltan's hands. He got up and held it out to me. "He wrote this for you as soon as he got back last year. Made me swear on the fuckin' fate of the

All Blacks' World Cup game that it would make its way to you," he told me.

I stared at the envelope, wishing I didn't have to take it. My shaking hand took it from Keltan's grasp. I set in in my lap, not looking at it. It was an emotional grenade.

Keltan handed one to Gwen, who snatched it off him, then stared at it as if she unsure of what to do with it. She looked back up at Keltan. "Were you...?" she started, then her breath hitched. "Were you there when it happened?" she asked brokenly.

Keltan's face turned tortured. "I was two trucks behind," he said quietly.

Gwen let out a stifled sob. "Was it...? Did he...? Was it quick?"

Keltan put his arms around her. "He didn't feel a thing, Ace," he said, eyes shimmering.

The room turned silent, with the sound of Gwen's sobs breaking it every now and then. I didn't know what to do, so I just stared down at the envelope in my hands, wanting to rip it into a thousand pieces and also pore over every word it contained.

I ran my hand over the messily scribbled '*Ames.*'

Suddenly Gwen's sobbing stopped and she jerked upright. "You're staying here for a while, aren't you?" she shot at him, wiping her tears away.

Keltan grinned slightly. "Yeah, G, I'm booked in at the hotel in town. I've got a few days here and then I'm heading up to LA to check out spaces."

Gwen perked up. "Spaces?" she repeated.

"Yeah, me and some buddies are opening up a security business up there."

Gwen paused for a moment. "You mean you're out of the Army?" she asked quietly.

Keltan nodded slowly. "It was well past time. It was one of the things Ian and I had planned...before. We were getting out and setting up our own shop well away from any fuckin' deserts," he said.

Gwen beamed. "That's so fricking cool! You can come and visit, and Belle can have her Uncle Keltan make sure she doesn't have a complete American accent," she babbled excitedly.

"Wouldn't have it any other way."

"And you're not staying at a fricking hotel," she continued on a frown.

"Of course not, he's staying here," I cut in and they both looked at me.

"I wouldn't want to put you out," Keltan said, "I'm perfectly happy with a hotel."

I smiled at him. "You're not putting me out. There's loads of room, and Gwen's just going to insist you stay with her otherwise. Trust me, you don't want to share a house with a screaming baby and a broody biker," I teased as Gwen scowled at me.

Keltan looked at Gwen, who had raised an eyebrow. He shook his head. "I'll get my shit," he muttered, defeated. Gwen descended on me as soon as he closed the front door.

"You sure you don't mind him staying, Ames?" she asked, looking concerned.

I waved my hand. "Of course not. He's your family and I can't subject him to hearing you and Cade having your crazy animal sex."

Gwen's cheeks reddened. How could she pop out a kid and still blush over sex?

"It's fine, he seems like a good guy. As long as you promise he's not going to murder me in my sleep we're good," I joked.

"Who's going to murder you in your sleep?" Brock barked.

I jumped. "Sheesh, we need to get you a bell or something. You're light on your feet for a huge fucking biker," I said.

Brock scowled.

"She's talking about Keltan—he's staying here while he's in town," Gwen volunteered. "He was going to stay in a hotel. Could you imagine that?"

Brock stared at her a moment then glared at me. "Yeah, I can imagine that," he muttered.

Uh-oh.

Gwen read the atmosphere. "You know what, we're going to stay here too. Belle has a portable crib I can put in my old room and I want to spend as much time with Keltan as possible," she said quickly.

I frowned. "That's too much hassle."

Gwen frowned back. "It's not. Plus I won't be doing any of the work. Cade will." She winked at me. Her gaze went down to the letter in her hand and her expression turned serious.

"Can you watch Belle for a few minutes for me, Ames? I've gotta go take this outside," she said quietly.

Brock stepped forward before I could get up. "I got her Gwen," he told her, cradling the little baby in his huge arms.

Gwen gave him a small smile before coming up to me and squeezing my hand. I gave her a weak smile before she left the room.

I glanced up at Brock, who had his eyes on Belle. I felt a slight pang at seeing him, in his cut, covered in tattoos, looking menacing as shit, directing a tender look at my niece. I ignored the fact that pang came from my empty womb. So not the time to get clucky, or wish for little Brock biker babies.

Plus, you had to have sex to get pregnant.

"You volunteered to have a fucking stranger stay in the house with you alone, Sparky?" Brock asked me quietly.

I clutched my letter in my hands. "He's not a stranger, he's Gwen's childhood friend for fuck's sake. It's not like I asked Ted Bundy to have a sleepover," I argued.

"Jesus, Amy." He shook his head.

"What, Brock? Have you got something to say?" I prompted, daring him to bring up the subject we had danced around the past week.

He stared at me, his eyes blazing.

Before he could open his mouth, Cade shot through the

door. I hadn't even heard his bike. Fuck, were these guys going to stealth school or some shit?

He registered Belle in Brock's arms and gave him a chin lift. "You good with her for a bit longer brother?" he asked roughly.

Brock nodded.

"Where is she?" he asked, his voice full of concern.

"Out back," Brock told him.

Cade nodded, gave one look to his daughter then went in search for his wife.

"You call him?" I asked after we had bathed in silence for a moment.

Brock nodded. "Figured he'd have my balls if he found out his old lady was going through this shit and I didn't tell him right away."

I laughed sharply. "Yeah, that's about right."

His gaze softened. "You okay, Sparky?" he asked.

I met his eyes, registered the tender look of concern in them, the love. I couldn't do it. Couldn't have his sympathy, his understanding for my grief.

I stood quickly.

"I've got to go," I declared, snatching my keys off the coffee table.

Brock's face turned hard. "What the fuck do you mean? You're not going anywhere." He stepped forward, but thanks to the baby in his arms he couldn't exactly tackle me.

I sidestepped away from him, darting toward the door. "I've just got to go, okay? I need some air. Tell Gwen to call if she needs me," I said before turning my back and almost sprinting out the door.

I started hyperventilating five minutes after I left my house. Tears blurred my vision after ten. I somehow made it up to the overlook of the town. The place where a sharp drop held the ocean on one side and the town of Amber on the other. I let out a breath of relief as I turned the car off, as I realized I was away from it. Above it all.

The letter was sitting in the passenger seat, staring at me. Yes, I knew inanimate objects could nott stare, but that didn't mean I couldn't feel its gaze. It meant I could hardly breathe thanks to the fact it took up all of the air in the car.

How long I stared at it, I don't know. Minutes, hours, seconds.

Deep breath, Amy, you can do this.

I touched it with shaky hands and slowly pulled out the paper from its dirty and crumpled envelope.

Ames,

I'm gonna start with the whole "if you're reading this it means I'm dead" intro. It's cliché as shit, but how else do you start one of these things? Fuck. I really hope you're not reading this. I pray that one day when I get back from deployment and I'm in bed with you we can burn this motherfucker together. But the best laid plans and all that.

So if you're reading this, I'm sorry, baby. I'm so fuckin sorry I left you. Trust me, it had to be something big and bad to rip me away from the prospect of us.

From you.

I would have fought with my last breath against that reaper. Know that. In my last breaths, my last moments on this earth it would have been your face I saw. Your smile, your hair, the way you look after I kiss you. It would be your laugh in my ears, the sound you make when you're frustrated, the first time you said you loved me. I would not have died happy, I tell you that. I woulda been pissed as hell. But I would have had those memories of you to make it that little bit easier.

I'm sorry I didn't quit when you asked me to. I'm so sorry I hurt you, sweetheart. The only regret I have in this world is not getting out of this place sooner. Of not doing it when you loved me. Only me. When the way you looked at me made me feel ten feet tall and the luckiest son of a bitch on this planet. But I didn't. That's on me. The hurt I put you through, that's on me.

You falling in love with someone else, that's on me too. Shit, that's fucking hard to write. But it's gotta be said. 'Cause I know you. I know you're sitting there feeling guilty as fuck for letting someone else in, for loving someone else, even now that I'm gone and everyone's expecting you to be mourning me for life. I'm telling you right now, cut that shit out. If I am gone, don't you fucking dare screw up your chance at happiness 'cause of the shit swirling in that pretty head of yours. If you are, you can bet I'm up in Heaven furious with you for that.

The thought of you with another man makes me want to punch a cinder brick wall. The thought of you unhappy makes me want to rip my own heart out. No matter what, I want you to be happy. When I come back to you I hope to God I can win you back. I hope you still look at me like I'm ten feet tall. But if you don't, if you love this other guy more, if he's what you want, I won't stand in your way. I'll fight for you, babe. To the end.

But I'm also man enough to admit when I've lost.

'Cause at the end of the day, that's what love is … loving someone enough to let them go.

So, babe, if you are reading this, let me go. Don't let shit get in the way. Be happy.

Know I loved you until the moment I took my last breath.

Always and forever, babe.

I don't know how many times I read it. I read it until it was too dark to see the letters on the page. Until my tears had made all the ink run.

Fuck! Fuck him! Fuck him for speaking to me from the goddamned grave. Fuck him ripping open every wound that was healing.

Just *fuck*.

He knew. He knew I loved Brock. He knew there was a chance that he wouldn't be coming home to me, and he wrote that anyway. My hands were shaking and I felt like throwing up.

Where did I go from here? I couldn't run into one man's arms after reading another man's words telling me he loved me until his last breath, no matter what his fucking letter said.

A bright light distracted me. I realized it was my phone. I picked it up to see I had a zillion missed calls.

Gwen's name came up.

"Hey," I answered shakily, my voice husky.

"Amy! Thank the fucking Lord," she yelled. "Yep, I've got her guys. Call off the search party," I heard her say to someone in the background.

I laughed without humor. "Very funny, Gwennie."

"I'm not kidding, babe, Brock was seriously about to put out an Amber alert for you. I've never seen his face get so red," she murmured.

My stomach plummeted, then I got irritated. "He saw me walk out the door. It's not like I was bundled into a van," I said sharply.

Gwen sighed. "Yeah, you know how these guys can be. I'm surprised he didn't insert an implant into your arm or something. I'm pretty sure Cade's done that to me. Either that or he's psychic. The bastard always turns up when I need him most," she joked.

"Yeah, well, he probably imprinted on you or some shit," I told her seriously. "The way he looks at you is inhuman sometimes."

Gwen giggled. "You okay, babe?" she asked, her turning voice serious.

I hiccupped. "Yeah. You?"

She paused. "Not really, but at the same time I am."

I nodded. Then I realized she couldn't see my nod.

"Where are you?" she carried on as if she heard my nod.

"Lookout above town," I answered quietly, looking at the lights of my home.

"Want some company?"

"Yes, please."

"I'll be there in ten," she said.

———

Ten minutes later headlights pulled up beside me. I leapt out of my car the same moment Gwen did. She yanked me into her arms and we both stayed like that for a moment. I didn't cry, I'd drained my tear ducts dry. I just let my best friend get some strength from me and I took some of hers.

We pulled back in silence and her hand grasped mine tightly. We both stood there for a while, saying everything and nothing while staring at the lights below.

"Want to go and get shitfaced?" she asked.

"Do I ever," I replied shakily.

"Good," she declared. "Believe it or not, Keltan makes a kick ass margarita. He's totally down for getting blotto."

"Aren't you not supposed to drink on account it making your boob milk curdle or some shit?" I asked her.

I was pretty sure she rolled her eyes, but I couldn't see in the dark.

I followed Gwen back to the house, dreading the reception I would get. I hated that Brock had made such a big deal over my leaving. I just needed a minute.

Could I not get a *minute* to friggin' process?

Apparently not, considering he was leaning against his bike with his arms crossed as I pulled up.

"Fuck," I muttered as I got out of the car.

"I'll just, ah, chill our glasses," Gwen said, pointing into the house and darting away.

I slowly walked over to Brock, who watched my approach but didn't move.

"Hey," I whispered.

He was silent for a moment. "Hey?" he repeated in a low voice. "That's what you start with after taking off for three fucking hours? *Hey?*" he exploded, pushing off his bike.

"Well, how was I to know you'd get all dramatic and act like I took off for good?" I snapped at him.

"How was I to know you didn't?" he yelled, pushing his hands through his hair. "Last time you took off, you did it for a fucking month, at the end of which I rescued you from a mass murderer. Then you almost bled to death right in front of me!" he bellowed.

"I wouldn't do that again," I told him quietly.

"Yeah, babe, really? How about if it wasn't your choice? How about Devon decides to take advantage of your little drive and put a bullet in your skull? What the fuck do you think I'd do then?"

"He didn't!" I yelled at him.

"But he fuckin' *could* have!" he roared back.

There was silence for a moment.

"I just needed a minute," I said softly.

He sighed and put his forehead to mine. I sank into his touch, needing it, craving it.

"You need a minute. You got it. Maybe I need a minute too," he muttered.

My stomach sank.

"I'll give you some time, babe. Let you get your head straight."

He gave me a firm close-mouthed kiss and then his body was gone. I blinked and stared at him as he got on his bike and rode off.

———

"Thanks for letting me stay, Amy," Keltan said, enveloping me in his arms.

"The way you make margaritas, you're welcome anytime," I told him once he had disengaged.

He smiled at me. "I get why he loved you so much. You're perfect for him," he said quietly.

I swallowed, unsure of what to say. Luckily he didn't seem to expect me to say anything, because he moved to Gwen to say his goodbyes.

It had been two days since he had arrived and I hadn't seen Brock. Gwen said that Cade had told her he was off on a "run." I wasn't exactly sure what a run was, but I knew it took him out of town. I missed him like crazy and all I had wanted to do was call him. But I didn't know what to say. He hadn't called me either.

I was terrified that it meant he was done with me for good. Done with the royally fucked up girl who had her parents and her dead first love to thank for her reluctance to jump into anything that threatened her heart.

Luckily Keltan was a distraction. He was a hilarious guy who was light-hearted and easy to be around. He was like a New Zealand version of Lucky. He got along with the guys easily, coming to a club party the previous night. I hadn't missed the way his eyes had followed Lucy the entire night, and the fact I had seen them in a dark corner together. I was so needing the goss on *that*.

Gwen and Cade did end up staying at the house with him, not so I could escape the wrath of Brock for having a man in my house, but because Gwen genuinely wanted to spend as much time with her friend as possible. I could tell she loved him like a brother and had missed him like crazy.

So I hadn't spent all of my time thinking of Brock. Only about ninety-eight percent of it.

After we had waved Keltan off, Gwen and Cade had left me to it, off to have crazy animal sex, no doubt.

I was cleaning the kitchen when the rumble of a Harley made me freeze. I didn't move as the front door opened and closed and the thump of motorcycle boots on the floor came towards me.

Brock appeared in the doorway. I raked my eyes over him. He was wearing jeans and a white tee, his cut over top. His hair was piled on top of his head in a messy bun and he had two days' worth of stubble on his face. He gaze burned into me.

"You're back," I said quietly.

"Yep," he answered.

All I wanted to do was run across the room and jump into his arms, but I couldn't. The atmosphere was strange. I was terrified he came here to finally break it off.

I didn't blame him.

But the thought made my knees struggle to hold my weight.

"Why did you go?" I asked him, hating how pathetic my voice sounded.

He stayed leaning against the door. "You said you needed a minute," he told me flatly.

Thankfully pathetic, lovesick Amy was quickly replaced by pissed off, irritated Amy. "Yeah, a *minute*! Not two fucking days," I shot out, my voice rising. "I needed a second to breathe, to process all the shit that had been dumped on me."

"Yeah, well, maybe I needed two fucking days to process," Brock bit out.

"Two days to fuck me out of your system?" I hissed.

Brock's eyebrow rose and his face darkened. "You really think that's what I was doing? Fucking whores?" he snarled.

I threw my hands up. "How am I supposed to know? You took off!"

"Yeah, well, I didn't exactly know where I fit in with your dead ex's best friend and his sister," he shot at me.

I flinched. "That isn't fair."

Brock ran his hand through his hair, snatching it out of its band. "Yeah, I know it's not fucking fair. I feel like a bastard for being jealous of him, of a fuckin' *letter*. But I can't do this. I can't spend the rest of my fuckin' life competing with a dead man!" he roared.

I lost it.

"You don't have to!" I yelled back, leaning into him. "You don't have to compete because there is no competition!"

My hands were balled at the sides of my body and I actively had to stop myself from pounding them against his chest. "It's you! It's always been you. The moment you pissed me off, the moment you weren't afraid to call me a bitch and not put me up on a pedestal was the moment you won. He loved me and I loved him. But comparing him to you is comparing a raindrop to a downpour. You consume me. And I don't know how to deal with that. Everyone has been expecting me to be ruined for life because the love of my life is dead and buried," I paused.

"But I've been miserable because the love of my life has been right in front of me this entire time, breathing and alive." My voice turned quiet. "And I feel guilty. I'm sick with it. Because I know I was it for him. But he wasn't it for me. I was going to tell him that. The day I found out he was dead I was going to tell him." I met Brock's eyes, tears in mine. "I was going to tell him that I couldn't love him enough, that I didn't love him enough. Not like I love you."

There was silence. I was breathing heavily and a single tear trailed down my cheek.

Brock's face was impassive. I didn't know what to do, what to say. I wouldn't be surprised if he wiped his hands of me. I'd been fucking him around for the better part of two years.

I deserved it.

Suddenly he moved. He pushed himself off the doorjamb to plaster his mouth on mine. His hands were in my hair, rough and desperate. His kiss was brutal, taking no prisoners as he whirled me around, slamming me up against the wall. His hand moved to cup my breast.

"Brock," I half moaned.

"Shut the fuck up," he growled, pinching my nipple.

I cried out in pleasure.

"Never again are you going to let some fucked up shit in your head keep me away from what's mine," he snarled, hand plunging into my panties.

I restrained a scream as his finger pushed into me, flooding my body with pleasure.

He bit my neck viciously. "You know how many times I've jacked off thinking about you, fuckin' furious at you but desperate for your cunt at the same time?" he muttered, his mouth still at my neck.

His finger inside me stopped and his eyes met mine. "Do you know how mad I am that I haven't been able to claim you for all this time 'cause of that shit?" he barked.

I stared back at him, unable to process my own emotions. His words were brutal, but the hand at my pussy was soft, rubbing me in circles.

His face moved closer to mine. "Do you also know it makes me love you even more that you're so goddamned loyal to your best friend you'd sacrifice your own happiness for hers?" He paused. "Even if the reason was bullshit."

He shook his head before kissing me again, soft and tender this time. His hands started moving in between my legs again. "So tight, like velvet, baby. Even when you get prickly and sassy on the outside I know my girl's always soft in here," he murmured in my ear, kissing my earlobe.

I could feel my orgasm building, threatening to overwhelm me.

"I'm going to spend every night for the rest of my life in this pussy, in *my* pussy. You hear that, babe?" he growled in my ear as he finger fucked me.

"Yeah," I murmured, barely able to get one syllable out.

His finger stopped and my eyes snapped open. His blue eyes blazed into mine. This time they seared my fucking soul.

"Say it, Amy," he demanded.

"Say what?"

"Say this pussy is mine, you're mine. That you're my fuckin' old lady," he ordered hoarsely.

"My pussy is yours, I'm yours," I breathed out as his fingers moved slowly.

"My what?"

"Your old lady," I continued as he rubbed my clit.

"Too fuckin right."

His hands moved again, bringing me close to the edge before they stopped. Before I could complain, he ripped my panties off me and unbuckled his belt, plunging into me, filling me. I cried out in ecstasy.

"Fuckin' love you, Amy," he grunted as he pounded into me, his large hand spanning my collarbone, the other biting into my ass.

"I love you," I moaned back just before my orgasm rippled through me.

And there it was.

Those three words I'd been so scared of.

Three words that had never tasted sweeter.

CHAPTER THIRTEEN

The next morning had me feeling uncharacteristically domestic, which may or may not have been due to the fact I was thoroughly fucked both last night and in the early hours of this morning.

After getting all of dirty secrets regarding Ian aired, I felt one hundred pounds lighter, which may have been the reason I found myself blowing hair out of my face and frowning at the burnt mess that was my first pancake. I glanced at the pan, then at the picture on my iPad.

"Shit," I muttered.

I had left Brock sleeping upstairs and for once, he didn't wake up. I wondered if he would keep sleeping long enough for me to run to a café to get breakfast and feign I made it.

Arms around my middle made me jump.

"Morning, baby." Stubble brushed against my check and I shivered delightfully, relaxing into Brock's chest.

"You're not supposed to be awake. I'm meant to be making you breakfast," I replied.

"Well, when I woke to the smell of smoke I thought I'd better come down and investigate. Need a fire extinguisher?" he asked dryly.

"The first pancake is always a disaster," I protested, trying to reach for the jug amongst my mess.

"I think this is more than a disaster and I fear for your safety if you have to attempt that again. Plus I fear for my stomach if I have to consume that," he said seriously.

I turned around to face him, frowning. "I just wanted to do something nice for you and now you're being an asshole. I'm tempted to force feed you," I snapped, trying to maintain a scowl while his attractive face grinned down at me.

He kissed me on the head tenderly. "I appreciate the effort, babe. But how about I take you out for breakfast and we can save both the house and our stomachs?"

I chewed my lip for a moment, contemplating what a disaster it would be if I attempted to salvage the ruined breakfast.

"Okay," I conceded. "As long as you promise not to spread around what a horrible cook I am."

Brock gathered me into his arms for a tight hug.

"Your secret's safe with me, Sparky—although how is it you've been able to sustain yourself all these years?"

"Well, I mostly eat salads and healthy crap that doesn't require many open flames, and I go out to eat when I can," I confessed, hoping he wouldn't be my turned off by lack of domesticity.

Wait. Where did that come from? Since when did I care whether or not a man approved of my inability to perform household duties?

Brock interrupted my freak out, and he did seem angry but not for the reason I thought. "We're going to fix that shit," he growled.

"What? Are you going to give me cooking lessons, Jamie Oliver?"

Brock's eyes narrowed. "No, I don't give a shit that you can't boil an egg. I don't mind cooking, and I don't mind taking my lady out and showing her off. What I do care about is the whacked up shit you've got about all that rabbit food."

I widened my eyes, leaning back in his arms slightly so I could meet his gaze. "What are you talking about?"

"You and depriving yourself because you think you need to stay at a size zero. That's stopping now. You're beautiful, but you're too fuckin' skinny. You've got amazing tits, but the rest of you needs some meat on your bones."

I opened my mouth to voice the myriad of problems I had with that statement.

"Now don't go spouting crap at me just yet. I'd take you any way you are, ten pounds lighter or a hundred pounds heavier, as long as you were happy. You can't tell me you're happy living off fuck all in order to satisfy some fucked up goal."

I pursed my lips. My perpetual dieting had been a part of me for as long as I could remember. I wouldn't say I had an eating disorder, but when you had a weight-obsessive mother whose skeptical eye noticed a mere pound weight gain plus a love of fashion, you stayed thin.

It had become second nature to me to deprive myself, although every now and then I would glare enviously at people gobbling down candy bars or French toast. But I didn't want this change to be perpetuated to please a man.

"You can't just tell me what to eat," I snapped at him.

Brock regarded me. "I'm not telling you what to eat. Eat whatever the fuck you want. That's the point. Enjoy life a little, baby."

I didn't want to get into an argument so soon after a reconciliation so I just rolled my eyes. "Whatever. I'll go and get dressed for breakfast." I tried to move out of his hold, but his arms tightened.

"What? You want me to go in this?" I gestured down to the skimpy nighty I was wearing.

Brock's hungry gaze travelled down my scantily clad body. "Fuck no, I would like to show my appreciation for that piece of nightwear, though." Hands traveled down my sides to pull me flush against him, his firm hands squeezing my ass. "I'd also like to kiss my lady good morning," he said softly, eyes moving over my face.

His mouth descended on mine and the kiss went wild, as if we hadn't had sex, three times in the past twenty-four hours. I was pushed back against the counter and bowls and spatulas scattered everywhere. I didn't care.

Brock's hands circled my hips, lifting me on the counter. I moaned as his hard length pressed against me in the perfect spot. I frantically pulled at his boxers, freeing him and gripping him firmly. Brock's hands shoved my nightgown up, revealing my bare core. I was impatient and guided him inside me.

He plunged into me. Hard.

I screamed and almost came right then and then.

"You feel so fuckin' good, babe, you're like velvet," he muttered into my ear, hands holding me securely while he thrust into me.

"Harder," was all I managed.

He complied and I scratched my hands down his bare back, reveling in the sharp hiss he emitted. A strong hand bit into my hip. I held onto him for dear life as he pounded into me, plates smashing on the floor.

His hand went to my neck and he grasped it tightly, his eyes on mine. We stayed like that, staring at each other while he fucked me within an inch of my life, no words needed.

My orgasm washed over me without warning and I cried out as I felt him empty himself inside me. He rested his forehead against mine; we were both breathing heavily.

"That's what I call a good morning kiss," I whispered.

Brock chuckled lightly and the vibration made me twitch as he was still inside me. His gaze then traveled down my body to reveal we were both covered in flour.

All of a sudden we were off the counter, Brock still inside me. I squealed.

"We need a shower," he growled.

———

After a very long and satisfying shower, I stood in my walk-in closet, contemplating an outfit for the day. I was meant to be at the store about twelve. It was only nine now so we had plenty of time for a breakfast date. My head snapped up from a perusal of heels (I started my outfits from the bottom up, considering shoes to be most important).

Date.

Brock and I had messed around for months, on and off. We had fought, made up, slept together, woke up together but did not go on one date. I was too busy trying to maintain emotional distance to even entertain the idea of a date. We hadn't even shared a proper meal together. How could I be in love with a man when I didn't even know if he liked mushrooms?

"Want to run something by you, baby." Brock's voice penetrated my thoughts.

I whirled around to see him leaning against the door to the closet. He did that well. Leaning, I mean.

"Do you like mushrooms?" I blurted.

He furrowed his brow. "What?"

"Mushrooms," I repeated impatiently, "do you like them?"

He looked at me a second before answering. "Not particularly."

"Good," I nodded. "Me either, they gross me out. What's your 'go to' breakfast? Are you a toast and jelly man or do you go whole hog with bacon and eggs?" I asked. "Or do you forego breakfast altogether and just suck down a coffee? On that note, how do you take your coffee?" I shot at him, pacing.

How could our relationship have been so shallow and so deep at the same time? I knew. It was because of me. Me and my fucked up-ness keeping Brock at arms' length, then keeping him away altogether.

Brock stepped forward putting his hands on my arms. "Take

a breath, Sparky, and tell me where all this is coming from," he said easily.

I took a deep breath. "We hardly know each other! We haven't been on one date and I don't even know what your favorite color is. Please don't say something like black. That's just stupid and it doesn't even technically count as a color," I babbled.

Brock's finger brushed against my lips, silencing me. "We know each other, Sparky. I know the sound you make when I make you come with my mouth. I know you come from a fucked up family but still manage to have a sense of humor and be a good person. I know you would do anything for your best friend."

He cupped my face.

"I know when faced with situations that would make grown men quiver in their boots you shoot off your mouth and show no fear. I know you, baby. The important stuff, anyway. The stuff that makes me know I want you." He paused. "I also know you're a crazy fuckin' driver, you hardly ever stop at pedestrian crossings, and you don't like kids apart from Belle."

I stared into his eyes, letting all that information sink in, trying not to sniffle like a girl.

"And for the record, my favorite color is red," he said, playing with the strands of my hair. "*Now* can I run something by you?"

I nodded, still mute.

"Since it's Sunday and the garage is closed, I got no work today. Plus club business is quiet so I was thinking after breakfast we could take a ride."

"Where to?" I asked, finding my voice and finding excitement at the prospect of riding with Brock.

Wow, I was the new and improved, Amy. Usually I would be grumbling about damage to my hair or limited outfit options.

"Anywhere, down the coast. We'll stop somewhere for lunch, just ride."

"That sounds awesome," I told him, getting excited at the

prospect of an entire day with Brock. Then my mind caught up. "But I can't," I said, watching his eyes harden slightly. "I've got to work at the store at twelve," I explained, not wanting him to think it was because I didn't want to.

He relaxed. "Babe, you own the place. I'm sure you can take the afternoon off."

I bristled slightly. "Yeah, but I've been a shitty owner lately. I took off for six weeks and pretty much left Gwen and Rosie to deal. I've got a lot to make up for."

"Well, for a week of that you were being held prisoner, so I doubt they'd hold that against you. Plus you've worked all of this week when you should have been fucking resting. Take the day, babe."

I contemplated it. It had been relatively quiet lately and we had hired a couple of new girls in addition to Rosie and Lily. I was only there to do some office stuff today so I could take the day.

"Okay," I said and Brock smiled.

I stared at him a moment. It wasn't as if Brock didn't smile a lot. He wasn't like Bull or Cade. He smiled around me, even laughed at me most of the time. But he had never directed a soft, tender smile at me like the one right now. I almost melted in a puddle at his feet.

He smacked my butt lightly. "Get dressed then, babe," He kissed me firmly then sauntered over to the chaise lounge in the middle of my closet to sit down.

I followed him with my eyes. "What are you doing?"

"Waiting for you to get dressed," he replied.

I frowned, puddly feeling gone. "You can't sit there and watch me get dressed—you'll distract me. Go and do some man thing to keep you occupied." I waved my hand in the direction of the door.

"How much attention do you need to get dressed, Sparky? Plus, I consider watching my woman getting dressed as a 'man thing' since I get to check out her rack while she does it," he said with a playful glint in his eye.

I stood my ground. "Have you *seen* my outfits? They require careful consideration. I'm not like a guy who can just throw some jeans and a tee on and look like a biker version of a Greek god. This takes work. Plus, I need to find motorcycle appropriate clothing, I doubt couture would cut it." I glanced at my racks.

Brock smirked full on. "Greek god?" he asked. I glared and he carried on. "I've seen what you wear, babe. And as hot as you look in all your fancy shit I'm more interested in what's underneath it. And I have no fuckin' clue what couture is, but jeans and a tee would suffice for bike wear. We'll get you a leather jacket on the way out," he decided.

"I don't do 'jeans and a tee,'" I informed him. "And I've already got a leather jacket," I pulled out a Balenciaga tan biker style jacket that held a special place in my heart.

Brock didn't say a word. He just raised his sexy but judgmental eyebrows and folded his arms, leaning back on the chaise. I decided to ignore him and turned around to find something else to wear.

———

Turned out I did do jeans and a tee. So maybe they were three hundred dollar jeans, and the tee was designer. Baby steps. I even wore *flats*. Granted, they were beautiful biker style boots tucked into my skinny jeans, but it was still a change for me.

After calling Rosie to let her know I wasn't coming in and eating a breakfast of French toast, Brock and I set out for the day. The feeling of being on the back of his bike, hurtling along the coast was one that rivaled anything else I had done.

The sore butt after an hour of riding was not fun, though. Plus, my thighs hurt slightly from being at a weird angle, but I wasn't telling Brock that.

We stopped every now and then to wander around little towns we passed through. To get the substance necessary for my existence, or as other people called it, coffee. We finally stopped at a little shack on the beach.

"What's this?" I asked, looking at the corrugated iron building that looked like a food truck.

"Lunch," Brock declared, stowing our helmets.

"Lunch?" I asked disbelievingly.

"Taste the crab cakes before you judge, Sparky. They'll change your life." He grabbed my hand, tugging me toward the shack.

"They'll change my gut bacteria, more like," I muttered.

Brock ignored this sarcasm and dragged me over, ordered for us, paid and then handed me my paper plate.

"These are the shit!" I declared after swallowing my first mouthful.

Brock merely smirked at me. I was getting used to this fun-loving smile of his.

We were seated at a picnic table on the beach. There were only a few people scattered around. It was peaceful and beautiful.

We ate in compatible silence, enjoying the food and the tranquil sound of the ocean.

"This is nice," I said, watching the waves.

"Yeah," Brock agreed quietly.

I kept watching the waves while Brock's tattooed hand played with mine.

After our amazing lunch, Brock drove us down a depleted-looking road and parked his bike in the shade of a tree. We had driven away from the ocean and now we were in a huge field, with no civilization to be seen. I pulled my helmet off, confused.

"What are we—" I started to ask, but Brock snatched my helmet and tossed it on the ground.

Before I knew it, Brock had pushed me back so I was half-lying on his bike.

"What are you doing?" I tried to protest again. The erotic glint in his eyes had me staying still, although I worried about the bike toppling over.

"Remember me telling you I was going to fuck you on the bike, Sparky?" he asked hoarsely, standing so he could yank off my jeans.

"Here?" I stuttered slightly, feeling immensely turned on but also hugely exposed.

What if a nice young family decided to come for a Sunday picnic under this very tree and I scarred some child for life?

"It's just you and me here, baby. You think I'd let anyone else see that beautiful pussy?" he murmured, pulling me up once he had divested me of my panties.

He manoeuvered me so I was straddling him, my bare core rubbing against his hard length. I moaned slightly before Brock clutched the back of my head to kiss me. I ground up against him.

"What if the bike falls?" I asked when he had released my mouth for a moment.

Brock gave me a dark look and his hand moved to stroke me between my legs. "You think I'd let you fall, babe?"

I shook my head slowly, trusting him.

His hand moved in circles as he built me up, not saying anything, not kissing me, just watching me. My breath started coming in pants, the combination of his gaze and doing something so private in the open turning me on like crazy. I moved in rhythm with his strokes, the fire from his touch overwhelming me.

"I need you inside me," I said brokenly.

Brock stared at me a beat before freeing himself from his jeans.

"Ride me, baby," he commanded roughly, lifting me.

The cords of Brock's neck were tight as he filled me to the hilt. I wrapped my legs around him tightly, finding my balance on the bike. Once I got it I started to move, slowly at first, then faster as my orgasm crept up on me.

"Fuck yes, Sparky," Brock grunted as I clutched his neck and rode him relentlessly.

I cried out through my climax, throwing my head back, Brock's hand steadying me. Brock thrust into me hard as I came down, filling me with his own release. We were both breathing heavily and Brock rested his forehead against mine.

"Love you, baby," he said softly.

I stared at him for a moment. "I love you too," I whispered.

———

I was curled up watching TV as Brock cooked us dinner and I felt it. Happy. Content. It wasn't like my life before love and loss and heartbreak wasn't good. It was. I had friends. I had money. I had a nice apartment. I had nice things. But there was a little piece of me that none of that could fill. A piece of me that in the darkest recesses of my mind I would only admit was in need of love. That was something that had been sorely lacking in my childhood.

I watched my parents around each other and saw no affection, only duty. I received bouts of it from my Uncle Garrett and I treasured it. But I spent so much time desperate for attention and love from the two people who are meant to give it unconditionally that I thought that there was something wrong with me. I tried to be perfect, to look perfect, to act perfect. But that didn't work — in fact my mother always found some kind of fault in my behavior or appearance.

So I changed tactics. I acted out, I caused trouble. Broke curfew. Cursed. That didn't warrant any more attention, not even discipline. So I decided to just be me and pretend it didn't kill me just a little inside that I couldn't get love from my family. Since then, I'd vowed never to be that vulnerable little girl, changing everything about herself in order to receive love. I made it impossible to feel that rejection by picking men I would never love — hell, I hardly even liked them. I used them then threw them away.

Even when I had Ian, it was a whirlwind kind of love, one that I knew couldn't last, but it took me by surprise and I went with it. And to my horror, I became that little girl, pleading for Ian's love, for him to stay with me, for us to be together. When he broke it off, although his reasons were honorable and ultimately because he loved me, all I saw was his rejection.

After that, I vowed to not let that happen again, to let that need for love turn me into a vulnerable mess. That's what fucked up everything with Brock. Now it was fixed. Now I was taking the risk. I'd said the words, I'd jumped off that ledge. And he caught me. And here I was doing something as domestic as watching TV with him, and I was happy. I wasn't in a fancy apartment in my glossy city. I wasn't clad in overpriced albeit beautiful clothes. But I had everything I needed.

"Amy?"

I shook my head. I had been retreating into it far too much these days.

"Yeah?" I glanced up at Brock, who was shirtless. My gaze didn't get past his midsection as I drooled over his tattooed six pack.

"My eyes are up here, babe," he said playfully.

I didn't move my gaze. "I know," I replied. I heard his chuckle and I licked my lips.

He knelt down and grasped my chin. "Keep looking at me like that and our dinner's going to go cold," he stated in a low voice.

I ran my hands up his rock hard abs. "Food's overrated," I declared.

Brock's eyes flared. "As much as I would rather eat your sweet pussy instead of dinner, you need it." His voice was firm and I pouted.

He sighed, pulling me off the couch. "You're going to kill me, woman. Eat. Then back to bed."

I smiled at him. It was genuine and it was full of all that love that was radiating through my body.

He stilled and his face turned tender. "You're fuckin' beautiful, baby." He kissed me firmly and directed me into his cluttered dining room.

"So," I said, chewing my amazing dinner.

Brock could cook. And he had a hot body and a hot face and was great in bed. Oh, and I loved him. I guessed I'd keep him.

"So," he replied in between mouthfuls.

"The Sons killed Jimmy, right?" I asked casually.

I had wanted to talk about this with Brock or Cade at some point, but with Ian's death and all the drama that followed it had kind of fallen by the wayside. Now that Brock and I were together, I wanted to lay it all out. I wanted to know everything about the club.

Brock had stilled and was staring at me.

"Don't worry. I don't have a wired stuffed down my bra, considering I'm not wearing one," I joked, forking some more food into my mouth.

Brock had put down his fork and I had his full attention. His easy gaze had gone and he was in full on biker mode. It was kinda hot. "How do you know?"

I chewed. "I'm not an idiot. Gwen shacks up with Cade and Jimmy mysteriously gets shivved not three months after they get together. I'm assuming you called in a marker or something like that." I waved my fork. "Is that what it's called? A marker? That's not important. I just wanted to thank you. Off the record, of course. Gwen would go gonzo if she knew I was condoning vigilante justice. She's a rare person who believes in justice and karma and stuff like that." I paused. "I don't. I believe that a person who tortured, scarred, and almost raped and killed one of the most important people in my life deserved to die." I shrugged. "If that makes me a bad person then I'm guessing I'll be sunbathing in Hell."

Brock was staring at me with that blank look on his face, but it was tinged with shock.

I decided to soldier on.

"I kept my promise on the first night we met. I promised that I wouldn't go poking around into the club's business since I was satisfied you guys weren't a bunch of misogynists who liked to hurt women." I stared at Brock. "But now we're..." I paused, "now we're dating, officially. I guess I need to know more. You know me too well to know I'm not okay with ignorance. Or lying by omission. I need to know it all. I suspect Gwen's the same, but she hasn't uttered a word about the club to me. So I guess what I'm saying is, if we're going to do this, it's full disclosure."

"Of all the things that I thought would come out of your mouth, that was probably the last thing I expected," Brock said after a second.

"Really? What about if I said I'd like to dress up like a clown and spank you with a paddle?" I deadpanned.

Brock didn't laugh. He seemed to be battling with something before he finally decided he looked at me with a wary gaze. "I guess I knew you wouldn't be content with the bare minimum," he sighed. "Yeah, the club was indirectly responsible for Jimmy's death. What else do you wanna know?" He clasped his hands together on the table.

I put my fork down. "Have you killed anyone?"

Brock's gaze didn't waver. "Yes."

I didn't flinch. I guessed I expected it.

"When I was a SEAL, I killed people in battle, on assignments. I was good at it. It was part of my job. Ironically, it's part of my job here."

"That's what you do for the club?" I asked quietly. "You kill people?"

Brock frowned. "It's not as cut and dried as that, baby. Contrary to popular belief, the everyday life of an MC isn't walking around shooting people. Well, at least not the Sons, 'specially now that we've gone legit."

I had suspected as much, I knew they had been involved in illegal activity and now they seemed to be keeping their noses clean.

"But there's exceptions. Our version of going clean may not match up with society's expectation. But we don't run guns. I suspect your little file said something 'bout that," he said.

I nodded.

"Yeah well, that was how it was when I first got in. I didn't blink an eye, to be honest. I'd grown up with the club — even though the Navy taught me a lot, I would never question my brothers. And it was the only place I belonged. I knew it ate at Cade, what we did, I knew he wanted to get the club clean the moment he took the gavel. I supported him. He's my best friend, I'd follow him to the gates of Hell."

He met my eyes. "But truthfully, I didn't give a shit. Whether we went legit or not. Sometimes the shit we had to do didn't sit right with me, but it was same as in the Navy. Sometimes I did stuff I didn't agree with. But it was for the greater good. It's how it is with the club. I believed it was for the good of the MC—I'd live and die for the cut. I didn't get Cade's desperation to get clean, but I stood by him. I didn't get it until the day a little spitfire redhead burst into my life." His gaze didn't waver from mine. "Then I got it. I got why he'd want to have a life that was free from the filth that sometimes got so deep it was hard to scrub off. How he didn't want the woman he loved to get any blowback from the club he loved. He wanted the best of both worlds. I got it."

Wowza.

His face was thoughtful, his expression tinged with melancholy. "Maybe even before that. When Laurie got killed, we all wanted retribution. To kill every last one of the motherfuckers that were responsible. Then I got this sick feeling, the feeling that somehow we were responsible. The club's actions led to a course of events that almost shattered us." His eyes were far away. "I didn't understand a love like that until you. And the thought of you copping shit because of the club—" He shuddered. "Stuff of nightmares, babe. Even with all the shit we went through, I went dark. I was pissed at the world, pissed at you, and loved you at the same time."

I inwardly flinched at this, at my actions causing him pain.

His expression was full of love . "Through all that I still didn't want to be a man that you couldn't respect."

"I respect you. No matter what," I whispered.

"Maybe not if you knew what I've done," he said with a hint of vulnerability.

I got up from my chair and walked around to him. He scooted his chair so it faced me and I climbed into his lap. "Whatever you've done, I don't care. I know what kind of man you are. My world's not black and white. I see gray," I said softly.

Brock grasped my hips. "My whole fuckin' world was gray until you came along and set it ablaze."

I smiled at him. "So the club?" I probed softly.

He got back on track. "We don't run guns. We've got some security shit we do on the side, protection, retrievals, stuff like that. That's along with the other businesses."

My eyebrow rose. I knew one of the "other businesses" he owned was a strip club. We had even had a confrontation at said strip club after I had been involved in a catfight with one of the strippers.

Wow, that was a white trash statement if I'd ever heard one.

Brock seemed to read my mind. "I didn't touch her," he said quietly. "That night, that waitress—I didn't fuck her. I just wanted to piss you off."

I let out a breath I didn't know I was holding. We weren't technically together when that happened, but we were sleeping together sporadically. Not that I expected monogamy.

"Retrieval?" I asked, cottoning on to an earlier statement.

"Yeah, since me, Asher and Bull are all ex-Navy, we've got

experience in hostage extraction. We still do a bit of that. High risk or high profile cases that can't have the police involved, people come to us." He paused. "That's how your uncle found us."

I was silent for a moment, the conversation turning to a subject I had been trying to broach for the past week. "Clark," I said and Brock's body tightened. "What's happening there?"

"Not enough," he clipped. "He's a powerful guy. And a fuckin' dangerous one at that. He's high on the scumbag food chain. We can't exactly roll in there and put a bullet in his skull, which was one of my earlier proposals. But we're working on it."

"By working on it you mean a plan for his murder?" I clarified.

"He needs to pay," was Brock's reply.

"As much as I agree with that statement, maybe he's not worth it," I said cautiously.

Brock's eyes snapped to mine.

"Easy, tiger. I just mean maybe it's not worth the consequences of A, trying to get close enough to him to commit said murder, and B, the blowback of actually murdering him," I told him.

Brock let out an angry breath. "You sound like fuckin' Cade."

"Well, great minds think alike," I said. "All I'm saying is maybe your thirst for revenge is clouding your judgment. Am I even at risk anymore?" I asked.

I already knew the answer to this. Well, according to my Uncle Garrett, at least. He seemed to think that my father was taking care of it.

"Clark's given the word that he won't touch you anymore," he gritted out. "But that's the word of a fuckin' psychopath, babe. And I'm not gonna let the man who hurt you keep on sitting pretty in his fuckin' mansion."

"Yeah, I know, you're a big bad biker and you need to send a message to anyone who fucks with you or anyone connected to you," I stated smartly. "But maybe you've got to settle for an alternate. Set a bag of poop on fire on his doorstep and run off."

Brock raised an eyebrow.

"Or maybe just burn his whole freakin' house down. I don't know, outlaw justice isn't my strong point. All I know is I'm pretty fond of you and I'm not happy with you putting yourself at risk in order to exact some kind of revenge," I said softly.

My true fear was starting to show. What if something happened to him when he was trying to defend my honor?

Brock read that too. "We'll sort it out, babe. And nothing will happen to me, okay?"

I nodded vaguely. "Can you please at least promise to try and let this one slide if it becomes too dangerous?" I pleaded, knowing I'd have more of a chance getting him to wear that pink tutu.

The look he gave me said I was right.

CHAPTER FOURTEEN

The weeks passed by in relative harmony. Brock and I relaxed into the rhythm of being a couple, although not without some kinks along the way.

One was Brock's insistence we move in together. I wasn't ready for that.

"We spend every fuckin' night together anyway," he argued.

"That's not the point. I *like* having my house. My space. It's too soon for an 'our,'" I argued right back.

"It's not too fuckin' soon—we've been together for a fuckin year."

"We have not! We've been officially together for like a *month*. Everything before that was a mess. We need time to be a normal couple and move at a normal speed."

"I don't give a shit about normal!" he shouted. "I give a shit about having my old lady in my house, in my bed, coming home to her every day."

I raised my eyebrow and put my hand on my hip, my female battle stance. "Oh really? *Your* house. *Your* bed. Coming home to *m*e. So you expect me to move into your house, don a Christian Dior New Look dress and hand you a martini at the end of every day?"

Brock's anger cracked for a moment. "I don't know who Christian Dior is, I fuckin' hate martinis and I don't give a shit who gets home first. I just care that it's *our* home."

I hated that my resolve all but shattered at the sweetness of his words. Even if they were delivered on a yell. "Well, maybe I like my house. Have you thought of that? I like my pool and my kitchen and my closet!"

Brock smirked for a moment. "I don't get how the kitchen factors into it, babe, since you only use it for booze storage, but fine. If you want to do that I'll move in here."

I stilled for a moment. "You'll move in here?"

"Yep."

"What about your house?" I asked.

"I'll sell it." He shrugged.

"Don't you like your house?"

"It's just a place to rest my head, Sparky. It's four walls full of my shit. As long as I've got my bike and I've got you I could be living in a straw hut and not be fazed, although I suspect you wouldn't be happy about that."

I was silent for a moment. "It's really fast," I said quietly.

Brock moved to touch my hips lightly. "It's not fast. We've been waiting for a year and half for this shit to work out right. It has. I don't want to waste any more time."

I was dubious about living with a man. I mean, I was a girl. I'd only lived with girls. What if he didn't put the seat down? Or left his chin whiskers in the sink?

"Okay," I said quietly. The hands at my hips tightened and he leaned in for a kiss. I placed my hand on his lips. "But you can't leave the seat up and you have to clean up your chin whiskers," I ordered.

Brock chuckled and kissed me.

Of course, this peace had been short-lived when he demanded to be in charge of household expenses. When I informed him that we were mortgage free he demanded to pay for everything else. I should have been expecting such an order, considering Gwen's similar experience with Cade when they moved in together.

"That's not happening," I declared firmly.

"Yes, it fuckin' is," Brock clipped.

"Look, I know you've got this 'me the man, I take care of my woman' thing going on, but it's not going to fly on this. In the bedroom, yes. When I've got sore feet and want a foot rub, yes. But not this. We can go halves," I conceded.

Brock's glare darkened. "Nope. That's not me, babe. I'll take care of it all."

I took a deep calming breath. "Brock, you know..." How did I put this delicately? "You know I come from money. It's not a problem for me."

"I don't give a shit," he said sharply. "It doesn't matter how much money you've got in the bank, I take care of both of us."

I stared at him. I knew he wouldn't budge on this. "If you don't let me win on this, I'll just do even worse things like buy you a ridiculously expensive watch every week," I said with an evil grin.

Brock glared, he knew I wasn't bluffing. "Fuck, you irritate me sometimes."

I smiled sweetly at him. "That's why you love me."

He shook his head, pulling me into his arms. "No, I love you in spite of it."

So that argument was won. I guessed I would pay for it somehow in some way I was yet to see. But now it was the first night of us living together and we decided to throw a party.

Well, I decided to throw a party. Things on the club front had been quiet and I had recently just lost my constant chaperone, so I guessed the Clark threat was being dealt with.

I had been slowly getting used to the role of old lady, not a title I was hugely comfortable with, but I was supremely happy with Brock so I guess I'd learn to love it. Evie, the biker queen, had even accepted me into the fold with open arms.

"Glad you two finally got your shit together. But you hurt him again I'll pull your shiny red hair out."

So maybe not so open arms, but she had offered me a mimosa after, so I guessed my hair was safe for now.

Gwen was ecstatic about the fact we were both old ladies and we spent evenings complaining over cocktails over some of the alpha tendencies of our bikers. Which was what we were doing right now.

We were slightly separated from the party — I was bouncing Belle on my lap, Gwen was making the most of having baby-free hands and was cradling a cosmo.

"Who would have thought we'd be biker old ladies and you'd have a freakin' *kid?*" I asked lightly, looking around at our adopted family who I wouldn't trade for any of the stuck up Manhattanites I had grown up with.

The exceptions were Ry and Alex, who I secretly hoped would patch into the Sons. I expected Alex was the right amount of badass for the leather, but I didn't think Ry would make the cut.

Gwen's face turned melancholy for a moment. I knew she was thinking of Ian. "Yeah, it's funny how life works, isn't it?"

"You okay?" I asked, knowing it was a stupid question.

She focused her gaze on me, then Belle, then Cade who was staring at her from his biker huddle. He had a sixth sense when it came to Gwen, it was freaky.

"Yeah," she said finally. "I never thought this would be my life. But I've never been so happy either, you know? I miss him though, Ames. I miss him every day."

I was silent for a bit. "Yeah, me too," I confessed.

She looked at me. "He wasn't *it* for you though, was he? It's Brock. He's your soul mate."

It wasn't a question.

"No," I whispered. "I loved him. I loved him in a comforting sort of way, the way that he would stay in my heart forever. If I hadn't met Brock and hadn't experienced the firestorm that it is to love him, maybe he would've been it. But you can't live your life on what ifs." I snuggled into Belle, inhaling her sweet little baby smell.

Gwen watched me. "No, you can't. You're happy, though."

I nodded, catching Brock's gaze from across the pool. He had an intense look on his face, watching me holding Belle. Uh uh. He was not getting any ideas.

"Yeah."

We sat in a comfortable silence.

The party was a success, and we had bundled a drunken Gwen and a sleeping Belle in with Cade as they were the last guests to leave. For once, I didn't overindulge in the alcohol. I wasn't pregnant. I was happy enough to thrive off the atmosphere of being surrounded by love.

Ugh, I was getting sappy as shit and I couldn't find it in me to care.

I snuggled next to Brock after he had made me a very happy girl.

Multiple orgasms happy.

He stroked my shoulder absently and I basked in the moment of domestic coupledom. Well, maybe I basked in the afterglow of freaking amazing sex, but it was basically the same thing.

"You want kids, Sparky?" he asked finally, breaking the silence and with a boom my bubble of happiness burst.

I knew that look by the pool would come back and bite me in the ass.

"I don't know," I said honestly and his hand stopped stroking.

He twisted me so I was lying on top of him and our eyes could meet. He scrutinized me.

"You don't know?"

"I'm twenty-freaking-five, Brock. I like my life. I like my boobs and I do not want them to sag. I like my clothes and I do not want to have them covered in spit up."

Brock raised an eyebrow. "You're seriously saying you don't want kids because of your tits and your clothes?" His tone was judgmental.

I tried another tactic. "Do you like my vagina, Brock?" I asked.

He was silent for a moment. "Is that a trick question?"

"No, it is not a trick question. I assume you do like my vagina —I'm relatively fond of it too. I am not fond of the idea of a baby hurtling out of it and messing things up," I told him plainly.

He watched me like he didn't know what to make of my comment. "So you don't want kids." The flat tone of his voice worried me.

"Do you?" I countered.

His hands tightened around my waist. "Fuck yeah, I do."

The words left hanging were the "with you" part. I ran my fingertips across his chest.

"Can we not just enjoy being us without moving at warp speed like Gwen and Cade? They're happy and they love Belle, but I don't want a baby coming along just yet. We can revisit this at a later date, if we don't murder each other by living in such close proximity. My ovaries aren't going to shrivel up any time soon, 'kay?"

I hoped he would be happy to end this conversation. We had just moved in together after two weeks of actually being a normal functioning couple. Talking kids was a little too much for me, especially when I didn't even know if I wanted them.

Brock was silent for a moment, as if he was contemplating this. He kissed my head lightly and tucked me into his side.

"Okay, babe, I get you. The subject's shelved."

I relaxed. Hopefully that was the last I was going to hear on that subject for a few years at least.

The way these guys moved, I knew I'd be lucky if I had a couple of months.

———

The next day I was humming along contentedly while packing groceries in the back of my car, feeling excited at the sheer amount of food in those bags I had deprived myself for years. I wasn't going to be munching down twenty Big Macs a day or anything, but maybe I wouldn't avoid pasta like I avoided Ugg boots.

I was distracted thinking about pasta and maybe even cheese, I didn't notice someone had approached me.

"You're looking well, Miss Abrams," a cultured voice stated politely from behind me.

Oh shit. Not again.

I whirled around to face Clark, my only weapon a jar of pasta sauce. I contemplated how effective throwing it at his head would be. My eyes darted around the quiet parking lot, I supposed I wouldn't be lucky enough to have a friendly law enforcement officer stroll by. Crap.

"What the fuck do you want?" I hissed angrily.

This was not okay. Could I not enjoy something as mundane as a trip to the grocery store without getting stalked by my ex-kidnapper?

He held his manicured hands up to placate me. "I'm not here to hurt you, Miss Abrams, nor do I intend to disrupt your life any more than I have to," he stated calmly.

I snorted, gripping the pasta jar. "Yeah, right. I'm going to believe a sociopath who *kidnapped* and *tortured* me when he assures me I'm safe. Do I look like I'm on crack?" I asked sarcastically, ignoring the fear curling in my stomach.

Clark regarded me. "I do regret that course of action more than you know, considering I lost ten of my men." He didn't seem too broken up about it.

"Sorry, should I have sent you condolence flowers?" I spat, feeling momentarily stunned at how many guys the Sons had managed to off.

Clark sighed. "As much as I enjoy this banter, Miss Abrams, I'm pressed for time. I'd like for you to do something for me."

I raised my eyebrows at him. Maybe this guy was on crack.

"Are you suffering from syphilis?" I asked seriously.

A chink in Clark's emotionless façade showed when he looked visibly confused. "I'm not sure I follow the reason for asking such a question."

"Well, insanity is a common symptom of the disease. Just ask Henry the Eighth. I'm thinking that waltzing up to me while I'm doing my grocery shopping, treating me like a business acquaintance and asking me a favor after detaining and nearly killing me is nothing short of insanity," I explained.

Clark's jaw twitched. "I do enjoy you, Miss Abrams. Under other circumstances I feel I would have enjoyed you in many other ways."

Ick.

"The situation the way it is, I feel that course of action has passed. What I would like you to do is call your boyfriend for me," he requested calmly.

"Yeah, I'll get right on that, after I call the police and tell them a murderer and kidnapper is shooting the breeze with me in the parking lot of the supermarket," I said, fumbling through my bag for my phone.

If only I had something useful in there like a taser or a gun. The only thing I had that could do some damage was some questionable lipstick colors.

Clark stepped forward and I retreated, smacking my head on the trunk of my car. I ignored the lancing pain through my skull and focused on the fact I was not getting freakin' kidnapped again.

"I would urge you the refrain from calling the authorities. We have existed without them thus far and I think that should be the way we continue, considering I could tie your boyfriend and his gang to ten murders," he threatened softly.

"Club," I blurted automatically. "They're a motorcycle club."

"Whatever they are, their efforts to sabotage my business and kill me are getting a little irritating. All I want is to talk to them and unfortunately I don't have many channels to do so. You are my only option."

"Yeah, so I'm just going to call them and tell them to come and have a little meeting with you and the twenty or so guys you have hidden somewhere to shoot them. Not gonna happen, no matter how much you get your little knife boy to try and persuade me otherwise." I crossed my arms defiantly.

My gaze wandered around the parking lot. A couple of people were walking in and out with their groceries. But they looked like normal, everyday people. I couldn't expect them to come to my rescue against a crime lord.

Clark's gaze watched my scan of the parking lot. "I give you my word that I am here alone, apart from my driver. I have no intention of turning this street into a warzone. I'm not into that kind of attention."

I chewed my lip, not trusting him for a second. I didn't want to put the men in danger. But I had a feeling he wasn't going to take no for an answer.

I glared at him. "If you're lying and one of those men gets hurt, I swear to you I'll find a way to burn your tasteless mansion to the ground with you inside it," I hissed.

Clark nodded.

I pulled out my phone.

"Babe," Brock answered.

"I thought we talked about this. That's not a way to answer the phone Brock. 'Babe' is not a substitute for greetings, answers to questions or explanations for actions," I said automatically.

"Okay. Hello, my beautiful, vivacious Amy, how are you?" he murmured.

I eyed Clark. "I'm not the best since I'm currently sharing the same air of Clark Devon and he won't let me leave, which means my ice cream is going to melt," I informed him calmly.

I heard his sharp indrawn breath, then curse. "Jesus, Amy, why in the fuck was that not the first thing you said?" he yelled and I flinched slightly. "Where are you?"

"In the parking lot of Trader Joes," I said. "Clark seems to want to have a meeting with you and the boys and it seems I'm his unwilling secretary. He's not my idea of a suitable employer—his health benefits suck," I told him, glaring at the pompous psychopath in front of me.

I heard Brock barking orders in the background. "We'll be there in five." He paused. "Are you okay, baby?" his voice softened.

"I'm fine. Pissed off, but fine."

"He's dead if he touches a fuckin' hair on your beautiful head," he growled.

"I'd rethink the murder plan due to all of the witnesses," I stated. "I'm thinking that's why Clark chose this particular location."

Another curse. "Sit tight. We're coming to get you."

I hung up and glared at Clark. "They'll be here momentarily, Mr. Devon. Can I do anything else for you? Open a vein? Oh no, wait, I've already done that. How about I pick up your dry cleaning?"

"If this meeting goes as I hope, Miss Abrams, this will be the last time you hear from me."

"A girl can dream," I muttered.

Silence descended upon us and I was itching to get out of this man's presence. What seemed like seconds later, the roar of motorcycles filled the air. They must have broken the land speed record getting here.

Brock pulled up close to us, leaping off his bike. He strode toward me, pulling me behind him and yanking a gun out of his waistband to point at Clark's head. Clark looked unruffled. I had to give it to him, the guy had a mean poker face.

I touched Brock's sleeve lightly. "Maybe not the best place to be pointing a deadly weapon at a man's head, sweetie," I said quietly, eyeing the parking lot.

"Give me one reason not to blow your fuckin' head off right here," Brock snarled at Clark, ignoring me.

Cade, Lucky, Bull, Asher, and to my surprise, Steg all flanked Brock, while a couple of prospects spanned the lot.

"A long stay in a state penitentiary would be a good motivation," Clark replied, tipping his head to the people walking out of the store, then to the cameras perched in our direction.

Brock seemed to struggle with that for a moment, not lowering his gun.

"As much as I would like to see this fucker's brains splattered on the sidewalk, I can think of some other things I'd like to spend shitloads of money on other than lawyer's fees," Cade muttered quietly, hand on Brock's shoulder.

All of the men seemed on high alert, resting their hands on their belts. Brock sighed, then lowered the gun.

"Get Amy out of here," he instructed Cade.

I clutched his arm before one of the men could drag me off. "I'm not going anywhere," I declared.

Brock's jaw hardened, not taking his eyes off Clark. "Yes, you fuckin' are."

I held my ground. "I'm the one that is involved in this whole mess. I'd like to see it to the end."

Brock sighed. "You got ten seconds then I disregard what my brother and my woman say and I do the world a favor," he hissed at Clark.

"I want to propose a truce," Clark said simply, unbuttoning his suit jacket in the weird way men did.

"Not gonna happen," Brock replied.

Clark didn't seem surprised at this. "I already know you are trying your hardest to make sure I don't see my next birthday. I assume you already know the resources I have at my disposal. Neither of us wants war, I'm sure. And I can guarantee you don't want to lose any more brothers." He glanced at Bull knowingly. "Or women."

The men all stiffened at the threat and Bull stepped forward, hand on his gun. Steg held him back.

"That's the last time you threaten my brothers and even

fuckin mention our women," Cade cut in calmly, "or I'll put a bullet in you myself. I don't care if I've got a whole bus full of witnesses."

Clark nodded. "Fair enough. I only wanted to point out that this is a fight that you neither need nor want. I would rather not have a nationwide motorcycle *club*," his eyes rested pointedly on me before going back to Cade, "interrupting my life. And I'm sure you could do without any complications resulting from this. So I would like to suggest a ceasefire."

"You took one of our women. Fucking *tortured* her. Nearly killed her. You really think we're gonna forgive and forget that?" Cade answered.

Clark shook his head. "I do not. I do suggest I will overlook the slaying of almost a dozen of my men and personally deliver the man responsible for the injuries Amy sustained during her stay with me."

"So you think handing us one of your foot soldiers is enough to forget what you did? Think again, old man." Cade glared at him.

"Rafael is not a foot soldier," Clark said calmly. "He is my son."

I hissed in a breath and this and even the staunch men were taken aback. This was fucked up.

"You think I'd trust a man willing to kill his own kin in order to save himself?" Cade bit out in disgust.

A glimmer of something flicked through Clark's eyes. "Why else would I hand over my son if I wasn't going to keep my word?"

There was silence as everyone chewed on this.

"You hand him to us, and any fuckin' inkling that I get you're setting your eyes in our general direction, it's war," Cade said finally.

Clark nodded. "I assure you we will never cross paths again. You have my word." He handed Cade a card.

All of the men simultaneously stepped forward as he held it out, Brock pulling me behind his back yet again.

Clark ignored this. "A number you can reach me on. You pick the time and place for our exchange."

He glanced around the group. "Good doing business with you, gentlemen." His eyes found mine. "As always, Miss Abrams, a pleasure. Be well."

"The pleasure was all yours," I snapped.

Clark turned around and got into his car. We all stood and watched it pull out of the lot.

"That guy is off his fuckin rocker insane." Lucky broke the silence.

"Back to the clubhouse. Now," Cade commanded. He looked at Brock. "Bring Amy. I'm getting Gwen and Belle. We're on lockdown until I'm satisfied this crazy fucker means what he says."

———

"I have to say I'm growing to hate these lockdowns," Rosie declared, sipping a margarita.

I sipped my own. "Me too. As much as I love a good margarita and the quality of the company, I'm not too fond of the 'not being able to leave' part."

"I know, and I had a date tonight." Rosie frowned down at her phone.

I perked up, loving to hear about Rosie's latest men. They rivaled the revolving door I had back in my heyday. I didn't know where she found them all, considering she had an entire clubhouse full of protective older brothers.

"This guy is a professional swimmer. You should see his arms." Her face was dreamy.

I myself thought her serial dating was an effort to forget about a certain law enforcement officer who had a serious hatred for her brother. That had dimmed slightly, however, with his fondness for Gwen and baby Belle. I suspected he still wanted to put Cade behind bars, but his friendship with Gwen had made him slightly less eager to have Belle grow up without a father. He came into the store sometimes bearing coffee and giving us some eye candy. His banter with Rosie was easy, but I caught the way she looked at him.

"Dreamier than Luke?" I asked mischievously.

Rosie's face snapped to me. "What are you talking about?"

I raised an eyebrow. "You know what I'm talking about. It's time you gave me the lowdown."

Before I could get the goss, Gwen plonked down beside me, snatching my glass. "So getting Belle to sleep in an unfamiliar bedroom was not the funnest thing in the world, especially when she decided that today was the day she was going to give me my first experience of projectile poop," she declared, draining my drink.

I screwed my nose up at this. Gross.

"Luckily I've got good reflexes. I would have had a minor breakdown if I got crap on this dress. It's vintage."

Gwen didn't look like one of those stressed out, sleep-deprived mothers with unstyled hair and a slightly crazed gaze. Her chocolate brown hair was shiny and falling around her face. Her outfit was, like always, perfect. And she had pretty much lost all of her baby weight, the extra she was still carrying actually looked good on her. The bitch.

"That's why I'm not having kids," I informed them. "That and I'm quite fond of how my vagina looks."

Gwen scowled at me. "My vagina looks great! Better than before, in fact," she argued defensively.

I patted her hand. "I'm sure it does, sweetie. You're just an exception to the rule. It's like playing Russian roulette with your downstairs area."

Gwen gave me a look. "It's also the most amazing thing, having a little human who you love more than life itself."

I shrugged my shoulders. "I guess you've got a point."

My mind wandered to how much I already loved Belle and to the day when Brock held her so tenderly. Maybe I would risk my vagina for having that with Brock.

"So." Gwen turned to me. "Cade had no explanation as to why this was happening. Since he was in badass mode, all I got were sexy grunts and orders. Spill," she demanded, changing the subject.

"Yeah, I didn't get any of the lowdown—even Lucky seemed grim. Tell us," Rosie chipped in. I wondered if it was more out of motivation to get the subject away from Luke.

I sighed and filled them in on the parking lot showdown. When I was done, they both gazed at me with mouths agape.

"So this guy is just handing over his freaking son? That is beyond cold. That's crazy!" Rosie exclaimed with a disgusted look on her face.

"Yep," I agreed, unable to believe this was my life.

We were in a biker clubhouse talking about the man who tortured me getting handed over to my boyfriend by his own *father*. My boyfriend, the sergeant at arms of said motorcycle club, was most likely going to kill said torturer.

This way a far cry from sitting around a table in Manhattan drinking overpriced cocktails and talking about the latest "it" bag. Granted, I had been away from my island for over a year and this isn't the first time I was involved in a club "lockdown," but it was the first time I was smack dab in the middle of it.

I frowned at the empty glass, feeling slightly miffed at Gwen for draining it. This, like so many problems in my life, was a job for alcohol. Glancing at Gwen, I realized she might have needed it more than me.

"You okay, Gwennie?" I asked softly.

She jerked up, her eyes focusing on me. "Oh yeah, it's all in the job description of being an old lady, right? Discussing a father setting up his own son's murder. A murder my husband will most likely be involved in."

"I still think I'd rather live this life than have to face nightly dinners with my mother," I replied honestly and Rosie smirked.

Gwen sighed. "That's the thing. Even with all of this, I wouldn't change it for the world."

Neither would I.

————

"Are we going to get to sleep in a room that hasn't seen more traffic than Grand Central station tomorrow night?" I asked Brock sweetly as I rubbed moisturizer on my hands.

He shrugged his cut off and placed his knife and gun on the desk across from his bed. "Can't say for sure, babe, but the prospect is looking likely," he replied, undressing.

I looked around his room. It was messy, like the last time I had been in it, but this time I was a verified "Old Lady." It felt different. I also felt vaguely sick thinking of the other women who had shared this bed after me.

Hypocritical, I knew.

"Sparky?"

I jerked back to reality and looked into Brock's eyes. "How many?" I asked.

Brock looked confused. "How many what, babe?"

"Girls," I said quietly. "I know I have no right to ask and I'm not going to claw your face off when you tell me the truth. I just need to know."

I hated myself for asking this. It was like emotional self-flagellation, but the unknown was worse.

Brock sighed and ran his hand through his hair before directing his gaze back at me. "You want the truth?"

I nodded, even though the sensible Amy shook her head internally.

"Those first few weeks, before I got a taste of you, before I knew what it felt like to be inside you, I tried to fuck you out of my system. Not gonna lie, babe, there were girls. But every time

I sunk into some bitch all I could see was red hair and the most beautiful eyes I've ever seen." He stroked my face. "After I got in there—" He slipped his hand to cup me between my legs.

I felt myself get turned on, despite the subject matter.

"After I felt what it was to be inside you I was fuckin' ruined, Sparky. All the shit we went through—sometimes I fuckin' wished I could forget about you, go back to mindless fucking." His eyes met mine, blazing. "I couldn't. You had me under your spell, baby. For months I didn't get to touch you, get to slip into your heat. I thought I'd fuckin' die from blue balls."

He smirked slightly. My breathing got heavier as his hand worked between my legs.

"I tried to forget long enough to fuck some sweet butt. I swear my dick shriveled up the moment I touched them," he murmured.

My shoulders sagged.

We were silent for a moment. I didn't miss the fact he didn't ask about Ian, about if I slept with him. Guilt washed through me.

"I'm sorry," I whispered brokenly.

He looked surprised. "For cluttering my dresser with perfume and shit? I don't care, babe. Fuck, I like it," he teased with a smile.

I paused then shook my head. "For everything. For pushing you away when we first met, for not letting you in ... then for completely blocking you out after Ian died."

"Babe—" Brock stroked my cheek.

"Let me finish," I cut in. "I was fucked up. Not only from Ian but from the train wreck that is my family. I'd never seen love, never received it, apart from Garrett. My family never showed it nor gave it. My father was never purposely cold, just indifferent. He was fond of me, but never actually let on he loved me. My mother was openly hostile. I couldn't figure out why. So I steered away from love, or more the rejection I would feel from not getting it—the rejection that I lived with for eighteen years."

"Your mother makes me want to seriously reconsider my stance on hitting women," he muttered.

I smiled dimly. "Yeah, well, I'm hoping karma kicks her ass when her next surgery gets botched," I said dryly. "Anyway," I continued, "when I met Ian, I let myself love him and he broke my heart. He did it because he was trying to protect me, but it was rejection in my eyes."

Brock had stiffened and was listening intently.

"So when I came here I was already bitter and I definitely didn't want love. I wanted sex. Hot sex with a guy that didn't treat me like fine china." I smiled at Brock. "I met you and got everything I wanted and everything I didn't. I fell for you. I was so angry at myself for letting it happen and angry at you that I tried to keep away, but I couldn't so I acted like a bitch in the hopes you'd decide you didn't want me."

"Nothing you could do or say could make me not want you, babe," he declared fiercely.

"Yeah, I get that now. I was starting to get it then when Ian arrived. And it stirred everything up, especially when Gwen found out and expected me to marry him. So did Ian. I didn't know how to tell either of them the only thing that came of his visit was that I knew I wanted you. I didn't want a freaking love triangle, but I didn't know how to get myself out of it." I took a breath. "When he died, I was too focused on taking care of my best friend and getting her home. I didn't stop to think about me. About you."

I placed my hand over the one he had on my cheek.

"I felt guilty, so when I came back I didn't know what to do with my feelings. I kept you away. Acted like an idiot for almost a year." I met his eyes. "I'm sorry."

Brock's stare was level, as if he was calculating my words and his response. "Babe, this is not all on you. The start of this ... it was fucked. I knew I wanted you for more than just sex, but I don't think either of us was ready. I let you keep me at arms' length. Then Gwen's brother turned up and there was obviously something between you. I was pissed. Pissed you let him in. Pissed he could take you away from me. 'Cause he was everything I wasn't. He was a hero—he didn't kill drug dealers and run guns. He could give you a life I couldn't."

His eyes never left mine as he continued.

"I thought that's what you wanted. Then when he died, it fucked with my head. I hated that you were hurting, feeling pain. A sick, fucked-up part of me was almost glad he was out of the picture, then I realized I would always be second best. That curdled in my stomach for a while. So I let you push me away. Tried to get over you. I couldn't. That night at Cade and Gwen's wedding you looked so beautiful, so fucking perfect. I knew I wouldn't give a shit if I was your second choice. I wouldn't care if I was your tenth choice as long as I had you." He grasped my neck. "This isn't all you, babe. But let's leave all that shit behind us and focus on the now, okay?"

I nodded, feeling lighter and happy. "'kay."

CHAPTER FIFTEEN

The next day, I was sitting on the couch at the clubhouse bored as shit. Gwen was napping with Belle, Rosie was nowhere to be found and the main room was uncharacteristically empty. The menfolk had gone off to do God knows what.

Probably to prepare a torture room for Rafe or sharpen their knives. I was of two minds about the fact my boyfriend was preparing to commit murder. Obviously Rafe was fucked in the head and a serial killer, he deserved to see justice for his crimes. But this was *murder*. Brock and the men had appointed themselves judge, jury, and executioner. It was a weird lifestyle to get my head around. The law and courts weren't who decided justice for them. They were.

Something that I was loath to admit was a part of me *wanted* this to happen to Rafe. I wanted him to suffer. To pay for his crimes in ways a lifetime stay in prison just couldn't do.

I was also terrified that this would be some kind of trap and my man and my family would be in danger. I had pointed out to Brock this morning that they had no way of actually recognizing Rafe since they had never seen him. My suggestion that I be there went over like a lead balloon.

"No fuckin' way in Hell are you getting within ten miles of that sick fuck," he growled.

"Well, I'm the only one who actually knows what he looks like," I'd argued.

"Draw us a fuckin' picture." His voice was final.

"Well, how else are you going to make sure he's not handing over some poor innocent gardener?" I folded my arms in triumph.

Brock cursed under his breath, whipping out his phone. He scowled at me and stormed off. He had come back ten minutes later and thrust the screen in my face.

"This the motherfucker?" he bit out.

I squinted at the blue eyes staring at me through the screen. I nodded.

"Jesus, I feel like I'm gonna have to handcuff you to the goddamned bed so I can leave without spending the whole day worrying you've done something stupid like go shopping," he muttered under his breath.

I crossed my arms and raised an eyebrow. "You handcuff me to the bed with anything other than sex in mind and I'll shave off your eyebrows while you sleep," I threatened.

Brock's eyes darkened and he stepped forward, grasping my hips and pulling my body flush to his. "You into that sort of shit, Sparky?"

I nodded slowly.

"Fuckin' hell," he muttered. "How am I supposed to leave you here knowing that shit?"

"That's easy," I purred. "Don't leave."

Brock stared at me for a moment, his face pained. "You're going to be the death of me, woman," he growled, yanking my mouth to his.

Unfortunately, he had left after laying a hot and heavy one on me, declaring he had "shit to do."

Hence me sitting on the couch, bored out of my skull. This

was a biker clubhouse for fuck's sake. Where was the drama? The skank fights, the orgies, or at least a small explosion?

I glanced at my phone — three p.m. A little too early to break out the cocktails.

"'Sup, Abrams?" Lucky sauntered into the room.

I could've hugged him. "Lucky! Thank Christ you're here," I exclaimed, standing.

Lucky grinned. "I knew Brock would drop the ball eventually and you'd want a real man."

I raised an eyebrow. "You couldn't handle me," I deadpanned.

He chuckled. "Yeah, you're probably right. Having you as an old lady is a full time job."

I smacked his shoulder. "You're an asshole. I can't wait until some woman comes in and turns your life upside down."

Lucky grinned. "That's never gonna happen, babe, I plan on being an eternal bachelor. It would be cruel not to share all of this with as many bitches as possible," he declared, gesturing down to his decidedly impressive body.

I laughed.

"What are you doing here, anyway?" I asked. "Shouldn't you be off doing whatever badass things you boys do that the delicate females can't possibly be subjected to?"

Lucky's grin dimmed slightly. "I'm here to make sure you haven't tunneled your way out of here with an eyelash curler, Brock seemed adamant you'd found a way to take down the prospects."

I placed my hand on my chest. "Why, little old me? I'd never defy the orders of my old man."

Lucky laughed. "Yeah, right. What you up to anyway?"

"I was about to set something on fire so my eyeballs didn't start bleeding from boredom," I informed him seriously.

"I've got something else in mind that doesn't include any pyromania," Lucky said, dragging me out of the room.

———

I closed one eye and squeezed the trigger, bracing myself against the kickback as I fired.

"Holy shit, I got him! Right in the balls!" I screamed, clapping my hands.

Lucky grabbed my wrist. "How about you don't clap your hands like a seal when you're holding a deadly weapon?"

I looked down at the pistol in my hands. "Yeah, okay," I muttered.

Lucky had taken me out behind the clubhouse to a grassy area I didn't even know was there. It was a mock shooting range and had what looked like scarecrows at the end of it. We had been out here for about an hour, Lucky showing me how to handle a gun and how not to accidentally blow my foot off. I had just succeeded in making sure a certain scarecrow could never reproduce again.

"It's kind of disturbing how good you are at that," he told me, reloading the gun.

I gave him a grin. "Make sure you tell Brock that just in case he gets any ideas about screwing around with a sweet butt."

Lucky shook his head.

"Gimme." I held out my hand for the reloaded weapon.

"Hold on a sec. You going to do what I taught you?" he asked.

I took the gun from his outstretched hand, checked the clip, reloaded it and turned off the safety. I turned towards the scarecrow and fired. A couple of my shots went awry, but most went to his head until it fell at an unnatural angle.

"I don't know whether to be turned on or scared as shit," Lucky said after I had emptied the clip.

I laughed. I totally thought I looked the part. I was wearing six-inch heels, skinny leather pants and a loose khaki shirt with lace inserts in the sides so you could see my longline bra underneath. Totally badass.

"I'm gonna have to say the second one, considering you just

taught my fuckin' woman how to shoot," a gravelly voice informed us.

I whipped around to see not only Brock, but Cade, Bull, Steg, and Rosie watching my little gun show.

Brock had his shades on and took a puff of his cigarette. His face was impassive.

"Hey, honey." I waved with my hand not holding the gun.

Rosie stepped forward with a huge grin. "Holy shit, Amy, that was awesome!"

"It was fuckin' something," Brock muttered.

"I was bored and Lucky thought it would be a good idea to teach me how to shoot," I explained.

"That's the only thing that came to your mind to entertain her, brother? A game of fuckin' checkers would've sufficed," he said, throwing his smoke to the ground.

Lucky shrugged his shoulders. "I stand by my decision."

Brock made his way over to us, taking the gun out of my hand and shoving it at Lucky. "I'll deal with you later," he informed him.

Before I knew it, I was over his shoulder and he was carting me back to the clubhouse.

"Hey! What are you doing? I was having fun," I argued.

Brock smacked my ass hard. "Yeah, babe, we're going to have a lot more fun once I handcuff you to the bed and fuck you for the rest of the night," he growled.

My stomach dipped. That was definitely more fun.

———

"So now that we're safely out of the clubhouse and away from the gossips that ride the bikes there, you've gotta spill," I demanded, glancing at Rosie who was sitting beside me.

She looked back at me innocently. "Spill about what? The fact that my room is far too close to Brock's and the walls aren't that thick?"

I turned my attention back to the road. "I can't help I'm amazing in bed," I replied airily.

Rosie laughed.

We had been temporarily released from the lockdown at the clubhouse. Well, maybe not *released*, but Rosie and I and taken an opportunity to slip out when everyone was distracted. We figured that going to get some more tequila was hardly life threatening.

Plus, I couldn't sit around the clubhouse twiddling my thumbs while I knew that the men were off at the meet with Clark. I was scared shitless. Hence the need for distraction in the form of alcohol. Considering we were almost back at the clubhouse and hadn't been attacked or shot at, I gathered that the men were just being way overprotective.

I turned my attention back to the Rosie-Luke situation.

"But seriously. I've watched you do goo-goo eyes at Luke for a freaking year now. What's the deal?" I eyed a car in my rearview mirror that was following way too close. Impatient asshole.

"I do not do goo-goo eyes," she argued.

"You're right," I agreed, "You eye fuck the shit out of him."

"He's hot. I'm a red-blooded woman."

I took my eyes off the black Mercedes. "So am I, sweetheart, and while I can appreciate that the man can wear the shit out of a police uniform, I do not undress him with my eyes." I paused. "Well, at least not *every time* I see him."

She sank back in the seat. "What does it matter? He doesn't see me like that. Plus he hates the club. The club is my family."

"That didn't stop Romeo and Juliet," I told her, putting my blinker on so the Mercedes could pass. Didn't they know I was trying to have serious girl talk?

Rosie glared at me. "Romeo and Juliet died in the end!"

I furrowed my brows. "You're right. Bad example. That doesn't matter. He's a guy. You're hot. He definitely sees you like that."

Before Rosie could answer, my attention turned to the black Mercedes which was in the process of passing me.

"Finally," I muttered. "Flip this guy the bird—he's been riding my tailgate since we left town," I instructed Rosie.

"Gladly," Rosie complied, holding up her hand.

I smirked...that was, until the Mercedes didn't overtake us, but instead rammed into us.

"Holy shit!" I screamed, trying to get control of my car.

Just as I did, another jolt sent us spinning out of control and toward a ditch on the side of the road. We rammed into something with a crash.

I struggled against the airbag, which was threatening to suffocate me, along with a whopping headache.

"Rosie? You okay?" I called, my voice muffled.

I heard a groan. "Yeah, I'm fine. I bit my tongue something wicked though," she said, her voice sounding weird.

"Is there a deflate button on these things somewhere?" I asked, struggling.

Thankfully, my door opened and my airbag deflated with a start. I gasped in a breath, turning to the good citizen who had saved me from suffocation via airbag.

"Thanks a million—" I started but froze when I came face to face with Rafe.

"You may not be thanking me later, Red," he said with a sick smile.

Before I could do anything, namely kick him in the balls, he held a taser to my neck and everything went black.

————

I woke up slowly, not liking the fact I was familiar with the after-effects of tasing. I was surprised to see my arms were not bound. I wasn't restrained at all, in fact. I creaked opened my eyes to see I was lying on a bed. A glance at my surroundings had me deduce I was in a sleazy motel.

Rafe sat on a chair on the other side of the room, watching me. The empty look in his eyes had me seriously freaked. No, actually the fact he had run me off the road, tased me, then kidnapped me already had me freaked. The vacant look in his eyes tipped me over to terrified

"You're awake," he declared.

"Unfortunately," I muttered.

"You've caused me a lot of trouble, Red," he said calmly.

It was then I noticed the knife in his hand, which rested on his thigh.

He narrowed bloodshot eyes at me. "You tricked me. I thought we had something special, but you lied."

He stood and I scrambled to the wall, standing. He didn't take much notice of that, he just started pacing.

"When you left, I couldn't fill the void, I tried. No matter how many girls I had. None of them were you." He screwed his nose up. "All pitiful creatures. Weak."

I swallowed, sickened at the thought of what he did to those poor women. He stopped pacing and his eyes darted to me. "Then I found out my father was willing to give up my life in order to get your biker scum boyfriend out of his backyard." Fury glittered in his eyes.

I darted my eyes around the room, looking for a weapon, or at least an escape. I focused on the bathroom door which was behind me. I prayed it had a strong lock and a window.

"So I have to leave. And you have to come with me. You'll forget about the biker trash and I'll forgive you for running off with them." His face twisted into an expression of sick arousal. "Of course I'll have to punish you. But we'll have a life together."

He looked like he was about to step forward so I darted into the bathroom. I caught the surprise and fury on his face as I slammed it shut and locked the flimsy lock. I whirled to see a small window, praying it was big enough for me to climb through. I scrambled up urgently, hearing Rafe's body smash against the door. I fumbled it open, pulling my body up. I was about to hoist my body through when I heard a crash and hands tightened around my legs. I screamed and struggled, hoping the walls of this place were paper-thin and that some citizen would call the cops.

I felt triumphant when my bare foot connected with Rafe's face and I heard a crunch.

"Bitch!" he screamed, yanking me roughly down from my perch.

I continued struggling against him until a blinding pain exploded in my cheekbone, the force of his backhand sending me hurtling to the floor.

His rabid face glared down at me. "Why did you have to do that?" he whined. "Now I had to mark your face. I hate to do that." He shook his head.

He knelt down, holding his lone blade against my throat.

"You try that again and I'll be forced to slit your throat, no matter how much we're meant to be together," he whispered softly.

"How long do you think you're going to be able to run for, Rafe? They'll find you. It would be better to let me go now— maybe you'd have more of a chance," I told him, knowing reasoning with a crazy person wasn't likely to be effective.

He laughed, and it was so unhinged it sent chills down my spine.

"I have no intention of letting you go. And they'll never find me. I still have connections," he muttered, almost to himself. "Now get up," he ordered, standing.

I debated the consequences of staying where I was out of pure rebellion, but I thought doing what the crazy guy with the knife said was probably the best course of action right now. Plus I didn't even want to think about the germs I was subjecting myself to sitting on the floor of a bathroom in a cheap motel.

I gently pushed myself up. My body ached all over, most likely from the car accident. Fear bloomed in my stomach.

Rosie.

"What did you do to her?" I asked desperately.

It took a second for Rafe to click. "Oh, the dark-haired slut in the car? I left her. As much fun as I would have had with that little piece, there wasn't time. Your fuckin' bikers were on their way," he declared, tugging me back into the bedroom.

My body relaxed slightly at the fact Rosie was okay. Panic crept back in as Rafe pushed me roughly onto the bed, dragging my arms up above my head.

"I hadn't wanted to use these," he informed me, pulling handcuffs from his belt. "I had wanted your hands free." I sickened at the erotic glint in his eyes. "But I think this is best for now."

I hoped the click of my restraints was not the sound of my freedom and dignity being locked away before I was raped or stabbed. I had to believe that Brock would come for me. Or at the very least the police would. Weird how I thought about Brock before the law.

"What's the plan here, Rafe?" I tried to distract his gaze from its travel down my body. "You going to torture me in some hotel with paper thin walls? Not the smartest idea you've had."

Maybe questioning his intelligence was not the best idea at this juncture.

A muscle in Rafe's jaw ticked and he dragged his gaze away from my breast. "Oh, this is just a stop along the way. I've got a couple of calls to make, then we'll be heading to the airport," he explained with a grin.

"The airport?" I repeated.

"You didn't think I'd be stupid enough to stay in America? Not when dear old Dad and the Sons still have their spies everywhere." He shook his head. "No, no, no, we're off to Columbia. I've got everything arranged, Red, don't you worry."

He bent to kiss me and I managed to swallow down the vomit as his hand groped my breast roughly.

He pulled back with a groan. "We'll have plenty of time for that. First I have to organize a plane."

He stood up and turned his back on me, unearthing a cell-phone. He moved to the corner of the room, speaking quietly into it.

Shit, shit, shit. Kidnapped again. Fuck. And by the same guy. This was so not my year.

I tried to quietly move the handcuffs, but they clanged loudly against the headboard. I was effectively trapped here until someone came to rescue me. *If* someone came.

Hours passed and Rafe had left. He had thoughtfully gagged me so I didn't get any bright ideas as to yell for help. I tried to thrash around the bed, clatter my metal bracelets loudly, but to no avail. I was not only trapped, but I really needed to pee. The door opened, revealing the dim twilight. I hoped it was leather clad bikers, but it was only a well-dressed madman.

"Sorry to keep you waiting, sweetheart, so much to do."

He dropped some bags by the bed and reached to ungag me.

I sucked in my first unobstructed breath in hours. "I need to use the bathroom, like pronto," I informed him.

He frowned at me. "Fine. But you try anything, you'll be sorry. And I'm watching," he smirked.

Once uncuffed, I rushed to the bathroom, so desperate his wily glare wasn't enough to stop me. As I was washing my hands he thrust a bag at me.

"Put these on," he demanded.

I wordlessly took the bag. I stared at him expectantly. Why I expected him to leave when the sick fucker had just watched me pee, I didn't know.

"I'm not going anywhere, Red. I'm going to enjoy every minute of watching this. It can be our foreplay until I have enough time to have my fun with you."

My blood chilled at the promise and I wore the reminder on my skin as to what his fun really was. "Your dad really fucked you up, didn't he?" I muttered.

Suddenly he pushed off the wall and his hand was at my throat, choking me. I clawed at him, trying to get oxygen.

"You don't speak a word about him, got it? We never speak of that man again," he hissed, spittle flying out his mouth.

I nodded the best I could and he released me. I coughed, gasping for air.

"Now put the fucking clothes on and don't say another word."

Okay, so Daddy was a sore spot for him, I mused, silently undressing. I tried to ignore the crawling feeling I felt from his eyes on me and the humiliation of baring my body to him. I slipped the black slacks and blouse on quickly, slipping my feet into flats. Obviously he had learned heels constituted a deadly weapon.

He stepped forward once I was dressed, pressing his body to mine. I felt his hardness pressing into me and his palm brushed my face with a gentleness I didn't know he was capable of.

"It's a shame you had to make me do that." He pressed into my tender skin lightly and I flinched. "You'll learn."

I itched to sling some sarcastic remark back, but I stayed silent, realizing my mouth could mean my death.

He gripped my arm and yanked it. "Come on, we've got places to go," he demanded.

As we got into the bedroom everything happened at once.

The door crashed open and Brock burst through, gun drawn. Cade and Bull followed.

Rafe yanked me against his body like a human shield and I felt a blade at my neck. "Don't move a fucking muscle, or I slit her throat and you watch her bleed out," Rafe said evenly, pressing the metal into my neck.

They all stared at me with hard looks on their faces. It was weird considering I had a knife at my jugular, but I somehow knew I'd get out of this. Brock would make sure of it.

"That blade pierces her skin, you're dead," Brock hissed, eyes on me.

Rafe laughed. "It already has. I've already seen the milky skin part and watched her face as I tore through it. I've felt her body and tasted her mouth--"

He was cut off by a muffled shot and something warm splattered my face. Rafe collapsed onto me and I would've fallen to the floor if it wasn't for Brock catching me, throwing Rafe's prone body onto the bed. I glanced to see he was missing half his head. Okay, I so didn't want to see that.

Brock framed my face with his hands, his eyes searching my body. "You okay, Amy?" he asked with concern.

A dull roar in my ears only caused his words to be slightly muffled and I couldn't quite answer. I vaguely registered his hands skimming my body, looking for knife wounds, most likely.

"Baby? Talk to me," he pleaded, his eyes frantic.

"Is that blood on my cheek and brains in my hair?" I asked in response.

Brock's face turned grim. "I had the shot, babe. Trust me, I never would have taken it if I wasn't sure I could make it," he answered.

"I'll take that as a 'yes,'" I muttered, screwing my nose up and fighting the urge to pass out. I wasn't going to faint, that was way too cliché.

"I'm going to need a shower in about the next five minutes," I declared.

Brock searched my face. "You're in shock."

"I'm covered in blood and brain matter, Brock. I'm painfully aware of that. I need it *off*."

I hated that my voice was bordering on hysterical. I always thought I'd be totally calm and collected if the situation of a dead body ever arose. Turned out I wasn't. The fact that my hands couldn't stop shaking was evidence of that.

Cade appeared at Brock's shoulder, his eyes doing the same inventory of me. He seemed satisfied and his attention turned to Brock.

"We got this, brother, take care of your woman," he muttered.

Brock nodded stiffly, "Come on, babe."

I paused. "What does 'we got this' mean? There's a freaking dead body lying here—he can't exactly check out without his frontal cortex. What are you guys going to do?" I glanced at Cade and Bull worriedly, envisioning them getting caught trying to dump a body.

They both look unruffled.

"They got it, babe. Let's get you out of here," Brock said softly.

I sank into his arms and let him guide me out, feeling exhausted. I gave Cade one final glance, hoping I wouldn't have to explain to his wife that he got arrested for murder.

Brock had driven me home in a club SUV and the ride was silent. I was barely able to keep my eyes open, adrenaline crashing at a huge rate.

"Gwen?" I vaguely heard him speak into a phone. "Yeah, I got her. She's fine. I'm taking her home." He paused. "I mean this in the best possible way, sweetheart, but don't come. She's in shock and she needs to sleep it off. I'll call you as soon as she gets some rest and you can see her."

I didn't hear the rest of the conversation, but I was pretty sure I heard a shrill threat on the other side of the phone before I passed out.

I groggily awoke as Brock carried me upstairs, directing us into my bathroom. He set me on my feet, supporting my weight as my legs felt like jelly.

"Can you stand while I get these clothes off, baby?" he asked softly.

I nodded and he peeled my clothes off. I stood naked, shivering for a moment until he helped me into the shower. He had taken his clothes off too and he stood naked under the spray. I relaxed as he scrubbed at my hair with shampoo, closing my eyes when the water turned red.

I deduced it was safe to open them after a few minutes when Brock's hands had moved to wash the rest of my body. All of a sudden the grogginess was gone, replaced by a carnal need. I needed to feel alive, reassured I was safe.

"I need you inside me," I told Brock and his head snapped up.

I expected him to argue, but his mouth crashed into mine and he lifted me, pressing me against the tile. I let the fire soar through me at his touch, clinging to him and the feeling he gave me. Seconds later he was inside me. I cried out at the brutal pleasure of him pulsing through me, filling me.

One of his muscled arms was braced against the wall, the other bit into my ass. His eyes were glued to mine as he pounded into me with the same frantic need I had.

It was silent, desperate lovemaking. Born out of a need to feel alive, to erase the horrors of the events I had just been subjected to. I forgot everything apart from the feel of Brock moving inside me, saw nothing but his blue eyes that were locked on mine. And when I came, all I tasted was his mouth as he kissed me in a way that branded my soul.

————

Afterward we were in the kitchen, Brock cooking me up a huge dinner. My stomach had loudly reminded me that I hadn't had anything to eat since that morning and I was not too keen on going to bed, having spent the entire day handcuffed to one.

Brock set the plate in front of me quietly. We hadn't said much since our hot survival sex in the shower, I still needed time to process everything.

He walked around the breakfast bar and kissed my head. "Eat, baby. I've just got to make a call then I'll be back."

"'Kay," I replied. He started to walk away, but I stopped him, grabbing his hand. "Thank you," I whispered. "For saving me."

Brock stared at me. "You don't need to thank me. I'll always save you. I'll always be there to get you. Without you there is no me, Sparky."

A warm feeling bloomed in my stomach at his words and he kissed me firmly on the mouth. "Eat," he commanded.

As tempted as I was to dig into the huge bowl of pasta, I had a couple of things to do first. I grabbed the home phone from its cradle and dialed.

"Hey, girl, after some soul searching I decided not to bleach my eyebrows. I don't even care what designer it's for. I can't do it," was Ry's answer.

"Good call," I replied. "Now I'm sorry I don't have the streaming video feed—trust me, you wouldn't want it anyway, but this was just a courtesy call to let you I was kidnapped again. Only for a couple of hours though and I'm safe and sound at home with a bowl of pasta," I told him.

There was silence at the other end of the phone.

"I promised I'd tell you and I didn't want some loudmouthed maid to get there first." I filled the silence, unsure of what to say. No one had ever rendered Ry speechless before.

"Ry?" I asked.

"I'm booking a flight to your freaking crime hotspot as we speak. This shit has to stop. I'm going to kick those motorcycle-riding, leather-wearing man gods myself. And I won't even enjoy it," he shouted, emotion in his voice.

I commenced in talking Ry down and reassuring him I was okay, then hung up.

I devoured half a plate full of pasta before an image flew into my mind. Rafe on the bed, missing his skull. Blood and brains in my hair. I barely made it to the bathroom before emptying the meager contents of my stomach. As good as the carby goodness was going down, it was not fun to re-experience.

It was especially not fun to have large tender hands pull my hair back halfway through my vomiting saga.

"Go away," I whined in between heaves, feeling embarrassed. "I've had plenty of experience with mild alcohol poisoning, which gave me the skills I need to hold my own hair back," I informed him.

I didn't get a response as I continued, he just rubbed my back soothingly. When I was done, he handed me toilet paper to clean my mouth and I stood on shaky feet. I was aware of my puke breath so I pushed past him, grateful I kept spare tooth-brushes in the medicine cabinet. After making sure I was minty fresh, I turned to a concerned biker.

"I'm not pregnant," I blurted, remembering Gwen's revela-tion through vomit of her bundle of joy. "Him, his body. It just popped into my mind and I couldn't stomach the food," I explained quietly.

Brock gathered me into his arms and stroked my hair. "It's okay, baby, I'm surprised that's the only reaction you're having. You've had one heck of a shock. I'm proud as shit at how strong you are. But you don't need to be. I'm here. You're safe. React how you need to."

I sank into his arms. "I'm good now. I've got you."

"For the rest of my days, baby," he murmured quietly.

EPILOGUE

BROCK

"You still sure about this? I can totally cause a distraction while you slip out the back," Lucky deadpanned.

Brock grinned at his friend. "I'm not the one who's going to be slipping out the back." His voice held a note of humor, but he couldn't help but worry about the glimmer of truth behind that statement. His girl had been skittish as fuck the past few days, he knew marriage scared the shit out of her.

Cade slapped him on the shoulder. "She's not going anywhere, brother," he said quietly.

Lucky laughed. "Where else would she find such a handsome motherfucker?"

The men all ignored Lucky and they poured a shot glass for each of them.

"Any advice for married life, brother?" Brock asked his best friend after he had downed his shot.

"Count your motherfucking blessings every day. And never criticize the shit she wears, no matter how much skin she shows. It's not fuckin' worth it," his serious friend answered.

After they had downed a couple more shots, Brock stood at the end of the aisle, waiting impatiently for his girl. It had taken them too fucking long to get here and he was anxious to make her his wife. Actually, he was anxious to get this shit over with and take her home so he could sink into his wife's golden pussy.

She had insisted on a big fancy affair, he wanted to go to Vegas and get her locked down the moment he put the rock on her finger six months ago — but, like usual, she got what she wanted. Not that Brock cared. Nothing much fazed him these days. Shit with the club was quiet, his best friend was happily married and had a kid with another on the way. His other best friend seemed to be less likely to drive his bike into oncoming traffic, the fucker actually smiled every now and then.

Plus, six months ago, the night before he asked Amy to marry him, he and Bull had gone into Clark Devon's mansion and killed the piece of shit. More precisely, Brock had let him bleed out after giving him six incisions on his thighs. No matter what promises were made, there was no way Brock was ever going to let that motherfucker die of natural causes.

His life was good. Fucking amazing. In his wildest dreams he never imagined he would get a life like this. He thought he'd been happy with his club, with the freedom, with the pussy he got. But when *she* hurtled into his life he realized how empty it had been. The light within her, the fire, it ignited every inch of him and he knew his life would be nothing until he had her on the back of his bike.

It wasn't an easy road. It was hard as fuck. But the best things in life were always the things which you would work to the death for. Die for. The things that tested every inch of your strength, 'cause once you got them, nothing would taste sweeter.

The music started and his attention moved to the doors. After Gwen and Rosie and fuckin' Ry sauntered down the aisle, she was there.

Her hair was loose and down, tumbling over her shoulders, wild and free like he loved.

Her dress.

Jesus fuck, her dress.

It was lace, pure white, with a plunging neckline that hinted at her fantastic rack. It hugged every inch of her glorious curves and made his cock harden instantly. His hand twitched and it took all of his willpower not to storm towards her and kiss the living shit out of her.

He refrained.

He got why Cade had pounced on Gwen the moment she got to him. As Amy approached, that's all he wanted to do. But he wouldn't have been able to stop. He would've fucked her right then and there in front of the entire crowd.

She reached him, smiling so bright he almost choked on how beautiful she looked.

"Hey," she whispered.

"You're fucking breathtaking, Sparky," he choked out, not even embarrassed his eyes were wet.

She blushed. He had never seen his girl blush and his cock pulsed in his pants at the sight of it.

"You're not too bad yourself," she whispered.

He eyed Steg, who was grinning at them both expectantly. "Wanna get hitched now?" he asked.

"Yeah," she replied.

He could hardly wait for Steg to mutter all the bullshit to get them married, all he wanted to do was make it official and drag his wife outta there.

Once the words "I now pronounce you man and wife," were uttered, he picked Amy up and strode out of the room. He ignored the catcalls and cheers.

"What are you doing?" She smacked him. "You are supposed to kiss me and then we're supposed to go to the reception."

He stopped on his way to the car. "Babe, if I had kissed you in there I wouldn't have been able to stop. I need to kiss you somewhere where I can rip that dress off and fuck you every way I can think of." He grinned as he saw the spark in her eye he loved so much. "And there's no fuckin' way we're making it to the reception."

ABOUT THE AUTHOR

Anne Malcom has been an avid reader since before she can remember, her mother responsible for her book addiction. It started with magical journeys into the world of Hogwarts and Middle Earth, then as she grew up her reading tastes grew with her. Her obsession with books and romance novels in particular gave Anne the opportunity to find another passion, writing. Finding writing about alpha males and happily ever afters more fun than reading about them, Anne is not about to stop any time soon.

Raised in small town New Zealand, Anne had a truly special childhood, growing up in one of the most beautiful countries in the world. She has backpacked across Europe, ridden camels in the Sahara, eaten her way through Italy, and had all sorts of crazy adventures. She's currently in New Zealand with her fiancé and two dogs enjoying her own HEA.

Want to get stalking?
Join Anne's kick ass reader group!
Website: www.annemalcomauthor.com
Email: annemalcomauthor@hotmail.com

ALSO BY ANNE MALCOM

THE SONS OF TEMPLAR MC

Making the Cut

Outside the Lines: A Sons of Templar Novella

Out of the Ashes

Beyond the Horizon

Dauntless

Battles of the Broken

Hollow Hearts

Deadline to Damnation

Scars of Yesterday

UNQUIET MIND

Echoes of Silence

Skeletons of Us

Broken Shelves

Mistake's Melody

Censored Soul

GREENSTONE SECURITY

Still Waters

Shield

The Problem with Peace

Chaos Remains

Resonance of Stars

THE VEIN CHRONICLES

Fatal Harmony

Deathless

Faults in Fate

Eternity's Awakening

Buried Destiny

DARK STANDALONES

Birds of Paradise

doyenne

Hush (Co-written)

RETIRED SINNERS

Splinters of You

THE KLUTCH DUET

Lies That Sinners Tell

Truths That Saints Believe

OUTSIDE THE LINES

Want to read more about Hansen & Macy? Get ready for a wild ride...

My life's not easy. I'll tell you that now. It's not neat. I don't fit into society the way most people expect me to and I don't color studiously between the lines, outside the lines is where I reside. The fringes of society is where I found my place, with the Sons of Templar MC. The life they lived gave me everything I wanted, and everything I needed. Most importantly, it gave me something I'd been lacking for over a decade—family. A place to belong.

Club girl—that was my title. There were other words for what I was, but I preferred the less derogatory version. Sure, I'd love to be an Old Lady. It's the dream. But, as someone who escaped into fantasy worlds when life got too much, I knew the difference between dreams and reality. I had resigned myself to the fact, I'd always belong to the club. It didn't mean I didn't crave one man in particular to claim me. To put me on the back of his bike and ride off into the sunset with the man who'd captured my heart the first day I saw him—Hansen. The dream where he'd finally see me and make me his, existed strictly in Macy's world of wonder. Until now. Until somehow my fantasy world and reality world collided and he looks at me in the way I'd dreamt of for a year.

Fairy tales usually had neat and happy endings once the hero and heroine got together. This wasn't a fairy tale. Hansen wasn't your traditional hero and I was the furthest you could get from a heroine. I feared my past might dictate my future. That my world outside the lines would go from messy to complete disaster.

Printed in Great Britain
by Amazon

82211470R00192